With This Ring

Books by Leona Blair

A WOMAN'S PLACE
WITH THIS RING

LEONA BLAIR

With This Ring

Delacorte Press / New York

Published by
Delacorte Press
1 Dag Hammarskjold Plaza
New York, N.Y. 10017

Manufactured in the United States of America
First printing

Library of Congress Cataloging in Publication Data
Blair, Leona.
  With this ring.
  I. Title.
PS3552.L3463W5   1984   813'.54   83–10150
ISBN 0-385-29274-0

With this ring I thee wed,
With my body I thee worship,
And with all my worldly goods
I thee endow.

—Solemnization of Marriage

Book I

1

Jesse Slayter walked briskly out of Pennsylvania Station, a porter scurrying behind him. He was a tall man, broad-shouldered and elegantly dressed. A black fur-collared topcoat hung open over his gray broadcloth suit. The high starched collar of his shirt shone in the early winter dusk. His eyes were dark and clear under the brim of his hat, eyes far more serious than the genial smile that broke through his black beard and mustache when he saw the Slayter carriage and the two men on the box.

"Welcome back, Mister Jesse," the footman said, touching his hat. "Here, you," he said to the porter, "stow those bags behind."

Jesse nodded. "Pearl Street first, Bob, then take the bags home," he said to the coachman, and tipped the porter before he got into the carriage. The door was closed behind him, the baggage was secured, and he heard the footman clamber back up to the box. He sat back on the plush-upholstered seat as the carriage started off in the direction of New York's financial district.

Jesse looked out the carriage window, but his thoughts were not on the stir and bustle of New York. He was thinking of a tall girl with pale blond hair, deep blue eyes and a generously curved figure, and his lips closed with anticipation around the stem of his pipe. Then he smiled, remembering his father's description of her: "Gorgeous," Jethro had said to him, "not one of your cold blondes, not even bovine like some of the Dutch."

But Jesse had been so skeptical he had arrived in Philadelphia too late to meet her before the Assembly ball. With just enough time to bathe and change for the evening, he had dispatched a note of apology to her father, pleading a business delay, and two sumptuous bouquets, with appropriate cards, to the girl and her mother.

When he had entered the ballroom that night he regretted, for the first time in his life, having been cavalier with a woman. She was wearing white satin trimmed with champagne lace the color of her hair, and looking at him with the kind of undisguised curiosity most maidens would never display. He was glad they were in the ballroom now; he would not have to wait very long to touch her.

He put one hand on her waist in the anticipatory hush before the orchestra struck up and felt desire rise in him as if he were a blundering schoolboy.

When the music started they began to waltz and the dance floor burst into color, the girls' dresses streaking the ballroom with lavender, old rose, pale yellow, misty green. The sound and the color lapped sensuously at his consciousness, and he watched Madeleine tilt her lovely head back, close her eyes and smile.

"I amuse you, Miss van Ryn?"

Her eyes stayed closed. "No, I was just thinking about the reason for your visit."

He was surprised, even in his delight, that she would mention the object of this meeting so openly. Girls of eighteen were never forthright about marriage.

"You seem pleased," he said, leading her expertly. She was a tall girl, but the best dancer he had ever held.

Her eyes opened, cornflower blue and dazzling. "Aren't you?"

He laughed softly and her eyes closed again. She was swept away in the music and the dance. He thought she was going to look that way in passion, and for tonight he let himself forget what a fool passion had made of his father, and his vow not to let that happen to him.

Again her eyes opened and there was nothing mysterious in the way she looked at him.

"Miss van Ryn," he said softly, "would you like some refreshment?"

"Yes," she said, "very much."

He led her, still waltzing, toward the outside of the dancing circle and then through an open door into a supper room with a long table, laden with party refreshments. A few elderly gentlemen sampling the champagne were the only other occupants of the room. He brought her some fruit punch and took a glass of champagne for himself. They walked toward the two-story-high windows at one end of the room and stood looking out on the snow-covered lawn.

In the next room the dance had ended and there were the rustlings, the scraps of conversation, the laughter of a large company enjoying itself, but in here it was very still. He turned his head and his eyes traced her profile, the slope of her neck, the curves of her shoulders and breasts.

She waited until his eyes returned to her face before she turned and smiled at him. Her mouth was full and sweet and there was just a hint of mischief in her eyes.

"Madeleine?" he asked.

"Yes, Jesse," she answered . . .

"Mister Jesse," the footman repeated through the open door of the carriage.

Jesse knocked his pipe against the fender of the carriage, put it in his pocket and got out. He glanced toward Trinity Church at the bottom of Wall Street, then up at a window on the sixth floor of his father's building near the corner of Pearl Street. *J. Slayter and Son, Merchant Bankers.* He went inside.

2

"Well?" Jethro Slayter demanded, as soon as his son opened his office door.

Jesse smiled carefully. His father always came straight to the point, often before Jesse was ready to say he had reached it. He walked to the big desk in his father's office and took a cigar from the humidor. He did not like cigars, but this one helped him keep his smile in place while he clipped it with a small gold instrument lodged in the humidor's lid. Then he moistened the cigar tip slightly and held the sulphurous flare of a match to its other end before he answered.

"She's perfect," he said.

The father leaned back in his chair, a gratified look on his thin, angular face. "All right, then," Jethro said. "When's it to be?"

"I just met the girl," Jesse said, laughing. "I haven't even approached her father."

"Van Ryn will agree." Jethro's hand tossed that aside with his cigar smoke. "So will the girl, by the look of you."

Jesse remembered the way Madeleine had stood at a window in Philadelphia with a yielding he could almost see, letting his eyes drink her in. "Yes," he said, determined not to show how pleased he was. "She'll agree."

"I knew it," Jethro said. "You're a damned good-looking fellow, even if you usually think more about stock-market figures than women's. In her case you won't find it difficult to do your duty and get us some sons for Slayter's." He gave Jesse a conspiratorial wink. Jethro was well past middle age, yet he thought of nothing but women when the market was closed.

Jesse was different. Women were usually passing fancies to him, not grand passions, not even the physical compulsions they were to men like his father. At twenty-eight Jesse would have married Madeleine van Ryn if she were plain as pudding, but now he really wanted to.

Besides, there were sound business reasons for the two families to unite. Society was part of business, and a woman like Madeleine on his arm would be as much of an asset to Slayter's as her connections.

"Not difficult at all," he said.

"High time you married and set about it, boy!" Jethro approved. "Look how many years of marriage it took me to get you." He did not seem to remember that Jesse's mother had been invalided, had eventually died of giving him a son.

"That's settled, then," Jethro went on, puffing on his own cigar with

13

relish. "She'll have a healthy dowry, but van Ryn will want an equally healthy settlement for her." Jethro clasped his hands behind his head and gazed at the lofty ceiling, which had looked down on generations of Wall Street Slayters, an attitude he always assumed when he was thinking deeply. The streetlight filtering between the tobacco-brown velvet portieres limned the planes of his face, with its web of wrinkles. He reminded Jesse of a somnolent hawk who could take rapid, lethal flight without warning.

There was no man on the Street more canny than Jethro Slayter when it came to business, but he had unfortunate luck with women. The second Mrs. Jethro was only a girl when she married, and not much more when she died in childbirth three years later, leaving Jesse a half sister, Philippa, and a half brother, Daniel. Since then his father preferred carousing with the lusty women of New York's demimonde—or even plain tarts—an activity in which his son only joined with any enthusiasm when he needed sex.

"We can make good use of all that money for the new land investments," Jethro was saying.

Father and son looked at each other. There was little resemblance between the two. The father was sandy-haired and sharp-featured and his chair seemed too big for him. Jesse was compactly muscular and his tall, broad-shouldered frame filled the chair he sat in, with one long leg crossed at an angle over the other knee.

"Madeleine's money will be kept in our bank," Jesse said. "I'm sure she'll leave the disposition of it to me."

Jethro nodded. "The more we offer, the more we'll get from van Ryn. I'd say two and a half million is about right, maybe three."

"I'll talk to him," Jesse said. "I'm going to Philadelphia next weekend."

Jethro regarded his son through half-lowered lids. "You talk to *her*. He's coming to New York tomorrow and I'll take care of the business arrangements."

Jesse's expression did not change, although the fingers holding his cigar tightened. "What makes you think I can't handle both?" he said.

Jethro chuckled. "You're supposed to be in love, boy, not thinking about filthy lucre. Van Ryn sets a lot of store on that girl; he's been holding her for the highest bidder *and* the best husband he can find. We don't want him suspecting our motives."

"Mine are completely honorable," Jesse said, his fingers relaxing. "She's the first girl I've considered marrying."

"Nobody said there wasn't honor among thieves," Jethro conceded. "But her money's important only for the short term; it's her connections that'll serve us in the long run. After all, someday you'll run J. Slayter and Son. It's time they stopped calling us 'the errand boy of Wall Street' for hiding whatever they want hidden and orchestrating their swindles for them. They won't be able to patronize a van Ryn connection. So," he said, sitting up in his chair, "you go down there next weekend with a bunch of flowers and your mother's star sapphire ring. I'll have seen van Ryn by then and the stage will be set for the most romantic proposal you can manage."

3

Madeleine peered between the watered-silk curtains of her bedroom, watching the snowflakes tumble down. The window faced a large park at the back of the house, but the snowy silence magnified every sound. She waited for the whir of carriage wheels, raising her head in anticipation when she heard anything, then relaxing into a reverie when the sound passed and white stillness closed again about the house.

It was still too early for him to arrive, but she had been ready since nine, when she had changed from her morning gown into a blue velvet dress the color of her eyes. She had been ready ever since her father summoned her to his study a few nights ago to tell her she was going to be married.

"To Jesse Slayter." She smiled.

"Yes, and I hope you're pleased," he had said from the depths of his wing chair. She remembered how the lamplight flickered on his frock coat, on the heavy chain and fob across his vest, on the seal ring he wore. "It's a fine match."

"I know. There's no one else I could marry."

He had been both surprised and pleased. "I'm delighted to hear that, Madeleine, but how can you be so sure after only two brief meetings?"

"I was sure I wanted to marry him the moment he asked me."

"Asked you?" He was shocked. "A decent man doesn't ask a young girl —he asks permission of her father to propose to her."

"He didn't ask me in so many words," she assured him. Her voice was warm. "It happened between dances—we were standing near one of those huge windows in the supper room. He just said 'Madeleine?'—it was a definite question." She smiled, her blue eyes sparkling. "And I said 'Yes, Jesse'—a definite answer."

Her father looked at her, seated in the velvet lady chair opposite his. It might tempt providence to think it so often, but she was certainly the most beautiful young woman he had ever seen. She looked like his own grandmother, Susannah van Ryn, whose portrait hung in the dining room of this house, but Madeleine was not just woodenly beautiful, she was warm and intelligent as well. He shook his head questioningly and she caught the movement.

"I know, I know," she said with happy resignation. "The kind of instant infatuation that turns into love happens in bad novels, not real life. I never expected it to happen to me, but I'm glad it did."

17

He reflected in silence for a moment. "It's true," he said finally, "that he's a charming man—although his father's an odd fish—and he has a brilliant future according to my acquaintances on Wall Street." He leaned forward, watching her more attentively. "But tell me why you love him."

"Isn't charming, very wealthy and respected enough?"

"Don't tease me," her father said, thinking that Madeleine might be innocent but not foolish. "Not enough for you."

She grew serious then. Her right hand played with a gold locket he had given her when she was sixteen.

"I love the kind of—I don't know exactly what to call it—sophistication, command—no, power, that's it!—that he has. He knows what he wants and takes it. The men standing near him at that ball were like cubs compared to a lion. They're all popinjays. He's a man."

So that explained it, her father thought. He sighed; he had hoped Madeleine would find more than that in the man she married.

"He's very like me," Madeleine was saying, to his relief. "What you call 'direct' and Mama calls 'scandalous.' "

"She was certainly scandalized at the way you two behaved the other night," he said, and they smiled together as they often did over Mrs. van Ryn's strict notions of proper behavior for young ladies.

"I know. Everyone was talking about us—but everyone's always talking. Why pay attention to them?"

"Come, now, Madeleine, the world needs its rules and regulations," he said.

She nodded. "Of course, but not nearly as many as it has. And how can anyone regulate love?"

Her father hesitated, disturbed at the depth and swiftness of her feelings. "Don't expect too much of love, my dear," he said, and then, knowing this was an impossible request to make of an eighteen-year-old girl with a mind of her own and a mindless passion for a man, he smiled, newly content with his decision. "But I mustn't scold you for falling in love with the man you're going to marry."

Now, with the windowpane deliciously cool against her flushed cheek, she was thinking how very much in love she was when her mother's voice interrupted her, talking in the nervous rattle that seized her before large events.

"Madeleine, you can't poke about here any longer, you have to be downstairs to receive him—the drawing room, or perhaps the green parlor, it's cozier. Now come along." She went on chattering while the two of them glided down the stairs of the gracious Georgian house, the short trains of their gowns slipping along behind them down the wide, curving steps.

Her mother preceded her into the green parlor, still talking. "I'm not sure if you should stand or sit—you're so tall, but then so is he, so I suppose it doesn't matter. Perhaps some needlework—but you do it so badly—or a book, yes, a book. Go and get something suitable from your father's study, there's a good girl, while I ask Daisy to bring you a shawl."

Madeline was through the door and across the hall to her father's study before her mother stopped talking. He looked up from his desk and smiled to see her.

"Ready for your young man?" He opened his great gold watch. "He should be here at any moment." He closed the watch and put it back in his pocket. "Still prepared to accept him?"

She nodded and went around his desk to kiss his thick fair hair, still almost as bright as hers.

"Mother sent me in for a suitable book," she said, purposely prim. "She thinks I ought to be reading when he comes to propose. What about *Wuthering Heights?*"

He took it down from the shelf and handed it to her. Simultaneously they heard the sound of carriage wheels and her mother's voice calling her back to the green parlor. She took the book and went quickly back to her mother, who arranged her in a cushioned window seat, draped her with a shawl and left her, at last, mercifully alone.

She waited, while the clock on the mantel ticked stolidly on, wondering why she felt so sure about this marriage. She had spent one romantic evening with him, then the whole of Sunday. She knew he had a half brother and half sister years younger than he was, that his family lived in a house— she suspected it was a very large one—on Fifth Avenue, and that the newlyweds would have a floor of it to themselves. He had not enumerated all of these details for her; they had emerged in conversation.

In the same way other things had emerged. He was quick, in mind as well as movement. He was not a romantic, as she was, but that was not a requirement in a man. He was well-educated but not very interested in the books and music that she loved. His love was business—and now, she was certain, herself. It was in the way he looked at her, in the electricity between them.

He seemed unacquainted with love, seemed to treat it as if it were a new book, with something unique to be discovered on every page. She was sure he had never been in love with any of his other women. She blushed, sitting there; it was an experience she wanted to share with him.

There was a rustle and she saw that he was in the room, with the door

19

only half closed behind him—the proprieties again. He started to speak, then shrugged and smiled at her, that brilliant smile of his that made words unnecessary.

They regarded each other in silence, amid the tasseled lamps and festooned draperies of the parlor, surrounded by mahogany whatnots and family photographs in ornate frames.

He walked to her and took her hands. "Marry me, Madeleine," he said.

She leaned toward him, took her hands from his and moved them slowly up along the broadcloth of his jacket and around his neck. The scent of crisp starched linen, cologne and pipe tobacco intoxicated her. His beard, when he kissed her mouth, felt strange and lovely. She had never been kissed before, except in her dreams. She sighed a little when it was over, wanting it to go on.

"Does that mean you will?" he asked, gently mocking, his strong hands holding her waist.

"Oh, yes, Jesse, it means I will." She laughed softly. "I must, or I'll be compromised."

He reached into the pocket of his vest. "This is for you," he said, taking her hand. "It was my mother's." He put the star sapphire on her finger, then looked back at her eyes. "How clever of my father to find a girl whose eyes matched this ring."

"I thought the choice was entirely yours," she said, surprised.

He led her to the pale green moiré settee that seemed too small for his frame. "The choice is mine, but he knew what I would do the minute I saw you." He took a tobacco pouch and pipe from his pocket, filled the pipe and tamped down the tobacco. "Now, when's it to be?"

She would have married him today. "June?"

He nodded. "We'll go to Europe on our honeymoon. I have business there."

She paid no attention to the mixture of business with honeymoon pleasures. The prospect of intimacy rippled through her again. She was both eager and apprehensive about it, with only the vaguest notions of what to expect. It was not a subject decent women discussed.

"I'd like to go to Italy," she said before she could blush.

"Anywhere you like. When we come back you can redecorate the house for us—we'd like that, it's a gloomy old place now." He kissed her hand. "You'll like living in New York, I'm sure."

She was sure she would have liked the North Pole if he were there, but her new life promised to be more inviting. A fine house on Fifth Avenue, a new circle of people—above all, this man as her husband. He had not said he

20

loved her, but she knew he did. They had understood each other from the beginning without words.

He came to Philadelphia every other weekend in the next months and his dark eyes followed her constantly. They were a stunning pair, the golden-haired girl and the dark-bearded man, both of them taller than average. They enjoyed the hush whenever they entered a room together; it seemed right to look as glorious as they felt.

Madeleine sailed through her engagement parties on a tide of anticipation. She floated through her gown fittings, unconcerned with trousseau linens, with china, silver and crystal patterns, impatient for the months to slip by until it was blissful June.

4

Madeleine drifted in a tub of lavender-scented water, a large towel spread across the bath for modesty's sake. Four maids bustled about her. Her luxuriant hair had been shampooed in castille soap and was being polished to a high gloss with soft flannel cloths. The day had dawned misty, but it would be clear by eleven o'clock, in time for the wedding.

"Come along, dear," her mother called from the bedroom. "You can't languish in a bath all morning or we'll never be ready. Daisy," she called to Madeleine's maid, "help Miss Madeleine out of the tub at once. I'll finish dressing and be back in ten minutes."

Averting her eyes, Daisy held a large soft towel while Madeleine rose with her back to the women and wrapped herself in it. No one had seen her naked since she was very small except herself, on the rare occasions when she appraised her body before the looking glass in her bedroom.

She went behind a screen to dry herself, very conscious today of her breasts and the joining of her thighs, glad that she had kept her skin soft all over with rose water and glycerine. Daisy passed her a sheer batiste shift trimmed with blue-threaded lace, and she dropped it over her head before she emerged from behind the screen, her shining hair in a cloud around her shoulders, her full bosom thrusting the shift away from her body. She put a lace shawl around her shoulders and went into her bedroom to have her hair dressed in a puffy "cottage loaf" just as her mother came back, in a flutter of mauve chiffon under a large silk hat crowned in velvet violets and tulle.

"Not so tightly on that side," Mrs. van Ryn told Daisy from her careful perch on an armless stool. "Leave some side curls, they suit her. All right, that'll do, now you girls be off and fetch the gown, I want a word with Miss Madeleine before I leave for the church."

The maids hurried out and Mrs. van Ryn regarded her daughter. "You look absolutely lovely, darling. We've rehearsed everything and it should all go splendidly."

"Mama," Madeleine said. "What is it like, being married?"

Mrs. van Ryn looked pained. "Really, Madeleine, your husband will tell you whatever he wants you to know."

"I wish I knew more," Madeleine whispered.

Mrs. van Ryn stood up and smoothed her mauve flounces. "You'll find out soon enough. There's some embarrassment to being a woman," she said, "but remember you're a lady; don't fuss, and it'll soon be over." She

23

smoothed a long white kid glove. "Now I must go," she said, bending to kiss Madeleine's forehead. "I wish you every happiness, darling." With a little wave she sailed out of the room as the maids came in with Madeleine's wedding lingerie and gown.

Tossing the shawl aside, Madeleine stood up in her short shift and was fitted into a long corset designed to shape her body into an S curve. After the busk was buttoned and the laces pulled tight, the maids drew fine white stockings onto Madeleine's long legs, fastening them to dainty suspenders attached to her corset. Then three petticoats were dropped over her cambric drawers and fastened at the waist by tapes. Pink satin padding was tied around her hips and beneath her arms, rounding her above and below a waist that looked tiny by comparison.

Finally the dress went on, to admiring murmurs from the maids. It had been restyled by Callot Soeurs in Paris from her great-grandmother Susannah van Ryn's gown of luscious white satin, framed in silver lace and embroidered with pearls.

The veil had been in the van Ryn family since they arrived from Holland centuries ago. It was of stiff lace, fastened to her high-piled hair and draped in folds around her face. Daisy clasped a dog collar of superb pearls around her neck, the five strands held rigid by spurs of diamonds. It was a gift from Jesse. Even her mother had been impressed.

"You look beautiful, Miss," Daisy said. "The most beautiful bride I ever saw."

"Oh, yes," one of the little maids gasped adoringly. "Like an angel, all white and gold and silver."

Once downstairs she was packed carefully into a carriage with her father, tall, dignified and dearer than ever for the hint of tears in his eyes. He said nothing, although he held her hand during the short drive to church. When the carriage stopped, she was handed out and led into the church on her father's arm. She was given a bouquet of white orchids and stephanotis, heard someone lining up the bridesmaids and ushers, the flower girl and ring bearer, and then, at last, the strains of the wedding march.

She walked in a mist of candlelight and calla lilies to where Jesse waited near the flower-banked altar. When he turned to watch her coming down the aisle, there was a look on his face that was more than delight over beauty coming to him. It was a look she would never forget. It would both sustain and mystify her until she finally understood it.

When the cake had been cut, the wedding clothes changed for travel suits, and the bouquet thrown to the people gathered on the grounds of her father's house, the celebration continued aboard a private railway car bound for New York with the Slayter family and their guests.

There was Jethro, birdlike and preening his feathers with satisfaction, myriad aunts, uncles, and cousins Madeleine still could not sort out, financier friends and partners of J. Slayter and Son, and her new sister and brother.

"Will you stay in America to finish school?" Madeleine asked Philippa, home from England where she had been attending school.

"Goodness, no," the girl replied in a thoroughly English accent. "One can't possibly live in a barbarous country like America." Her thin face, very adult for a girl of sixteen, softened as she looked at Madeleine. "If I were as beautiful as you, of course, it wouldn't matter. As it is, I'll do better in a country that makes more of wit."

"Beauty isn't something I accomplished," Madeleine said, "even though I'm glad it happened to me."

Philippa smiled, looking almost pretty. "Then I won't value you for that alone." She moved her head in her father's direction. "He will, though. He thinks women are inferior creatures except when it comes to children."

"I didn't marry *him.*" Madeleine smiled. She was aware of her father-in-law's admiration for her, but she was accustomed to men's admiration by now.

"And a good thing too," Philippa told her. "Jesse's not at all bad; he has a certain style." She studied Madeleine. "You're really in love, aren't you?"

Madeleine nodded. "More than most women, from what I've seen."

Philippa smiled again. "Well, I wish you happy, I really do." She glanced around the crowded railway car. "Look after my little brother, will you?"

They both found the boy, brown-eyed and too solemn for a fourteen-year-old, standing near his father. He seemed fascinated by Madeleine, but too shy to say much to her.

"Of course I will," Madeleine promised. "I'd look after you, too—but you're a lot older than I am."

They laughed together, unlikely friends, and the train rolled on toward New York. It seemed many hours before Daisy helped Madeleine to undress and put on her billowy white silk nightgown, put the wedding jewelry away in the special case she always carried with proud responsibility, and brushed out Madeleine's heavy blond hair at the dressing table.

Finally she put the brush down and looked at her mistress in the mirror.

"If that's all, Miss," Daisy said tentatively, clasping her capable hands over her starched white apron. Her round eyes regarded Madeleine with affection and virginal apprehension; she was only a few years older than Madeleine and still unmarried.

25

Madeleine smiled and turned to the girl who had cared for her so intimately for many years. "Yes, Daisy, dear, that's all—and thank you for all you've done to make this day so lovely."

"Oh, Miss," Daisy said, tears in her eyes. "I'd do anything for you. I do hope you'll be happy." Her lips trembled dubiously at the ordeal awaiting Madeleine tonight.

Impulsively, the two young women embraced each other, then Daisy hurried out, leaving Madeleine alone in the hotel bedroom, waiting for her husband.

5

Jesse hesitated before he tossed the white nightshirt aside and put on only a robe of dark blue China silk. He glanced at the chased silver watch his valet had put on a table, along with his billfold, pocket comb, tobacco pouch and pipe. Half an hour had elapsed since he had left Madeleine with her maid. In another five minutes she would surely be ready.

He filled a pipe, then thought better of it and slipped it into the pocket of his robe. He always smoked after sex, sometimes before, but this was his wife, and he did not want to offend her if she disliked the odor of tobacco.

"My wife," he said aloud, trying to get used to it. He crossed the room to look out at Fifth Avenue under the streetlights. His father's house was mere blocks away on the same avenue, but he had not even considered spending his wedding night there. Jesse felt too much a son in his presence. He had no wish to be called "boy" on his wedding night. Perhaps things would be different now that he was a married man—except for the fact of consummation.

He stirred, excitement rising in him again at the thought. He had managed to restrain the physical desire he had felt for Madeleine from the first moment he saw her in that ballroom in Philadelphia, but he would be able to let it free in minutes now. Still, he wanted to treat her gently, and that was something that had never concerned him. Before he met Madeleine, Jesse had reduced sex to sensations: warmth, wetness, a gathering of force and its uncontrollable release, then a vague repugnance. Women, to him, were regularly necessary in bed, even pleasant to see in drawing rooms, but they were not stimulating. They had nothing to do with money and power.

Madeleine, though, was different. She was entitled to special consideration because she was his wife and would be the mother of his sons, and because—he might as well admit it—the sight of her had created more than a powerful erotic need in him.

He had expected her to be a lovely bride, but when he had turned to see her this morning in the church, she had been so virginally radiant, yet so powerfully female, that he had been more than proud; he had been fiercely triumphant that she was his, that no other man had any right to her.

He crossed the room swiftly and tapped on her door. She was sitting at the dressing table and she stood and smiled at him as he came in, the sheer folds of her nightdress drifting around her. In seconds he was holding her close against him, feeling the roundness of her uncorseted body, kissing her

27

mouth now without restraint. Her lips parted readily under his. He felt himself hardening against her and saw the surprise on her face.

"Don't be afraid," he whispered, his voice heavy with the craving of his body. "Come to bed. I won't hurt you."

She slipped under the bedclothes while he turned off the light, removed his robe, and got in naked beside her. Her nightdress was tangled about her legs.

"Let me take this off," he said and she nodded, holding up her arms so he could lift it over her head. Then he held her and kissed her again, letting one hand play over her breasts lightly until she relaxed. He cupped her breasts more firmly and let his tongue brush the nipples. When she sighed contentedly, it excited him beyond control and he moved to lie over her, parting her thighs with his knee, then searching with his body until he found the way into hers.

"Oh, yes, that's wonderful," he said, partially inside her. "But don't pull back, Madeleine, please, let me in."

He slid his hands under her, tilting her body up to his, and went deeply inside her. The surprise of penetration had made her tense and tight around him. Soon he was not conscious of sensation, only of drive and heat and the soft body under him, enclosing him. He erupted out of himself with a groan and a long shudder.

His head dropped on the pillow next to hers and he lay for some moments, breathing heavily. Then he lifted himself, still inside her, to look at her in the dim light from the street.

"Did I hurt you?"

Her blue eyes, wide and misty, looked up at him as she shook her head. He lowered his head to kiss her, very differently now, then pulled himself from her and lay at her side, slipping an arm under her shoulders.

"It was a surprise, I know," he said, and she answered yes, moving into the curve of his arm. "You were very brave about it." He had a strong urge to smoke, but resisted it. "It'll be easier after this first time, you'll see."

"Are you happy, Jesse?" she whispered.

He chuckled. "I'm surprised you have to ask."

"You've been so quiet since this morning. I think the last words you said to me were 'I will.' "

He reached for his robe, took the pipe from its pocket, and lit it before he gave her the only answer acceptable under the circumstances. "You were so incredibly beautiful I didn't know what to say." It was, amazingly, true.

"You might have said 'I love you.' " He was relieved to hear the smile in her voice.

"With all those people listening?"

28

"Not then—just now."

"Didn't I?" He smiled down at her through the curls of smoke. "Well, I do. You've just had ample proof of that."

She was quiet a moment, while he stroked her hair. "I like your sister very much," she said.

He laughed. "You're about the only one who does. My father calls her a sharp-tongued, angular wench."

"She's very bright," Madeleine insisted. "Extremely intelligent. When she marries I'm sure she'll have a 'salon' and entertain all the cleverest people in London."

"Husbands are hard to come by for women who are too intelligent."

Madeleine laughed. "Did you choose me because you thought I was stupid?"

"Of course not," Jesse said, hoping she would not ask why he had chosen her.

"I'm glad of that," she said. "I love your little brother too. He has such huge, serious eyes."

Jesse knocked the ashes out of his pipe and put the tray on the bedside table. "He's not serious, he's spoiled. My father never disciplines him, gives him whatever he wants. It's made a stubborn little beggar out of him." He turned to kiss her again. "Now you must sleep. The ship sails at ten and we must be aboard by nine at the latest." He smiled contentedly. "Good night, Mrs. Slayter."

He was soon asleep. Madeleine lay warmly against him, luxuriating in their naked closeness. She had been surprised at the way a man's body grew and hardened to penetrate a woman's, but it all seemed natural once it was done.

She had always supposed that what had just happened would be more exciting, that it would be in some way as ecstatic for her as it seemed to have been for him—the way his body shuddered at the end, the sound he had made. But if he was pleased, then so was she.

Married! She was well and truly married to a man she adored. She sighed blissfully, settled even closer to him and fell asleep.

6

"The house is magnificent," Philippa said to Daniel, toying with a biscuit and savoring her sherry. "Madeleine's completely transformed the old mausoleum. No wonder you all dote on her."

They were sitting in the garden behind Jethro Slayter's mansion, waiting for Madeleine to come down from the nursery, and for Jesse and his father to finish changing and join them for a drink before dinner. Philippa, brilliantly stylish and very conscious that her husband, Elton, was Lord Lucas and an English peer, seemed older than nineteen. She had Jethro's features but on her they suggested wit, not cunning.

"What good is doting?" Daniel said glumly. "She's alone most of the time."

Philippa shrugged. "So are a lot of women."

"A lot of women don't seem to care," Daniel said pointedly.

His sister laughed. "I'm enjoying my little junket without Elton, if that's what you mean."

"You're not in love with Elton, is what I mean."

Philippa raised an eyebrow. "I'm quite fond enough of Elton, but of course Madeleine's mad about Jesse, I know. You'd think she'd have got over that after three years of marriage and a child, the way everyone else does." She took another sip of sherry. "You're very observant, I must say. Are you falling in love with your sister-in-law? Oh, don't scowl, she's the most gorgeous creature in the world, and the nicest, and you're the romantic type."

"I'm not in love with her," Daniel said quietly. "I just like her a lot. I thought you did too."

"Of course I like her!" Philippa was impatient. "I just can't get exercised about a woman who has everything she wants—including a daughter and a husband she's dotty about."

"*She* doesn't complain," Daniel said. "I'm the one who thinks she's lonely." He stood and began to pace slowly under the huge elm tree that shaded them.

Philippa regarded him attentively. He was already as tall as Jesse, but much slighter, not so squarely built. He didn't have Jesse's saturnine good looks. He had light-brown hair—that was from their mother—with a

31

square jaw and a fuller mouth than Jesse's, a more finely modeled brow and thoughtful brown eyes. She found him less open than Jesse, but somehow more sincere. Jesse's charm was easy to see; you had to look for Daniel's. He was too serious for a boy of seventeen, she thought, and extremely sensitive. "I sometimes wonder how you got born into this family," she said.

"What do you mean by that?"

She gave him one of her rare soft smiles—he thought she would have used it more often if she knew how it transformed her face. "You're just so different from Jesse and me," she said. "We're content with ourselves; all we want in life is more of what we already have, and we don't look much beyond our noses. You do."

"All Father ever thinks about is money," Daniel said, "and before Madeleine came along, so did Jesse."

"The way we spend money," Philippa said languidly, "it's a good thing they do."

"You know what I mean."

Philippa nodded. "It's true they're both in love with their lovely little banks, but that's the way of the world. Elton's got his title and his estate, after all."

"And what have you got?" Daniel asked her, curiously intent.

"Him—my position in society. Two grand houses, one daughter and, with any luck, a son next time out to carry on the title and no more childbearing after that." She leaned back in the chair, stretched her arms up to the elm tree and laughed. "Then I'll have all the time I want to go about, wearing gorgeous clothes and talking to interesting people—perhaps a love affair later on, who can tell?"

Daniel blushed painfully.

"Good heavens," Philippa said archly. "I can't really have shocked you. Father let me know, in that heavy-handed way of his, that you'd lost your innocence. Quite proud of you, he was."

"It's just the sort of thing he *would* be proud of."

"Maybe he thinks you take after him when it comes to women. He killed off Jesse's mother and ours with all those miscarriages too close together. Some lucky woman's alive today because he decided he likes brothels better than marriage." Philippa leaned forward and refilled her sherry glass from the tray on the lawn table. "Anyway, that's not the sort of thing I meant by having an affair."

"I hope not," Daniel said.

"Oh, everyone has them or risks being bored to death by marriage, but don't fret, love, I'm still faithful to my lord. I'm sure that's not what's bothering you—or Madeleine's 'loneliness' either."

32

"No, you're right, it's Father."

"Well, you can't be blamed for that." His sister was very matter-of-fact. "I always thought he was odious. He never paid any attention to me, thank God, I'm only a girl, but he's always been madly fond of you. It makes Jesse jealous, I can tell you, but I can't see why it should bother you."

Daniel stopped his pacing, his head just grazing a low branch. "He'll buy me anything I want, but he'll make me go to Yale and then come into Slayter's, no matter what *I* want to do."

"Ah," Philippa said, "so that's it. What *do* you want?"

"To study art—to be an architect." He looked at her in abject defeat. It was sad to see in so young a man.

"Have you told him?"

"Yes. He laughed at me, said I couldn't build a chicken coop, much less a house."

"You've got a year before Yale," she said without much conviction. "Perhaps he'll change his mind."

"You know better than that," Daniel said.

"Well, maybe he'll die—then you'll have Jesse to deal with and he won't care."

Daniel looked at her in shocked admiration. "You don't care what you say, do you?" He considered her suggestion, then shook his head. "It wouldn't make any difference. Jesse gets more like him every day."

"Not really. Jesse doesn't care what anyone does as long as it won't interfere with Jesse. It's one of his most admirable traits and you'd do well to follow his example." She held out her hand to him and he took it. "People pretend to admire a sensitive soul in this world, Daniel, but they always trample it to death. Cheer up, little brother, things may not be as bad as they seem—and here comes Madeleine. You can worry about her."

They both turned to watch their sister-in-law coming across the lawn from the house. The slanting rays of late-afternoon sun cast a deeper glow on her apricot gown, on the pale gold of her hair. One hand shaded her eyes and the sunlight sparkled on the sapphire ring she always wore. She moved with quiet grace.

"Amazing," Philippa said. "A 'still unravished bride of quietness.' She was a lot more perky at her wedding—and mine." She raised her voice to call to Madeleine. "How's Susannah Bess?"

"Asleep, I'm glad to say." Madeleine reached them and took a chair next to Philippa's. "I could do with a sherry."

Daniel poured it for her. "You tire yourself out with Susannah."

"He's right." Philippa nodded. "That's what Nanny is for."

33

Madeleine laughed. "I know—my mother says I'm acting terribly middle class—but that child's so adorable I can't keep away."

"What does Jesse say about her?" Philippa asked.

"That she's the marvel of the century. He's still in raptures after a whole year—and I thought he'd be disappointed that I had a girl."

"Wait another year until she's two," Daniel said. "He'll read her the financial pages."

7

"You were right," Jesse said to his father with no preliminary greeting. He sat down across from Jethro at their usual table in Luchow's. Jesse, just off the train from Chicago, wore day clothes; Jethro was in evening dress, obviously ready for a night out. "They're flat broke and ready to take whatever price we offer."

Jethro chortled. "Did you close the deal?"

"Yes, at thirty-five."

"Well done, boy, well done!" Jethro signaled the waiter to bring another glass. "You've put your father-in-law's nose out of joint—it'll teach him not to poke it into Slayter's." He stopped talking while the waiter filled Jesse's glass with Burgundy and left the table. "You'd have thought we were trying to steal Madeleine's money!"

Jesse tasted the wine appreciatively. "We *did* appropriate it for a long time, didn't we? Anyway, we've doubled it for her now and bought Susannah part of a utility company, so van Ryn can't say anything."

Jethro nodded. "By the end of this week he'll need financing from us."

Jesse put his glass down. "What did you do?"

"Didn't bother to tell him we were pulling out of those silver mines, starting a bear raid."

Jesse was very still. "But why? What good can it do us to have Madeleine's father penniless?"

Jethro looked at his son and wagged his head slightly. "The man was too curious, you know that. And he's got notions, doesn't approve of speculation, thinks bear raids in the market are immoral. We'd have had him around our necks like an albatross. This way we'll support him—he can't question the hand that feeds him, can he?"

Jesse thought it over for a few seconds. What could he tell Madeleine?

"I suppose he needed a dressing-down, but I didn't expect you to go that far."

"Neither did he." Jethro cackled.

"Madeleine will be upset. You know how she looks up to her father."

"Just remember one thing," Jethro said, ignoring him, "if you let people predict what move you're going to make, you'll be off Wall Street in a week.

Now let's talk about utilities. The way this country's growing, they're just what we want, provided we pick the right cities."

"And provided you guess the right direction of growth," Jesse added, "as I did."

"What do you want as a reward, a gold medal?" Jethro demanded.

Jesse kept his expression very calm. "I'd like more autonomy at Slayter's," he said evenly. "I've earned it, but you still have the last say in everything I do."

"Hell, boy, you'll have the whole shebang as soon as I'm dead. What's your hurry?" He smiled wickedly. "I know, it's power you're after, you can sniff it, can't you? Well, you'll have to wait, the way I did. My father lived to be eighty-seven—had five wives to my two, the last one seventy years younger than he was—I think he died of her!" His smile faded. "You'll just have to wait," he said again. "It's not as if you'll have to share it. Daniel doesn't know one end of a company from the other. You'll have to take care of the lad," he added with concern. "He's not like you."

Jesse finished his wine amid the convivial noises of the restaurant, filling with glossy women and men in evening clothes. He did not feel in the least convivial. Even the shared exhilaration of his successful mission to Chicago, to outwit other bidders for a company, had evaporated. He was still just his father's vassal, not an empire builder in his own right—and directed to be his brother's keeper into the bargain! Jethro had always been besotted by his younger son for no reason at all that Jesse could determine. Daniel was sly and secretive and made no attempt whatever to emulate their father—and that was all Jesse had ever done.

He set his glass down, refusing more wine. "It's time I went home," he said blandly, no indication of his feelings apparent in his face or his voice.

"Eager for your lady's charms?" Jethro said.

"Very," Jesse answered. Actually he was not thinking about sex, but he was damned if he'd tell his father so.

Jethro's furrowed face had gone sour with an envy he never bothered to conceal. "If I had a wife like yours, I wouldn't be so hot after an old man's power as you are."

"Then maybe I won't be so 'hot' in the morning," Jesse said. Madeleine was the one thing his father hadn't owned before he had, couldn't make him wait for, couldn't overindulge the way he did Daniel. She was the one winning hand Jesse held, and because of her he managed to say a polite good night to Jethro before he left.

Take care of Daniel! Jesse thought angrily, as his cab rolled up Fifth Avenue. *Let him take care of himself.* Only two things softened his bitterness: One day his father *would* die and Slayter's would be his, and while Jesse waited, he had sole possession of a woman his father wanted.

The hansom dropped him at the curb in front of the house, and he paid the man and went inside, letting the butler take his coat, hat, gloves and cane. It was late, past ten o'clock, but he went directly to the nursery to see Susannah.

"Good evening, Nanny," he said softly to the woman when she looked in from the next room. "How has she been?" He looked down at the dark-haired sleeping child, and the woman reflected that if anything could make Mr. Slayter even handsomer than he was, it was looking at his little girl.

"Busy as a bee, as usual," she whispered, smiling. "That child is into everything. Madame taught her three new words today."

"Did she?" Jesse was as interested as if his entire fortune were at stake. "What were they?"

"Baby, honey and blue."

Jesse smiled. "I'm tempted to wake her up to hear them."

"You mustn't do that," Nanny said seriously. "We don't want Miss Susannah forming bad habits."

With a last look at Susannah, Jesse left, wondering what bad habits a sixteen-month-old girl could form. He followed the gallery that bordered each floor of the four-story mansion. It was a bright and elegant house, since Madeleine had replaced the heavy old furniture and dark-hued carpets and draperies with pale blues, soft beiges and white. Their own bedroom, their two dressing rooms, his study and her private parlor were on the second floor, across the stairwell from the nursery. Jethro lived on one side of the third floor and Daniel on the other, with guest rooms between them. There had been no guests since Philippa's visit last summer and the house was quiet with Daniel away at school.

There was a crack of light under the door of Madeleine's parlor and he knocked briefly and went in. She looked up from the book she was reading, tossed it aside, and came to greet him, reaching up to shower kisses on his face.

"I've only been gone for a week," Jesse said, smiling down at her.

"It felt like a year to me."

He walked back to the sofa with her. "You ought to get out more," he said.

"And do what?"

"Whatever it is women do—shop, play bridge, gossip."

Madeleine shook her head. "None of that is nearly as fascinating to me as you and Susannah—and you know it. Now tell me about Chicago."

He filled his pipe and she sat down beside him. "It wouldn't interest you —it's just business."

"Try me," she persisted. "Father wrote that you were both interested in some utility company."

Jesse pulled on his pipe. "I wish he wouldn't bother you with things like that." He glanced at her. "Your father's affairs are in a bad state."

She looked very worried. "I thought something was troubling him. What will happen to him, Jesse?"

He took her hand. "Nothing at all, you're not to worry. We'll take care of him. Do you think I'd let him go under without lending a hand? Life will be easier for him, letting us run his affairs."

She looked very doubtful. "My father is a very independent man. He likes to run his own affairs."

He said nothing for a moment, trying to master his anger with Jethro for acting without so much as a word to his own son.

Because he knew I'd object, he thought, and flushed because Jethro cared very little for his son's objections. It had taken Jesse many years and a hugely successful deal to voice the demands he had made tonight—and he had been refused. He moved in his chair as if he could escape the realization of how ineffectual he was.

Madeleine's voice was low, but insistent. "Isn't there anything you could have done to keep him from going under?"

"Of course not," Jesse said, too tartly. He saw her face and softened his tone. "You know I'd have protected him if there had been any way to do it, no matter what the business considerations."

He put down his pipe and took her face in his two hands. "Trust me, darling," he said softly. When her eyes continued to search his, he kissed her mouth lingeringly, letting his hands slide down her neck and stop at the buttons of her velvet robe. He waited for her eyes to close, as they always did whenever he touched her like this, and for the searching gaze to stop.

"Lord, I've missed you," he whispered. "Come to bed."

She felt his hands on her body and she began to tremble in anticipation. She had been waiting for him all day, all week. She felt his lips against her breasts as he unbuttoned the robe, and she leaned back against the arm of the couch, drawing him down to her.

"Come to bed," he said again, and she complied, although she wanted him to make love to her there, on the couch, in the same kind of passionate urgency she felt herself.

It took him longer tonight and she felt very hot between her thighs when it was over. She wanted more, but she had no idea what "more" was. She

38

only felt, for the first time since her marriage, that there was a corner she had not turned, a hill she had not climbed. *It must be me,* she thought.

"Talk to me," she said to him. "Tell me what you're thinking."

He looked at her with what bordered on impatience. "What is there to talk about?"

"Are you happy, Jesse?" she asked, needing to hear him say it more than ever tonight.

"Do you still need to ask me that?" He reached for the pipe he kept in the table near his side of the bed. "Nanny says you taught Susannah three new words today."

"Yes," Madeleine said, a little hurt that he had gone first to see his child and not his wife. Then she felt contrite—to envy her own child, to question her own husband! He hadn't told her about her father because business affairs were far too complicated for her to follow, because he wanted to spare her. Suddenly she thought again that something must be wrong with her, and then she thought she knew what it was. "Did she tell you what words they were?"

"Blue, honey—I forget the third—oh, yes, baby. Why those?"

Madeleine smiled; her strange feelings of moments ago seemed foolish. "There's going to be a new baby—I hope it'll wear blue, but until we know we'll call it 'honey.' "

He kissed her reverently, as if she had done something quite miraculous, and she felt too replete in his arms to worry about anything, even about her father's troubles. She was Jesse's wife, she was carrying Jesse's child again, her loyalties belonged with Jesse. Of course she trusted him; there was no reason in the world why she should not.

8

"You're looking very merry these days, Madame," Daisy told her one day a few months later.

"Oh, Daisy, I feel like a girl again," Madeleine laughed, "even with this." She pointed to her rounding belly, then pressed her fingertips to her mouth when Daisy blushed. "Do forgive me, Daisy, I didn't mean to embarrass you, but you'll see how very natural these things seem once you're married."

"Yes, Madame," was Daisy's only answer, as she blushed more deeply than ever. She was going to marry Bob Harris, the Slayters' coachman. "And about time too," old Jethro had said, when he was told. "They've been making calves' eyes at each other for years."

"Marriage is the most sublime state in the world," Madeleine kept saying —and these days it was. Jesse's pride in the expected child was endearing and the way he cherished her intoxicating. She could not help being more playful, despite her growing bulk. Jesse was more attentive and Jethro differently so.

"A daughter's well enough," Jethro said one night, "but we want a son from you this time." He was paternal now, not the least bit gallant, a tendency that had often disturbed her in the past.

"And a son you shall have," she told him happily.

"How can you tell?" Jesse demanded.

"I just know," she said with utter conviction, sipping her wine. She watched the two men look at each other, obviously convinced and in a state of almost religious awe, and she laughed delightedly. "If you two could be as sure of your market as I am of my son, you'd own all of Wall Street."

Jethro snorted appreciatively and Jesse smiled. It was the most amusing evening the three of them had ever spent together.

"Are you happy, Jesse?" she asked him that night in bed. Her belly was well-rounded by now and her breasts taut and heavy.

"Very happy," he said.

"Here," urged him, taking his hand. "You can feel the baby moving." His hand rested firmly on her until he felt the flutter and nodded. She pulled it to her breasts, aroused by his touch. "Jesse," she said, "make love to me."

"It might hurt the baby."

"No, no, it won't," she assured him. "It's only five months. Please, Jesse, I want you to."

41

He looked at her as he had when she wanted strawberries last week, and in the same way, it occurred to her later, he complied with her whim; pregnant women were not to be thwarted.

In whatever spirit he did it, the experience was electric for her. Her sensitive nipples were rigid before he touched them; her body, engorged by the weight she carried, responded the second he penetrated her and she shook with pure pleasure. He was alarmed by her movements, then overwhelmed by his own, then anxious at the sounds she began to make, sounds he had heard from other women who were paid to make them. He would have withdrawn, but she held him to her until her trembling peaked and stopped.

"Oh, Jesse, I love you," she murmured. Her mouth reached for his, but he drew his body carefully away. "What is it?" she asked, still clinging to echoes of exquisite sensation.

"I'm not sure that's safe," he said. "I'll speak to the doctor tomorrow. That never happened to you before."

Apparently the doctor thought it was a risk, and Jesse slept in his study until Jonathan van Ryn Slayter was born. If Jesse adored his daughter, he idolized his son, often gazing at him with the same satisfaction he showed when he had engineered a difficult business negotiation for his father.

The charmed life of her pregnancy was over and Madeleine spent her days with her children and her evenings in the constant round of New York social life. Occasionally she took the children to Philadelphia to visit her parents, but although her mother was the same, her father was very changed since his retirement. He had aged terribly and seemed ill and listless. There were no confidential talks and no little jokes for them to share.

"You never laugh anymore," she said to him one evening in his study.

"Nor you," was his reply.

"Life in New York doesn't encourage merriment," she told him.

"Life—or the Slayters?" He said it lightly, but there was something serious behind it. She knew it was a trial for her father to be supported by her husband, and again she wondered how much Jesse had to do with that, if he had really tried to prevent it. It would have been impossible for her to side with one of them against the other, and something told her that if she knew everything about her father's bankruptcy, taking sides was what she might have to do.

She could not appear to take sides in New York, either, in the rivalry between Jesse and Daniel. Actually, it was Jesse who craved his father's approval; Daniel had no interest in it.

"You know, Jesse," she said softly to him once when they were alone in her parlor. "Your father wouldn't know what to do without you."

42

He looked at her quizzically, as if she were speaking in a foreign language. "He spoils Daniel for fun, but he needs you."

Jesse turned back to his newspaper. "I'm sure I don't know what you're talking about," he said.

She made one last attempt. "I'm talking about love. I love my own children differently."

"When it comes to love," Jesse said, smiling brightly, "I defer to your judgment." He put down the paper and came to kiss her cheek. "You women know more about love from the day you're born than men will ever learn."

There was something lost inside Jesse; Madeleine had seen many glimpses of it before his pride closed over it like quicksand. Someday he would trust her enough to share it with her.

9

Sunlight struggled through the windows of the Slayters' crepe-swathed carriage. It touched on Madeleine's unrelieved black, on the stark white collars Jesse and Daniel wore and on the white ruching that trimmed Susannah's dress and the inside of her bonnet. The child held Madeleine's black-gloved hand and listened intently to the argument between her father and her young uncle. Actually, Jesse was calm; it was Daniel who argued.

"Look, Jesse, there's no reason to fuss about where I go to school; it can't make any difference to you."

"It made a difference to Father," Jesse answered. "Everything he always told you is in his will. You'll attend Yale and then come to Slayter's, or you'll be disinherited."

"But you're his executor," Daniel fumed. "You can change things."

Signs of annoyance ruffled Jesse's calm. "He's barely in his grave, Daniel! Are you going to keep on fighting with him, even now?"

"Not with him, with you. I thought finding him dead in a"—he glanced at his four-year-old niece—"place like that was the final straw, even for you."

"Daniel," Jesse said in a warning voice. "You go too far."

The younger man flushed angrily. "I go too far? *I?* Don't you think running everyone else's life the way he did is going too far?"

"You're still his son and you're still a minor. He has that right."

"Nobody has that right—and it seems I'm not his son, I'm his property, just as you are. I'm surprised he didn't leave you yourself in his rotten will."

Jesse's self-control was visible. "That's enough, now hold your tongue."

Madeleine leaned toward them. "Please, don't argue with each other. Why not let him do as he likes, Jesse? It can't make that much difference."

His eyes glittering, Jesse looked at the lovely face under its swooping black-plumed hat, astonished that she had taken Daniel's side against him. He almost said so, but he held himself in check.

"It may not seem to make any difference, Madeleine, but a man has to have the right education to take his place in the world. Making mud pies in a Parisian garret is not the right education." He looked from her to his angry brother. "Daniel is my responsibility now, and I have to do what's best for him, no matter what he thinks he wants."

45

"Damn it," Daniel said, beside himself. "I'm twenty years old! I know perfectly well what I want, and it isn't to row through Yale and then crouch behind a desk at Slayter's for the rest of my life. I'd feel like a caged animal." He shook his head. "There was nothing you could do to help while he was alive, Jesse, I understand that, but you don't have to play his game now. You're in charge, or aren't you?"

No, Madeleine thought, *he isn't*—and with a cold chill she thought of her father's premature death the year before, and the feeling she increasingly had that he had died of grief, not illness. Even though Jethro was dead and buried, he was still in charge of Jesse's life, as he must have been when he made that ruthless decision to dissolve the van Ryn fortune. Jesse could have interfered then—warned her father, done something—but he hadn't, any more than he would now, for Daniel.

She looked at Jesse, waiting for his answer, but he said nothing, reaching for Susannah to put her on his lap. "You mustn't be frightened by all this," he said to his daughter. "Your Uncle Daniel is not himself."

"He looks the same," Susannah said, uncomfortably.

"Outwardly, perhaps," Jesse explained patiently. "The inner man is changeable at his age."

Susannah nodded quickly, as she usually did when Father explained things to her, although she wondered if everyone had a man inside who was different. Mummy often asked her if she really understood or was simply trying to please her father by pretending. Susannah couldn't see any difference.

"Do you really mean you won't even consider what Daniel wants," Madeleine asked in a voice that sounded hollow, even to her.

Jesse only patted his daughter's cheek approvingly and settled back in his seat with her, ignoring Madeleine. He turned to his half brother with insulting patience. "There's no point to this discussion. I'm not going to defy my father's wishes the very day he's buried."

"Why not? For all your fawning on him you thought he was a crude, revolting old tyrant, just like everyone else."

Jesse's calm broke. "My opinions are my own business! I don't remember sharing them with you. You didn't find him crude and revolting enough to refuse everything he showered on you from the day you were born. He spoiled you rotten—and you loved every moment of it. You'll have enough to live like a gentleman, even with your extravagant taste, provided you don't upset your own cart by being foolhardy. A few acceptable drawings don't make an architect."

"Spoken like a true Slayter," Daniel said, cuttingly.

"You're as much a Slayter as I am," Jesse retorted.

46

"To my everlasting horror, yes, I am," Daniel snapped. "But I loathe it and you wouldn't change it if you could."

The two glared at each other, at an impasse. Susannah stirred in the uneasy silence. "Am I a Slayter?" she asked, trying to divert them from their quarrel. She hated quarreling. It was one of the few things that could make her feel uneasy, even when her father was right there at her side.

Daniel slumped back against the carriage seat with an unintelligible curse. Jesse straightened his jacket and brushed invisible lint from his immaculate lapel. He seemed not to have heard Susannah's question, and a warning pressure from her mother's hand kept her from asking again.

The carriage turned into Fifth Avenue and Susannah began to hear other noises again: the squeak of the springs, the clop of the horses' hoofs, and the clatter of traffic. She was sorry that her uncle was "not himself." It seemed amazing to her that he would dare to argue with her father. It was foolish to argue with a man who was always right and who explained things so carefully. Susannah understood a lot of things about Father. She wondered why her mother didn't.

"All right, Jesse," Daniel said finally, in a voice that made him sound even older than twenty to his niece. "I'll finish Yale and then I'll come to Slayter's and I hope you'll regret it as much as the old man's going to." He said no more; when the carriage stopped at the mounting block in front of the house, he sprang out without waiting for the footman and walked rapidly away.

Servants handed Madeleine down and lifted Susannah out. "I'm going to see Jonathan," the child said to her mother, waiting for a nod of permission before she started off. "I want to tell him all about it." Susannah and Jonathan had their own means of communication no one else could share.

Jesse turned to his wife when they were alone. Black made other women haggard, but it only emphasized Madeleine's fairness, the luster of her hair and the softness of her skin. "How could you side with Daniel against me?" he demanded, his mouth rigid.

"Oh, Jesse, I didn't! I just thought it didn't matter that much, that he might as well have what he wants; he'd be less bother to you that way." She was shocked by his vehemence and amazed at her own need to be conciliatory.

He was only slightly mollified. "He's always had what he wants! This time it could ruin his life."

Madeleine dropped her wrap and took off her gloves. "Is architecture such a shameful profession?" She had never been so careful of what she said.

47

"No," Jesse said, not looking at her. "If he really wants it badly enough," he went on, brightening, "another two years at Yale won't stop him, and at least he'll have a gentleman's education." He came to her, touching her cheek with his lips. "I must be sure he has that much, Madeleine, you can see that, can't you?" He looked at her beseechingly. "Help me with him, Madeleine, he'll listen to you."

Madeleine's blue eyes misted. He was asking her to help him and he had never done that before. She put her arms around him, trying to push everything else away.

"Of course I'll help you, darling," she said against his cheek, thankful that he could not see her face. She held him as if the Furies were after him and she could save him.

Then Susannah called and Madeleine left him to go up to the children, moving slowly with the weight of what she had to acknowledge about the man she had married.

"You mustn't cry, Mummy," Susannah said anxiously, one small hand stroking her mother, the other touching the little boy in Madeleine's lap.

"Yes, darling, I know." Madeleine made herself stop crying because life had just tipped the balance for Jesse and everything he had always wanted was his—except the one thing he needed most and would never have: the gift of it while his father was still living.

After what had happened in the carriage today—Jesse's imperious will to direct lives and destinies after his own fashion—Madeleine was convinced her husband had inherited Jethro's character along with his empire. How much of Jesse Slayter had been lost when he traded his principles for his father's approval? She wondered if there was anything of Jesse left for her to save.

"Mummy, Jonnie's crying," Susannah said reproachfully.

Madeleine shifted her son's weight in her arms. "He's tired, darling, he must have his nap." She touched Susannah's little face, so like Jesse's with its intelligent dark eyes, its silky black brows.

"Maybe he'd like a nice cup of tea instead," Susannah said, offering Nanny's recipe for adult disasters.

"You know he doesn't drink tea, my love," Madeleine said. "Please ring for Nanny for me."

Susannah did it, reluctant to have her favorite toy put to bed, but yielding to the inevitable. "I know he doesn't," she said with serious determination, "but you have to try everything, don't you?"

When Nanny came in, Madeleine handed Jonathan to her and gazed at her daughter. But of course! Jethro was gone now, she and Jesse would be alone together, without even Daniel to stir Jesse's bitterness. She and Jesse would travel to Europe alone, they would be by themselves at Southampton.

No, she thought, *I can't just let him go, I love him.*

"You're right, Susannah," she said, holding out her arms. The child ran to her and Madeleine swept her onto her lap. "You have to try everything to help someone you love."

She pressed her cheek to Susannah's glossy black hair and felt the little arms hug her hard. "You're a very clever girl, Susannah Bess Slayter. Has anyone ever told you that?"

Susannah nodded, her face radiant. "Father."

Jesse stirred the library fire and a secret little smile lit his face. It had taken a long time—he was thirty-four years old—but he wasn't "old Jethro's boy" on the Street anymore. No one would ever address him as "boy" again, although, in a strange way, he kept listening for that raspy voice.

Then he thought of the new deference his colleagues showed him. It excited him physically to be suddenly conscious not only of his power but of his complete discretion to use it however he chose.

He felt desire stir in him. It might be unseemly for a man to have sexual intercourse with his wife on the very night of his father's funeral, but he wanted it and he would have it.

Besides, no one would know.

Book II

10

If anything, Jesse's new prominence on Wall Street kept him busier than ever, and when the war broke out in Europe, he was even less inclined to share the most important part of his life with her.

"Do you realize," she told him one night when the war was making headlines all over the world, "that the only place we meet alone is in bed—and not even there every night!"

"I'm out so late. I'd rather sleep in my dressing room than disturb you." He had just lit a pipe, as he always did after sex. "I was going to suggest a separate bedroom—it would be more comfortable for both of us."

"It's more uncomfortable to me to sleep alone," she said. "I might not see you for days on end that way."

He was very patient with her. "You have to understand that there are more important matters for me to consider than where I sleep."

"Oh, I know the world couldn't possibly turn without you, but neither can I."

He replaced his pillows and smiled, looking down at her. "We've been married for over ten years. Marriage is not a romantic novel."

"What is it then? A business deal?"

He used another match. "In a way. It's a mutually beneficial arrangement between suitable partners."

"My God, Jesse, I'm a woman, not a corporation! I need to be considered, not negotiated."

He was quiet for a moment, puffing. "Is that how you'd describe what just happened here?" His gesture covered the rumpled bed. "A negotiation?"

She sat up, letting the sheets slip down, exposing her breasts. "Just about," she said. "It was the outcome that mattered to you, not the person you were dealing with. I might have been any woman. You didn't seem to know you were making love to me."

"Are you pregnant?" Jesse asked hopefully.

She threw back the covers and got out of bed. "No, I'm not, and it's obviously not that time of the month, either. I know very well what I'm saying. You may not realize it, Jesse, but you've locked me out of your life, everywhere but here—and sometimes I feel as if you've done it here, too, in a strange way that has nothing to do with infidelity."

53

He watched her through the pipe smoke, admiring her nakedness, but his mouth compressed in annoyance at this scene. Then he looked at her helplessly. "I wish you'd tell me what you want of me that I haven't given you."

She came back to the bed and got into it. "Yourself," she said. "Oh, I know you won't understand that, I hardly do, either, but you're everything to me."

"That's not true, Madeleine, you have the children."

She shook her head. "And you have the world to run, but it's not the same thing. I should have been a bank."

He smiled, that charming smile of his, and his hand reached out to stroke her bare shoulder. "You're fussing because I don't want to disturb you late at night. Is that reasonable?"

She lay down, sighing. "No, not at all, but love is not reasonable. I love you all the time, not just a few nights a month. I suppose I want you to love me in the same way, and certainly enough to sleep next to me every night, whether or not you want to make love."

"All right, Madeleine," he said, knocking the ashes from his pipe and sliding down on his pillows. "I'll sleep here no matter what time I get in." Again he was patient and resigned.

"Now I feel like an utter fool," she said, knowing that where he slept had nothing to do with how he felt about her, how he thought about her. His silence in the bed was eloquent: how could a man be expected to deal with these tiresome domestic scenes when he had important things to do?

The next day she started redecorating a bedroom for him. He said nothing about it, but he showed his approval with a yellow-diamond necklace set in gold filigree from Cartier.

"If only I had your talent for business," Madeleine told him, "I'd have held out for the whole store."

"I'll buy it for you," was his reply. He was amused by the joke. At times like this, when he looked at her long enough to consider what she said, when he smiled that brilliant smile, she knew the other Jesse was there in him, the one she had married, the one she still loved.

"Some day I'll find the key to you, Jesse Slayter," Madeleine said.

"There is none," he said disarmingly. "I'm as you see me."

"I won't believe that," she said, going to kiss him, to feel him near, half convinced she was talking nonsense. Yet, when the moment passed, she went on looking for her first love in him.

She could not discover it. He came to her bedroom with the same regularity as before and their life together went forward as usual, while Europe became more deeply mired in war. Jesse was reluctant to discuss any of it at home, not even when Daniel joined the French forces while on his grand tour of Europe.

"But he's your only brother!" Madeleine protested. "Aren't you concerned about him?"

"Just as much as he is about me," Jesse said darkly. "And that's the last I want to hear about it."

More and more he withdrew into the little circle of his own content, a sealed circle that had its center in the raging conflict in Europe. The investment possibilities of a world war preoccupied him almost totally.

Madeleine took the children to museums and zoos, to plays they could understand and later, when they were old enough, to operas and concerts. They were delightful companions, Susannah with her perpetual curiosity and Jonathan with his sweet nature.

Madeleine seemed younger than she was. It came of being with her children so much and of sharing their unfolding. The children, by a reverse sharing, seemed older.

As months drifted into years, Madeleine knew she must try to be content with whatever she had of Jesse. The worst of him was, to her, the best of other men.

11

"Hurry, Anna, please," Susannah told her maid. "I don't want to be late."

The girl finished buttoning Susannah's low-waisted navy serge middy, straightened her pleated skirt and tightened the ribbon holding back Susannah's heavy dark hair. "The Mister likes you to be tidy," she told the impatient eleven-year-old under her hands. "And there you are, Miss Susannah, all ready and with twenty minutes to spare before he's off to his business."

Susannah raced for the stairs. She hated to miss a minute of Saturday breakfast, when her father often lingered over a second cup of coffee before he went to his office. There was no rush for her to get off to school today, and she would do her homework while he was gone. The market closed at one o'clock on Saturdays and she wanted to be free if he had any time to spend with her. She kept her fingers crossed, hoping he would.

She stopped at the bottom of the stairs, looking down at her black cotton stockings and polished high-buttoned boots. She made sure the black grosgrain bow that peeked out from either side of her head was straight, then walked decorously into the breakfast room.

It was different. Even the sounds of silver on china, of coffee being poured and crisp rolls crumbled, were different. Jonathan sat stiffly in his chair, his porridge untouched before him. Her mother's hand, emerging from the pleated organdy undersleeve of her morning gown, hovered over a porcelain cup of milky tea, but the cinnamon toast she favored for breakfast sat forgotten on her plate.

"What's the matter?" Susannah asked, her voice more tentative than usual.

Her father, the only one of them proceeding calmly with his breakfast of grilled kidneys and toast, looked at her. "Good morning, Susannah. Sit down and have your breakfast."

She obeyed, after saying good morning to her mother and Jonnie. She took some scrambled eggs from one of the covered dishes on the sideboard and settled into her chair.

The silence continued.

Jonathan looked across at her, his blue eyes brilliant with tears he was trying not to shed. "Uncle Daniel's been wounded," he said.

Susannah swallowed hard, both at the forbidden mention of her uncle's name and at the frightening reason for Jonathan's disobedience. She looked anxiously at her mother.

"It's his leg, honey," Madeleine said, taking a letter from the pocket of her blue velvet gown. "Aunt Pippa says he might lose it." There was another silence in the room, then Madeleine looked at Jesse. "How can you be so indifferent?" she asked him, whispering, as if she knew she should not have said it.

Susannah watched as her father plied his knife and fork with exasperation. "Come, now, Madeleine, you know how Philippa exaggerates for dramatic effect! Daniel will recover." He finished the kidney with precise motions of his jaw and poured another cup of coffee for himself from the small silver pot with a long handle that appeared at his place on the breakfast table each morning. "You can't pretend this was unexpected. Boys who run away to war get wounded. I'm surprised it didn't happen sooner."

Jesse looked up then, glancing around the little circle of stricken faces, and his expression changed to bewilderment at their reaction, so different from his own. He was impatient.

"What's the matter with all of you? You're making a tempest in a teapot."

For what seemed many moments, no one spoke, then Jonathan, his eyes blazing, said, "I'll bet you're glad it happened."

"Oh, Jonnie, no!" his mother said. "You mustn't say such things about your father."

"Why not if they're true?" the boy insisted. Then the courage of his short burst of temper changed to a plea. "His own brother's hurt and he doesn't even care!"

Jesse was very quiet, the way he was, Susannah thought, when he concentrated hard on something. His dark eyes flashed momentarily at his wife. Then he looked at Susannah, pushed his untouched coffee cup aside and took a pipe from the rack on the table near him.

"Of course I care about Daniel," he said, his hands busy with the pipe. "I've been angry since he went to war without so much as a by-your-leave— and worried, too, but I try not to show it." He lit his pipe then put a hand out toward his son. "When there's a war on, my boy, a man can't lose courage, no matter what happens. You can see that, can't you?"

After a moment Jonathan nodded, his eyes still on his cold porridge.

"I'm going to get more news of him today from the War Office in Washington," Jesse went on, "but in the meantime we must all carry on as usual and not let down the side, the way your Aunt Philippa says." He watched Jonathan nod again, then turned to Susannah. Her dark eyes, so like his own, waited.

"Susannah, how would you like to come to Pearl Street with me this morning?" he said.

"Oh, yes, Father," Susannah breathed, her doubts vanishing. "I'd rather do that than anything else in the world!"

"You wouldn't object?" Jesse said to Madeleine.

"I don't know—a little girl in that atmosphere?"

"Oh, Mother, please!" Susannah said, as quietly as she could. Her father didn't like importunate children.

"I'll keep her in my office with me and we'll lunch at Sherry's when the market closes." Jesse smiled faintly at Madeleine. "It will do her good"—he waved his pipe—"after all this."

Her mother nodded finally, and Susannah clasped her hands in utter bliss. To spend a whole day with her father—and in his office where she so longed to go! To watch him at the magic he did, changing the world with numbers on bits of paper! He had explained some of it to her, but she had never seen him actually doing it. "I hope you don't mind, Jonnie," Susannah said to her brother. "You and Mother can still go to a museum this afternoon. Jonnie? Are you all right?"

"Of course he's all right," her father said. "Once he's finished that cereal, he'll be fine." He got up from the table, tall and handsome, tailored to a turn. He patted his son's head and the boy looked up with an unfathomable expression. Then he walked to his wife and bent to kiss her cheek. "Why don't you and Jonathan meet us for lunch at Sherry's? We'll make an afternoon of it, the whole family."

"I'd like that," she said. Her eyes and her voice were neutral.

Jesse raised her hand, opened it, and slowly pressed his lips to her palm. Susannah, watching them, flushed. She was impatient to be gone.

"Forgive me," her mother said softly, in that husky voice she only used with her husband.

"Nonsense." He tossed it off now, smiling. He looked even more handsome when he smiled, Susannah thought. "You were upset, we were all upset." He straightened. "Come, Susannah, it's time we were going."

Eagerly, she started out of the room after him, turning back for a moment to ask soberly, "Where was he wounded?"

"Ypres," Jonathan said.

"When?"

"Two months ago."

She nodded sadly and went to get her hat and coat, thinking that her uncle might already be dead or—she shivered—without a leg. She willed herself not to cry at either possibility. Her father didn't like "scenes." He would never take her to Pearl Street if she behaved like a baby.

She was quiet and preoccupied as she followed him out of the house.

12

"What are you thinking about?" her father asked when they were settled in the Rolls-Royce.

"Father, will Uncle Daniel come home?"

"He doesn't tell me his plans," her father said, rather distantly.

"Maybe he would if you asked him to." It was at that moment that she turned away from him, as if she could find a reason in the sunshine outside for her father's implacability. On the plush of the car seat her hand lay curled in defenseless, injured trust.

Her father took it, opened it out like a spool of ribbon, and placed it securely between his own. She could feel his eyes upon her, but she could not look at him. Finally, he said, "He never loved me, you know, even as a boy. I never knew why. It was always a bitter hurt to me." His voice was very low, as if he were ashamed at this admission of rejected love.

She turned to him quickly, snuggling her head close to him, knocking her bowler hat back on her shoulders where it dangled, held to her by an elastic as she was held to him by love and admiration and pain for this pain she had never known he felt.

"*I* love you," she whispered passionately, hugging him. "I will *always* love you and I'll never let anyone hurt you, not ever. I understand how you feel, Father, I really do."

He touched her cheek when she looked up at him, the devotion in her dark eyes reflected in the look on his face, that look she always tried to summon, so celestial did its love for her feel. She had never felt this way in church; God did not make her feel like this.

Then she sat up, smoothed her hair and replaced her hat, retrieving her dignity and giving him back his own. He opened the small leather case he always carried and began to study some papers. Susannah concentrated on the scene along Fifth Avenue, the more completely to compose herself, and stealthily dried her eyes with the handkerchief that was always pinned inside her skirt pocket.

It was a clear, tangy day, the kind Susannah loved most in New York. The great establishments lined Fifth Avenue like Grenadier Guards, sparkling monuments to the city and its wealth. They passed the Lewisohn house, with its private gallery on the top floor. Her father would not mingle socially with the Lewisohns—they were Jews—but her mother had taken her there to tea one afternoon. Farther on, next door to the Plaza, the Astors' huge

61

French château loomed. She loved Mrs. William Kissam Vanderbilt's enormous mansion at 660 Fifth Avenue—and thought of poor Alfred Gwynne Vanderbilt who'd gone down with the *Lusitania.*

The big Rolls sailed past Delmonico's and Sherry's, past Tiffany and Altman and the Waldorf-Astoria Hotel on Thirty-fourth Street. There was a jumble of traffic—automobiles and carriages, trolleys and the jitney taxicabs that charged five cents for a short ride—as the car continued down toward the financial district, finally rolling to a stop at the corner of Wall and Pearl at fifteen minutes past ten.

Breathless with anticipation, Susannah followed her father into the Pearl Street entrance, around the corner from Slayter's Bank, into his private elevator and up to the sixth floor.

There was a muffled buzz of activity when the elevator door opened and they walked along the deep carpets of the corridor. The atmosphere of masculine power, however restrained, excited her. The place had an odor of leather, wax, dusty files, and tobacco smoke. She saw some boys, no more than fourteen years old, sitting in a row of chairs, and knew they were the runners, ready to carry messages worth millions of dollars anywhere on the Street at a simple command. They wore Slayter's livery.

She followed her father into his office, admiring the great globe on a stand beside the chair facing his desk, the lofty ceilings, the banks of books. Sometimes the men who sat in the client's chair were famous, she knew that. Their faces peered out of newspapers. Sometimes, she had gathered, they were so important that only men like her father knew who they were.

"Why don't you sit there?" Jesse said, pointing to a small desk and chair near a window. "I'll give you a balance sheet to look at. See if you can make anything of it after all I've told you about large corporations."

Susannah nodded, taking off her hat and coat. Her father put them in the closet with his own things, sat down at a desk as solid and as neat as he was, and handed her a folder from his top drawer.

She sat down at the desk and stared earnestly at the sheets of numbers he had given her, trying to make some kind of sense out of it and failing utterly. How complicated business was! What must banking be like? The telephones on her father's desk rang a few times and he placed several calls, but other than that he worked quietly at his desk, sometimes giving orders to the clerks who came in.

She looked up at her grandfather Jethro's portrait on the wall behind her father's desk and thought she was the luckiest girl in the world to belong to this family. She must tell Jonnie all about it; it would be his someday, thousands of years from now when her father was old—but he would never be old.

The large clock in the corner finally tolled noon and her father looked up.

"You're so quiet, I'd forgotten you were here. Did you make anything of that company's condition?"

"Not really, except they have more liabilities than assets. I wouldn't have anything to do with them."

He shook his head. "That doesn't decide everything. We must think creatively. What do they produce? What kind of machinery do they own? How can they fit in after the war?" He took out his pipe.

"Let me," Susannah said, going to his side. She took the pipe and began to fill it expertly.

"Your hands will smell of tobacco," he warned, smiling.

"I don't care, it's a lovely smell. I'll only marry a man who smokes a pipe. Here." She handed it to him and he lit it. "What will happen when the war's over?" she asked.

"We'll use all the new processes we learned from the war—they call it technology—to produce a flood of merchandise, and we'll sell it to the workers who earn money producing it." He leaned back in his chair while she listened, fascinated, a tall, intense child on the brink of adolescence. "We'll be a creditor nation for the first time and we'll lend money, at interest, to other nations, just the way a bank does."

"Who'll we lend to?"

"England. France. Germany."

"Germany?"

He studied her. "You must learn to be realistic about certain things, Susannah. Just because there's been a war, trade between nations won't come to an end. Trade is the lifeblood of this planet," he said, underscoring the importance of what he said with his pipe stem. "Trade and investment capital, pumped by the banks through the international system. Do you understand?"

"Yes." She hesitated. "But, Father, the Germans did such terrible things. How can we forget that?"

"Everyone does terrible things in a war—and not nearly so bad as what's reported to get the people into a fighting mood. Never believe what you are told, Susannah. Always look for why you have been told it."

Susannah pondered that. "You mean those stories about the Belgian babies being bayoneted were lies?"

"I'm sure of it." He looked at her steadily. "Heaven knows what the German public has been told about *our* soldiers."

Susannah shook her head. "If we've all been made to hate each other, why would we lend to them and why would they borrow from us?"

He was patient. "*We* don't deal with the mobs, Susannah, we're above

63

that. We deal with bankers, financiers, honorable men like myself who have no more committed such acts than I have."

He always explained things so well, Susannah thought, both satisfied and comforted. Then something else struck her. "You can't explain that to everyone—I mean to all the investors. Won't they refuse to lend money to Germany?"

"They'll invest money with us," her father said. "We'll invest it in Germany, or anywhere else where it'll earn a good profit." He stood up, smiling again. "That's enough for today, little financier. Let's tidy up and take a little walk around the Street, then we'll go uptown to meet your mother and Jonathan."

She nodded, then clasped her hands to hold her eagerness in check. "Father, please may I come here again next Saturday?"

"Not next Saturday," he said, and her heart sank. "There are more things for young ladies to learn than the banking profession. Let's say the first Saturday in every month—except in the summer of course, it's too hot for you to be in the city then. What do you think of that?"

She was overcome. "I think it's wonderful, and you're the best father in the whole world!"

"Susannah," he said softly, patting her hair. "You must not repeat the things I tell you here, about Germany and such. People don't understand as you do."

"No, Father," she vowed earnestly, a neophyte on the brink of initiation into the temple. She would never betray him, she told herself fervently, never.

13

Just as Jesse had predicted, Daniel did not die and did not lose his leg; but his recovery was long and slow and he stayed in a French hospital throughout the war. He was still there when the Armistice came in November of 1918.

"He still doesn't write to Father," Jonathan said one rainy day the following spring when he and Susannah were alone in the music room. Madeleine had transformed it from a guest room on the third floor when Jonathan's talent for the piano became apparent.

"You can't blame Father for that," Susannah said.

"Father could write first. After all, Uncle Daniel's the wounded one. He could ask him to come home."

Susannah looked at her brother, standing near her at the high brocade-draped window and watching the April rain. He was taller at ten than she had been, but he had the look of a puppy who had still to grow into its paws. Fortunately her own paws, she often told herself, were somewhat smaller; she was going to be as tall as her mother, but Jonnie would be taller still—and handsome. Even on a gray day his blond hair glistened.

She had adored him from the moment he was born, but she was aware now that their characters were vastly different. She was protective of his impulsive, loving nature; she herself thought there was more safety in restraint.

"Perhaps he will when we're all in England next month," Susannah said, and watched Jonathan brighten visibly. "Now go back and play the Bach for me again. It sounded very good, you know."

She listened to the Bach Invention with part of her mind, thinking of the coming trip eagerly. Maybe her father would take her to see "the Old Lady of Threadneedle Street," as people called the Bank of England. And she would see her Aunt Philippa, and Uncle Elton, whom she hardly remembered, not to mention their children—three little Lady cousins and a four-year-old Lord, the youngest of Aunt Pippa's children and the twelfth heir to the title.

She settled contentedly into the window seat. She was almost thirteen and really a woman now, although having to go through proof of it every month was a nuisance. Only her mother and her maid knew *that* happened to her;

65

she thought she would die if her father and brother ever found out. At least her chest remained inconspicuously small and all other evidence of womanhood, thank heaven, was hidden by her clothes.

Best of all, her father took her to Pearl Street on the first Saturday of every month, true to his promise. She had learned so much since that first trip that he often called her downstairs when there were guests for dinner and let his friends quiz her on financial matters.

"That's quite a daughter you have there, Slayter," the men said, waving their glasses of sherry when she had answered what they considered a difficult question.

"Very tall, but doesn't look a thing like Madeleine," was what the women said, but Susannah was content to look like her father and let Jonnie be the beautiful one. Her mother said Susannah was just as beautiful, but Susannah didn't really believe that and anyway she didn't care. In her father's world smart was a lot more important than beautiful.

"Bravo!" she said, when Jonathan had finished. "Someday you'll be a great concert pianist and I'll come to hear you and clap and clap."

He smiled and her heart sang to see him. She wanted to tell him how much she loved him, how he made her feel happy just because he was there, but it would have embarrassed her.

Oh, please, she wished intently, *let him be happy.*

14

"There's nothing so English as a garden party," Madeleine said to Philippa, "especially in the heart of London. I think I'll give one in New York when we get back."

She sat down abruptly and removed one pale mauve shoe with a flourish. "All the shoes I bought in Paris pinch."

The two women sat on the rear terrace of Philippa's town house in Stanhope Gate, watching servants clear away the genteel debris of the afternoon's party. The soft twilight of an English summer began to gather.

It seemed to Madeleine that she had talked about New York incessantly since she arrived here with the children—and without Jesse. Business had kept him from making the crossing with them—"And that's such a lame excuse," Philippa had remarked, "that it must be true." It was a great disappointment, all the same. Madeleine had looked forward to being alone with Jesse on the crossing, with no office for him to rush to each morning, no business dinners to keep him away until all hours of the night.

She made herself chatter now to keep Philippa from opening a long-avoided conversation. "I'm amazed at how many people came. Don't most of your set retire to the country for the summer by this time?"

Philippa smiled, her clever, sharp-featured face and her angular figure somewhat softened by the years. "They came to see you, darling," she said. "You're the talk of the town."

Madeleine put her head back and closed her eyes. "Oh, Pippa, really, you exaggerate."

"Not at all. The most beautiful woman in London—and untouchable because she's in love with her absent husband! They all think it's a shocking waste." She let her eyes shift toward Madeleine without turning her head. "There's little Lord Tate, for one, so mad in love he's ready to abandon his dogs and his title for you."

"He's only twenty-five!" Madeleine opened her eyes, startled.

"What of it? You don't look any older. Or you could choose someone a bit longer in the tooth. There's not a man alive you can't have." She was both proud and envious as she said it.

"I don't want anyone but Jesse," Madeleine said, giving in after a month of artful dodging. Once Pippa set her mind on getting to the bottom of things, nothing could divert her.

"I'm sure Jesse's even more devilishly attractive than ever," Philippa was

67

conceding, "now he's got all that power, but from what the children say—and *you* don't—it sounds as if he's changed."

"Yes, he has," Madeleine admitted. "But I haven't." She watched Philippa take a cigarette from a white alabaster box on the table and wished she herself could be as precise and practical in mind and movement as her sister-in-law. Philippa's assurance was as crisp as her apricot organdy dress.

"I hear Elton," Madeleine said, willing him to come out, "talking to Jonnie in the conservatory. He's the dearest man." *And you're an impossibly observant woman.*

"He has his points," Philippa agreed. "After thirteen years of marriage and four children, he still quite carries me away on the nuptial couch—although you'd never guess it to look at his aristocratic Lordship."

Madeleine blushed. "I'll never get used to the way you talk about things like that."

"You would if you lived here," Philippa said, puffing on her cigarette with relish. "I know they're all very proper in America, but that's only in public, surely."

There was no reply from Madeleine. The telling silence lasted until Philippa sat bolt upright, going to the heart of the matter as usual. "You don't mean to say Jesse's never carried you away!"

"I don't think so," Madeleine said in a small voice.

"My star and garter, there's a shock," Philippa said, extinguishing her cigarette. "I never suspected *that*—he's such a magnificent specimen. He used to patronize all the best bordellos with our sainted father." She looked at Madeleine, shaking her head slightly. "I used to call you the 'still unravished bride of quietness,' thinking you had no temperament at all. I should have known better, the way you look, like a fertility goddess."

"Stop now," Madeleine pleaded. "Elton's coming out."

Philippa's voice dropped to a whisper. "Jesse's a damned fool, in love with his bloody banks. It's fine for the family fortune, but terrible for you." Her voice rose as her husband approached. "Hello, you old darling, are you perishing to get off to the country?"

Lord Lucas smiled affectionately at his wife. He was wearing white flannel slacks and a blazer, but Madeleine always saw him in the brass and crimson of a guardsman, mounted on a charger with his sword at the ready to defend King and Country and the Virtue of Woman.

"I'm happy wherever you are, my dear," he said to Philippa as he sat down next to Madeleine. "I've been talking to young Jonathan," he said. "A fine fellow, but sadly disappointed Daniel isn't coming. His uncle is a hero to the lad, although he hardly remembers him."

"Better an absent hero, alive, than a dead one buried in some forgotten field in France," his wife countered, trying to hide her own disappointment that her brother still lingered on the Continent. "I don't think he's fully recovered yet in spirit, never mind his poor leg."

"I thought he would come when Jesse didn't," Madeleine said.

"Surely that fence has been mended by now?" Elton showed his surprise.

"It is a very high fence," Philippa remarked. "Well, never mind, we mustn't be gloomy." She stood, shaking out her ruffles. "It's time to have a bath and a rest before we change for dinner. Come along, Madeleine."

Madeleine replaced her shoe and stood, wincing a little. "How can anyone dance in French shoes?" She smiled at Elton. "Change your mind and come out with us. You and I can watch while the others make spectacles of themselves."

"Not I, my dear," Elton said, rising and towering over her. "I have work to do. But you must go and have a good time while you can, it'll be quiet enough in the country."

They left him on the terrace and went into the house and up the stairs. Elton took his position in the government very seriously.

"Still," Madeleine said on the stairs. "It always amazes me how married couples lead separate social lives in England."

"Marriage doesn't guarantee two people are anything alike." Philippa paused. "As you should know," she added pointedly. "All right, don't look so put upon. I'll stop. If you take my advice, though, you'll have some fun for yourself—and there's no opportunity like the present." She kissed Madeleine's cheek in a rare display of affection. "Cheerie-bye, darling, be ready at nine and wear something scandalous."

Madeleine stopped to look in on Susannah and her worshipful younger cousins. Susannah was taller and less girlish than her cousins; she would never have their frilly kind of femininity, but she was a beauty already.

"What are you young ladies doing this evening?" Madeleine asked them.

"We're going to read *Frankenstein* in the tower," Lady Carola said.

"By candlelight!" Elspeth added, faint with shivery expectation. The youngest of the three, Alexandra, looked too frightened to speak.

"Oh, children," Madeleine said, bending to comfort Alexandra. "You'll all have nightmares for weeks! Really, Susannah, I don't think you should."

"It was their idea," Susannah said. "I'm not in the least interested in some silly old monster."

"It will be all right, Aunt Madeleine," Lady Carola assured her. "Jonathan will be there."

Ah, Madeleine thought, a juvenile romance, for all she's two years Jonnie's senior. Her eyes met Susannah's and a little glimmer of amusement passed between them, a little complicity between mother and daughter. She loved those moments; whatever the reason, it made their closeness all the more apparent.

Then Madeleine went to her room, where Daisy waited to help her undress. She lay down to rest on the chaise longue after her bath and considered the idea of going to bed with another man—although, heaven forbid, not Lord Tate. He was too reminiscent of the youths she had known before she married Jesse. If she were ever to be attracted to someone—and that, of course, was impossible—it would be to a man, not a boy.

The idea no longer made her blush. Infidelity did not seem such a heinous offense in sophisticated Europe. People kept romance, which in Europe meant eroticism, distinct from marriage—probably avoiding a lot of disappointment in both areas, she reflected, with a cynicism that was new to her, and she dozed off until Daisy came to wake her at half past eight.

"I don't think I'll wear the blue tonight," Madeleine said, and pointed to a froth of chiffon already put out with its accessories. "Let's try the new white one—if I can still get into it after all these English sweets."

She stood, wearing only silk bloomers with tiny satin bows at the thighs, sheer silk gartered stockings and white brocade shoes that, mercifully, did not pinch. Bare-breasted, she stepped into the dress Daisy held for her, none of the old modesty left between them. Madeleine couldn't be modest with the woman who dressed her, knew when Jesse had been in her bed, had been there when both her children were delivered.

"Thank heaven," Madeleine said as Daisy fastened the heavily embroidered silk dress. "It closes! I'll have to start slimming, though, for these new fashions."

The dress was a sheath, close-cut to the knee, with a long flounced overskirt of silvery tissue. It was completely backless. A hint of bias drapery across the bodice did little to hide the fullness of Madeleine's bosom. Her breasts moved when she walked to the mirror, as did her long legs, thrusting under the silk.

"Lord," Madeleine breathed, looking at herself. "It really *is* scandalous, isn't it?"

Daisy shook her head loyally, her lips pressed firmly together, a nondescript woman with thin brown hair who was rendered even more insignificant by the black uniform she wore. She had a square set to her thin shoulders, magical hands that could mend lace or quiet a headache, and eyes that missed very little.

"Nothing is scandalous on you, Madame," she said. She had taken to addressing Madeleine in this way after their first trip to Europe on Madeleine's honeymoon, when she found it to be the fashion among continental ladies' maids.

She held out one shoulder-length glove to Madeleine, helping her to ease into the rich, powdery-smelling kid. "Madame always looks elegant in white," she said, observing her handiwork with satisfaction.

"Remember, Daisy, how you dressed me in white on my wedding day?"

The maid went on busily with the second glove. "Madame is just as beautiful now as she was then."

"Maybe," Madeleine sighed, "but does it matter, Daisy, does it really matter?"

Daisy's brown eyes looked up and took on the sadness in Madeleine's. Our dreams, the two women said to each other in one of their silent exchanges, what becomes of all our wonderful women's dreams?

"Oh, my dear Miss Madeleine, don't cry," Daisy said, the way she had when Madeleine was a young girl. "You mustn't cry, not just before a party." She put her arms around Madeleine. "Hush, now, it will be all right, you'll see, things will change now the war's over, he'll have more time."

She reached for a handkerchief and patted Madeleine's tears away, then expertly used a powder puff and some of the black kohl that was now in fashion to repair the damage. "You must go out and have a good time tonight."

"Lady Philippa says I'm to flirt with a very young man," Madeleine said bleakly.

Daisy colored, plying a small gold-handled comb, but her reply was firm. "Milady is a very sensible woman." She fastened lustrous pearl earrings in Madeleine's ears and put two perfectly matched pearl-and-diamond bracelets over her gloves, chattering all the while. Then she handed her mistress a small hand-painted silk handbag and put a wrap of white panne velvet bordered in white fox over Madeleine's arm.

"There," she said, "Madame will have a lovely evening. I'm sure of it."

She closed the door behind Madeleine before she dried her own eyes with a large, sensible handkerchief. "Can't he see she's perishing for love of him?" she muttered, beginning to put things away. She had said it often enough to her own Bob Harris who, bless him, knew how to love a woman better than most.

"The gentry don't have much truck with our kind of love," Bob would declare. "From the day I was took on as coachman to the old man I remarked it."

"It's all those banks and things," Daisy always said. "Just like his father, he is."

"Wasn't always."

Daisy didn't want to know. "She shouldn't've married him—my old Mister knew it when it was too late. She deserves better, dear as she is."

What was it like to sit there unnoticed, like a roast on a sideboard, getting colder every hour, every year? Mr. Slayter should have married a woman who cared as little about love as he did; there were plenty of them in New York society, flashy and cold. A cold man, he was, behind those good looks and that smile.

Daisy had tidied the room, been downstairs for her supper and was long back and nodding in an armchair when Madeleine came in, slightly disheveled and trailing the velvet wrap behind her like a standard fallen in battle.

"I have a terrible champagne headache," Madeleine said, "and I think I heard something tear while I was learning to dance the Kiki Kari—or was it the Shimmy?"

"Never you mind," Daisy said, taking the wrap. "I'll mend the dress in the morning. Here, now, out of it and into your wrapper. Come and sit down and I'll massage your poor head."

After a while, as happened so often, their eyes met in the mirror above the dressing table, and Madeleine shook her head in a tiny, almost imperceptible movement, before she relaxed again under Daisy's soothing fingers.

There now, Daisy said to herself, *it's just as well, my little Miss, it's no flirtation with a young scamp you want, it's the love of a real man and I pray someday you'll have it.*

15

There was a burst of laughter from the men surrounding Susannah, and Madeleine dismissed the butler and made her way through the guests across the summer drawing room, its high French doors thrown open to the mild weather.

Susannah, looking flushed and uncomfortable, stood near her father. She was as tall as Madeleine now and seemed several years older than fourteen. It was difficult to dress her without making her look awkward.

"What's all this?" Madeleine asked. Several men turned to her with apparent respect, but their eyes lingered on her with another impulse. The new afternoon dresses were soft, far more revealing than prewar fashions, and ever since corsets had gone out of style a man could feast his eyes on curves unfettered by canvas and whalebone.

Madeleine Slayter was a rare feast; she was one of the most beautiful women in New York, yet there was a quality about her, as of a golden wine, safely bottled, its warmth and flavor surmised but not yet released. There was not a man among them who had not dreamed of releasing that essence, and in his fantasies each was certain she would yield only to him.

"Your daughter, Mrs. Slayter," said a distinguished gentleman, moistening his lips, "knows more about the market than some of my junior partners."

Madeleine nodded. "I know. Her father has taught her a great deal."

"She learns quickly," Jesse said with satisfaction. "It's astonishing for a girl."

"Blood will tell," one of the other men offered. "Girl or not, Slayter, the apple doesn't fall far from the tree."

"What does the young lady think about projected market conditions for the last quarter?"

It always amazed Madeleine, this interest her daughter took in financial matters. She herself left her household accounts to the housekeeper. Still, Susannah was too mature now to be trotted out before a crowd of men, even at an afternoon party in her own home on a pretty summer day. She glanced at Jesse, then reached a hand to Susannah.

"Come along, darling, I need you. Gentlemen, you must look elsewhere for investment advice today." She smiled sweetly and the circle opened, letting mother and daughter pass.

Susannah came willingly, still uncomfortable and slightly confused. Mad-

73

eleine knew she had never felt ill at ease with her father's friends before, but adolescence was a trying time, particularly for serious young girls who looked older than they were.

"What did you need me for, Mother?"

"Nothing, darling, I made it up." She smoothed Susannah's glossy hair. "You're supposed to have fun at a party. I thought you'd answered enough questions."

"I'm used to it," Susannah said, without much conviction. Today it had been embarrassing to stand there, giving out information like a ticker tape, when she was so conscious of her body.

"You're right, of course," Madeleine said immediately. "Oh, dear, I suppose I'm old-fashioned, but I don't think you ought to do that anymore, so I took you away." She was interrupted by two women who came to admire her gown and exclaim over Susannah's height.

Susannah felt more awkward than ever. Little as she cared for most feminine pursuits—dresses, gossip, and boys—she longed for womanly assurance. She wanted to arch her neck, the way Grace Dawes did; her own felt far too long, like *Alice-in-Wonderland's*. She would have liked to stand as loftily as Margaret Phelps, but she was taller than most women as it was. She still slumped, whenever her posture would go unnoticed, to hide her breasts, which had popped out last summer in England, as though the climate there were more conducive to breasts.

As soon as she could, she slipped upstairs in search of Jonathan. She found him in the music room, practicing scales.

"Come on back down with me?" she invited him hopefully.

He shook his blond head and went on with his scales. "I don't like parties as much as you do."

"Who says I like parties?" Susannah objected, sitting next to him on the bench.

"Girls like parties. They can show off. I'll bet Father was showing you off again."

"That's business," Susannah said loyally. "Most girls show off in other ways, you know, flirting and all that. I'll never flirt, it's dumb. Anyway, I'm in no hurry to be a 'wife-and-mother.'" She said the words derisively. "That's where flirting leads."

"And I don't want to be a banker," Jonathan said. He looked at her and after a second they both nodded. It was nothing new, this sharing of confidences, even if they were secretive with everyone else.

"Really, Jonnie, being a wife and mother's not all that marvelous," Susannah said.

"Mother's marvelous! She's a lot more fun than Father, you said so yourself."

"Well, she *is* more fun, but he's more fascinating."

"All he cares about is Slayter's."

"Because it's one of the most influential investment houses in America and that means the world! Father has more power than the King of England, maybe more than the President. Power is more important than fun."

Jonathan supposed she was right. "But I'll never be like him, Sassie," he sighed, using his name for her. It was the way he pronounced Susannah Bess when he was a baby. "I don't want power, I hate business and I don't understand banks."

Susannah brushed his misgivings aside, as usual. "Someday you will, I'll help you. You'll be just fine when you grow up. I can tell."

They left it at that, Susannah absolutely sure and Jonathan lulled by her assurance. It was hard for Jonathan to explain to anyone how his father made him feel. Jesse was an awesome figure, like God with a black beard. Jesse spoke a different emotional language, the way Susannah did, but Susannah understood Jonathan and he didn't think his father ever would.

They settled down now to play duets and Susannah forgot the unwelcome burdens of her fourteen years and was content to be a child again with her brother.

Outside Madeleine strolled in the garden with Dr. Edward Driscoll, one of Jesse's brokerage clients and a fairly recent addition to New York society. He was a Bostonian who had decided to practice in New York—"I couldn't breathe in Boston after four years in Vienna," he had told her—and, like any single man, he was in great demand among New York hostesses. He was an attractive man with a quiet manner and she liked talking to him.

"Your daughter is extraordinary," he was saying now. "Is your husband grooming her for his brokerage house?"

"Of course not," Madeleine said. "He would never let her work."

"Then why bother to teach her all that?"

"I don't know—she has an aptitude for it and he's so proud of her."

"She might be very disappointed," he observed.

Madeleine nodded, saying nothing but aware of his perception. She had often said the same thing to Jesse, but he always brushed aside her concern.

"Are you?" he asked.

She looked at him, confused. "What?"

"Are you disappointed? Or has life brought you everything you dreamed it would when you were her age?"

She laughed. "Of course not."

"Tell me what dreams haven't come true," he said seriously.

She hid her temptation to answer him. "You don't really expect me to reveal that to a stranger."

He would not accept it. "Nonsense, we've known each other all winter."

"Party conversation doesn't transform strangers into friends," she said, although it seemed possible with him. They sat down on a bench at the end of the path.

"No," he sighed. "I suppose not, but I don't feel like a stranger with you, Madeleine."

It was unexpected from him. "Don't, please," she said.

"I've tried not to—and God knows you haven't given me any cause to presume—but I can't help it. You don't have to do anything about it, but will you please just let me say it?"

It was the most open approach she had ever heard. There had been many others, but so sly and devious that they were repugnant to her, although she knew that most husbands the world over had mistresses and some wives took lovers after they had produced legitimate heirs. She sometimes thought about things like that on silent, sunny days in Southampton, waiting for Jesse.

"What's the point, if you know I won't do anything about it?"

"Confession is good for the soul," he said ruefully. "I thought I knew just what to say, but now that I have the chance I feel like a schoolboy. Anyway"—he gestured with a long, graceful hand—"I think you're the most delightful woman I have ever met—and the most beautiful, that goes without saying—but you're like an unfinished statue, half in and half out of the marble. The first time I saw you I thought, she wants to run and she's standing still, she hears some inner music, but she doesn't dance to it."

It was such an accurate description of how she felt that she looked at him with new interest, almost as if to tell him he was right. Then she looked away.

"It's true, isn't it?" he said, rather sadly.

She nodded.

"Damn it," he said, more to the flowers and shrubs than to her. "What are you going to do about it? Are you going to leave all that you are trapped inside a block of granite for the rest of your life?"

"What else can I do?"

"Meet me tomorrow," he answered quickly.

She blushed. "I already have a luncheon engagement tomorrow."

"Damn lunch," he said. "It's true I want to make love to you, but if you don't want it too, then I just want to talk to you, to hear about you, to know you better than I ever can at parties."

She turned to study his face. It was more open and engaging than handsome. Young as he was, there was gray in his curly brown hair. His hazel eyes looked at her with a longing that was not entirely sensual, with an anxious concern that touched her. He had achieved a better sense of her in a few short months of occasional conversation than Jesse had in sixteen years of marriage, and she felt drawn to him in a way she had never experienced with anyone else.

Unbelievably, she agreed to meet him and listened while he told her where, her eyes on his mouth, wide but sharply defined. She wondered what it would be like to kiss him and knew then she would not stop at talking tomorrow. Then they walked back to the house, and she presided over the rest of the garden party as if nothing had happened.

She had only an hour to herself before dinner, and she spent it in a fever of torment, torn between her love for Jesse and the temptation to talk to a man who knew what she was really like, to let him make love to her in ways she had often thought about and had been ashamed to think.

The prospect made her weak with desire, alone in her room, and grateful for the first time that it was Daisy's day off. When the dressing bell rang she bathed her face, smoothed her hair, and changed from her voile garden gown to a loose chiffon Fortuny. Then she arranged her face in a normal expression and went down to join her family.

16

"Where were you two all afternoon?" Jesse demanded of his children at the gleaming mahogany dining table. "Jonathan disappeared almost immediately and Susannah not long after. I missed you."

"It was a grown-up party," Jonathan said, with a smile that was dazzling, even to his father. Jonathan was his mother's image, he was only twelve but his looks were startling already. It was impossible to scold him when he smiled like that.

"Nonsense," Jesse said, not in the least inclined to scold. "An afternoon party is a good way for both of you to socialize. In a few years you'll be out in society and you must know how to behave. Half of the world's business is conducted at parties."

"I behaved pretty well today," Susannah said, with a look at her father. "Didn't I?"

He smiled. "Yes, you always do. Your uncle will be surprised to see what a lady you've become."

"Uncle Daniel?" Jonathan was eager. "Is he coming home?"

"Next month," Jesse said.

"Then he's recovered from his wound?" Jonathan asked.

"It's almost three years since Ypres," Jesse reminded his son. "He recovered from it long ago. I can't imagine why he didn't come home sooner."

"Maybe he doesn't want to be a banker," Jonathan offered, daring in his feigned innocence.

"He's a Slayter," Jesse said, responding as he usually did. "If he doesn't want to be a banker, he's a damned fool."

"No, he's not," Madeleine said. She rarely interfered in any discussions about Daniel, but her tone tonight was very definite. "He's a very brave man."

Jonathan agreed. "I think he's swell."

"Don't use slang," Jesse remonstrated. "Of course he's brave, but he's still a fool."

"Someone had to fight that war," Madeleine said.

Jesse took a spoonful of his dessert and ate it neatly. "There are many ways to do that and for Slayters a filthy trench in France is not one of them. He enlisted while he was still on his grand tour, long before *we* were involved in the fight. No matter how you look at it, that's damned foolishness."

79

"Is he going to stay this time?" Susannah asked.

Jesse looked stern. "I'll do everything I can to make him see reason and responsibility. He inherited half of Slayter's, as I did. If my equity has outstripped his it's because I've worked at it. I made at least five million over champagne and cakes this afternoon—by no means a disagreeable way to do business. He can do likewise."

"He won't stay," Madeleine said. "He's more comfortable in Europe after all these years. Philippa said he was more affected by the war than he let us know."

Jesse always laughed whenever his half sister was mentioned. "Frivolous Philippa! Her mind is always on her wardrobe. What can she know about it?"

"I think *she's* swell, too," Jonathan said, and Susannah shot him a warning glance. "Sorry, Father," he apologized, and was immediately absorbed in his apple tart.

"Why doesn't Uncle Daniel represent Slayter's in Europe if he wants to stay there?" Susannah asked. "You said just last week that a lot of investment capital will come from there, now that the market's on the rise."

Jesse's brows relaxed. "Now there's a thought!" He was surprised it had not occurred to him before. Daniel had never been a threat, with his absurd notions about architecture; but now, as a man and a war hero, he might be a nuisance. Jesse had plans for German investments that a war hero might not approve of. Putting his brother in charge of an unimportant, though suitably prestigious, level of European operations would solve the whole problem neatly.

"Very clever of you, Susannah," he said finally, to her great pleasure. "It works out very well." He turned to Madeleine. "I think he'll be happy about this; it'll keep him busy, help him to forget the war. Try to persuade him, will you? He won't listen to a word I say."

She nodded and, when they rose from the table, said she had a headache and went to her room. She had surprised herself by defending Daniel, yet Jesse now seemed sincerely concerned about his brother. Perhaps Daniel had no need of her small defiance.

Now she was on the brink of a far greater act of defiance and wondered if she would really go through with it. What could the doctor offer her that was worth disloyalty to every one of her values and an affront to her dignity?

"I want to know you better." Jesse had never said that to her, Jesse had never seen that she was only half alive. She was alive now, her body throbbed with life.

She hardly slept and was awake with nervous anticipation long before Daisy came with her breakfast tray.

"Did you and Bob enjoy your Sunday?" Madeleine said, trying to get interested in her toast.

"A lovely drive in the country, it was," Daisy said, opening the satin draperies and coming back to settle the tray. "What shall I put out for you to wear today?"

Madeleine suddenly thought she ought to wear something easy to take off. She flushed and buried her face in her teacup. "I'll decide that after my bath," she said, and watched Daisy go into the bathroom. The sound of running water and the fragrance of scented oil made her impatient with food, and she tossed back her bedclothes and got out of bed, carrying a second cup of tea.

She went to the closet where her day dresses were carefully arranged according to color, and stood there looking at them until her bath was ready. She decided on a simple, side-buttoned linen in smoke-blue, and a wide straw hat.

Dressing after the bath, her heart pounded as she considered again all the implications of adultery with each garment she put on—and then refused to consider them as she imagined each one being taken off.

"Is anything wrong, Madame?" Daisy asked.

"I don't know. I was thinking I might just undress and go back to bed, I have so many calls to make today." She stood there hesitantly, aware, as she had been for a long time, of the intimate touch of silk underclothes against her flesh. Her breasts and her belly tingled. She looked at Daisy and blushed furiously.

Daisy held out her gloves and handbag. "It's such a beautiful day," she said, as if she were only talking about the weather!

"Yes," Madeleine said finally, "it is." She took the gloves and handbag from Daisy.

"Shall I call the car?" the maid said uncertainly.

"No, I'll take a taxi." Madeleine's eyes were hidden by the brim of her hat, but they were glowing with erotic appetite. A part of her, long suffocated under gowns and furs, was stirring.

She left the bedroom, wanting to breathe, to run, to turn the corner she had always sensed was there and had felt so near yesterday afternoon in the garden.

17

She took a taxi to a small hotel near Union Square, announced herself as "Mrs. Driscoll," and was shown to a quiet, pleasant room on the third floor to await her "husband." She was early and she felt awkward, not knowing what to do while she waited. Should she undress and get into bed? It seemed so crude now, but it would make things easier later.

She took off her hat and gloves and sat like a schoolgirl on the small love seat near the window, more positive with every minute that passed that a bed was the last place for her to be with anyone but Jesse.

Then she heard the key in the lock and looked up to see the doctor, with no suggestion of a welcoming smile on her face.

"Thank heaven you came," he said softly, closing the door behind him and shooting the bolt. "I'm sorry to be late." He tossed his hat and cane aside.

"You're not," Madeleine said. "I was early." She looked around. "It's a very pleasant place."

"No, it isn't," he said, "it's awful. No hotel in the world is good enough for you, but it was all I could think of." He came toward her hesitantly. "Madeleine, let's not stay here. We can take a drive through the park or go boating on the lake, only don't look like that, please, I can't bear to see you so uncomfortable."

She smiled up at him. "You really mean that, don't you?"

He nodded, his hazel eyes fixed on her. He was waiting, ready to do whatever she wanted. Suddenly she wanted him to kiss her, and although she said nothing, he seemed to know it. He knelt beside her, put his arms around her, and kissed her lightly and sweetly at first, then with warmth, slowly, as if he intended to kiss her for hours. It was the languor of it that aroused her; it was not urgent, but deep and quiet and expectant. The urgency was hers. Now that he had kissed her, she was avid for him to do more.

Then his head rested on her shoulder while his hands unfastened the top buttons of her dress. He kissed the hollows of her throat, then her mouth again, with infinite pleasure. The desire she felt within her had always come at the end of sex with Jesse, not at the beginning like this.

She sighed and he picked her up and put her on the bed, undressing her slowly. Then he leaned over her, watching her face while his hands caressed her, watching her eyes close when he encountered the inner folds of her

83

body, lingered, searched, and stroked until she approached a pleasure she had felt only once before, when she was pregnant with her son.

She forgot where she was, what she said, how she moved. She let him wander all over her, and almost cried with pleasure several times before she reached for him, an instinctive reaching that was followed, when he came into her, by an instinctive thrusting of her body to claim his, until another kind of ecstasy possessed her. When it faded they lay coiled together, tired and replete.

He brought her a glass of water from the pitcher on the dressing table, then moistened a towel in the bathroom and patted her body gently, cooling her where he had just made her feel so warm.

"You have a light touch," she said to him, smiling with her eyes closed. "You must be a good doctor."

"The very best," he said confidently. He took the damp towel away, came back to bed and they lay still, talking of anything: trivia, people they knew, fashions and plays and cities in Europe.

"Do you know," she said to him presently, "I've never just talked to a man like this before."

"Before they all have just one thing in mind." His hand grazed her breasts. "But surely afterward . . . ?"

"There's never been an afterward like this. You're the first."

He turned his head to be sure she was serious. "I'm honored," he said. "You must be devoted to your husband."

"I love him," she said sorrowfully. "There's no way to describe how much."

"But?" he looked at her hopefully.

It seemed far more of a betrayal to tell him than to sleep with him, but she had come too far in intimacy to hold back now. "Sometimes I think he doesn't know I'm alive unless I'm in his direct line of sight—and even then . . ." She moved restlessly under the sheet that covered them. "This will sound foolish, I know."

"Go on," he said quietly.

"I think any decorative woman who could raise his children and preside at his parties would have pleased him just as much, that he didn't choose me for what I am, but for who I was."

He raised himself on his elbow and looked down at her. "You must know how lovely you are; he must have known, too."

Her blue eyes pleaded with him to understand. "There's more to me than what you can see," she said. "There is to anyone. I don't just lie down and look beautiful; I laugh too, I cry sometimes. My father thought I was clever, even amusing. I read books; I have opinions I'd like to share with the person

I love most." She shook her head. "He has no idea what I'm really like. Even when he listens, he doesn't hear."

She sounded so lost that he gathered her into his arms, more as he would an abandoned child than a passionate woman. "I would like to know what you're really like, Madeleine, far beyond what I've already discovered."

"And that is?"

"That you're a delight, not only to love but to see and be with and know. He's a damned fool to want only the passion in you."

She shook her head again. "He doesn't even know it's there."

"But just now—" He stopped, incredulous.

"He never made love to me the way you just did. I had no idea I could feel like that, act like that." She looked down at her still widespread thighs under the sheet.

"My God," he said. "These damn fool men who divide women into the sexual and the marriageable!"

"I don't think he has a mistress," Madeleine said, "except for Slayter's. He doesn't have time for women. My sister-in-law says he's in love with his banks. I want him to be in love with me—just part of the time, in love with me."

He lay back for a while, one arm still protectively around her. He was silent so long that she turned to see if he had fallen asleep, but he was gazing at the ceiling.

"What is it, Ned?"

He sighed. "Something simple and banal, but it complicates things. You see, he's in love with his banks, you're in love with him and I—I'm in love with you."

"Oh, no," she said, torn between happiness and concern for him, grateful to have him and unwilling to hurt him. "You don't really mean that, you can't be."

"Can't I? And what if I am?"

"Then we couldn't ever see each other again." Her lost air was gone, she was very definite. "I want you to be my lover, Ned. I want you to be my friend, but that's all you can be."

He waited a long moment before he agreed. "All right, Madeleine. I'll be your most loving friend for as long as I can bear to be only that."

"Show me, Ned," she whispered, throwing the sheet back. "Show me how loving you're going to be."

18

The house was quiet when she got home late that afternoon, and Madeleine was relieved; surely the intensity of those hours had left some mark on her face, and she needed time to regain her composure before dinner.

She climbed sedately up the stairs, then closed her bedroom door and whirled around to lean against it, clasping herself with her arms. She laughed softly with the sheer delight of the memories in her body, with amazement at the well-being that flooded her.

Then she looked across the room at her bed and her smile faded. She had been unfaithful to her husband and that was nothing to rejoice about. She had broken her vows.

How had it come to this, from the magic of a ball in Philadelphia one night sixteen years ago? And yet there had been signposts all along the way, markers that foretold it, even her own pathetic appeals to Jesse in an attempt to forestall it—all of that before she had known what it was for, this clamor in the flesh she had felt so often.

"I must give him up," she whispered, and knew she could not give Ned up, not yet. She needed not only the physical release but the caring closeness of a man who wanted her and made her glad she wanted him.

She went to the window overlooking the garden and that fateful bench. "I must be a very wicked woman if a husband like Jesse and good works aren't enough for me," she said aloud. Then she wondered what Ned would say about such wickedness.

Reluctantly, she saw it was time to bathe and change for dinner. It would have been voluptuously satisfying to keep the evidence of that afternoon on her body—she was too fastidious to bathe in a hotel tub—but what if Jesse should want . . . ? But she would have to refuse him; it was beyond her to sleep with a lover and her husband in the same day.

She rang for Daisy, removing the modest jewelry she had worn. "I'll wear that dark blue chiffon with the white ruching around the neck," she told the maid, "the one you call my convent dress."

"Madame is looking very lovely this evening," Daisy said later when the dress was on and she was arranging Madeleine's hair. Daisy always said that, but this time Madeleine quickly bent her head to examine the perfect finish of the ruching at her wrists. When she went downstairs she reminded herself to govern her face and her eyes; she always showed everything she felt.

87

Neither Jesse nor the children noticed any change in her. She would tell Ned about that tomorrow too. There were so many little things she wanted to tell Ned.

"It's time you thought about moving out to Southampton for the summer," Jesse said that evening in the library. "The days will be getting sultry before we know it."

"It's dull in Southampton," Susannah said.

Madeleine's heart sank. Ned had a practice; he could never come to Southampton to see her. "Daniel will be here soon," she said, remembering suddenly.

"Next month," Jesse said. "Surely you don't propose to wait for him? He can join you out there."

"Will you stay on in New York?"

"Of course"—he nodded—"until mid-August. The market takes no notice of the heat."

"I'd rather stay in town," Madeleine said. It was what she always said and it was still true; she tried not to think of the new reason.

"So would I," Susannah said. "Oh, let us, Father, please. We can ride in the park and go to museums and even to the visitors' gallery at the Stock Exchange." She turned to her brother. "It'll be fun, Jonnie—and we can meet Uncle Daniel's ship at the pier and throw confetti."

Jonathan smiled, always ready to second his sister and his mother. "Sure, Sassie, I think we should stay right here—and keep Father company."

Jesse looked at each of them in turn. It was as close as he came to being sentimental and Madeleine knew why: No one but her had ever clamored for Jesse's company before. At Jonathan's age he had been shunted off to school, and when he was a young man he had been prized for his ability, not for himself.

Don't you see? she almost asked him right there. *Don't you see how much it means?*

He nodded agreement, then smiled when they applauded his decision. Madeleine had never loved him so much.

The children had gone upstairs and she was pretending to read a book when she felt Jesse's eyes on her. She raised her head, unaware that the very dress she had chosen for its severity only set her off physically. There came from this blond woman reading quietly in an armchair of her library a healthy eroticism that seemed to illuminate her naked white body through its covering of indigo chiffon. A sudden pallor spread over her face as she understood his look.

"Jesse, I have a terrible headache again. I think I'll go up now," she said quickly.

He hesitated, then stood when she passed him and kissed her cheek. "I'm sorry," he said, "I hope it will pass." He took her hand.

"Yes, yes, of course. By morning I'll be fine." She managed a small smile, trying to avoid his eyes.

"How beautiful you are, Madeleine," he said, as if he had never noticed it before. Then he loosed her hand and let her go with "Good night, my dear, sleep well."

In the safety of her bedroom once again she paced the floor nervously. How desperately she always waited to see that look! And how much she loved him, no matter what she had done! But it was impossible to sleep with him tonight; it would have debased her and humiliated him, whether he knew it or not. More than anything, she would have missed the new magic that still echoed inside her, and she might not have been able to hide that from Jesse.

"Lord, what a tangled web," she murmured. Now she was using quotes, like Philippa! What would Philippa have done tonight? You had to be sophisticated to handle adultery—or cynical—and Madeleine was neither.

Was that adultery today, that sweet wildness, that freedom in a man's arms? She sank down on the edge of her bed, the dress an inky pool against the pale silk sheets. She remembered the muslin sheets in the hotel and shook with wanting them under her again while Ned made her careless of where she lay or how.

There was a tap on the door and Madeleine got up hastily from the bed, relieved to see it was only Daisy. "Hello, Daisy," she said happily, then noticed the look of confusion on the maid's face. "What is it?"

"Mr. Slayter said you had a bad head; he sent me up to help you." Daisy was struck again by how different her mistress looked tonight. Uncanny, it was, different from how she had ever seen her.

The two women, one questioning, the other radiant, looked at each other. Then a spark of comprehension widened Daisy's eyes and her chin lifted, just a little.

Madeleine seemed to nod her head, although Daisy realized later she had only closed her eyes affirmatively for an instant. "I'll need your help," Madeleine said softly, and waited, leaving the woman to make her own decision.

Daisy turned away to fetch a dusty-rose gown and peignoir from the armoire. "You've had that since the first day your mother, heaven rest her, took me into service. I was that frightened, Miss Madeleine, until I met you and you were so kind . . ." Daisy chattered on, saying everything by saying nothing about it, until, the gown and shoes neatly ranged in the closet, the jewelry put away, the dainty silken underthings placed in a satin slipcase to be hand laundered tomorrow, she said good night and left.

Drowsing in bed, Madeleine heard Jesse come upstairs and go to his own room. She knew she would give the world to have him love her the way Ned did and her life would never be complete until he could.

19

She had no illusions about the nature of her love affair. When it was over, she would still want Jesse. If Ned had given her something she treasured and would no longer do without, he still hadn't changed that fact.

She tried not to discuss Jesse with Ned; they talked of other things. "I think passion is more powerful than guilt, especially for a woman," she told him one day. They were lying in bed in the little studio in Greenwich Village Ned had rented for them, eating grapes.

"Why especially for a woman?"

"It's what we're reared to do, after all, inspire passion in men—even though the message is carefully camouflaged."

He put a grape into her mouth and kissed her. "Explain."

"Well, when I was a girl we weren't supposed to be sexual. We didn't know anything about it if we'd been properly brought up, but our clothes accentuated our waists and hips and exposed our breasts. What were we supposed to think of all that? And why are ankles coming out of hiding now after two thousand years and dresses being made of fabrics that wouldn't cover what those corsets used to accent? What are we supposed to think of all that now—except that our primary role is to entice men."

Ned laughed. "Biologically, it is, to keep the species alive, but your ultimate goal is pleasure, and exciting men is preliminary to that. Haven't you heard the rumor that women are sexual too?"

"The rumor hasn't reached Wall Street yet," Madeleine said, bringing Jesse into this bed despite herself.

Ned's face clouded, as it always did when the third party to their love affair was mentioned. "I don't know why you think it ever will," he said.

"Because he wasn't always like this," Madeleine told him, putting the grapes aside. "There was something wonderful in him once, but before I found the way to make it grow, he changed."

"When?"

She shivered a little. "It was gradual, but mostly when his father died."

"Not a very nice man, from what I've heard." Ned put an arm under her shoulders and pulled the bedclothes up higher.

"He was the coldest man I ever knew," Madeleine agreed, moving closer to Ned. "I could never tell what he was thinking, but he was capable of almost anything."

Ned hesitated before he said it. "That's exactly how I've heard Jesse described."

She looked away, not wanting to agree, yet there was no denying it was largely true. There was Jesse's complicity in her own father's ruin, long ago when he could have helped, and then more fundamental changes that could not be explained merely by his new position in the world. He was different. She could never question anything Jesse did now, the way she used to; yet how else would she ever reach him?

She turned back to Ned, her blue eyes questioning, both needing and dreading to understand more.

"If you can't win someone's love," Ned said, "you can become that person, you can fill the void by encompassing him, in a manner of speaking. Primitive people swallow the qualities of the animals they most admire by literally eating their brains and hearts and testicles. They become what they most want and then they don't need to want it anymore. It can be done with a personality too."

Madeleine's eyes widened. "That's—evil and inhuman."

"It's primitive," Ned said. "It may even be evil, but it's very human. A brave bull's testicles are still a prized delicacy in Spain."

"Well, we're not in Spain," Madeleine protested, "and I'm sorry I ever started this. I don't want to think about anything morbid when I'm with you." She kissed him. "I just want us to be happy."

"Madeleine, it isn't that easy."

"Yes," she whispered, close to him, "yes, it is, it has to be."

20

"You've changed," Daniel said to Jesse. *He's still a handsome bastard,* he thought.

"So have you, it's been years." Jesse offered his brother a cigar, but Daniel refused and Jesse waited while he lit a cigarette instead. "Lean ones, by the look of you."

Daniel smiled. "Fat for Slayter's, from what you tell me. Father would be very proud," he added, in a tone impossible to qualify. He inhaled deeply on his cigarette and watched Jesse. *He's figuring out the best way to handle me,* Daniel thought, sitting back in the chair in Jesse's study. He had refused to go to the office on Pearl Street. *Doesn't he know he's absolutely transparent to me? That business with his pipe, now—it's not only for effect, he's playing for time, trying to make me nervous.*

"I suppose it's time we talked about your future," Jesse said at last.

"Only if you can't restrain yourself."

"I see your wit's become as English as your accent," Jesse said, with his flashing smile. "There's the matter of Father's will, after all."

"Blast Father's will," Daniel said pleasantly, but his brown eyes were strained. Jesse *had* changed, in a subtle way he could not yet qualify. This man would never lose his temper, as he once did the day of Jethro's funeral.

"He wanted you here."

"You don't."

For once Jesse was nonplussed. "That's an odd thing to say. I remember a peppery argument the day of his funeral precisely because I *did* want you here."

"Then let's not have another one. After all," Daniel said sardonically, trying another tack, "you can't overlook how badly I've been injured. Even Father wouldn't insist on putting me behind a desk in my condition. No one on the Street expects you to."

Jesse looked utterly perplexed. "Well, I was only going to suggest that you represent Slayter's in Europe, but if you really aren't up to it . . ."

"Do you mean that?" Daniel leaned forward eagerly.

"Of course I mean it," Jesse said, apparently sincere. "I was trying to figure out what you'd like and I hit on that. It solves everything, doesn't it— your wishes, the conditions of your inheritance." He smiled confidentially. "My conscience."

"It certainly does." Daniel's expression altered as he reassessed his

93

brother. "You *have* changed, Jesse. You didn't much like me as a child. I never knew why."

Jesse shrugged. "More your imagination than anything. Best forgotten." His dark eyes were watchful.

"Yes," Daniel agreed, looking at his well-manicured hands. "About this arrangement—in what countries would I represent you?"

"England and France, I thought, to begin with. It's where you have the most contacts"—he smiled—"among the idle rich."

"Not Germany," Daniel said, unsmiling. "I don't want anything to do with Germany. If you take my advice, neither will you. They're a thoroughly bad lot."

"Daniel, the war's been over for two years," Jesse said reasonably. "Aren't you carrying a grudge a little too far?"

Daniel was adamant. "No, that's the one condition I have to make."

Jesse raised both hands in surrender, his pipe clenched between his teeth. "All right, all right—you'll have nothing to do with Germany. Agreed?" His smile flashed again. "Now let's talk of other things. How're Philippa and her Lord?"

Daniel made himself exchange small talk until Madeleine joined them. She was just as lovely, Daniel thought, but not the same in herself as when he had graduated from Yale and gone abroad, first for the grand tour of Europe that every young gentleman of fashion took, then to fight for France when the war began.

Madeleine seemed to be playing a part, that was it, a controlled and regulated part, as if she must smile so, move so, behave just so. He wondered if Philippa's old assessment, that Madeleine was unresponsive, was right; she had said nothing about their sister-in-law's private life before he left England for this visit, so Philippa's impression obviously hadn't changed.

Yet it was hard to discount his childhood instincts about Madeleine and Jesse; they had never been wrong yet. Still, Jesse had denied disliking him, had come up with this splendid scheme to resolve the problem of Daniel's future to Daniel's liking. Had he been wrong about Jesse, too? Philippa was coming over soon for a long visit. She would find out about Jesse. Nothing escaped Philippa.

When Susannah and Jonathan came to insist that their uncle referee a table tennis match in the garden behind the house, Madeleine looked uncomfortable.

"Come along with us, you two," Daniel said, impulsively. Her relief told him as clearly as words that she had no wish to be alone with Jesse, when that had been her only wish for so many years. He didn't want to know why.

94

He would be glad to go to Southampton in the morning and leave Jesse behind.

"Go with them, Madeleine," Jesse said. "I have some papers to look over before dinner." He watched the little group move off, slowly, to accommodate Daniel's injured leg.

He smiled contentedly. He had handled his brother with skill, letting Daniel himself refuse to have anything to do with Germany. Jesse was preparing that terrain with care, and he was sure that Slayter's would soon be a large investor in Germany, that it would float many loans—well-hidden behind American companies—for German industrialists. The less his brother knew about that, the better. The last thing a financier needed was a relative with "principles"—like Madeleine's late father—poking about. He must remind Susannah to keep his views about the German investments confidential.

He relit his pipe and picked up a folder of papers. *It would take a better man than you to outwit Jesse Slayter,* he thought.

Men had weaknesses. The thing to do was use them to his own advantage —or, where it concerned his family, to protect them from themselves. Daniel's weakness was the need to defy their father. Jesse had let him think he was succeeding. Jethro's had been twofold: a lust for women and a tendency to spoil his younger son. Jesse had inherited neither flaw.

Madeleine, like all women, was weakened by her need to be loved—she would do anything for him if he gave her new proof of love by sleeping with her on two consecutive nights or telling her more often how beautiful she was. Using Madeleine's weakness was easy and pleasant.

Children were difficult until their characters formed, but he knew Susannah basked in his approval, in the assurance he gave her that she was "different" and not to be understood by anyone as well as her father. He had not yet determined what Jonathan needed—he was not easy to read—but Jesse was watchful. When Jonathan's particular weakness surfaced, his father would be there to protect Jonathan from himself.

He stroked his beard thoughtfully. His own weakness, he confessed to himself, had been a tendency to sentimentality that would have been fatal to a financier, but he had overcome that when his father died. He had enormous discipline: Any man who could control his lust with a woman like Madeleine had strength of character. His own father had been deprived of character by lust.

He had made up his mind early on in this marriage not to yield to his wife's powerful attraction, either in her bed or in his mind. Those thoughts of her that came upon him unawares, intrusive as they were, would have pushed a lesser man beyond the bounds of conventional sexual behavior, would have made him another slave of passion.

He shook his head briskly, as if to clear it, opened the folder and began to read.

21

"Lovely," Jesse said, still breathing hard against her shoulder. "You're a lovely woman, Madeleine."

It was the first time they had been to bed together this summer. Now Daniel was gone and Jesse was in Southampton for the few weeks' holiday he permitted himself each August.

He drew his body from hers and rolled back to lie at her side with a small sigh of content. She thought how different this had been from the infinite variety of kisses and the sounds of rapture she experienced with Ned. Jesse was virile—and predictable and decorous. She simply did not evoke passion in him. Since she could sense that it was there, she knew the fault was hers.

"I'll be glad when we're all back in New York," Jesse said. "Distance seems to have made strangers of us."

Apprehension darted through her and she warned herself to be more natural. "I'll be glad too," she said. It was true because she longed to be with Ned. No wonder men made such a fetish of virginity and fidelity in wives. Comparisons could be disastrous. Still, she must not make more of Jesse's shortcomings than of her own. She was the one guilty of adultery, after all, and her only excuse was that she had a rival for Jesse's affections: Slayter's. And business was the first thing he talked about tonight when his pipe was lit for the ritual postcoital smoke.

"I never had a chance to tell you that I've settled it with Daniel," Jesse said.

Once she would have been overjoyed to have him talk about his business affairs with her. Tonight she had to make herself show interest.

"I did as Susannah suggested," he went on. "He'll do very well representing Slayter's abroad. He's become some sort of minor authority on art history, antiques, that kind of nonsense, and he knows half the aristocracy in England and France. Philippa and her Earl were good for something, after all."

Madeleine put her own thoughts aside. She liked Philippa and she had a great compassion for Daniel, forced so roughly into a life he did not want, first by his father, then by his brother. "He's a fascinating young man," she said to Jesse. "Jonathan followed him around like a puppy the whole time he was here."

"Fortunately he wasn't here long enough to give Jonathan any ridiculous ideas," Jesse said. "My son has quite a different future from my brother's."

The shadow of possible trouble for Jonathan made her careful of what she said. "You wouldn't force Jonnie as your father forced Daniel?"

"I won't have to. My son has good instincts, like his sister."

"They're both much too young for anything but fun and lessons now, anyway." She was determined to protect their happiness as long as she could.

He agreed with her. "Jon's well enough at boarding school. Perhaps Susannah should go too, she needs finishing."

"I'm not the one who calls her downstairs to perform for a crowd of cigar-smoking men!"

"You think she's too grown-up for that?"

"She's fourteen—and looks sixteen, she's so tall. Brandy and cigars aren't quite the thing, are they?"

He nodded. "I'll stop it then. I appreciate your concern, Madeleine."

"My concern?" She laughed drily. "She's my daughter, not my affiliate branch, and I love her. You have an odd way of speaking."

"I know—it's a carry-over from the Street," he said, absently. He smoked silently for a while. Then he said, "I'm really very glad Daniel's taken care of. It keeps to the spirit of my father's will, if not the letter."

"You were never very much concerned with your father's spirit, thank goodness."

He got out of bed. "No, but I'm sure he would be very pleased with what I've made out of Slayter's." He put on his pajama bottoms and smoothed his almost unrumpled hair and beard. Then he took her hand and kissed it. "Good night, my love. I have to get up early to go sailing with the children in the morning—I promised in a weak moment. Sleep well."

When he was gone, her smile twisted into tears in the half-light. Except for a telltale warmth on his pillow and the traces he had left in her body, he might never have been there tonight, might never have been so close without really touching her at all. She cried for a while, then dried her eyes and lay there thinking.

She would go on seeing Ned whenever she could, but she would be totally discreet. Her children were at school most of the time. Jesse was at his office all day. She never questioned him about his luncheons and he had never been interested in hers. She loved him, but she could no longer live on the few anxious hours she had with him. They were too infrequent and too sterile.

There were other hours now, vivid with warmth and laughter, when decorum was as outmoded as the corsets she'd been married in, when she was held as softly and as firmly as she needed to be.

98

She was more exquisite than ever, one of those women whose beauty peaks after thirty. If Jesse noticed the riper loveliness of his wife, he never mentioned it—not even on the day a few months later when he discovered the reason for it.

22

"I wasn't in Saratoga with Grace over the weekend, Jesse," Madeleine said. They were headed downtown in the Pierce-Arrow to an impromptu dinner Jesse had arranged with Grace and Clarence Dawes. The weekend would be mentioned; she had to tell him or risk letting him make a fool of himself with their friends. He would never forgive her for that.

"Really? Where were you then?"

When she didn't reply he turned to look at her, noticing now how pale she was and how her hands plucked nervously at the fox trim of her velvet cape. A faint gleam in his eyes told her he suspected what was coming, but refused to believe it. "Where were you?" he repeated, coldly this time.

She felt like a butterfly being slowly impaled on a pin. "In Atlantic City— with a man," she said.

He glanced at the partition separating them from the chauffeur, then back at her. His face was rigidly controlled and his eyes veiled.

"I'm telling you so you won't say anything to—to embarrass yourself with Grace and Clarence tonight."

One heavy black eyebrow rose with contempt. "How thoughtful of you," he said, studying her with the icy calm his business associates half joked about. "What do you expect me to do now, play the outraged husband?"

"Yes," she said desperately. "Get angry with me, tell me what a rotten wife I am—anything." When he didn't answer, she whispered, "You might ask me why."

"No need," he said, shaking his head abruptly. "I can only assume you have the instincts of a harlot, since I haven't given you cause." He stopped, then said explosively, "My God, you've had everything a woman could want—the finest clothes, jewels, cars, houses!"

"That isn't love," she said, knowing as she said it that he would not understand why. "I loved you, Jesse, but you hardly seem to know I'm alive except when I'm being a society mother or an occasional wife."

"You're a woman! What the devil more do you expect?"

"The feeling that I matter to you, that no other woman could have made you happy!" Her voice dropped. "You never really know I'm there, not even when you come to my room, and that's been less and less ever since you've had your own." Her hands opened helplessly. "Your only real passion is Slayter's, and you talk more about it to Susannah than you ever did to me. We've never just talked to each other."

"Is that what you did in Atlantic City—talk?"

The contempt on his face drove her from shame to anger. "Part of the time, yes! And you wouldn't believe the rest!"

"Shut up," he said, deadly quiet, and she knew it was cruel to hurt him like that and impossible to make him understand.

"Oh, Jesse," she said sorrowfully, her anger melting to regret. "Why can't you love me?"

"This is hardly the time to ask about love," he said tonelessly.

"I've always asked about it. You never answered."

"We have different ideas of what the word means," he said shortly, "and yours isn't worthy of my wife."

Her heart lurched. "Do you want a divorce?"

He was silent for a few moments, then he appeared to have made a decision. "Let's understand each other now, Madeleine. I'm not going to disgrace my name and my children by the first divorce in my family's history. A divorce could ruin Slayter's—scandal is the one thing that doesn't mix with money. If you force the issue and we have to live apart, you'll never see my children again. Do you understand?"

She nodded silently, understanding all too well. As long as no one knew, he didn't care what she did. She was no more important to him than that.

"Just one more thing," he said, still ominously calm.

"Yes, Jesse."

"This subject is not to be discussed again—ever."

Jesse meant what he said. He would never mention it again. He would never touch her again, either.

He withdrew from Madeleine completely, although he was still the same attentive husband in public and when the children were at home with them. He was at her side in public; it was only when they were back at home with all the doors closed for the night that she felt so terribly alone with her guilt.

23

"You can't go on this way," Ned told her. "If he won't divorce you, then leave him."

"You know I can't do that. I'd never see my children."

"Not for a while, but surely they'll understand when they're old enough."

"What? That their mother was the scandal of New York and they were laughingstocks at school because of me?"

"Come on, darling," Ned insisted, "he's entitled to part of the guilt too."

"Not in a way my children would understand. What would I say, that he was kind, undemanding, showered me with gifts—and didn't know I was there, even when he slept with me? Who would understand anything like that? He doesn't and he was right there all the time, why should anyone else? They'll hate me as much as he does."

Ned looked at her with sad comprehension. "I think you still love him, far more than you do me."

"It's true I still love him, but it's not the same as you, Ned, it's not the same." She turned to him. "I've stopped trying to understand how I feel, anyway, I just have to live with it—and with you, if you'll let me, whenever I can."

She managed to see Ned often. Jesse devoted himself to his business more than ever, explaining to the children that a boom was starting in American business that would change the economy of the world. Slayter's would help direct that boom.

"And," he said one night at dinner, "I've bought your mother a present, a colonial mansion on the Hudson."

"What about Southampton?" Jonathan said. He loved the swimming and sailing out at the beach.

"Too many people," Jesse replied, glancing at Madeleine. "Willow Hill has the most beautiful grounds I've seen up there, riding trails, a duck pond, a sizable wood. We'll put in tennis courts and a pool, and you can go boating on the river. The house needs a lot of work. It has to be completely restored and redecorated."

"Good," Susannah said. "Mother loves that kind of thing, don't you?"

Madeleine agreed with outward enthusiasm, knowing the house on the Hudson was in the nature of a punishment, a banishment to keep her away from evil opportunity, not a real present or an attempt at reconciliation.

But it was a beautiful house and she was soon immersed in restoring it.

Jesse came to Willow Hill only on summer weekends. He was free the rest of the time to dine with his colleagues or work on his files until the wee hours —even, she supposed, to patronize a discreet brothel with the same arid regularity as he had patronized her.

She asked him only once to forgive her. "I'll do anything to make it up to you, Jesse."

"I don't know what you're talking about."

"Then there's no hope," she said softly, "not if you won't acknowledge it."

"There's every hope," he told her. "We're a model family. I've expanded my father's company tenfold since he died. Susannah is an intelligent girl and Jonathan a delightful boy. You're the beauty of New York, a devoted mother and a perfect wife. There's every hope."

"I don't know what he means by that," she worried to Ned when she saw him in New York. "Every hope of what? Hurting us?"

"He's trying to frighten you," Ned said. "He's never even asked you who the man is."

"I'm sure he thinks there are at least a dozen," Madeleine said bitterly. "How can he know me so little?"

She knew Jesse watched her constantly when they were out together, looking for a smile or a glance that might tell him who her lovers were, but she was sure his pride prevented him from hiring a professional detective who would lead him to Ned.

Only Daisy knew when Madeleine was not out shopping or visiting the art galleries, although neither woman ever alluded to it openly.

"Bob has an early call to Pearl Street this evening," Daisy would say. "Do you have any errands for him?" Come home early, she was telling Madeleine, before he does.

Madeleine hated having implicated Daisy. Sometimes she thought the whole game was not worth the candle, that it would be better if she left Jesse, but she worried about her children, particularly Susannah.

"She's been following him around like a serious little owl ever since she was eleven," Madeleine told Ned. "They have 'business secrets,' things he's always said women can't understand. Susannah must think I'm a complete fool."

"She doesn't think he means you," Ned comforted. "Children put their parents in a special category, separate from the rest of humanity."

"You're probably right," Madeleine conceded, for Ned's sake and her own. "But what kind of woman will she turn out to be? It's impossible to tell what she's thinking. She imitates him, down to that guarded expression that

104

keeps Wall Street guessing! Jonnie calls her the Sphinx, but he can call her anything."

"So can you. You take her much too seriously."

Madeleine tried, but the atmosphere between Jesse and herself was strained, heavy with his hurt and his frustrated revenge. She knew he had never waited so patiently and implacably for a coup in the market as he was waiting to punish her.

The worst of it was that he would never comprehend why she had humiliated him, why she had been unfaithful. "I gave you no cause," he had told her in the car that night. "And there's many a woman who'd agree with him," Madeleine said one day in Ned's little flat in Greenwich Village.

"Only the taking women, not the giving ones, like you."

Madeleine crossed the little studio and kissed him. "Ned, my dear, dear Ned, I don't know what I'd do without you."

He averted his face. "I don't want gratitude, Madeleine. I want to help you through this because I'm half responsible for it, but it can't go on forever. I won't accept that." He took her hands from his shoulders and stepped back, a little away from her. "I don't want to be your 'dear,' Madeleine. I want you to feel the same passion for me that you do for him."

"But I do," she insisted, "you know I do! More than I ever had with him."

"I said *for* him, not with him. I want you to look at me the way you look at him, as if I were a lord of creation, even if I know I'm not and no man is. You've confused his power with the man himself and you're in love with it. It's enough for a lot of women, but not for you. You can't live with it." He turned away from her. "I don't know how much longer *I* can live with it."

"I do love you now, Ned," she said pleadingly. "I didn't at first, it started with loneliness. I even hoped Jesse would notice me out of jealousy when he found out." Her voice faded to a whisper. "Don't be angry, Ned, but I used to pretend sometimes that you were Jesse, talking to me, listening to me, even making love to me. Now I know it's you."

She went close to him and put her arms around his unyielding body, her face against the silk dressing gown covering his back. "I do love you, darling. He's like a habit or a fever to me, he's wanting what I can't have. It'll take a little time, while the children still need me, to get over the habit." Her arms tightened around him in a vain effort to enclose him. "Can you wait for me just a little longer?"

She could feel him trying to resist her, then he turned to her against his will and lifted her in his arms.

"Damn it, what a fool I am," he said, looking down at her with eyes that worshipped and rebuked her at once. "Well, I'm a fool then, but out of love,

105

Madeleine, not weakness." He kissed her fiercely and carried her to the bed. "I won't wait forever."

For the first time her response, ardent as it was, was more to the man than to his body. Her passion was not solely for what he did, but for what he was, and she knew she held in her arms not power or wealth but someone, a person, a man. Like a great bell somewhere deep inside her, the first knell of her need for Jesse began to toll.

24

"Strength of character," Jesse told his children one Saturday afternoon when the three of them were horseback riding in Central Park. "That's what makes a person, man or woman. Beauty is a useless commodity—except in a horse."

Jonathan laughed shortly.

"I'm quite serious," Jesse went on, with a glance at his son. "You want to get your values straight. Look at your sister. She has something better than beauty."

"Susannah's beautiful!" Jonathan insisted, with such force that his horse's ears first rose, then flattened.

"Of course," Jesse agreed carelessly. "She has an interesting face, but she has intelligence and breeding and that's a kind of beauty too, the kind that lasts." He looked proudly at the slim girl riding beside him in a full-skirted black riding coat and fawn breeches. Her hair was pulled back in a black velvet snood. A starched white stock and black derby and gloves completed the austere costume.

"Uncle Daniel called her the dark lady of the sonnets," Jonathan said doggedly, "and that's a whole lot more than interesting." He was in one of those stubborn moods, Jesse saw, that sometimes possessed this otherwise good-natured boy.

"He once said you were Ganymede," Susannah reminded her brother, trying to smooth it over, "and you hated it."

"Your uncle was not acquainted with either individual," Jesse remarked drily, making both of them laugh. "It takes more than good features to get you through life, you can take my word for it."

They began to trot the horses, twigs popping under their hoofs like bullets. It was a cool April and the air was invigorating. Sunlight filtered through the barely budded trees and the voices of children at play came to them from the park.

"Really, Jonnie," Susannah said when they slowed their horses for a moment at a crossing. "I know Father thinks I'm pretty enough for all practical purposes." She smiled, mediating between the boy and her father, as they crossed. "Come on, now, there's the long path, race me to the bend."

Jesse watched them go, thinking she *was* lovely, but it was safer for her not to dwell on it. She was slender as a larch tree, with eyes even darker than her shining hair and an ivory complexion. Her long lashes cast extraordi-

107

nary shadows on her finely molded face and her mouth had just enough fullness to gentle it. She was growing up. Men would notice Susannah before too long and he had to protect her from herself. She couldn't marry just anyone on a romantic impulse. And if any of Madeleine's lechery lurked in his child, he intended to stifle it before it was too late.

They finished their ride, had some hot chocolate at Rumpelmayer's, and decided to walk back to the house where Madeleine waited for them. It was still difficult for Jesse to act naturally with his wife for the children's sake, but he felt it necessary to protect what was his by playing a part.

He was locked into this humiliation by the greater shame an open scandal would make, and for the first time he was grateful for the example his father had set him. It had kept Jesse from losing his head over Madeleine, even in their most intimate moments. Now the sight of her made his gorge rise: no one had ever made a fool of him before.

Susannah was his comfort. Jonathan was at boarding school, only home for occasional weekends, and difficult to know, no matter how charming he could be. Susannah went to day school and Jesse spent more time with her now that she was fifteen than he ever had before, even to shopping with her for dresses.

"Not that one," he told Susannah later that week when they were choosing dresses at Arnold Constable. "You don't want to look like a pink pincushion."

"It's the sort of thing the other girls wear," Susannah said.

"You're not in the least like other girls. Show us something simpler, please," Jesse told the saleswoman. "Without ruffles and in a color better suited to my daughter's complexion."

The dozen dresses he chose suited Susannah's style, he thought. They made her look different.

"Your Aunt Philippa will approve when she comes," Jesse said, "you'll see."

"You always say she's frivolous," Susannah reminded him. She loved to catch him out in a contradiction.

"About everything but clothes. She knows what suits her, never mind what other women wear. You'll never be like other women," he told her as they walked to the elevator. "Empty-headed, with nothing but romance on what passes for their minds."

"I suppose I'll never fall in love and get married," Susannah said, "will I?"

"You won't 'fall.' You'll marry someone who's worthy of your respect and confidence."

She looked at him with that dark gaze that was sometimes as skeptical as his own. "It doesn't sound very exciting," she said.

"Excitement is for shopgirls and peasants," Jesse answered. "What is popularly called love is moral weakness. It makes a person utterly defenseless." He smiled and gave her his arm as they left the store. "Don't worry about it, just trust me. I'm the only one in the world you can trust completely."

"And Mother and Jonnie," Susannah added.

"Yes, of course." He handed her into their waiting car. "Let's stop in at Cartier for some trinkets to go with those dresses."

He always included a gift for Madeleine on these expeditions. He had to keep up appearances, no matter how difficult that was, and after all she was still his wife.

His, damn it! Sometimes he shook at the mental picture of other men, faceless and priapic, enjoying her generous body, using what belonged to him. It was unbearable, but he had never let her know what he felt and he would not show it now. His caution with her—and everyone else—had been vindicated by her treachery.

While he waited for Jonathan to reach the age of reason and take a son's rightful place at his side, he had his daughter to mold out of soft, feminine clay—Susannah, whose need for his approval was boundless, precisely because he had not given it too lavishly.

Book III

25

1922

There was nothing unusual about the way that day began.

Susannah took a book from the library after lunch and set off for one of the graceful trees that gave Willow Hill its name. For a time the tinkle of Jonathan's piano followed her across the expanse of green grass, but when the lawn dropped toward the Hudson, she could hear nothing but the lazy sounds of summer. When she was settled under a weeping willow near the pond, the book seemed too heavy in her hands. She felt bored and idle. Any girls she knew on neighboring estates preferred to gossip about boyfriends and babies; she had enough of that at school.

Finally she dozed while the breeze, warm and dry, fanned her face and jollied the mourning tree. When she opened her eyes the sun was in its downward parabola. She brushed the bits of grass from her skirt and started back to bathe and change before her father arrived.

She decided to take a shady shortcut around the back of the empty guest cottages. It was silent in the heat. There were no bird calls, no rustling sounds of rabbits and field mice, not even the sound of buzzing flies.

Then she heard a voice, warm and throaty—her mother's. What would Mother be doing here at this hour—at any hour? She was about to call out when she heard what Madeleine was saying so earnestly, in a way Susannah had never heard her speak before.

"You know I love you, darling, but there's nothing we can do. He wouldn't hear of it. At least we have this. It's better than nothing."

"It's not enough," a man's voice said despairingly. "I don't want to share you."

"But you don't, not in that way."

"Not in any way!" Susannah recognized the voice now. It was Dr. Driscoll, one of her father's brokerage clients. "Damn it, Madeleine, do you know what it's like to leave you here with him? We're both living a lie and it's worse than wrong, it's stupid. You can't live with an arrogant bastard like Jesse Slayter. He doesn't deserve you."

Susannah was breathless. A wave of anger stifled her. How dare her mother meet this man in such a place and talk about Father like that? She was Father's wife. She belonged to him!

". . . not now," Madeleine was saying. "It was such a risk for you to

113

come here today, don't waste it. We can talk in town, but not now, not here when I can touch you."

"Oh, God," the man's voice said in a different way. "When you touch me like that . . ."

Susannah half turned to leave. Then she glanced down at the soft earth around the cottage and knowing it would cushion her footsteps, she went closer to look through a corner of the curtained window.

She could see the woman's body and his through the sheer white curtain, but their heads were hidden by the window frame. They were both naked on the bed and shining with perspiration. The woman was lying on her back, her long legs parted, one hand hidden somewhere between their bodies. Both the man's hands were visible. One of his arms circled the woman and his hand came around to nestle on her full white breast, gently fingering its tip; the other was stroking the hair between her thighs as if it were a kitten.

Susannah edged back against the side of the house, unable to move away. She could no longer see, but she could still hear her mother's lazy voice as it gave way to another sound, a demanding little sound, muffled and furious, almost as if she were being hurt. But it was clearly not pain she felt. It was some mysterious, indescribable kind of pleasure.

After a while her mother whispered, "Yes, oh please, yes," and a few seconds later the man repeated the same words until he stopped with a last, deep moan that sounded beyond his power to control.

There was utter silence then, except for their breathing. Susannah shrank into the outer wall, her face still furiously red, but with something that was more than anger, more than outrage. It was a sensation she had never felt before, an impulse in her body for which her mind had no name.

When the voices inside began to murmur again, she moved softly out of earshot and then ran the rest of the way to the house. She locked the door of her bedroom, dropped onto the bed and lay there until she was breathing easily.

Should she tell her father? She couldn't! It would shame him—and how could she say such things to him? She had no words to tell him what she had seen. How could her mother do such things with a man?

But at the back of her mind another thought flickered. This indecent handling of each other, this shameful cleaving of bodies, must be what came after the kisses, even the mere suggestion of kisses, in the books she was allowed to read. It was this, according to her friends, that drove men and women to risk everything, despite honor and loyalty and anything else that mattered. Something as mindless and degrading as this. It was why women exposed their breasts with low necklines and men flushed at the sight of them. It was what men wanted with women, all men.

She hated it, all of it, the waiting and the whispering about it, the dreaming and wondering about the man who would undress her and invade her body. She tossed restlessly on the bedspread, feeling its chenille nubs as if they were spikes.

She wished again that she could have been a boy, like Jonathan. Boys had no such problems. All they wanted was a woman to handle, the way that man had handled her mother. This was "love," the traitor emotion her father had warned against.

Too agitated to lie still, she sat on the edge of the bed, wishing her father was there. She wanted to sit on his lap and be cuddled, the way she once had, but she was sixteen, a woman now, even to her father.

She was very like her father, as dark-haired as he was, with the same high cheekbones and a silky echo of those heavy brows that made his handsome face so distinctive and so powerfully masculine. Her mouth, though, was more like her mother's, and she was as tall as Madeleine too, but Susannah would never have to diet the way her mother did. She had high breasts and slim hips, the kind of figure that was in fashion now, not Madeleine's turn-of-the-century voluptuousness.

But Madeleine was beautiful in a way most women could never hope to be. There were many lovely women in New York, but Madeleine was matchless. If Susannah's complexion was as smooth as ivory, Madeleine's had the look of coral-tinted cream. There was a richness about her mother's body, a luster to her hair and her velvety arms and breasts that was in no way maternal. To Susannah it was unthinkable that her mother's body had ever been swollen with a child, although she must have seen it that way; she had been two years old when her brother was born.

Jonathan had been her most precious possession from the moment she saw him, tiny and trusting, his little star of a hand holding hers. He was her only confidant. She loved him with a tenderness that had no awe in it, such as she felt for her father, and none of the vague resentment she had some-times felt for her mother.

It was more than resentment now; she hated Madeleine for shaming her father. He was different from the other men and he deserved a better wife than he had.

"I have to get away from her," Susannah said, her voice muffled by her cupped hands. She had objected to going away to finishing school before, but she could not stay near her mother now without showing what she felt

115

to Jonathan and her father. She had to protect her father—and find a way to stop Madeleine.

She fell back on the bed again. "How could she? How could she?" She cried, her voice muffled by the pillow. It was a question she would never ask aloud because she did not want to hear the answer.

26

"It frightens me," Madeleine said to Ned. She sat in a chintz-covered wicker chair in the cottage, sponged, dressed and ready to go but unable to leave until she had absorbed what had happened to her.

"Why? Because you love a man who loves you, for a change?"

She crossed her arms and covered herself protectively. "I feel as if I've won a treasure hunt I didn't even know I was on." He was waiting for more than that and she knew it, but she said nothing, hugging herself in the chair. Adultery was an enormous burden to Madeleine. Their secret hours together were only momentary bright patches in her gray cloud of guilt.

And there was always Jesse. If another man loved her, why didn't he? Perhaps she should have tried harder to reach him, to keep his armor from growing thicker every day . . .

". . . have to tell him," Ned was saying firmly. "Then you can get a divorce and marry me."

"It isn't that easy. He hates me, Ned. It's made him very cold and angry with everyone but the children, and I'm afraid he'll turn it on them someday. How can I just walk out and leave all of them?"

He stood, his hands jammed into his pockets. "All of them," he repeated. "But you really mean Jesse. I suppose he wasn't cold and hard before he found out about us? You still want to believe he's the big, handsome teddy bear you thought you married, with a thorn in his paw, and someday it'll fall out and you'll heal his wound and everything will be roses—just the way it *never was,* Madeleine." His face was stormy. "He's not that man anymore. Maybe he never was, but you yourself told me he hasn't been for sure since his father died. The one chance he ever had was you—and he never took that chance."

He lowered his voice then, as if to show her that he did not speak in anger alone. "I want you, Madeleine; he doesn't. For some reason the challenge to win him still has some fatal attraction for you." He shrugged. "I've had all I can take. You know I'm leaving for Vienna at the end of the summer. I hope you'll come with me, but I'm going, with you or without you." His determined calm abandoned him. "Don't let anything happen to us, Madeleine, for heaven's sweet sake, don't let anything happen."

"I'll try, Ned," she told him, her hands moving as if they were searching for something to hold on to. "I promise, I'll try."

They parted with nothing resolved except the necessity to take the fatal step soon, and the impossibility of finding any solution that was not disastrous one way or another. Finally she sighed and rose to go, looking around the cottage again to be sure there were no traces of the afternoon. In spite of her problems she felt the ineffable contentment of the love that caused them. There was nothing in life—no laughter, no dream—that was not better because of love. She was glad she had taken the chance and let Ned come here this afternoon.

When she reached the house she took a last look back over the rolling green lawn and the graceful trees before she passed the four soaring white columns and went inside. It was cool and pleasant in the vaulted entrance hall with its curved staircase sweeping upward along the right-hand wall. The drawing rooms were on the left and led to the music room and a winter garden. She could hear Jonathan still playing as he had been when she left the house just after lunch to meet Ned.

She went up the stairs and into her large, square room with its polished plank pine floors gleaming under hand-hooked rugs. Starched white muslin curtains fluttered at the long windows. Willow Hill was pure colonial, a "Southern plantation" house, and she had spent a long time and a lot of energy finding every authentic article in it. Even Jesse said it was a showplace—one of the few compliments he paid her these days.

Daniel said it was a "marvel" from the sketches she had sent him, and for some reason Jesse valued his brother's opinions, much as he disapproved of Daniel's way of life. She rang for Daisy, glad that Daniel was expected in a few days for his first visit in two years. He would ease the tension in the house. It was hard to pretend they were a happy family.

She looked up when Daisy came in, unaware that her eyes were troubled and her face strained.

"Listen to Master Jonnie," Daisy said. "He plays like Saint Peter at the gates."

"He's very talented, isn't he?" Madeleine smiled. "It isn't only because I adore him, Daisy; everyone says the same thing."

"And so they should, the hours he spends at it," Daisy unhooked the back of Madeleine's blouse.

Jonathan's rapt devotion to music was worrisome. Jesse had no idea he spent so much time at it. He hadn't expressly forbidden it yet, but Madeleine knew someday he would. It would break the boy's heart to give up music, even to please his father.

"Has Susannah come back?" Madeleine asked.

Daisy nodded. "Forgot her dignity and went flying up the stairs the way she used to, about an hour ago."

Madeleine smiled. "Sixteen is such a confusing time for a girl, even one as mature as Susannah." In many ways Susannah tried to behave like Jesse, but she was far too intelligent to take kindly to the domestic future Jesse planned for her. Madeleine had wanted nothing more than to be Jesse's wife and the mother of his children. Susannah shared her own father's patronizing opinion of domesticity. She was bound to rebel sooner or later.

"It's high time all of you rebelled," Ned had told her not long ago.

"And then what? Where do we go when we're social pariahs? The 'other women' never get invited to parties. They're a threat to every virtuous wife and a prey for every husband with a wandering eye."

"You know where you'll go," Ned had insisted. "You'll come to me."

What was she going to do about his insistence that they stop the charade and marry? He was right; after two years it was no longer an affair. Ned was a man Madeleine loved enough to marry.

But could he take the place of her children? Madeleine could not contemplate such a loss, not even to have Ned. She would have to tell him so. No matter what he said, it was better for them to meet secretly than not at all. Somehow she would persuade him not to go to Vienna to study with Dr. Freud. Ned was not like Jesse, who never changed his mind.

"Where's Madame's scarf?" Daisy asked suddenly, sorting through the clothes Madeleine had been wearing.

"I—I don't know," Madeleine said nervously. "I must have dropped it."

"Never mind," Daisy soothed. "I'll go along the path and find it."

"Thank you," Madeleine said softly, knowing she was far too agitated. She might have dropped the scarf on a perfectly innocent walk. "Oh, Daisy," she said, clasping her hands.

"It's a small thing, you mustn't fret. I'll be back in five minutes and I'll tell Master Jonnie to stop playing now, it's near time for the Mister to be arriving."

Madeleine watched Daisy go, her gratitude to this woman beyond expression. She leaned against the dressing table to stop herself from trembling. It would probably be easier if Jesse found her out; the decision would no longer be hers to make, but that was not what she really wanted.

She knew what she wanted, from moments of fantasy she had never confessed, not even to Ned. She wanted Jesse to drop his mask, just for once, and acknowledge her as more than a possession, as a person.

After a while she began to prepare for the evening. Jesse would be here soon, bearing his myriad disapprovals with him. Even so, Madeleine always wanted to look as beautiful for him as she could. Briefly, she wondered why that was so, then she shook her head and put the old question aside.

27

Even from the quiet of his lofty oak-paneled office Jesse could feel the contagious electricity of the Street. Since the Great War America was, indeed, a creditor nation and Wall Street was gaining ground as one of the world's new financial centers. It had always been the focal point of Jesse's life.

Today, on a sultry Friday in August, he could literally feel the Street winding down for a long summer weekend. Many men in the financial district had already gone to join their families in the Hamptons or Newport or on the cool heights of the Hudson, but even in summer Jesse never left his office on Friday until the closing bell sounded on the New York Stock Exchange and the ticker, pristine under its glass dome, had brought forth its last scrap of information. It was enough of a concession to miss the Saturday morning market.

It was still early afternoon, two hours before he would lock his desk with the gold key on his watch fob, take his straw boater from the closet and go down to his waiting car to be chauffeured to the train for the pleasant journey upstate to Willow Hill.

Now he was immobile behind his massive mahogany desk, listening intently to the slender, foxlike man who sat stiffly on its other side in a matching green leather armchair, one arm on the large globe that stood near it. Jesse did not speak when the man paused occasionally, but merely nodded his impressive head to show he understood what Karl-Dieter Veidt was saying in his accented English.

None of it was new to him. The German chemical industry led the world in technology. They had proven it during the war by producing synthetic nitrates to make gunpowder when the British blockade cut off supplies of the natural stuff. The laboratories that had produced aspirin, Salvarsan and the first synthetic blue dyes to equal natural Chinese indigo had turned their genius to war with explosives and poison gas.

"I'd far rather they used their genius for something else," Susannah had remarked when he began explaining it to her. "And I don't understand why private industry would organize. You always say organizing anything leads to Bolshevism."

"Ah, this is the exception that proves the rule," Jesse had gone on. "This industrial organization coordinated Germany's wartime effort as no bumbling government bureaucracy could have done."

"They lost the war," Susannah had observed with relish.

"Because they were not allowed to direct it. The government did that and governments are run by elected officials—with all the shortcomings of the people who elect them. Business is run by men of skill and talent."

Fascinated as she was, Susannah had not accepted that. "There must be some competent men in government."

"Only the ones industry puts there," Jesse had insisted, and had continued her instruction about the *Interessen Gemeinschaft der Deutschen Teerfarbenindustrie*—the Community of Interest of the German Dyestuff Industry—of which Herr Veidt was a representative.

"A puny emissary," one of Jesse's partners had remarked, "for such a powerful group."

"Don't judge an organization by its emissary," Jesse had reminded him. "Not by his size, anyway. Look at his eyes."

The group Veidt represented was very powerful and very clever. Virtually every man-made object on earth was colored by its synthetic dyes, and its technology was so intricate that even those who got their hands on the descriptions were incapable of interpreting them. Du Pont had been forced to lure I.G. Farben scientists away from Germany with high salaries just a year ago, to work its patents.

But what did Karl-Dieter Veidt want of him now? Jesse stirred slightly and the German seemed to sense his impatience.

"Of course you are aware of all that," the wire-thin man said, his hand turning the globe on its stand. "I am here on behalf of the I.G., to introduce myself in the event we might share future interests."

Jesse looked purposefully skeptical. "Now that Du Pont has the scientists to compete in the dyestuff market, what possible future interests could we share, aside from watching our stock in the industry grow?"

Veidt pursed his thin lips. "That is difficult to say at this point. There is always expansion and there are—other products, other technologies."

Jesse leaned back in his chair and lit his pipe, his dark eyes watchful. "And other large American companies to develop them."

The other man nodded. "Just so. Too large and too, shall we say, eager. We prefer to purchase our own facilities in your country and direct the development ourselves."

"I see," Jesse said. "That way you control the patents *and* the know-how."

Veidt inclined his head to indicate that, as a man of few words himself, he appreciated the quality in others.

Jesse continued to wait, his eyes fixed on Veidt's pale gray irises behind silver-rimmed spectacles. Finally Veidt came to the point. "If we pursue this

122

expansion we would like to arrange financing by a bond issue floated through your firm."

Jesse smiled glacially. "Why Slayter's in particular? A half dozen others would do as well."

"Of course, insofar as money is concerned. But your firm has a special reputation for handling, shall we say, delicate matters of this kind."

Jesse nodded at his waiting visitor. "We are discreet." The war had ended only four years ago; anti-German sentiment still ran deep in America. "Discretion has its rewards," he added pointedly. The price of avoiding a public outcry or a federal investigation had always been high, but there were ways of raising money without trumpeting its final destination to American investors all around the country.

"Just so," Veidt said again, a smile stretching a thin arc under his long, patrician nose. "We understand each other perfectly."

Jesse nodded again, saying nothing.

"Then I shall call upon you if our expansion comes to pass." Veidt stood and offered a pale, sinewy hand. Jesse shook it, then walked with Veidt to the door of his office and instructed his personal secretary to show Herr Veidt out.

Interesting. It had been an interesting exchange. He made a note in his tiny, precise script to buy more Du Pont stock on Monday. If the Germans were concerned enough at American competition in dyestuffs and "other technologies"—meaning more than the explosives, fertilizers and pharmaceuticals already developed from it—then Jesse was willing to sink more capital into the most qualified contender in America. He might also pick up some shares in the I.G. companies.

He stretched. Even if nothing came of this meeting, he was busy all the time. The economy was beginning to run at full tilt. Finding goods to buy in America was no longer the problem it had always been. What people wanted now was fast money to buy what was offered to them.

For Jesse the excitement and the potential were mercurial. Every day was a new challenge to him, one he knew he could meet. This office, with its tobacco-scented leather chairs and heavy velvet drapes, was where he felt most comfortable. He rarely looked at the paintings on the walls—two Renoirs and a Rousseau Daniel had given him—although he was aware of the portrait of Jethro Slayter hanging just behind his chair. The lessons his father had taught him were unforgettable—in this room particularly.

"Power," old Jethro used to say, "is most effective when it's quiet. Only an anxious whore uses rouge and bangles; a successful one doesn't need them. On this Street the houses with the most power make the least noise, see?"

Slayter's made very little noise. There were firms with their own gymnasiums and masseurs, private chefs and stewards to attend the partners, and fleets of cars. Here on Pearl Street Jesse and each of his nine partners had private offices, rather than a row of roll-top desks in a huge Partners' Room as was the case at Morgan's. They met once daily to discuss their separate projects and then retreated to their offices.

From the quiet outside his door Jesse knew they had all gone. It was a few minutes past three. The ticker was quiet.

"Blake," Jesse called his private secretary.

Willis Blake's florid face appeared in the doorway. His sack suit was wrinkled and his collar wilted, but Willis Blake was a very sharp young man; without him and his sweaty brow Jesse's business life would not have run with such well-oiled precision.

"Is the car downstairs?"

"Yes, sir," the young man nodded, his earnest face showing no hint that this exchange, repeated at three o'clock every Friday afternoon in summer, was superfluous. Of course the car was downstairs. It was worth Willis Blake's job for it to be anywhere else, and the job carried more than its munificent salary of seventy-five dollars a week. It carried inside information on what stocks to buy and when to turn them over for the best profit.

Jesse was locking the small private safe behind a panel in Jethro's desk. "Then I'll say good-bye until Monday morning," he said. He took his hat from the closet, closed the door carefully, and surveyed the vast plateau of his desk again to see that no confidential papers marred its order. The memo pad was not confidential. Du Pont stock was out of Blake's reach and the initials I.G. meant nothing to him. He knew Blake was a prize sneak; if he could make anything out of such sketchy information, he was welcome to it.

Jesse went through Blake's office and down the corridor to a private elevator that dropped him smoothly to the lobby at the corner of Wall and Pearl streets. He looked crisp and cool in his gray, single-breasted shantung jacket and his loosely cut cuffed trousers. In the glaring sun outside his chauffeur held the door of a Rolls-Royce Silver Ghost open for him. There was a fresh carnation in each of the silver vases bolted to the sides of the car, just forward of the windows.

With a nod to the chauffeur by way of greeting, Jesse settled into the back seat, lit a pipe and let the hot breeze fan his face while the car rolled toward the Grand Central depot.

The city was fairly busy, even in the August heat. Heat didn't bother Jesse, he ignored it. His attention was on the streets filled with trolleys, motorcars and a few horse-drawn vehicles. They passed the Woolworth Building, the tallest in the world. They passed small patches of green where women and nursemaids aired their charges, most of them uninterested in exercising their two-year-old right to vote. Jesse had always considered the vote for women sheer lunacy, although his wife supported it. Madeleine, however, was no criterion of womanly behavior.

There were private houses nestled between fine shops as they approached the terminal on Forty-second Street, and speakeasies behind sober facades.

"Prohibition's another lunacy," Jesse told everyone who listened to him. "It's time the politicians and the women stopped meddling and let finance run the country. We're the only ones qualified. Washington is a colony of clerks; anyone who's elected is answerable for tenure to an ignorant mob."

"That doesn't sound much like Jeffersonian democracy," Susannah once said dubiously.

"Jefferson didn't live in the twentieth century," her father told her. "Money is what decides everything in the long run, not philosophy, and no one knows more about money than a financier."

At the station he dismissed the chauffeur, walked through the huge building to his platform, and boarded the Pullman car where he removed his hat and settled himself for the trip to Willow Hill.

The car was almost empty. There was no one he knew and he was glad of that. He wanted to reflect on a few matters without interruption, particularly on the possibilities opened by the enigmatic Herr Veidt.

He wondered what his father would have said about such a vague proposition as Veidt's. His father might have had some faults, but he was the best judge of men Jesse had ever met. In the twelve years since his death—Jesse grimaced at the memory of Jethro sprawled naked on a whore's musky bed —there had been times when his father's opinion would have been very welcome.

On the whole, though, Jesse felt that his judgment was as sound as his father's—better, when it came to women. He ignored females as he did heat and other discomforts. Women were so unimportant in the grand scheme of things. He was not ready yet to do anything about Madeleine, his concentration was needed elsewhere. Jesse held the past and the future of a long line of Slayters in his hands; he had no time to waste on a woman who had made a fool of him while she pretended to love him.

He sat up suddenly in his Pullman chair, aware that the train was slowing at his stop. He was in command of himself again, the lines of rage at his wanton wife erased from his face. He had the Slayter jaw, square and heavy, and old Jethro's mouth as he grew older and smiled less, a streak of determination half hidden in his neat beard and mustache.

125

Bob Harris was waiting at the station with an open landau and a pair of horses.

"Evenin', Mr. Slayter."

"Good evening, Harris."

"Hot in the city, Sir?"

"It's always much cooler here."

Bob flicked the reins and the horses started out. Jesse enjoyed the ride. In fair weather he always preferred a horse-drawn carriage to one of the motorcars. The horses clopped along roads old and new, under trees in full leaf sprayed by the rays of the setting sun.

"All quiet this week?" he called to Bob Harris.

"Yessir, as usual. Master Jonathan's gettin' brown as a berry, boatin' on the river. Miss Susannah has her books when she's not off with her brother."

Jesse smiled, thinking of Susannah, a very different smile from the bleak one he had given Herr Veidt. The child had amazing intelligence for a female. A pity he could no longer put her through her economic paces to astonish his friends. It was not the proper place for a young girl who would be married in a few years' time.

His smile faded and was replaced by an expression of uncertainty. Jonathan was not interested in business and it was Jonathan who should have been. One day soon Jesse would put a stop to his son's mooning about over music. He was behaving more like Daniel, who had no interest in money except to spend it. But Jesse was wary of his brother; Daniel was no fool. It was a relief he didn't meddle in Slayter's. He was due home on a visit from Europe on Monday. Jesse wondered if he would stay this time.

"I'll want you in the city this week, Harris," he reminded Bob. "Mister Daniel is arriving, he'll probably need a car."

"Yessir, Mr. Slayter." Bob was curious about two brothers who acted more like strangers.

Jesse looked at his pocket watch. They did not dine until eight and he felt the need of some exercise here in the fresh, green countryside.

"You can stop at the bottom of the lane, Harris," he said. "I'll walk up to the house."

Jesse walked along the lane, not very eager to see Madeleine and resume the appearance of a happy husband glad to be reunited with his wife. It was getting increasingly difficult, especially in the summer when he had the welcome respite of the business week to relax and be himself, well removed from her.

The lane skirted the lawn and he tried to observe the improvements the

126

gardeners had made during the week. Willow Hill was a prime property, a sound investment. Houses like this would never be built again.

He kept on until he had passed the house and then he turned from the lane toward the white gazebo on the top of the back slope. His feet sank gratefully into the thick, freshly cut grass, and he was almost at the gazebo before he saw Madeleine sitting there, unaware of his presence.

She was like a statue, still as stone on the circular bench. She was in semiprofile to him, her hands lying passively in her lap, her eyes lowered. She was a beautiful woman, unravaged by time and lust. She looked virginal, as she had on the first night he saw her, and that, astoundingly, aroused him.

She had already changed for dinner. The dress was white organza, sprigged with hand-embroidered flowers, daisies, perhaps, or daffodils, it was hard to tell at this distance. A flounce bordered the shoulderline to hide the swelling of her breasts.

In his mind he approached her and undid the bodice, letting it fall to her waist. In his mind she looked down at her full, white breasts, then up at him.

"Kiss them, Jesse," she said, "kiss them the way you've always wanted to."

He sank to his knees next to her in the gazebo. He kissed her open, eager mouth first, then her perfumed breasts, urging the nipples with his lips and his tongue until they stood erect in the warm summer breeze. It smelled of grass and sun and woman.

He pulled the dress from her to expose the navel, the rounded belly, the dimpled buttocks and downy thighs.

"Kiss me, Jesse," she said again, "kiss me the way you always wanted to."

He stood there, watching her, and swallowed hard. He had always been able to master desire. The only mistress he wanted—power and the prospect of more power—was already his. Madeleine's appeal was not to him, he told himself, but to his glands. He did not want her; he wanted to settle his account with her.

Silently he turned and retraced his steps away from her to the lane and back to the front entrance of the house.

127

28

From his bedroom window Jonathan saw his father stop, gaze intently at Madeleine for many minutes, and then silently walk away.

He knew then that he had not been imagining it, that something had changed between his parents. It had been going on for a long time, yet there had been nothing he could put his finger on, nothing specific he could discuss with Susannah, until now.

He turned from the window, still puzzled by that scene on the lawn, and finished dressing for dinner. He liked the fit of his first informal dinner jacket even though the stiff wing collar was a nuisance, but he wasn't thinking of that now. Automatically, he straightened the bow of his tie and stood near the highboy, trying to tame his thick wavy hair with gold-backed brushes engraved J vR S—a gift from his father last Christmas and just like the set Jesse used himself.

Jonathan never paid much attention to his looks. It was something everyone else did for him. It made him feel like some kind of hollow puppet, a shell with nothing inside it. After all, what he was had nothing to do with how he looked.

It angered him to hear his mother's friends call him "magnificent, a young Apollo." And the lamentations of Susannah's schoolmates that he was too young for them annoyed him too. Those girls were as foolish as Susannah said they were.

He felt more comfortable at school where he was one boy among many. His friends liked him because he was generous with his possessions and good at sports, not because he was good-looking.

If he had been asked to describe himself, he would have said he was taller than average, with blond hair and blue eyes like all the van Ryns—and left it at that. He would not have said that his features were so arranged as to create a face of near-perfect male beauty. There was something about him quite apart from his thick wheat-colored hair and his sea-blue eyes, his straight nose, white teeth and healthy tanned skin, something that made people like him even better when they knew him. He had no idea that his perfect face reflected kindness, intelligence and, above all, his rare sensitivity.

"But you're no saint," Susannah used to say in her dry way when only she had been punished for something they both had done. "You just look like one."

Maybe Susannah could solve this riddle. He settled his jacket, shot his cuffs and crossed the hall to his sister's room. She must be nearly ready by now. It was almost eight o'clock and Jesse did not like latecomers to his table.

She was at the window seat, dressed in a blue silk gown, her thick straight hair pulled back and tied with the same darker blue velvet that banded the long, slim dress. He was surprised to see her sitting there so quietly, doing nothing. Susannah seldom sat still without a book, and she was always eager to go downstairs early on Friday evenings to welcome Jesse.

"Hello," she said to him over her shoulder, something not quite right in her voice.

"How long have you been sitting there?" he asked her, wondering if she had seen their parents too.

"Only a few seconds. Why?"

"Didn't you see them out there just before?" He pointed down toward the gazebo.

When she shook her head, he told her what he had seen. "It was strange, don't you think? He didn't even say hello. He just stood and looked at her in that frightening way he has, and went away. There's been something different about them for a long time now. I thought you might know."

Susannah watched him intently. Her lips parted nervously several times, as if she wanted to speak and couldn't. It was unlike her. Then she stood up and smoothed her blue dress.

"Nothing's wrong, don't look so worried, Jonnie. He probably didn't want to startle her, that's all."

He went closer to her. "Are you all right?"

"Yes," was all she said.

He was unconvinced. "Where'd you go this afternoon?" he asked, after a few moments that seemed longer.

She tilted her head toward the window and the near-dark outside. "Walked down to the pond and fell asleep under a willow." She looked at him with some of the familiar spark dancing in her eyes. "I almost went skinny-dipping the way we used to at Southampton."

"Why didn't you?"

She blushed. "I can't! I'm not a baby anymore."

He smiled. "You look the same to me."

"Well, I'm not and it's no joke, either," she said furiously, although he knew her fury was not for him. "In two years I'll be trotted out and presented to society like a side of beef at the Chicago stockyard. I'll be done up in white like a vestal virgin, and I'll have to flirt and make stupid conversation with a lot of stupid boys so one of them will marry me." Her

130

foot in its white stocking and silk sandal tapped against the wood of the window seat in anger. "That's what women have to do," she finished. "Make men want to—to marry them."

"I thought you decided to go to college first."

She shook her head impatiently. "Father's still not convinced."

"Ask Mother to help you," he suggested. He had always asked his mother to intervene for him with Jesse.

Susannah was very still, all of her fury contained now. "No," she said, sharply.

"Why not?"

"Because—I don't want to. Anyway she wouldn't be able to do any good."

A muffled gong sounded downstairs.

"We'll be late," Susannah said.

He took her hand and they started for the door. "Listen, Sassie, you're not getting married until you're good and ready." He opened the door and let her precede him to the landing. They could see shadows from the drawing room projected into the hall. Jesse and Madeleine had gone down already and he lowered his voice. "If you want to go to college first, I'll make him send you. I'll tell him myself." Then he added ruefully, "If I can't make him listen, Uncle Daniel will."

Susannah smiled, as if she had just remembered her uncle was coming. She gave a short nod and they went downstairs arm in arm to join their parents.

By the time dinner was over, Jonathan was sure there was something very wrong and that Susannah knew it too, might even know what it was. It must be something awful if she couldn't even tell him what it was.

The three of them now, his mother and father and his sister, were locked into cross-currents that did not include him, some unspoken battle he didn't understand, but which threatened him very much. He was frantic to do something to make things better, to put them back the way they used to be, but he was helpless to change something he didn't even understand. He didn't go off to play his piano after dinner; his father didn't like that and he wanted to keep his father as happy as he could for his mother's sake.

His only solace was the imminent arrival of his Uncle Daniel. Daniel was the only person Jonathan knew who wasn't impressed by Jesse Slayter, the powerful financier.

Daniel's ship would dock early Monday morning, too early for Madeleine and Susannah to go to the pier. Jonathan decided to go into town with his father, leave Jesse at his office, and then go to meet his uncle on his own.

29

Daniel leaned against the ship's railing and watched the *Mauretania* move slowly toward her berth. He hadn't been back for two years, and each time he returned, the feeling diminished that America was "home." The longer he lived abroad, the more at home he felt there. Curiously, his patriotism waxed and waned in reverse proportion to his location. When he was in America he found a lot about it to criticize; when he was abroad he defended Americans against the invidious generalities used to describe them.

People who had mistaken him for a European said he was the exception who proved the rule.

"You're too divine to be American, darling," his sister, Philippa, always declared, in an accent that had been upper-class English even before she married Lord Lucas. "It was a mercy Elton met you before he clapped eyes on that preposterous father of ours, or he'd never have proposed to me."

Daniel had always been convinced that nothing would have come between Lord Lucas and his sister's staggering dowry, but he never said so to Philippa. He didn't defend his father, either. He had despised Jethro when he was alive and wouldn't stoop to the pretense of mourning him after he was dead.

Jesse had never asked him why he chose to stay so far away. Jesse didn't want to hear what he must know: America, for Daniel, was full of their father's presence, a presence too repressive to live with, dead or alive.

Even so, the Slayter propensity for making money had emerged. Daniel's services, as a "representative" of Slayter's, sent many clients to Jesse's door. But Daniel's real pride was in his growing eminence as an art historian and a respected connoisseur. Whatever he collected increased in value almost daily. He might have been consoled by the knowledge that old Jethro would have considered all of it "women's work," but Daniel himself had not yet fully examined his motives. He only knew that it was a joy to spend the fortune amassed by a man he loathed. "He was a user of men, an abuser of women," he'd said to Philippa again just before he sailed.

"Oh, come darling, don't dwell on it—it's morbid when the old goat's been dead for twelve years!"

"You're right, it *is* morbid, but I *am* that old goat's son."

"You're nothing like him—we're changelings, you and I. Jesse's like him."

Daniel disagreed. "Jesse's not gross, and he's certainly not lecherous."

133

"I'm not so sure of that," Philippa said after a moment's reflection. "But he's gone cold now, angry cold. He doesn't really care about anyone, any more than Papa did. You weren't imagining, both he and Madeleine have changed, I saw it at once when I was there last year. Oh, they're still a gorgeous pair, I grant you, but with Madeleine it's springtime with the sap flowing—and Jesse looks as if he's been preserved in ice. I'm sure I don't know how Madeleine lives with him, they're as different as chalk and cheese, unless, of course, Madeleine's finally taken a lover for herself."

"I wouldn't blame her if she did, but she's always been too much in love with him."

"That," Philippa had pointed out triumphantly, "is what comes of a love match. You would never do anything so foolish."

"I shall never marry at all, I'm very fond of my own company."

His sister thought he should marry. "You're thirty-two, after all," she had told him. "It's time you settled down, even though half the women in society would be prostrate if you did. I really don't understand what makes you so attractive," she'd gone on, studying him. "You're not handsome, actually, with that craggy face. Thank God I got any prettiness there was. Your cheekbones are too high and your eyes far too cynical for a proper cavalier, but of course you've got a marvelous figure and that limp is positively Byronic."

The cane Daniel carried was still a necessity, not a sop to fashion, although Daniel always dressed in the latest style. He braced himself with it now, against the gleaming deck.

The ship had come alongside the pier and was edging her bow deeper into the berth. The small crowd of people waiting there were indecipherable still, like bits of clumped confetti in the distance.

"What a barbarous hour to arrive," a woman's voice said in cultured tones.

Daniel turned and raised his hat with a smile. "Good morning, Your Grace," he said. "I trust you passed a restful night."

The Duchess smiled back enigmatically from under the brim of a pale panama hat, its shallow crown garlanded with silk flowers in the same tints as the softly printed chiffon dress she wore. The dress was fluid, with a many-layered skirt floating in hand-rolled handkerchief points around her slim calves. Four long ropes of dazzling pearls cascaded from her arched neck. She was so thoroughly aristocratic, standing there, that it was difficult for Daniel to envision her as she had been last night and all the nights of the crossing, totally disheveled and stark naked, whether they were making violent love or eating caviar omelettes in her cabin.

"Well, there they are," she said languidly, gesturing toward the welcomers on the pier. "I can't see the Duke yet, but I know he's there. His devotion is simply too disgusting. Hardly lets me out of his sight, more's the pity." Her eyes glanced up at Daniel again.

He looked moderately rueful. Although they got on splendidly in bed, neither he nor the Duchess would suffer if they never met again and both of them knew it. Most of Daniel's affairs were passing ones with married women, sophisticated, worldly women like this one. It was safer.

"Who is that exquisite young man, I wonder," she was murmuring. "The tall blond princeling in the beige blazer."

Daniel's eyes followed hers to the people they were now close enough to see. A wide smile transformed his strong-boned face. "A bit young, isn't he, my dear?"

"At least seventeen," the Duchess said, "judging by his height and those shoulders."

"He's fourteen," Daniel said, waving to the boy. "He's my nephew Jonathan."

The Duchess shrugged, her gaze still on Jonathan. "He'll grow up very quickly, I'm sure, with you to help him." Then her eyes shifted and she fluttered a long handkerchief at someone. "Oh, God, I knew it, there's the Duke, still pale as suet."

Daniel kissed her hand gallantly and said a few appropriate words of farewell. Then he walked as quickly as his lame leg would permit to the nearest debarkation point and waited impatiently until the gangway was secured. He was the first passenger off the ship, greeting his nephew with a bear hug.

"Damned nice of you to come, Jon! I hadn't expected anyone at this hour."

"I came to town with Father this morning. The car's over there. Harris will see to your baggage."

He walked with his uncle to the Rolls that had chauffeured him and his father to the city this morning. They got into the car and turned to look at each other more carefully.

"You haven't changed, Uncle Daniel," the boy said affectionately.

Daniel was thinking that the Duchess had not exaggerated the youngster's looks. He was extraordinarily handsome, but it was not the gilded, wooden appeal of the Arrow shirt advertisements. His face reflected a depth Daniel had known was there for a long time, but had feared would be altered by the pace of American life and the demands it would make on a boy in Jon's position. "You've changed, Jon," he said.

Jonathan only nodded, apparently impatient with any reference to his appearance. "I just kind of shot up," he said.

135

"I didn't mean that," Daniel said, taking a cigarette from a black lizard case. "I meant something else, something I should have guessed from your letters. You seem older, not just taller. But I remember people were always telling me I'd changed." He lit the cigarette with a lucifer. "I didn't like it, either."

They both laughed and Jonathan looked more at ease. "Gosh, it's good to see you, Uncle Daniel. I hope you're going to stay awhile this time."

Aware of the anxiety beneath Jonathan's eagerness, Daniel didn't say he had already booked his return passage for a month later. "I'll be around for quite some time. Now tell me how you all are."

He gathered that things continued on their usual course in his brother's house. Jesse was more absorbed in business than ever, Susannah hated learning to paint watercolors and play the harp, and Madeleine was either meeting people or reading books Jesse described as "radical."

Daniel laughed when he heard that. "Your mother was never political."

"She is now. She voted! Father was furious."

"Good for Madeleine! I wonder what's got into her."

"I don't know," Jonathan said. He seemed relieved when Daniel left it at that and went to see his baggage through customs. He was still silent when his uncle returned and the chauffeur loaded the bags into the trunk of the car.

"Where to, Sir?" the chauffeur asked.

Daniel glanced at his nephew's troubled face and immediately abandoned his plan to spend a few nights in New York.

"To Pearl Street first, Harris," Daniel directed. When the chauffeur had started the car, he turned back to Jonathan. "I must look in on your father. Can you amuse yourself for an hour or two before we head for the country?"

Jonathan's face cleared. "Sure! I have some errands to do for Mother and Susannah."

Their conversation was less tense during the drive to Wall Street. Jonathan was still interested in hockey and motorcars, in Babe Ruth's batting average—and in music. The one thing he never mentioned, Daniel noted, was banking, not even when they reached the financial district and pulled to a stop at the corner of Wall and Pearl streets. "Pick me up at"—he glanced at his wristwatch—"noon, Jon. And buy two pairs of goggles for us somewhere. I have a new Stutz sports car waiting, a real beauty. We'll drive up in that."

He got out of the car and limped into the lobby of the building. It still gave him the suffocating sensation he remembered from his boyhood. Then it had simply been oppressive, like his father; now he recognized the other-worldly smell of money.

136

"Money doesn't care who it goes to," his father used to say, and he was right. It didn't care from whence it came, either. It ruled people, wrecked them, eased them, seduced them, and moved on, without carrying a trace of its history when it changed hands. Daniel approached the elevator, trying to put his discomfiture aside, but it was too deeply rooted in memory. There were times when all his bitterness ran together and he was unsure of its target—his father, his brother, or himself. It permeated his life. He was not a happy man and he did not intend to curse anyone else with his melancholy, particularly not a woman if he loved her.

After the war it had been easy to obey his father's will by dabbling in Slayter interests abroad. He knew his leg helped; even Jesse couldn't deprive a wounded man of income.

He thought his brother had another reason for indulging him, one Daniel hadn't yet fathomed. He didn't agree with Philippa that Jesse was as ruthless as old Jethro. There was something hidden behind Jesse's facade, as if he had been terribly hurt a long time ago. Jethro had never been hurt.

Philippa had laughed merrily at that theory. "There is nothing behind Jesse but more Jesse, my poor innocent," she had told him patiently. "He'll walk over anyone to do as he wishes, the way Papa did."

"What's Jesse ever done to you?"

"Nothing, that's the point. He doesn't care enough about me to do anything. But you—there's another story. You're the conscience he never had. He'd be delighted to be rid of you. As for Madeleine and the children," Philippa had summed it up remorselessly, "they haven't a chance if they get in his way."

Daniel wondered, now, as he got into the elevator, what had happened to worry Jonathan so much.

30

"You look as if you were born there," Daniel said. His brother sat firmly behind the big desk while Jethro's oily eyes surveyed both his sons from the portrait behind Jesse.

Jesse's eyes traveled over his brother, slim and elegant in clothes tailored in Saville Row. "And you as if you'd been born in Europe."

"Not quite. If I had been, I'd be heavily invested in the American market. I understand from your new clients that you make it very easy."

Jesse nodded. "Even for small investors; we're willing to extend credit, to let them buy stocks on a margin as low as ten percent of the total."

Daniel lit a cigarette. "Is that a good thing? Whatever happened to the American revulsion against buying on credit?"

"Profit happened," Jesse said expansively. "It wins every time. We're producing new things to buy and people don't want to work night and day and save for ten years to get at them. They buy them with their market profits, and we keep building new factories to supply them with new things."

Daniel changed the subject. "Your son's a remarkable boy. You must be very proud of him."

"He's more interested in his piano than anything else. At fourteen I was reading the financial journals."

"I'm told Susannah does that." Daniel concealed his disgust that Jesse saw no merit in music.

Jesse was smiling. "Yes, she's a true Slayter, reliable and bright. She'll make some man a good wife. She has breeding and intelligence."

Daniel nodded. "Philippa showed me the new portrait. Susannah looks like a Renaissance noblewoman."

"How is Philippa?" Jesse asked in what was clearly an afterthought.

"Thriving. She always loved the English and they don't come more English than Lucas."

Jesse lit his pipe. "I always thought he was a fop."

"Perhaps he is, but he does no one any harm."

"Not much recommendation for a man, is it? To be harmless is to be ineffectual."

"You mean like me," Daniel said quietly.

"Not at all." Jesse pulled on his pipe. "I never thought you were ineffectual, even if I can't comprehend anything you do. The war, for example."

139

"It was something I had to do," Daniel said, suddenly angry that Jesse would question the best thing in his life.

"Risk your life? End up with a bad leg? Why would any man have to do that?"

"There was a war on, Jesse. It had to be fought."

"Fools go out in the mud. There are other ways to fight a war."

Daniel looked at his watch. "Jon will be waiting," he lied. "Will you be coming to Willow Hill?"

"On Friday."

"Then I'll keep all the gifts until you get there." Daniel took his cane and got to his feet, awkward and aware of his lameness under his brother's eye, as if his limp were new, not five years old. "No, don't bother, I can see myself out."

He was impatient to leave that office, to leave his father, his brother and his old, shattered hopes. He vowed he would never come here again. The very atmosphere was inimical to him.

"Other ways to fight a war." Jesse meant money, of course. He always meant money. Wasn't that why wars were fought in the first place?

He got into the elevator and dropped gratefully to the street level. Coming out of that dark lobby into the sunny street was like breaking the surface of water to breathe air again. Jonathan wasn't due for another half hour, but it was easier to wait there than inside.

31

They had lunched at Delmonico's and were well on the way to the country before Daniel asked his nephew what was troubling him. He listened quietly to what Jonathan said.

"That doesn't sound serious, Jonnie. Married couples always have their ups and downs."

Jonathan looked doubtful behind his goggles. "Not for two years. It'd be better if they argued even, but they never do. And why did he just stand there and look at Mother like that?"

Daniel wondered if Jesse had begun to follow in their father's outrageous footsteps. "Does Jesse stay away from home a lot?"

Jon shook his head. "Never, except for the office. Mother's the one who's always out with those new people I told you about, the ones he doesn't like. But why should he care what she does during the day or if she has a better time with *her* friends than with his?"

A possible answer flashed through Daniel's mind. Madeleine's new friends might not be political radicals but what Philippa called "Bohemian," a polite euphemism for the sexually adventurous, the "free thinkers." But he was not about to speculate on that to Jonathan.

"What does Susannah say?"

"Nothing, but I think she knows. She and Father hardly looked at Mother the whole weekend. It was awful." Jonathan was glum.

Daniel touched his nephew's shoulder. "Perhaps you're exaggerating, old fellow, but I'll try to help if I can."

Jonathan nodded. "Just having you there will help." He hesitated. "When you find out what's wrong, will you tell me?"

"If I can," Daniel said.

"I'm not a baby," Jonathan reminded him.

"No, you're not," Daniel agreed, surprised again at Jon's perception. "I was dodging and I'm sorry. Look, I'll tell you anything you ought to know, but there might be nothing to tell, so cheer up. Try your hand at the wheel, why don't you? There's not a car in sight and she's a real honey."

Jonathan drove the rest of the way, changing gears with the smooth rhythm of an athlete. Driving relaxed him visibly and he was in better spirits by the time the Stutz pulled into the driveway at Willow Hill. Jonathan leaned on the horn, shouting to his mother and sister.

141

A slim young woman leaned out of the window of the upstairs hall. "Uncle Daniel! I'll be right down."

"My God, she's a young lady," Daniel said.

"Don't tell *her*—she hates it." Jon pointed to the end of the open veranda. "There's Mother."

Daniel watched Madeleine come through the columns and down the broad, shallow steps. How had he ever thought of her as merely lovely? She was one of the most beautiful women he had ever seen, and there was something about her that he recognized instantly, from years of experience. It was a quality some women have regardless of beauty, dress or manner. She had the warmth, the radiance, the tremendous allure of thoroughly awakened sexuality. It had not been there when he last saw her, two years ago, and his brother could never have brought it to life. Madeleine had a lover, he was sure of it. Philippa, as usual, was right.

For a moment, as she walked toward the car, Daniel almost envied the man, whoever he was, but Madeleine was the kind of woman who demanded everything of a man and Daniel had absolutely no intention of involving himself with such a woman. There was no one in the world he would risk his freedom for, except the boy sitting next to him who reminded him so much of himself.

Over Madeleine's shoulder when she leaned to kiss his cheek, he saw Susannah come out of the house. Any question that Susannah, too, knew about her mother vanished at the look the girl gave Madeleine, a silent burst of anger and contempt before she suppressed it and smiled at her uncle.

Daniel had a sinking sensation. The war had been a mad tea party compared to what was happening in this family.

32

"Help me, Uncle Daniel," Susannah pleaded. "If I have to be finished at all, like a piece of furniture, I'd rather it happened in Europe."

Daniel looked at her appraisingly. "You're very direct, Susannah. Any other young lady would have gone about it very differently."

"Why? It's a terrible waste of time."

They were walking near the pond at Willow Hill, and she was not as poised and controlled as she had always tried to be. "Miss-ish," Philippa called her, "a *Mare Frigoris* like her father." Daniel had never thought Susannah was frigid, but she had always had a quality of calm, even as a tiny girl. It had been born of knowing exactly what she could expect of the world. She no longer seemed so certain.

Privately, Daniel was convinced she would be better off away from her mother. It was clear it demanded all of Susannah's discipline to hide her distaste for Madeleine. During the week the girl was rarely in the house and directed all of her conversation to himself and Jonathan. Madeleine, usually so sensitive to her children's moods, seemed not to be aware of it; she was in some vortex of her own, a vortex, Daniel was absolutely sure, with a man at its center. It was obvious to him that somehow Susannah knew about it.

So did Jesse, the weekend had shown. His attitude toward his wife had once been patronizing and proprietary; now it was withdrawn and almost openly contemptuous.

Last time, Daniel thought, I'd supposed the marriage had hit a civilized level of indifference after almost twenty years; now I can see it's an undeclared war.

One of the banes of mankind, he reflected, was linking the honor of a man to the virtue of a woman, without reversing that standard. Susannah seemed to accept the idea; she was on her father's side, as if she had to protect him. It was at once gallant and pathetic. Jesse needed no protection.

"I'll do all I can," Daniel promised her. "I'd like to chaperon a damsel like you. I just hope you're not in real distress."

She covered it well. "Not unless boredom qualifies."

"Would a Swiss finishing school tempt you?"

"Yes, yes, anywhere—as long as it's not in America."

"Will your mother agree?" He whipped at a reed with his cane.

"She doesn't matter," Susannah said in a way that reconfirmed his suspicions. "It's Father you must convince."

He would not insist on the whole truth as the price of his compliance. She had a right, at sixteen, to choose her own solution to this problem. Jesse was due again this evening and Daniel was determined to speak to him in any case. It was time to put the pretense about his banking career to rest. Jesse would agree. Even if Daniel were not his brother's conscience, as Philippa always said, he knew Jesse preferred to run Slayter's on his own, without even lip service to his brother-partner.

He waited until they were out on the lawn after dinner, when the last sun streaks lightened the sky and as much tranquility as this family would ever know descended upon them.

"I've come to a decision," Daniel said quietly. "I'm going to live in Europe permanently." He was obviously addressing Jesse and neither Madeleine nor the children interfered. "I've exhausted my usefulness to Slayter's, and my time would be better spent advising people about antiques, not investments." He smiled, making his importance as a banker minimal. He was so relaxed, lounging there, that only Jonathan noticed how deeply the tip of his cane was embedded in the lawn.

"I don't like the idea of a Slayter becoming a remittance man," Jesse said darkly, as if he heard Jethro's voice in his ear.

"Nonsense," Daniel said equably. "I don't need what I earn as your 'representative.' I can live very comfortably in France on the income from my capital." He waited to see if Jesse would object. The capital was part of Jethro's legacy and it had strings attached to it. As executor, Jesse might pull the strings that bound Daniel to live officially in America or, at the very least, to maintain his connection to the company. If Jesse thought of the will, he gave no sign. He merely scoffed. "The way you spend money, your income won't suffice and your capital will be gone before you're thirty-five."

"Not if you invest it for me," Daniel suggested, and waited again. He watched; Jesse's face was shadowed but his posture shifted as he considered the ramifications of all of it.

"Oh, come on, old man," Daniel said when he could wait no longer. "I'll never get the hang of your business and we both know it. Accept it. I'd only be in the way." *He'd be delighted to be rid of you,* Philippa had said. He could only hope that she was right.

Jesse got up to relight a lantern. They were all quiet, waiting for him. Finally he shrugged. "Live as you like. I'm not going to stand in your way." He smiled warmly.

"I knew I could count on you," Daniel said, more relieved than he showed. "I'll be traveling quite a lot. What must I sign to give you control of my shares?"

Jesse's expression changed. Daniel could almost hear one of old Jethro's

144

most fervent commandments ringing in the air: "Never, under any circumstances, give another man control of your money!" But apparently it was an offer Jesse could not resist. Whoever controlled Daniel's shares might vote them any way he chose.

"Don't you want to know where your money's invested?" Jesse demanded, as if it were a last consideration.

"I'll trust you for that. People are always hounding me for market tips as it is. Now I can honestly say I haven't a clue and let them take their business straight to you."

Jesse watched his brother for a moment, thinking that if Daniel didn't want to know his money was invested in Germany, so much the better.

"All right," he said. "I'll have the papers prepared if that's what you want." A match flared as he lit his pipe and the cicadas began piping almost as if he had ordered them. "I still hope you'll be coming to us regularly."

Daniel shook his head. "Unlikely, but ships sail both ways. Once I'm settled you can all come to me. I've seen a property I like in the south of France."

"We might," Jesse agreed. "There are any number of people I need to see in that part of the world."

Susannah stirred in the shadows and Daniel spoke again. "I'd like to take Susannah with me."

Jesse was startled. "What?"

"She tells me she has to be 'finished.' What better place than Europe? There's a fine school in Switzerland and I'd be grateful for her company during the holidays—and all of you for the summers." He lit a cigarette.

Jesse turned to his daughter, who said nothing except for the eager look in her eyes. Then he looked at Madeleine, who seemed as surprised as he was. If there had been any plotting, he saw, it was between Susannah and Daniel. Madeleine had nothing to do with it.

"She seems so young to go far away," Madeleine began. "There isn't time to get her ready . . ."

"Nonsense," Jesse said, as if her reluctance banished his. "All right, Daniel, it's a fine plan. She'll do well, as always. You won't have much chaperoning to do."

"Father!" Susannah was ecstatic. She crossed to his chair and bent to kiss his forehead, her face aglow as it used to be when she was very small and he brought her a toy on Saturday afternoons and played with her for hours. "You're the most marvelous man in the world!"

"That's because I have the most marvelous daughter," Jesse said. His daughter's admiration seemed like balm to him. Susannah filled the hollows left by his wife's betrayal and his son's lack of interest in Slayter's.

145

Jonathan had gone to sit on the arm of his mother's chair; only Madeleine was less than content with the thought of Susannah's departure.

"Come on, Jonnie," Susannah said, avoiding her mother's eyes. "Let's plan all the things I ought to see." For a moment she turned back. "Thank you, Uncle Daniel. I'll try not to be any trouble."

He laughed. "You've never been any trouble, Susannah." He waved the two of them off, then looked at Jesse and Madeleine. "I suppose I should have asked you first in private, but she would have accused me of moral cowardice. Please, don't worry about her, either of you. I'll take the best care of her."

"Will you stop in England to see Philippa?" Madeleine asked. "Susannah likes Philippa."

"If you've no objection." He glanced at his brother. Considering Jesse's opinion of Philippa, that was an unfortunate suggestion, but Madeleine seemed less concerned about annoying her husband than she had been during many years of marriage. "She can help fit Susannah out with uniforms and the like." He waited for Jesse and was rewarded with a nod. Apparently the English aristocracy was acceptable to Jesse, even if it had permitted his flighty half sister to marry into it.

"I'd better plan to go back to New York with her on Monday," Madeleine said, rising from her chair. "We can make a start on shopping." She looked at Daniel for a moment. "I think you've probably done the right thing. She seems so restless lately." Her hands moved distractedly. "Sixteen is a difficult age." With a quiet good night to both of them she withdrew to the house, leaving Daniel and Jesse together in the flickering light of the lanterns.

"You handled that brilliantly," Jesse said. "I had no idea you were a master of diplomacy."

Daniel lit another cigarette. "It seemed perfectly straightforward to me—and acceptable to you. She needs finishing. American debutantes are still diamonds in the rough. She'll be the first Slayter to be presented at the Court of St. James. Elton will arrange it when she's eighteen."

Jesse tilted his handsome head, smiling faintly at his brother. "I was referring to the way you handled your own future."

"The same things apply—straightforward and acceptable." Daniel wondered briefly if Jesse would go back on his word. "I hope you didn't have other plans for me." He left the matter of their father's will unspoken.

"I never make plans for you," Jesse said sardonically. "You don't take kindly to it."

For a moment they looked at each other with something resembling

146

understanding, as if they were making a mute agreement. *I'll leave you to your own devices,* Jesse seemed to be saying, *if you'll leave mine to me.*

"I'm content to make plans for my son," Jesse went on, making the warning clear: *Jonathan is mine, don't interfere.* He was soft-spoken, urbane, but there was a chill in him that put Daniel on his guard.

"He seems to like school," Daniel said noncommittally, feeling strangely young and plunged backward in time again, as if he were talking to his father.

"He's a fine athlete and a favorite with his classmates," Jesse was saying. "By the time he graduates and makes his grand tour he'll be the most popular young man on the Street. He'll have a network of school friends for his business connections and one of their sisters for his wife. That is the way a life is managed."

Appalled by the management of yet another person's life, Daniel did not object. He only commented on Jonathan's extraordinary good looks.

"He inherited a manly version of his mother's looks," Jesse said, "but fortunately not her unruly temperament. Susannah is the more headstrong of the two."

"Whom shall she marry?" Daniel said in the manner of a fond uncle. The night hid his face. Tentative, docile Madeleine unruly? Susannah, who would die to please her father, headstrong? Jesse had been deaf in his complacency before and now he was blind as well.

"Someone worthy of her," Jesse was saying. "She may be headstrong, but she isn't foolish."

They sat on in silence together. They had taken each other's measure. There was nothing more to say. It only remained for both of them to act. It seemed to Daniel that their story had run its course; Susannah's and Jonathan's remained. As for Madeleine, only a miracle would free her.

33

"No, Anna, I don't want that one," Susannah told her maid over a pile of new underthings. "I hope they don't wear navy blue serge jumpers to school in Switzerland."

Susannah put the lace-trimmed lingerie into a drawer of one Vuitton wardrobe trunk. "I'll choose the dresses—you pack my riding things. And, Anna, please take anything you like when I've gone."

"Oh, thank you, Miss," the maid said, wondering if she would be dismissed as soon as Miss Susannah left for her new school so far away in Europe.

"The underwear too—especially the bloomers." Susannah laughed. "I always hated bloomers."

The room was cluttered with trunks, packing boxes and tissue paper. Piles of dresses, gowns, hats, shoes, gloves and coats almost obscured the peach silk bedspread under its matching canopy. The family had come back to New York in late August to prepare Susannah for her sailing with Daniel at the end of September. Her excitement almost obscured the relief she felt at getting away from the dullness of school in New York—and away from her mother. She stopped sorting clothes for a moment, not looking forward to the moment of truth she still faced with Madeleine.

But it was something Susannah had to do, no matter how difficult it was going to be. She owed it to her father.

She resumed packing, shaking out each of her new dresses and admiring it in the mirror before she put it on a wooden hanger in the second trunk. The new clothes made her feel different, more aware of how she moved, just as the new underthings made her more conscious of her body. Crepe de chine chemises and step-ins felt nothing at all like muslin bloomers and camisoles.

She had already put the heavier fur-trimmed suits and coats at the back of the wardrobe trunk. She kept the narrow tweed skirts and hip-length sweaters up front for the crossing, along with all of her evening dresses. Most of them were pastels in silk or taffeta, with little or no beading. Brilliant colors were unsuitable for young girls and black velvet had been out of the question since she'd worn full skirts, white stockings, starched petticoats, and high-buttoned shoes. Foolish, that little girls could wear black and young ladies could not. One of these days she was going to wear bright red if she wanted to.

Susannah frowned at herself in the mirror. "Young lady." It was such an insipid stage of life, just like pastel colors and lessons in the domestic arts. But at least she could learn something useful in Europe. She could perfect her French and German. That would be good preparation for college. If her father had been persuaded to let her finish school in Switzerland, he would certainly let her go to college. Her uncle would help with that too.

She had Daniel to thank for many things, not only the prospect of her first ocean crossing and her escape. It had been easier to tolerate her mother when there was someone else around, particularly a man like her uncle. He was a special person, even her father thought so, odd as it was for Jesse to respect a man who preferred art to business. He was not as handsome as her father, but he was just as attractive, maybe more so in a certain way. All summer long the women guests at Willow Hill had clustered around him.

"They look like a clutch of peahens, preening," Susannah told her brother. "It's ridiculous. Can't they see he isn't interested?"

"He doesn't seem to be," Jonathan agreed. "But if I think he's swell, why shouldn't they?"

"God, but you're innocent," Susannah clucked.

"No more than you," was his reply, but he had blushed furiously. That blush had given Susannah the answer to the problem of controlling Madeleine. At first it seemed a terrible way to go about it, using Jonnie to threaten her, but she could think of no other way and time was running out. In a week she would sail for Europe, chaperoned by her uncle until she reached her final destination—Les Cours Sainte Agathe in Montreux—for her first semester. She would be in Daniel's charge during all the holidays too. Her parents and Jonathan were coming over for the long summer vacations.

Susannah hummed happily, her cares momentarily forgotten. She felt brand new—new clothes, new school, new cities and countries to see.

There was a tap on the door and her mother came in. "You're making progress, darling. Want any help?"

Susannah almost refused, then reconsidered. Jon was out with Daniel, her father was at his office. It was an opportunity not to be missed. She nodded at her mother and spoke to the maid. "I think those boots need polishing, Anna. Will you take them down now?" The maid gathered up high boots for breeches and chukka boots for jodhpurs and left mother and daughter alone.

Madeleine went through the dresses in the trunk. "They're really lovely, Susannah. I think you'll have enough, but you can always get what you need on your holidays. Your Aunt Philippa will shop with you in Paris if you like." She sat down and her blue pleated skirt, the same hyacinth color as her eyes today, fanned out around her. "Now tell me what I can do."

150

Susannah watched her mother for a moment with a pounding heart. She looked like a Madonna sitting there, with her hair in soft, full waves around her face. The waves were natural, like Jon's. All Susannah had been able to see that day at the cottage was what that man had done to her mother's body, but he must have rumpled her hair too. The memory of those male hands on Madeleine gave Susannah the courage to speak, even though she turned away.

"There *is* something you can do," she said, more viciously than she had intended. "You can stop your—your carrying-on with Dr. Driscoll."

Madeleine's face paled before she could hide it with her hands. She tried once or twice to speak. Finally, through her hands, she whispered, "I'm sorry, Susannah, oh honey, I'm so sorry."

"Sorry?" Susannah's voice was low and angry. "Do you think you can do a thing like that and then just say you're sorry?"

"Susannah, there are some things—"

"Don't you dare tell me I'm not old enough to understand. I understand that you have no excuse to be unfaithful. Father isn't, I *know* he isn't."

Madeleine's hands pinched the pleats of her skirt. "It isn't spite. That's not the only reason these things happen."

"Then what *is* the reason?"

Madeleine searched frantically for something to say, but finally she shook her head. "I can't. I just can't. You're only a girl—he's your father."

"And your husband!" Susannah's expression was a mixture of shock and disgust. "And with that man—it was only for—for *that!*"

"No," Madeleine said. "It's much more than that."

"Oh, stop it! You can't love two men, not even you."

Madeleine shook her head again helplessly. "All right, Susannah, there's no point in this. I'm just sorry you had to know about it."

"I told you that 'sorry' isn't enough. You have to stop seeing him."

Madeleine was more upset than ever. "But it doesn't concern you, Susannah . . . It won't change anything whether I see him or not. What does it matter now?"

"It matters to me," Susannah said. "Someone will find out if you keep on and Father will be humiliated. I won't let that happen to him, ever. He doesn't deserve to have all those men laughing behind his back because his wife is a—" She turned away again, unable to say the word. "And you can't pretend to agree just because I'm going away. There's a way to be sure you'll keep your promise."

A silence stretched between them, filled with love and hate, disillusion and regret. When Susannah could not bear another second of it, "I'll tell Jonathan," she said abruptly, despising herself for using him. Madeleine

151

gasped and she spoke as fast as she could to get it out and finished and done with quickly. "I will, I'll tell him before I leave unless you swear to stop."

Madeleine looked at her child with unbelieving eyes. "Do you really hate me enough to hurt Jonnie like that?"

"Yes, I do. I think you're despicable. But I have to protect Father—and Jon too. He goes to school with a lot of boys who might hear about you. If you're not going to stop, I'd rather tell him myself than let him hear it from them—or see it, the way I did."

Madeleine covered her face again. "For God's sake, don't say any more, please. All right, Susannah, I swear it, I won't see Ned again." Her voice broke as she said it. She got up to go, but before she left she took a flat leather case from her skirt pocket and put it on the chair. "I almost forgot," she said absently. "I came to give you this."

"I don't want anything from you," Susannah said, still unable to look at her mother. Somehow there was something wrong with all of this. Madeleine wasn't behaving like a brittle femme fatale. She seemed lonely and young and very sad.

"They're pearls," Madeleine said, ignoring her daughter's refusal. "They were your great-great-grandmother Susannah's and I wanted you to have them for your first grown-up crossing."

Susannah said nothing, unable to utter another word.

"I hope you have a wonderful time, Sassie," her mother said. "I hope all your dreams come true."

Susannah heard the door close and brushed away the tears. No one but Jonnie had called her Sassie for a long time. It brought back happier days when she thought her mother was the most wonderful woman in the world —the way Jonathan still did. She could never have told him, she could never have hurt him like that. It was strange that Madeleine had believed she could.

She picked up the case her mother had left and opened it, looking at the string of creamy pearls without really seeing them. She had seen them often enough in a portrait of her great-great-grandmother Susannah van Ryn, another blond lady in a velvet hoopskirt. She wondered if she had been as proper as she looked.

She closed the case and started to put it in the night chest near her bed. Then she tossed it instead into a drawer of the trunk and slammed the drawer shut. She went on with her packing. She had done what had to be done and she kept telling herself she was glad of it.

Book IV

Book IV

34

Susannah heard the telephone ring on the dormitory's second-floor landing and she put down her index cards and waited.

"Susannah Slayter, telephone," a voice called, and Susannah smiled. Charles Benedict called at nine thirty every night and she waited more eagerly for him than she wanted him to know.

"Old Faithful," said the girl who handed her the telephone, and Susannah sat down on the top step of the landing.

"I have marvelous news," Charles said the moment he heard her voice. "Old Pritchard's gone, young Pritchard's only sixteen. That leaves Dad the ranking partner of the firm. It's clear I have a great future and good prospects for enormous wealth, so will you marry me?"

He had been asking her to marry him for two years, ever since they'd met at a house party in Newport two summers ago. It was the first summer she hadn't spent in Europe with Daniel or Philippa and it had been boring until she met Charles.

She laughed. "Shouldn't you mourn poor old Pritchard for a decent interval?"

"He didn't die, he just retired," Charles said, "but if you keep on saying no, you might have to mourn me. How are you tonight?"

"Grinding away at my economics paper. How are you?"

"Middling. Most of the country's too prosperous to need a shy country lawyer."

"A likely story. Last night you were deep into corporate law and now you're Honest Abe."

Charles sighed. "I need someone to keep me steady. Why won't you marry me?"

"I will, Charles—but not right after graduation, not so soon." Her voice took on the excitement her future plans always aroused in her. "I don't want to sit at home planning menus and selling tickets to charity balls. I'd rather be going to Slayter's with Father every morning. The way women are investing in the market these days, I'd be a great asset to our brokerage house. Women prefer dealing with lady brokers; that's why so many firms are hiring them now."

"Not Slayter's."

"Slayter's has been waiting for *me*."

"I still can't see your father hiring a woman, not even you. He has a solid reputation on the Street, mostly for what he's against: Bolsheviks, government interference in finance, and women in business—even Smith College graduates."

"Well, I'm not just another woman," Susannah said.

"Amen to that." He said it in an intimate way that made her feel warm inside. "That still doesn't mean he'd let you work for him, no matter how much he's taught you."

"I suppose you think he's right," Susannah said, her temper beginning to rise. "I suppose you think women have no place in business."

He denied that. "But I don't run Slayter's—or Wall Street. Even if you did get into the firm you'd hate pushing papers around. You'd want some power and I know he'll never give it to you."

"You don't *know* anything about it," Susannah insisted.

"Neither do you. Why don't you ask him what he's planning for you?"

"Because I already know!"

There was a pause. "Look, Susannah," Charles said. "I know you think I'm trying to rope you and tie you down. I'm not—I just want to marry you and love you. What you do with your days will be your affair, except on weekends. I don't want you to be hurt when all your plans are shot down, that's all." He waited a moment for her to answer, then said ruefully, "I'm sorry I badgered you again. I swore I wouldn't."

After a second she was able to speak evenly. "It's all right, really."

"No, it isn't. Don't be polite, Susannah. If you hate me, go on and say so."

She managed to put a smile in her voice. "I don't hate you at all. I just have a lot of work to do, so I'm going to hang up. No, Charles, I don't want to argue anymore. Good night."

She put the receiver on its black hook and started up to her room on the third floor, whispering angrily to herself on the stairs, "Why did I cut him off again like that? One of these days he might not call back."

She wanted him to call again. She was in love with him.

Why couldn't he just give her a year or two at Slayter's—she refused even to consider that he might be right about Jesse—before they were married? It would be a good marriage too, but first she wanted to make all her hard work lead to something else, even for a little while, something different from marriage, not necessarily better.

Back in her room she tried to concentrate on her work again, then put the light out with a sigh. She opened the window, lit a forbidden cigarette, and sat waving the smoke out and looking over the campus of Smith College, its sturdy old trees illuminated by a full moon. From time to time a girl's laughter broke the studious hush in the dormitory and was quickly stifled. A muffled radio in the next room broadcast someone's nasal rendition of "I Can't Give You Anything But Love."

She loved Charles, she had known that from the moment she met him. The feeling was what the French call a *coup de foudre*—and what her father often said was more the province of shopgirls than women of class and substance. In her secret heart Susannah felt like a shopgirl every time she thought of Charles and like a wanton whenever he touched her.

He had a way with women, or maybe it was more accurate to say he knew his way around women. Girls were instinctively drawn to men like him, whether they were handsome or not.

Her best friend, Gemma, called him "gorgeous." He was certainly good-looking. He was well above Susannah's height, although not as tall as Jonathan. He had brown hair and hazel eyes, a healthy complexion, and a sportsman's physique, more muscular than Jesse's and not as broad.

But there was more to Charles than looks. He was exceptionally bright. He had graduated from Harvard and finished law school by the time he was twenty-two. For the past two years he had been a junior member of Pritch-ard, Benedict, Merritt, and Phelps—Gemma's father—where the elder Benedict was now the senior partner. Charles had more charm than was fair for an intelligent man.

He had never gone beyond kissing her, as if he refused to demean her by making love in a car. There were many times when she wished he would, but his code forbade the seduction of the girl a man would marry and he had decided to marry Susannah.

There was a knock on the door. "Mind if I come in?" Gemma Phelps asked.

"I wish you would. I can't do any more work tonight. Sit down and have a cigarette."

"Thanks, but I'm working on an apple for the moment." Gemma tried starving herself to stay slim and savagely crushed her breasts with a Boyishform bra, but she remained stubbornly voluptuous, even in her wool serge robe. "I came to hear about the nightly siege of Lochinvar."

Susannah looked woebegone. "I was nasty to him, as usual—and he was nice to me."

"Well, one of these days you'll settle down with him and be as nice as you please."

"I want to be! It's just that I want this chance to *do* something with all the hard work I've put in. If I get married, all I can be is a wife."

Gemma eyed her carefully. "Sometimes, when you talk about getting

157

married, you don't sound like you at all." She shook her head. "I could understand that with some of the others, maybe, but Charlie's special."

"I know that." Susannah played with the window curtain. "I just don't want to get married right out of school."

"What if he won't wait?" Gemma asked quietly. "What if he marries someone else?"

"I'll die," Susannah said flatly. "I'm mad about him."

"Well, tell him so," Gemma counseled, as if the entire problem were solved. "Then he'll wait for you."

"You can't just tell a man you're in love with him!"

"Why not? They're all tickled pink to hear it."

Susannah stirred in the window seat, looking for an explanation. "It isn't that easy for me, Gem. It's all there, inside, you know? I just can't seem to make myself say it." She perked up deliberately, with a little smile, as if she had exposed too much of herself. "I can't see myself all frilly and feminine, cooing and batting my lashes. I'm not the type."

"I hope not!" Gemma laughed. "But you don't have to be. Just look him in the eye and tell the man you love him straight out, as if"—she searched for an appropriate comparison—"as if you were bidding for his stock." She laughed again, delighted with herself.

Susannah caught Gemma's infectious laughter. "Lord," she said, "what a trouble men are."

"Yes, but think how dull life would be without the creatures." Gemma studied Susannah seriously again. "Why don't you go and call your fellow back?"

"He's not mine!" Susannah said, impatient again. "Not yet."

"Okay, okay," Gemma said. "I was only trying to help."

Susannah sighed contritely. "I know, Gem, and I'm sorry. But you have to be very careful of love."

"That's too profound for me. I want all I can get."

Susannah was silent. Gemma, it was rumored, had a lot more experience with men than she should have. It might be true, although they never discussed it.

Susannah moved restlessly. "At this rate I'll never finish my paper."

"I haven't even started mine. I'm going to Europe after graduation and I can't think of anything else but that."

"Gemma! Graduation's not until next June and it's only November!"

"But I've never been!" Gemma protested. "I wasn't finished there, like you."

"I needed finishing too." Susannah laughed. "What a baby I was when I sailed away with Uncle Daniel."

"So you always say," Gemma observed, "but you came back as pure as when you left."

"Not quite, I learned there's a big difference between what most people say and what they do." People only pretended to obey the rules, particularly in England where Philippa said they absorbed hypocrisy with their wet nurses' milk.

Susannah smiled at Gemma, thinking how much Philippa would like her when they met—and Daniel too. "My Uncle Daniel says you can do anything you like provided you do it with style, and he's usually right."

"I'd love to meet him," Gemma said, "and his Condesa too." She laughed. "I can imagine your face when he told you about *her!*"

"Well, I'd never met anyone's mistress before." Susannah refused to think of her mother in that vaguely glamorous context.

"Maybe it's better being a mistress than a wife," Gemma said. "Why don't you suggest that to Charlie?" She held up her hands in exaggerated defense. "All right, I'll go quietly," she said to Susannah, "but it's a brilliant idea."

Susannah sat in the dark after Gemma had gone, wondering what to do about Charles Benedict. Maybe she *would* have more freedom as a wife; so many women did. Daniel's Condesa had lived apart from her husband for years before his death. Philippa had a lover—never mind that she really adored her husband, Elton—and that was perfectly acceptable for a married woman, even though it wasn't the kind of freedom Susannah wanted. She did not want a lover, she wanted a husband, she wanted Charles.

But first, she wanted to work at Slayter's.

With a decided little nod of her head, she snapped on the light and sat down at her desk.

35

The hills and trees were draped in Christmas snow, but inside the train, rushing from New England toward New York, it was warm and comfortable. One of its cars was a private Pullman with a den, a bathroom, and a spacious dining area. It was completely deserted except for four young woman seated at a bridge table in the den, utterly absorbed in their game for the past few hours.

They were obviously favored by fortune. Their clothes were new and fashionable, from their French couture dresses to their custom-made shoes, and they were not in the least impressed that a private railway carriage had been attached to the train today for their particular use. The girls had been shuttled to and from Northampton in this style from the time they started college together almost four years ago; their families preferred them not to mingle with strangers, even the better sort who traveled in parlor cars.

"Five hearts!" Gemma Phelps said triumphantly to Susannah, who smiled at her partner.

The other two girls groaned. Mary Jane Quigley and Katherine Morley not only roomed together, they studied, traveled, and dated together too. Now they were both lamenting Gemma's bid.

"Stop wailing, you two," Susannah said. "It's your bid, Mary Jane."

"What's the point of playing it out? We're going to lose the rubber." Mary Jane stood and stretched, her small body fragile in a short navy wool-crepe sheath. Her green eyes sparkled and a few freckles were visible through the powder on her small tilted nose. "Let's stop and have a drink. We'll be in New York in an hour."

They left the table and moved to four of the six capacious club chairs that furnished the den, swiveling to face each other. Katherine rang for the porter and asked for the champagne her father had ordered from his bootlegger especially for his daughter and her friends. Then she looked from one girl to another and smiled.

"What a collection of knees!" she said. "If skirts get any shorter people'll be able to see Trafalgar Square."

"Don't be coarse." Gemma smiled back, crossing her silken legs. Only breeding kept her from being vulgarly seductive. She had dark auburn hair, a wide full mouth, and she responded to men like a flower in the sun. Today she was wearing bright red, simply cut and very much a la mode, but still a magnet for all eyes.

161

"Katherine's right," Susannah said in her low voice. She had the art of soft speech; it commanded attention because people had to lower their own voices to hear her and she always looked as if she had something intelligent to say. "This is the first time in the history of western civilization that women have exposed their blasted knees, but skirts won't get any shorter. All this exposure has lost its shock value."

"No one can accuse you of dressing for shock," Gemma Phelps commented. "That dress is at least two inches longer than mine."

"Everyone's dress is longer than yours," Katherine observed, watching the porter wheel in a trolley laden with a bottle of Dom Perignon in a cooler, four glasses and a tray of petit fours. "Anyway, Susannah's tall enough to get away with it."

Gemma sighed. "I know, I know. Susannah can get away with anything, even wearing black. That's Balenciaga, isn't it?"

Susannah nodded. Her black skirt was slim; the hip length jersey worn over it had white trompe l'oeil collar and cuffs hand-painted on it, with a large painted white bow on one hip. Her hair was dark and shiny, cut in a short, waved shingle. She had tossed her white felt cloche onto a chair with her Harris tweed coat. She was as well-curried and sleek as a thoroughbred. There was no longer anything girlish or tentative about her. Her figure was as clearly defined as her face, with none of the still-unformed features of childhood. Only the people who really knew her, and they were few, recognized a certain wariness about her, a kind of waiting for the next surprise life had in store for her, and a suspicion that it would not be entirely pleasant.

At twenty-two Susannah needed very few ornaments to be noticed. Even her makeup was minimal: a light touch of vaseline on her eyelids, a trace of grease rouge, Rachel powder and a medium-dark lipstick. She wore mascara only in the evening. Even without it, her eyes were striking, dark and constantly observant. She had learned to keep her face under control, but her eyes sometimes gave her away.

"Here's to Christmas," Gemma said, leaning forward with her glass.

"No, let's toast graduation," Katherine insisted.

"How about my wedding?" Mary Jane asked; she was getting married in June.

They looked at Susannah. "Never mind," Katherine said, "we all know what Susannah wants."

They touched glasses and drank, then settled back in their chairs.

"The question is," Katherine said, "will her father let her have it?"

"I should think he would," Gemma said. "He's been drilling her about the boring old market for years."

"Your father frightens me," Mary Jane told Susannah. "I'd never dare ask him for anything."

Susannah smiled. "He's not frightening at all. He's reserved, that's his way, but he's a wonderful man."

"Handsome," Gemma said, raising her eyes to heaven. "The strong, silent type."

"Oh, Lord, she's off again," Katherine said, laughing.

"Sex," Susannah said. "That's all anyone talks about now. Sometimes I wish we had never discovered Freud."

"Then let's talk about something else," Mary Jane pleaded. "How about your dresses for my wedding? You haven't even chosen the colors for your gowns and we have to have four fittings over this holiday or we'll never be ready."

By the time the train reached the city a decision had been made about the bridesmaids' gowns and four appointments recorded, in the handsome leather-bound diaries they all carried, for gown fittings at the Quigley mansion. At the station they dispersed to the four chauffeured limousines waiting for them.

Once inside the Slayter Rolls-Royce Susannah forgot her friends and basked in the electric atmosphere of New York. She loved the city as no other. Paris had never appealed to her; it was as cool and lacquered as the French. Rome was like an overgrown village. Only London had that unique mixture of simplicity and sophistication that Susannah loved in people, as well as cities.

"Is my brother home yet, Harris?" she asked the chauffeur.

"Yes, Miss, he came day before yesterday with his friend."

That would be Victor Kastenberg, a German student Jonathan had invited to spend Christmas with the Slayters this year. There had been some misgivings about the suggestion—Jesse usually objected to harboring Jews —but he had made an exception in this case. Susannah wasn't sure whether Jesse did it because Victor was Jonathan's closest friend at Yale, or because the Kastenbergs were important in the German chemical industry. Her father rarely did anything out of pure sentiment, but then no one could resist Jonathan.

That seemed to be true of Madeleine, as well. It was difficult to dislike her mother, no matter how violently she objected to what her mother had done. Even the nature of Susannah's objections had changed. What Madeleine had done was no longer so shocking—it seemed that most of the world did it —it was that she had done it to Jesse that Susannah couldn't forgive.

It was still difficult for them to relax when they were together and they avoided being alone. Yet there were times when Susannah wanted desperately to comfort the loneliness she sensed in Madeleine, to say, "I don't really hate you, I don't know what I feel, but I don't hate you."

When the car stopped at home and Harris came to help her out, she touched his arm impulsively. "How are you, Bob? How's Daisy?"

His square, florid face was creased by a large smile. "Very well, thank you, Miss Susannah. It's nice havin' you and Mister Jonnie home."

"Not half as good as it is to be here." She left him with an affectionate smile.

164

36

While her maid unpacked, Susannah looked around her room with approval. The peach silk bedspread and draperies were gone and the little-girl decor with them. The bedroom was furnished with Louis XVI antiques she had bought with Daniel's help during her travels through Europe. Susannah didn't like the new trend in decorating that was all the rage in London. She preferred beautifully crafted old furniture to glass and lacquer.

The telephone rang and Susannah picked it up from a square marble-topped nightstand.

"Is that my girl?" a deep voice asked.

"Hello, Charles," Susannah said, smiling. "How'd you know I was home?"

"I make it my business to know where you are at all times. But you haven't answered my question: Are you my girl?"

Susannah sat down on the bed and kicked off her shoes. They had come very close to sleeping together during a football weekend at Cambridge and even the sound of his voice excited her. "I couldn't be anyone else's, could I?"

"No," he said, "you belong to me." His tone was light, but not his meaning. "I'd like to take you to dinner tonight."

"I can't, Charles. It's my first night home and I want to spend it with my family."

"Then invite *me* to dinner."

Susannah laughed. She had never met a man as determined to have his own way as Charles Benedict and she loved that about him. "Come for coffee afterward," she suggested. She wanted some time to talk to Jesse at dinner, even with Jonathan and his friend present.

"Done!" Charles said. "But you must come for a ride through the park in a hansom with me afterward. It's something to see, all covered with fresh snow."

"I'd like that. You think of the nicest things."

"I think of you," he said, serious again. "You're the nicest thing."

"Naturally," Susannah said, taking refuge in banter as she usually did when she was touched. "I'll expect you at about nine thirty."

"Nine. I can't wait until nine thirty."

When she hung up, she lay back on the bed, trying to determine what there was about Charles Anson Benedict III that made her want to sweep him into her private preserve, the part of herself she always kept inviolate and secret.

She wondered what sex would be like with Charles. Sometimes she felt terribly burdened by virginity and wanted to have it gone so she could get on with the rest of her life instead of thinking about it so much of the time.

It crossed her mind that Madeleine would know what to say, what to do, why she felt this way about Charles—it was sex, yes, but it was so much more than that. But Madeleine was the last person she would ever consult about sex. Philippa, perhaps, or the Condesa . . .

"Oh, to hell with it," Susannah said aloud. "I have to stop thinking about it, tonight at least."

She went into her bathroom and turned the gold dolphin taps on full. She always relaxed best in a tub of hot water.

37

"Are you receiving?" Jonathan called through her bedroom door an hour later.

"I'm doing my nails—come on in," she called, looking up with happy anticipation. She reached up to hug him, careful of her nail polish, feeling his cheek cold and fresh against her own. "You look in fine fettle."

"And you look beautiful." He tugged his tie loose. "How was the homecoming trip?"

"Fine—we played bridge half the way and drank champagne the rest."

"There's a big bunch of roses for you in the hall waiting to be brought up," he said, "from good old Charlie, of course. Are you going to marry him?"

Susannah laughed. "If I married every man who sent me roses I'd be a bigamist. No, I'm not going to marry him, not yet, anyway."

He sat down and lit a cigarette. "That's a relief."

"Why? Don't you like Charles?"

"Better than most who run after you. I just don't want you to leave home." He looked anxious at the idea.

For a second she thought he might have heard something. "Where's Madeleine?" she asked.

"Still out, probably at one of her artsy meetings in the Village. She tells the funniest stories about all those people—and knows a lot more about art and literature than they've been able to teach me at Yale."

Susannah fanned her fingernails. "Father says this new explosion in the arts has produced more bizarre people than masterworks."

"I like bizarre people," Jonathan said. "They fill life with ideas, with new words and music."

"You're a hopeless romantic." She smiled fondly and gestured at the envelope he had brought with him. "What's that, a love letter?"

"You make romance sound like a terminal illness. There's nothing hopeless about me." He smiled his fantastic smile and opened the envelope. The smile faded and he passed the note to his sister to read. It was from a woman he scarcely knew, inviting him to cocktails in an arch fashion that made it clear they would be alone.

"By God, I'll grow a beard and wear my hair in ringlets one of these days," he exploded.

"Don't bother," Susannah advised him. "It won't change a thing. Anyway, you appreciate beautiful women. What's wrong with women liking handsome men?"

Jonathan scowled and waved the perfumed paper. "This one doesn't even *know* me, what I'm like, I mean. I don't appreciate women just because of their faces."

"Yes, I'd heard your interest in women is all-embracing," was Susannah's wry observation, provoking a good-natured laugh from her brother.

Jonathan *did* like women. He had had his first adventure one summer in France when he was sixteen, Susannah was sure of it. She'd heard he'd been involved with one woman or another ever since—women, not girls—and he was a man of twenty.

"How's Father?" she asked.

"Deep in figures, as usual. I took Victor down this morning to see the Slayter sanctum sanctorum and they talked forever about the German investments."

"Father has been consistently right about the German investments," Susannah said. "Even back in 'twenty-three when the German mark was over four billion to the dollar."

"Father is always right about money," Jonathan conceded, taking another cigarette from the crushed packet in his breast pocket.

"It's important," Susannah insisted. "The Germans are doing research now that will earn a king's ransom."

"What if they fail?"

"Father says they never fail."

He smoked in silence for a moment. "Uncle Daniel doesn't trust the Germans. He thinks they have a natural tendency to conquest."

"All men have a natural tendency to conquest, if you ask me," Susannah said, thinking of Charles.

"*I* haven't," Jonathan said.

"You don't need to, people just fall at your feet." She winked at him to make a joke of it, but it was true. "Has your friend Victor?"

Jonathan laughed. "Not Victor. He just wants to sit in a dusty old lab, discovering formulas."

"Well, there you are then—*he's* German," Susannah said. "Light one for me, will you?"

"Funny about Father," Jonathan said, obliging and passing her the cigarette. "He doesn't like Jews but he was as nice as pie to Victor."

"Victor's father is connected to I.G. Farben."

Jonathan looked at her intently. "Isn't that a dumb reason to like a man, because of his business connections?"

168

"Of course, but that's how Father is. I don't like his prejudices much, either. Did he say anything at all about my Christmas present?"

Jonathan got to his feet. "Not a word—you know he never shares his little secrets. You still hoping for a desk plaque that says Susannah Slayter, Lady Broker?"

"You can't blame a girl for hoping, can you?"

"I guess not. Well, I'm off to have a bath and dress for dinner. Come down early and I'll introduce you to Victor. He's dying to meet you."

"I'll be there." She smiled. "Here, take your love note." She sailed it to him and he caught it expertly.

"What'll I tell her?"

"Accept—and take Victor and a few more of your Yalie friends with you. That'll cool her ardor."

He threw his head back and laughed heartily, then nodded his agreement and left the room. Laughing herself, Susannah began to put on her makeup, humming with high spirits. It was fabulous to be back in New York! She could hardly wait to be alone with her father, to find out what was happening in the center of power. Slayter's partners held directorships in three railroads, six public utilities, four insurance companies; they had seats on the boards of twenty industrial corporations and their foreign investments were constantly expanding. All Susannah wanted was a toehold in the brokerage house and a chance to use everything Jesse had taught her.

38

The maitre d' stood behind Madeleine and helped drape her sable coat over the chair's velvet-upholstered back.

"Tea, Mrs. Slayter?"

"Thank you, yes." She nodded and he snapped his fingers for the waiter, bowed and left her.

The Palm Court of the Plaza was not as busy as usual. Most of the people who took tea there were still out Christmas shopping. Madeleine had started and finished early this year and had needed only a few last items this afternoon. She pulled a small note pad, between gold covers, out of her purse and began checking off her completed list.

Madeleine had found two simple but handsome silver frames for Jesse with a new photograph of Susannah in one and of Jonathan in the other. It would have been a greater hypocrisy than she could manage to give him a likeness of herself and the children all together; Jesse found it difficult enough to look at her even in public, when he had to. He made a great effort in public. No one would have guessed they were tied together legally and in no other way since the night she told him she had a lover.

Eight years had scudded by, like ashes covering the ruins of their marriage, and Jesse was still as remote as the North Pole. If she had once seen anything but contempt in his eyes—even angry curiosity about why she had been unfaithful—she would have moved heaven and earth to make him understand, forgive and take her back. She did not expect him to forget; no man could dismiss the ugly fact of having been cuckolded. She often wondered why most women considered male infidelity something apart from marital love, why they just "put up with it." Yet she, too, had their roles been reversed, would not have been surprised as much as hurt, and she would have forgiven him.

But it was pointless to think about all that. Madeleine gave her head a little shake and went on reviewing her list.

For Jonathan there were several things: Royal Stewart lap robes from London for the new sports car Jesse was giving him; an ebony riding crop with a silver handle; an imported cashmere robe for the cold winters in New Haven; a Cartier wristwatch he had admired.

The waiter brought a silver pot with the Darjeeling tea Madeleine favored, a graceful Sheffield service, and some paper-thin fluted lemon slices artfully arranged on a lace doily.

"Would Madame care to see the pastry cart?"

Staunchly, Madeleine shook her head and tried to enjoy the lemon tea that was her penance for an overindulgence in pastry last summer in Europe. She would never have a flat chest and flapper hips, but at least she no longer looked dumpy in a short chemise dress. Jonathan denied she ever had.

She smiled, thinking of her son. He had shot up to his full height in his teens, but it was only after he started Yale that his features had sharpened into the angles of maturity. His thick hair was still blond, his brows slightly darker, and his eyes the same deep blue as hers. He had a changeable face. Sometimes he looked a total Sybarite, devoted solely to pleasure, despite his almost-square chin and the strong sweep of his jaw.

The nicest thing about him was that he made everyone, men and women, feel more attractive when he was around, when logically they should all have felt lumpish and dull by comparison.

Madeleine sighed. She felt lumpish by comparison with her daughter, although that was far from Susannah's intention. She made no more effort to impress or discomfit people than Jonnie did. Yet she had a crisp, efficient, no-nonsense manner that by implication frowned on frivolity, even though she had a wry sense of humor.

Susannah was not vain or haughty, she was—Madeleine searched for the right word and again failed to find it—competent? Assured? Self-sufficient? At any rate all the things Madeleine was not. All Madeleine had ever been, it seemed, was beautiful. She had never felt competent, she was not sure of herself, and she was certainly not self-sufficient. Beauty needed to be appreciated or it had no use; it was not, as Emerson would have it, its own excuse for being. She even thought of her one attribute in the past tense; at forty-two she was past her prime.

She felt the tightness starting at the back of her throat and her eyes filled with tears. Sometimes she missed Ned so much that it was physically painful. She was always thinking she had seen him; she had thought so today as she came into the Plaza. She leaned forward to look at the dark-haired man again, but he was hidden behind a potted palm. With a little sigh she sat back in her chair.

The last time she heard his voice was when they parted six years ago, both of them angry and heartsick that they would never be together again. She heard some months later that he had left New York and was studying psychoanalysis in Vienna. Every time she went to Europe she cherished the dream of meeting him by chance at one of the world's crossroads—the Cafe de la Paix or Doney's or the Ritz in London. She never had. She combed the marriage announcements in the newspapers, but there had been nothing there about him.

Her life seemed pale and gray, a vast and lonely terrain with no one to share her thoughts or feelings. She and Jesse dined out most of the time in a silent conspiracy to avoid being alone with each other. She spent most of the days in the Village with a group of people who were avant garde in their tastes—musical, artistic, literary—and sexual.

She still hoped, at times, that Jesse might forgive her. Any relationship was better than emptiness. The echoes of twenty years are not easily quieted, and she still wanted from him what he had never given her: that wonderful side of himself that had somehow been lost before she ever really had it.

When he looked at her with that frightening glitter in his eyes, it was impossible to discern all that he was feeling. Contempt, certainly, but there was something more. Had he been any other man she would have said it was unvarnished, carnal lust.

When that look was on his face, she was caught between her desire to put things right between them, to have a husband and a marriage again, and a ferocious need for Ned's honesty and integrity and uncomplicated love. Jesse had never loved her the way Ned did. Sometimes she was desperate, watching moments and years she would never live again pouring out of her life.

The sound of the little orchestra reminded her where she was. She dabbed at her eyes carefully, because of the mascara, and sipped her tea and tried to listen to the waltzes they were playing, but that didn't seem to help.

There was one thing she could be proud of: She had kept her promise to Susannah. Susannah had never questioned Madeleine's adherence to her promise, and that showed an implicit trust in her mother's word that was a compliment.

The tea was flat and boring. She thought she might allow herself just one pastry—and looked up to find the waiter beside her with a sealed message on a silver tray.

39

The sight of her name—*Madeleine Slayter*—in that special handwriting, startled her. She kept her eyes on the tray, extended and waiting, but her hands went first to her cheeks, then to her hair, then vaguely toward her coat, as if she would put it on and flee. She was not prepared for this, even if she had been dreaming of him for six long years.

Finally she picked up the envelope and read the four words on the card inside. "May I join you?"

She did not dare to look around and find him, see him in a crowded room across the heads of strangers. She told the waiter, "Yes, please tell the gentleman yes." Then she sat and waited, feeling fragile as crystal, as if she might splinter into tiny pieces from inside. She was perfectly still, but it seemed to her that she was running down a long, dark hall to where he waited for her in sunlight, his arms reaching to close around her.

"Hello, Madeleine," Ned Driscoll said as he took a seat across the small table from her.

She was still running, but not much nearer to him. "Hello, Ned." Her cheeks flushed and she traced odd shapes on the white cloth with her teaspoon. It seemed she would go on making marks on the linen forever, but then she raised her eyes and looked at him. She was startled because he had a full beard now, like Jesse's. She remembered the touch of his mouth and her lips moved. She wondered if he loved her still, or if he had married some woman who could never want him half as much as she did. Inside herself she moved a few steps closer to him. "How are you, Ned?"

He started to speak, then shook his head. "I can't. I can't make small talk with you. I thought I could, I thought I could carry it off like a man of the world, but I can't. I still love you, Madeleine," he said, so simply that she nearly cried. "I tried to love someone else, but it's no good."

She was in his arms, even though they sat sedately at the little table cluttered with tea things. "It's been no good for me, either," she said. She had forgotten how sweet it was to say exactly what she felt.

"Jesse?" he asked.

"The same. I play my part, he plays his." The words were simple, but they were heavy with her emptiness.

"Will he divorce you now?"

The waiter, bringing more tea and a setting, interrupted her. It gave her time to see the implications of this terse, coded, intimate conversation in a public place with a man she loved and needed, now more than ever. When the waiter left them, Ned was still waiting for an answer.

"I don't know," she said. "I don't think so."

"Then will you leave him?"

"How can I? You know what happened . . . Susannah."

His eyes still had not left her face. "Your children are grown now, soon they'll be married. Are you going to waste the rest of your life for something they'll probably understand and accept once it's done?"

"Oh, Ned, please, please! You make it sound so simple, but it isn't."

"Yes, it is!" His voice sharpened. "It's your *life*, Madeleine, the only one you'll ever have. You've wasted enough of it on him already."

She was silent again, knowing he was right, wanting to leave this place with him and never look back. It *was* that simple, but her son's face made it impossible and her daughter's voice, saying things she could not bear to hear again. And God alone knew what Jesse might do . . .

Ned moved in his chair and she put out her hand, not quite touching his. "Don't go, Ned, give me a little time."

"I'm not going. It's hard to sit here without touching you. Madeleine, I can't let you go on the way you are. I want to live with you, I want to love you, I want to make you strong."

"I know, Ned, you always did." She thought she would faint with longing to touch him. He had put more meaning into these few moments than she had known in all the empty years since last she'd seen him. She wanted him as a child wants a place called home. She wanted him because she wanted to live, not scratch along in her dusty solitude to the end of her days. "All right, Ned, I'll talk to him as soon as the children go back to school."

He shook his head impatiently, but she stopped him from speaking. "No, I want this time with them. It might be the last time I'll see them. I want this Christmas with my son and daughter. Then I'll speak to him, I swear it."

His voice was even softer than it had been. "Can we see each other?"

She hesitated; the thought of love with him was overpowering. She shook her head. "No, not until I tell him. I promised Susannah and she believes in promises. It's the only thing she's naive about. Whatever I do, I want to do it honestly."

He searched her face, trying to be sure she was hiding nothing. "All right," he said finally. "You arrange things as you think best, but if you need me when the time comes I'll be there. He's a dangerous man."

"I know, darling," she said, not noticing how easily the endearment came to her lips, how naturally she leaned toward him. Then she glanced around anxiously, remembering where she was and with whom.

He noticed it and rose to leave with a formal little bow. They looked for

176

all the world like casual friends. "I'll be in touch somehow," he said, and left her, striding rapidly through the Palm Court's fussiness. She loved the way the back of his neck looked, the way he walked. It was so much easier to be honest and brave when she was looking at Ned.

She would wait until the holidays were over and talk to Jesse then. In the meantime she had a gift, a treasure that nothing else on earth could match: Ned was back, he loved her, he wanted her with him.

They had said so little to each other; she still didn't know where he lived, whether he still practiced medicine, so many other things. Yet in their brief exchange everything important had been clear between them. She loved him for this priceless kind of understanding. The thought of how it would be to lie in his arms made her hands tremble. She sipped some cold, tasteless tea to steady herself.

She reached for her coat and the waiter sprang to help her put it on. There was no check; the charge and an appropriate tip would be put on the Slayter account, as usual.

She nodded at the maitre d' on the way out, her cheeks flushed and a spring in her step that had not been there when she came in. She was not thinking of how she looked, only of how she felt.

40

Jesse and two of his partners, Clifton Sailes and Thomas Thurgood, made fairly steady progress on their way out of the Stock Exchange Luncheon Club. They exchanged cordial, if restrained, nods with several of the nineteen Morgan partners, then greeted other financial giants—people from Harris, Forbes and Dillon, Read—even a Goldman, Sachs partner who was someone's guest. If Jesse, along with the rest of Wall Street, was anti-Jewish and anti-Catholic, he never let bigotry get in the way of business.

Finally the three men acknowledged a rotund gentleman with rosy cheeks sitting at the Standard Oil table. It was a bare acknowledgment, nothing they could discuss until they were out of the building, although the visitor was well-known to all three of them.

"Excellent kidney pie," Clifton Sailes said as they crossed the spacious room with its handsome early-American prints, its array of silver tureens, and its atmosphere of purposeful animation. Sailes was big and husky with small, sharp eyes and abnormally large hands; a trencherman, he was almost as interested in food as he was in women. In any case, food was a safe topic in this club on the seventh floor of the New York Stock Exchange. Secrecy was everything on the Street.

"Best clam juice cocktail in New York," Thomas Thurgood offered. Thurgood never said much of importance, but he was a good listener; he had been placed on the Street by his father to keep him out of trouble, but he proved to be an asset. He virtually blended into the woodwork wherever he was, and people, ignoring such a nondescript individual among all the titans, tended to talk more than they should have.

Outside the building the three men buttoned their fur-collared overcoats and held on to their homburgs against a biting wind. It was just steps along Broad to Wall Street, where they turned right in the direction of Pearl. The ground they walked on was valued at seven hundred dollars per square foot, a low estimate in Jesse's opinion.

A seat on the Exchange itself had been two thousand dollars in 1871, one hundred and fifty thousand dollars in 1926. Now it was five hundred thousand dollars, enough to keep the riffraff out. It was a closed world, three quarters white, Anglo-Saxon, and Protestant, in which its members were born, schooled, lived, married, and died. They were envied, admired, imitated, and, above all, respected by their countrymen. They took themselves very seriously.

179

The three partners didn't speak again until they were in their private elevator on their way up to Slayter's much-expanded premises. Thomas Thurgood brought up the oil issue.

"I think our oil boys are getting nervous over this—what's it again, the way the Germans make coal into oil under high pressure?" Thurgood's brow was artfully furrowed; he knew the name as well as anyone.

"Bergius," Jesse said. "The Bergius-Bosch process."

Thurgood nodded. "The oil boys'll be sitting on a lot of useless wells if it succeeds."

"The wells are running dry as it is," Sailes reminded his colleagues in his pontifical style. They needed no reminder. The Federal Oil Conservation Board had been established to deal with an ominous fact: America was down to a four-year supply of oil.

"Precisely," Jesse said. "Which is why Germany—and, in particular, I.G. Farben—is crucial. Whoever controls the patents for strategic materials controls the world."

"That bothers me," Thurgood said, impulsively for once.

"It shouldn't," Jesse replied. "I.G. Farben is run by businessmen, not patriots. They speak our language. They want to control markets, yes, but also to keep order."

"I'm sure we can expect another visit soon from your Mr. Veidt," Thurgood said.

There was a silence. Slayter's had floated many issues to capitalize German companies, using dummy corporations with innocuous American names—or Ambrose-Sentinel, the huge management company Jesse had just set up. Most of the partners thought Jesse played the German cards too close to his own chest and none of them liked Karl-Dieter Veidt.

But of course they had been trained to do business for money, not love.

They dropped the discussion while the elevator rose to the highest of J. Slayter and Son's six floors. Here was the partners' conference room newly decorated, but still the same, with its gleaming brass spittoons, large leather chairs, and dark-brown draperies. There were ten handsomely appointed private offices guarded by ten private secretaries in smaller offices. There was also a private dining room, a business library, a billiards room, a gym, which provided Jesse's primary physical exercise, and a special enclosure for the international tickers. New York prices were kept up to the minute by special messengers from the Exchange floor whenever the tickers in each of the private offices fell behind because of the volume on the floor.

The men separated, each to his own domain. Jesse nodded to Willis Blake in his outer office. Willis was almost bald now, but managed to stay relatively tidy.

"Any calls?"

"A list is on your desk, sir." Sometimes Willis "forgot" things on purpose, inconsequential things, to pander to Jesse's fondness for finding small faults. It was little enough to pay for the inside information that was making Willis richer every day.

Jesse hung his coat in the closet and straightened the lapels of his charcoal-gray suit. Lapels were fairly wide this year and trousers somewhat narrower. Jesse's shirt was white, his tie pearl-gray, his stickpin a gray pearl. There was a white Swiss-lawn handkerchief in his breast pocket; its hidden monogram, JTS, was hand-embroidered in gray silk. The T was for his mother, Bess Talbot, for whom Susannah Bess was named. He looked at his watch—she must be home by now.

He leaned down to open the panel that hid Jethro's old safe and unlocked the small, steel door with the key he always kept in his vest pocket. He removed a heavy white vellum envelope containing Susannah's Christmas gift. In it were two valuable documents: a certificate for another large block of shares in J. Slayter and Son, made over to Susannah, and the deed to a fine town house on Eighty-second Street just off Fifth Avenue. He knew his daughter would appreciate a solid piece of real estate more than a trinket. He had brought her up that way. The house would do very well for her when she married, and that must be soon after her graduation. She seemed to have made her choice, and he would make the engagement announcement at the Slayter open house on New Year's Eve.

Jesse would have preferred one of the young men on the Street, young Prescott, or one of the Brown Brothers people. They were Anglophiles and Susannah had grown fond of her Aunt Philippa, for some reason. But Susannah was partial to Charles Benedict. A legal branch might not be a bad idea—he made a note. What with the new National Banking Act and the constant meddling of the Federal Reserve Board in Washington, a legal mind in the family would be an asset.

The trouble with young Benedict, however, was that he did not take direction easily. Still, as long as Susannah married decently, and soon, she could marry whom she chose. Jesse prided himself on the freedom he allowed his children. Eventually, he would find a way to make Charles Benedict more pleasing to him; Jesse always molded people to please himself.

In another envelope were a similar stock certificate and a keepsake set of gold keys to Jonathan's new car. Why the boy wanted a Stutz when he could have had a Marmon or a McFarland was beyond Jesse, but he was an indulgent father and his son had earned it.

"You're doing splendidly at Yale," Jesse had told him during the Thanksgiving recess, while they were exercising together in the company's gymnasium. "You have a crowd of friends who'll be useful to you later on, all of the right sort too, except for this new lad, Victor Kastenberg."

Jonathan had gone off to shower without any reply, but he raised the subject an hour later in Jesse's office. "Victor will be very useful," he said. "He's a lot smarter than the rest, for one thing." He had lounged in the chair across from Jesse, his attitude as startling, Jesse remembered, in the disciplined sobriety of Slayter's, as his extravagant blond handsomeness.

"He's a Jew."

Jonathan had risen, giving his father one of those blue gazes that were more steel than sky and made him seem much older.

"Ordinarily," Jesse went on, "I would discourage intimacy with a Jew, but Veidt tells me the Kastenberg Chemie is very valuable for its research skills and at this point research is paramount. So I'm going to allow this Christmas visit."

"Thank you, Father," Jonathan had returned, making it sound like something other than gratitude. Jesse remembered him standing there, tall and elegantly dressed. A polo coat hung from his shoulders with just the right degree of nonchalance. That day his white shirt, under a blazer, was pinstriped with blue. His tie, of garnet cashmere, was held by a gold pin under his deep, white collar. His trousers were fawn twill. It was conservative casual dress, yet Jonathan was as out of place there as a peacock in a farmyard and it had given Jesse pause. He had once thought the same of Daniel.

He had been very much aware of his son's reserve with him that day, just as he had noticed Jonathan's superb physique in the gymnasium earlier, a strength and an animal grace that made Jesse thankful he had kept his own figure in trim. But, as with certain animals, he had the feeling that Jonathan's reserve masked a temper that would have to be tamed if his only son was to make a success of his life. It required a different technique from the one to which Susannah responded.

"Just remember," he had told Jonathan before they left the office. "We do business with all sorts of people, but we wouldn't want to embarrass our friends at home, would we?"

"No," Jonathan had replied, lighting a cigarette. "I wouldn't like having Victor embarrassed in my own home."

It was another of his deliberate twists of Jesse's meaning, but Jesse had chosen to ignore it. He had effectively stopped Jonathan's musical nonsense by the sheer, pointed weight of his refusal to recognize it. The boy still played—rather well, too—but there was no longer any question of his taking it seriously.

It was how Jesse had so effectively dealt with Madeleine for the past eight years—by ignoring her.

Now he replaced the envelopes and took a slim blue velvet box from the safe, but did not open it. It was a necklace of sapphires set in diamonds for Madeleine, the sort of gift his children expected him to give their mother. The sapphires were the color of Madeleine's eyes, but they sparkled as hers had not done for many years. Obviously the excitement of adultery had been short-lived and she missed Jesse's attentions.

For the first time in many years the idea of a reconciliation with her did not seem impossible. If she regretted her transgressions, if she had learned her lesson and was sufficiently chastened . . .

If not, let her live with her remorse, he had no need of her.

He buzzed Willis Blake and began returning his calls, but his hand stroked the velvet box as if he were touching Madeleine's thigh.

41

"We're early," Jonathan said to Victor Kastenberg ten days later. It was Christmas Eve and they were in the family drawing room on the second floor of the house on Fifth Avenue. The lamps were lit and a fire sighed inside the Georgian fireplace, but it was the towering evergreen, ablaze with Christmas decorations, that dominated the room.

"We'll have a drink while we're waiting," Jonathan went on. "Whiskey or gin?"

"Brandy if you have it."

"Of course we have it. Prohibition wouldn't dare invade these hallowed halls."

Victor smiled, shaking his head in mock perplexity. "I cannot understand you Americans. Here you are, one of the most respected families in New York, and you proudly flout the law as no good German would."

He had a slight accent, but it was not obviously German, nor was his appearance. Victor Kastenberg was of average height, slight build, and wiry strength, like a bowstring, stretched and waiting to project something—an idea, an opinion, his energy—wherever he chose. His brown hair was thick and curly, defying any attempt to slick it to the patent-leather smoothness so favored by young gentlemen of fashion. The rest of him was stylish, lean and graceful, immaculately tailored in English dinner clothes: white tie, stand-up wing collar, starched white vest, satin-faced rolled lapels, and satin stripes down the sides of his full-cut trousers.

Jonathan opened a bottle of Remy Martin VSOP on the small bar-trolley near a Chippendale sofa. "Prohibition is a stupid law. My father says people shouldn't obey stupid laws." He poured some of the amber liquid into two small snifters and handed one to Victor. "Here you go, down with stupidity, long live Yale!" They touched glasses. "Merry Christmas, Victor, I'm glad we're spending it together."

"So am I. Christmas is a special time in Germany. I'd have been home-sick."

They sipped the brandy, savoring its smooth texture and rich taste. It was part of Victor's appeal, Jonathan reflected, that he was not embarrassed to admit to feelings most young men would consider unmanly. Jonathan had decided it was because Victor's manly authority needed no proving. Victor knew what he wanted; he directed his own life, even at twenty. Jonathan admired him profoundly, even as he envied him this freedom to decide his

185

own future. Jonathan had no such freedom. He had to make his father proud of him.

"What's your Christmas like at home?" he asked Victor. "Do you have a tree?"

"Of course—although without the Christ child and the star of Bethlehem."

"I didn't know a tree was standard gear in Jewish homes."

"We're not very religious," Victor said. "Anyway, religion's got nothing to do with nationality. We're German and in Germany Christmas is the most important family holiday of the year." He looked up at the small crèche on the mantelpiece, admiring the tiny, beautifully crafted figures sent from Italy long ago by Daniel, when his niece and nephew were still children. "I sometimes forget they were all Jews."

Jonathan laughed. "So do a lot of people."

"Too bad they didn't quite deliver."

"How so?" Jonathan loved to listen to Victor's views on many subjects. They were different, the kind of thing most college men either didn't think about or never discussed.

"Well, look at the evidence. Where are all the lions and lambs lying down together? Where are all the plowshares? All I see are the same old swords. It wasn't supposed to be like that after the Messiah came. Now, if your father didn't keep his promises, if *he* didn't deliver a good return on invested capital, or whatever the hell he calls money, where would *he* be?"

"Where would who be?" Susannah's voice said from the door. She came toward them across the silk-paneled room in a sheath of royal-blue crepe de chine, split at the knee to show a froth of chiffon underskirt in an impressionist print of every blue from indigo to turquoise. Panels of the same chiffon floated from her shoulders to the floor. Diamonds flashed from a bracelet and dangling earrings. She was as vibrant as a shaft of light.

"You look fabulous," Jonathan told her. Victor nodded agreement.

Susannah whirled around, making the chiffon panels fly. "It's gorgeous, isn't it?" she said with undisguised glee, one of those breaks in her usual reserve that so endeared her to her brother. "Now tell me, where would who be?"

"Oh, it was a theological discussion," Victor said lightly. "Of no importance on Christmas Eve."

Susannah smiled, going toward the bar-trolley. "Theology is not my long suit," she said, pouring whiskey into a tall glass and adding a dash of soda water. "If you ask me, religion's responsible for half the trouble in the world."

"And the other half?" Victor asked her.

186

"Men," Susannah said crisply. "They always want women to do something women don't want to do."

Jonathan winked at Victor. "I understand now. Charlie's after her to marry him again."

"Still," Susannah amended. "He never stops. And don't call him Charlie, he hates it."

"I don't blame Charles a bit for asking," Victor said. "But is there any hope for him?"

"Later, maybe," Susannah said, as if she had made up her mind with difficulty and needed discipline to stick to her decision.

"Then he has my sympathy," Victor said.

Susannah glanced at him, saw that he was being gallant in his oblique, continental way, and smiled. She liked Victor. He was quick and very bright. He didn't seem two years younger than she was. Jonnie still did in some ways. It was her brother's vulnerability, she realized; he could be hurt so easily, but anyone who hurt him would have his sister to reckon with—and his friend, she concluded, turning her dark eyes briefly to Victor's. She was glad of this friendship. Jonathan needed it.

The three of them were admiring the tree and trying to guess what was in the beribboned boxes around it when Jesse came in, pleased with his children's anticipation, even momentarily pleased with young Kastenberg. He helped himself to a highball and came to survey the mound of packages.

"We don't open our gifts until midnight," Jesse said to Victor. "It's a Slayter tradition."

"Drives me mad," Susannah complained mildly. Her eyes were on an ivory vellum envelope with a thin red satin ribbon and a red wax seal. It was exactly like two others marked for Jon and her mother—those envelopes appeared every year—but Susannah's was bulkier. She wondered if her father had extended a formal invitation to her to join Slayter's. He did things in an old-fashioned way she found charming, usually. Tonight she would have appreciated a direct, verbal approach.

"Here's Mother," Jon said, and the others turned to Madeleine. She was standing in the doorway as if she were memorizing what she saw.

The room, which had seemed old-fashioned as a backdrop for Susannah, settled like a perfect frame around Madeleine. Carved woods, opulent draperies, sculptured ceilings and silken rugs became her. She belonged to another age and had she been wearing a Gibson Girl gown it would not have been surprising. The coral chiffon she wore, warm as apricot liqueur, was gathered into a delicate ruche of petals around her throat and wrists; it glowed against her skin and her burnished hair. Her eyes looked purple by contrast. Her tapered fingers wore rings of pearl and angel-skin coral. She needed nothing more, with such a dress in such a color, with her perfect face so like Jonathan's. Jesse's face was flushed, looking at his wife. Even young Victor was gazing at Madeleine.

Susannah moved forward impulsively; Madeleine looked so defenseless, so in need of protection from adoring men of all ages. "It's a beautiful dress," she said when she reached her mother's side. It was not really what she meant; it was Madeleine she was concerned with in a way she was shocked to recognize as maternal. She could almost have forgiven her mother everything then.

"Good evening, everyone," Madeleine said, still framed in the doorway with her daughter beside her, as different as two women can be, but with more than their height to show they were mother and daughter. They had the same smile, the same warmth, but they expressed it so differently that people rarely noticed any similarity between the two of them, only the obvious contrasts. Madeleine was candle glow; Susannah electricity. The mother was *belle époque;* the daughter *art moderne.* The woman belonged to the past while the girl foreshadowed the future.

Jonathan beamed at them. "You two are sensational. You ought to be in pictures!"

There was a sound from Jesse indicating disapproval of such an idea, but he made no comment beyond asking Madeleine what she wanted to drink.

"Sherry, thank you," she said, going toward Jonathan. "Merry Christmas, darling." She kissed him, the two blond heads close for a moment, then she turned to his friend. "Victor, I'm so glad you're here with us."

Victor Kastenberg replied by kissing her hand.

"Smooth, isn't he?" Jonathan said. "Very chic."

"You didn't click your heels," Susannah teased. "I thought all Germans were heel-clickers."

"Nonsense." Jesse handed a crystal glass of pale Amontillado sherry to his wife. "That's a stereotype."

"Well, sir," Victor said, "the Prussians are heel-clickers and they're much admired in Germany. It's a logical mistake."

"I don't much care for Prussians," Madeleine said, smiling at the young man.

"Why not?" Jesse demanded. "And how many Prussians do you know?"

"Only one," she said, "and only for an instant. That Herr Veidt."

"Oh, him." Victor was disdainful. "The unfrocked general."

Jonathan agreed. "I don't like him either."

"He has no blood in his veins," Susannah said. "Only lymph."

"Nitrates, more likely," Victor said, observing how well Jesse Slayter controlled his annoyance. Victor had taken an instant dislike to Jonathan's father, and knew it was mutual, but that it would never surface on either side for Jon's sake. He relished the elder Slayter's ire. Provoking it without appearing to do so amused him. "Veidt lives and breathes chemicals."

"Well, let's not talk about him," Susannah said, noticing Jesse's attitude. "It's Christmas Eve."

As if on cue, the butler appeared from the hallway to announce dinner.

"It's about time," Jonathan said. "I'm starving. Come on, Mother, Victor and I will take you in."

The two young men went ahead with Madeleine and Susannah followed on her father's arm. "I can't wait until midnight," she told him. "I'm dying to see what you've given me for Christmas."

"I think you'll be pleasantly surprised," he said. "But I wish you'd let your hair grow."

Susannah was startled at the non sequitur, then she laughed delightedly and pressed her father's arm. "Honestly, Dad, you're the bee's knees."

"Ridiculous expression," Jesse said. "And don't call me 'Dad.' "

42

It was a long and leisurely dinner, a Slayter Christmas banquet: shrimp bisque, a roast goose with oyster stuffing, an assortment of vegetables dressed with butter, herbs and almonds, a soufflé Grand Marnier, dried fruits and nuts, and a fine bottle of wine with each course.

The young men kept them merry—even Jesse laughed at their pranks at Yale. Yet under the gaiety there were cross-currents that Victor, a perceptive outsider, could sense.

He thought Madeleine was exquisite and altogether delightful, the kind of woman who was a comfort to a man, although she did not appear to comfort her husband or to be of much interest to him either. Perhaps it only seemed that way to Victor because he disliked Jesse. He was not yet certain just why, aside from the Jewish thing. Curious, how Jews were socially acceptable in Germany and still segregated here in the land of the free. But Victor was accustomed to the Jewish thing by now, and there was more than that old saw at the root of his dislike. Maybe it was because the man was going to ruin Jon's life . . . and Susannah's too, if her father kept her out of Slayter's.

Susannah was the most interesting young woman Victor had ever met, unique in his experience, as this country was unique. He was curious about Charles Benedict, who was expected much later this evening after Christmas dinner with his own family. He had seemed nice enough in the few casual meetings Victor had had with him during this holiday, but he must be more than nice to interest a girl like Susannah. Jonathan liked him and Jonathan's instincts were usually right—except, of course, about his father.

Victor made a hobby of studying people, but Jesse Slayter was difficult. The only thing one could read about him was approval or disapproval, not the reasons for it. His real essence was as carefully cloaked as his wife's.

Suddenly Victor missed the open affection of his own family. It was as small as this one—he had only one sister, Marietta, nine years younger than himself—but they were all comfortable with each other, not like these people. He felt really sorry for Jonathan, the best friend Victor had ever had.

Dinner finished, they drifted back into the small drawing room where a fresh fire had been lit. There were all the appearances of good cheer. It had been a long dinner and it was almost midnight.

There was a subdued bustle as the gifts were opened and wrappings scattered all over to exclamations of delight from everyone. Susannah was astonished at the dress Madeleine had ordered from Paris for her; she kissed her mother, rather self-consciously, Victor thought. He could not decide, from one moment to the next, whether Susannah genuinely loved her mother; there was no doubt regarding her feelings for her father.

Victor was touched by the wristwatch—just like Jonathan's—that Madeleine had put under the tree for him, and he shared the merriment when Jon realized with a whoop what kind of car the gold keys represented.

"I don't know how to thank you, Father," Jonathan said when he'd calmed down, eyeing the keys with love. His delight in the gift had made him a boy again. Then he turned to Madeleine. "Or you, Mother." He went to kiss her. "Shall I help you put that marvel on?" he asked, looking at the sapphire necklace she was holding with an air of wonder.

She shook her head, smiling gently at him, then looked at her husband as if she might find something in his face that had not been there before. "I'd like your father to do that," she said.

Jesse rose without a word, humoring her. He could not refuse in front of the children, even though she had somehow misinterpreted the gift, had seen a message in it he did not intend. Why this should be so just now, he did not understand. She had received many lavish gifts from him since their estrangement, accepting them for what they were, the kind of thing a man was expected to give his wife, but now she was looking at him as she once did, before things ended between them. It was a beseeching look as if she wanted him to help her, but in what way he could not tell.

He bent to fasten the necklace and she put her hand over his as he finished, drawing it to her shoulder. She turned her head and her lips brushed his fingers. He colored, hesitated, then leaned over and kissed her cheek.

"It's exquisite, Jesse," she whispered, looking up at him. "Look, it matches my ring." She tugged at a chain around her neck and showed him the star sapphire he had given her the day he asked her to marry him.

"How clever of my father to find a girl whose eyes matched that ring," he said, too softly for the others to hear.

"Yes, Jesse," she said, willing herself to be that girl again, as young and as innocent.

His dark eyes looked at her as they had that day, as if he wanted to forget what they had suffered through since then. He was not the kind of man to decide anything so important on an impulse, she knew, but he nodded at her with a flash of his old smile.

She was interrupted by her daughter, saying incredulously, "What on earth is this?"

They turned to look at Susannah, poring over two separate sheafs of paper she had just removed from one of Jesse's vellum envelopes.

Jesse smiled. "I'm sure you know a stock certificate when you see one," he said happily. It was a customary gift from Jesse to his wife and children. It reduced his tax liability considerably and did not affect theirs. Moreover, under the laws that forbade a brokerage house to buy shares in its own affiliate bank, and thereby influence the price of the bank stock, the shares were "bought" instead by family members and the voting power consequently remained intact: Jesse voted all his family's shares.

"I mean *this!*" Susannah said, waving the other papers. "This deed to a house. What do I want with a house?"

"Every young couple needs a house," Jesse said smoothly. "You and young Benedict will want a place of your own as soon as you're married."

Jonathan and Victor exchanged a look; Madeleine leaned forward in her chair, a worried frown on her face.

Susannah stood, scattering the pile of ribbon and tissue paper in her lap. "I'm not planning to marry Charles."

"That's just as well," Jesse said. "He's a sight too cocky for my taste. But whomever you marry, you'll have your own house. Now who is it to be?"

She shook her head. "I don't want to marry anyone—not for a long time, Father."

Jesse's contented air vanished. "Nonsense," he said. "You'll marry as soon as you graduate, and high time too. As long as you marry a decent fellow with good connections it doesn't matter which one you choose."

"How can you say a thing like that?" Jonathan demanded. "It matters a hell of a lot." But Jesse ignored his son. He was watching Susannah, as if waiting for her to come around to his point of view, as she had always done before when he voiced it.

"I don't want to get married," Susannah said, duplicating her father's firm expression. The others watched as if the two of them were under a spotlight on a stage. The tension between them was building, as the man and the girl, so much alike, approached each other, hacking their way through a forest of opposing convictions.

"Indeed? Then what *do* you expect to do with yourself?"

"Work at Slayter's, of course. It's what I've always wanted."

"Work? At Slayter's?" Jesse's shock was apparent to all of them now.

"Why not? You've said yourself I'm smarter than half the men you hire. You've always told me that."

"But whatever made you suppose I would want you to work there?"

"You did," Madeleine interrupted, in a tone neither of her children had

193

ever heard before. She moved toward her daughter. "I've been warning you for years that you were misleading her."

Jesse's eyes flicked over her warningly. "Stay out of this, Madeleine. This is no time to meddle in my business."

Madeleine could read the full meaning of what he said. She was virtually certain she had touched him somehow, a few seconds ago, that there was a chance for understanding at last, if she were careful. She was equally sure that if she opposed him now there would be no hope. Yet there was Susannah, whom she had already hurt so terribly, and who was about to suffer a cruel rejection by her father. Madeleine gave up one battle and joined another.

"My daughter is as much my business as yours," she said.

Susannah looked at her briefly. "Please, Mother," was all she said, before turning back to her father. "*Have* you misled me all these years?"

"Not at all. You were interested, you had an aptitude for my work. I merely developed it."

"But why, if not to let me use it?"

Jesse pulled out his pipe and began to fill it from a humidor, his eyes on the bowl.

My God, Victor thought, *Susannah hasn't got a chance, but how will her father handle it?*

None of them noticed Charles Benedict, who had been standing just inside the door for several minutes. They stood there, like actors frozen in place while the curtain rose, until Jesse looked up at his daughter.

"Of course I intended you to put it to use," he said—and Victor thought, *that's a bloody lie*—"but you must trust me to know when." Jesse walked to Susannah and took her hand. "You know Slayter's has a conservative reputation; we attract a lot of business because of it. I can't put a young, unmarried girl in an executive position, not even my own daughter. The clients aren't ready for it."

Susannah held her ground, looking at him. "There are over thirty lady brokers on Wall Street already."

"When you come to Slayter's, it won't be as a brokerage clerk," Jesse scoffed. "You'll be dealing with countries and corporations, not housewives. You're not a lady broker; you're different."

She hesitated, caught between his logic and her own, and he pressed his advantage. "You know it's for the firm's best interests, or I'd let you do as you like. I always have—Europe, college, anything you wanted. Won't you do this for me and wait, just for now?"

She sighed, then nodded slowly. *She's putting a good face on,* Victor thought, *but the sparkle's gone.* She suddenly realized that Charles had come in and was watching as intently as the rest. "All right, everyone," she smiled. "You can all relax. I promised Charles to go sleigh riding with him, so if you'll all excuse us . . ."

The group in the drawing room watched them go. "How could you do that to her?" Jonathan demanded. "She's been dreaming about Slayter's since she was ten!"

Victor, standing at his friend's side, wondered again how Jesse was going to handle this; it was not like Jonnie to show such naked anger.

"You can't blame me for people's dreams," Jesse said reasonably. "It's time everyone came down to earth." His eyes lit briefly on his wife, but there was no warmth in them.

"Do you know what she'll do now?" Jonathan said, desperately. "She'll marry Charles, whether she really wants him or not."

Jesse's dark eyes noticed the look of cynical appraisal on Victor's face and dismissed it. "Jonathan," he said, "I think you're confusing your sister with ordinary girls. She wouldn't marry anyone unless she wanted to, and Benedict is the only man she cares anything about, you must know that." He waited a moment, then went on—*confidentially,* Victor thought, *man to man.* "It's a man's world; Susannah will be better off in it if she's married to Benedict."

"I thought he was too cocky for your taste," Jonathan said suspiciously. "I thought you didn't like him."

Jesse laughed. "*I'm* not going to marry him. I'd never tell either of you whom to marry. Susannah can do anything she likes—within reason—but I don't call it reasonable for your sister to be involved with a bunch of sweating, swearing men every day, until she's married and a little older." He smiled fondly. "Look, Jonnie, you may look like a varsity hero, but I know you're a lot smarter. If she were in your care, you'd feel the same way, any man would."

Jonathan turned away, reluctantly convinced. Victor looked at Jesse with a little smile and a congratulatory nod of his head, as if he were saying *well done, you've fooled them all brilliantly.* Then he put a hand on Jonathan's shoulder. "Let's take a spin in the new car, Jonnie, the air will do you good."

With a last, questioning look at his father—the look of a man in a boy's face—Jonathan followed Victor from the room.

There was silence in the room except for the roar of the fire. Madeleine went to sit near it, shivering slightly.

"The truth," she said to Jesse, "is that you have no intention of letting Susannah get anywhere near Slayter's and never did. You tell Jonathan he's 'man' enough to see what's best for his sister, but you'll never give him any authority, not even over his own life."

195

Jesse was gathering up the documents Susannah had left lying on her chair. He folded them, returned them to their envelopes, and put them with Susannah's other gifts.

"Would you care for a nightcap?" he said to Madeleine.

She shook her head. "I was hoping for something more—you, the way you used to be."

"There's been no change," Jesse said, authoritatively, as if they were discussing the stock market.

"I think there has," Madeleine said.

"You're a fool, Madeleine, if you expect me to care for a woman who constantly betrays me." He was not as calm as he had been.

"It happened years ago, Jesse! One affair isn't a constant betrayal!" She looked at him carefully, then her face changed. "You're not talking about that, are you? You're angry because I tried to help Susannah tonight."

"Susannah tonight, Daniel years ago, certainly Jonathan soon. Your one affair—if there was only one—is part of a pattern."

"In other words you demand total loyalty—no ideas or opinions that conflict with yours, no mistakes."

"If the rest of the world sees fit to give it to me, it's the least I expect in my own home."

"I'm not the rest of the world, Jesse, I'm your wife, but I can't agree with everything you do."

"I know that," he said sharply. "You go out of your way to prove it. Those impossible people you see, your political ideas, your slavish admiration for all this new modernism. It's not the kind of thing my wife should be involved in."

Her blue eyes looked at him sadly. "I think you care more about all that than about my—my infidelity. Oh, Jesse, were you really that wonderful young man I met one night, who was so much more exciting than the rest, simply because he didn't try to be better than they were? Everyone fell in love with you, the way I did. What happened to you? Why is power the only thing you care about? Why could you never share what you cared about with me?" Her eyes filled with tears. "Jesse, did you ever love me?"

He watched her, his face working. He started to turn away and then, as if he could not stop himself, he said, "Yes," angrily, "for all the good it did me, *yes!*" Then he walked rapidly out of the room.

She sat by the fire for a while, then reached up to unclasp the necklace from around her throat and let it slip heavily to her lap. It was hopeless, absolutely hopeless. She had never been as lonely as this. She thought of Ned and the comfort he could give her, but she had made a promise to Susannah and she would not break it while her daughter still needed her.

43

Susannah sat in the rattling hansom, rigid with anger, talking more to herself than to Charles.

"Why does he treat me like a child? Is that how I seem to him?"

"Susannah, it's the way most men treat their daughters."

She shook her head, making her diamond earrings dance furiously. "He ought to know better, he's a brilliant man."

Charles handed her a handkerchief. "About business, yes, not about people."

She looked at him then, absorbing that. It was true. She had protected Jesse from the truth about Madeleine for years, but it was something he should have sensed, somehow. As he should have sensed her own aptitude, and Jonathan's reluctance, to work for him.

There were still tears of unvented anger in her eyes. "You know, I've worshipped him all my life."

"Worshipping a man's gods doesn't give you access to his temple. It doesn't make you over in his likeness, either."

She looked at him questioningly over the handkerchief.

Charles shrugged. "You try to be as calm and cool as he is, but you're not. You care too much about too many other things. You're more like your mother than you are like him."

"Leave Madeleine out of this," Susannah said stiffly. "She has nothing to do with it."

"She *did* try to help."

"All right, she did, but it did nothing to change his mind. I've worked and studied for years, and he still thinks I'm too young to handle it." Her shoulders relaxed and dropped. "It's hopeless, I know," she said, the full edge of her disappointment already blunted by the inevitable.

"He's proud of you, if that's any comfort. He's like the Cheshire cat in *Alice in Wonderland* when you're around, preening himself because you're clever and beautiful—and *his.*"

"Marvelous," Susannah said, her voice still shaking. "I'm the cat's pajamas but I still can't get through life without a caretaker."

"He wants you to be protected."

"You're as bad as he is! You've been ranting about taking care of me for months."

"But I want all of you," Charles said, "including your ambition and your brains."

She hoped he really meant it. "Do you mean you'd let me work if we were married?"

"I've told you so a dozen times!"

"It couldn't be at Slayter's, you know. He'd never let me work there. I'd be just another working woman in some other brokerage house."

He put his hands on her shoulders and turned her toward him. "I love you, Susannah. I'd do anything to make you happy." His hand stroked her face. "I'd like to take that hurt look away. You'll never regret marrying me, I promise you that."

"I know that, Charles, and I could never marry anyone else. But you don't have to marry me to go to bed with me, you know. You can sleep with me whenever you want to—tonight, if you like," she said, pretending a worldliness she did not feel.

He was quiet for a moment while a snowflake drifted into their hansom cab as it trundled through the park. Her head was on his shoulder and he kissed her hair. "I don't want to make love to you so you can get even with your father. That isn't all I want you for anyway."

"Why *do* you want me?" She relaxed against him. "I'll make a rotten wife. I hate the domestic arts, charities bore me, and I can't stand parties."

"I want you because you're lovely and smart and sweet and stubborn all at once—and honest too."

"You forgot faithful, Charles. I'll be faithful."

"I should hope so!"

She moved away from him then, observing him from her side of the hansom cab. "You'll have to be too. I know some people don't care about that, but I do."

"For God's sake, Susannah! You haven't even said we could take the vows and you're already assuming I'd break them. That's inadmissible."

"Don't be legal, Charles."

"Don't be insulting, Susannah." He sounded almost angry with her. "Your father disappointed you, but I'm not your father. When I make a promise I keep it."

She answered so quickly that she was surprised to hear what she said. "He never promised me Slayter's."

"Not in a notarized document, but he let you think it could be yours. Why are you defending him when you were angry enough to hit him a few minutes ago?"

Confused, she sat back in the cab abruptly. "I'm damned if I know," she said. She was quiet, puzzling over the strange nature of her loyalty to her

198

father, no matter what he did, while the cab rolled through Central Park. She felt very tired suddenly; all the electric energy that had buoyed her up for many anticipatory months was gone. She leaned against Charles again. "I do love you, Charles," she said, the words coming more easily to her lips than she expected. "I love you very much." It was as much as she would risk, in emotions or in words.

He was quiet at first, but he held her closer. She heard him breathe deeply, as if he were suddenly at ease after a long period of stress. "Then marry me," he urged her gently. "Marry me soon."

"Whenever you like."

"After graduation then. This isn't much of a proposal—I had planned a garden in the moonlight with a vulgarly large ring—but at least you can be a June bride."

He made no attempt to kiss her. He spoke lightly, but the occasion was serious for both of them. They were emotionally spent but very comfortable together.

I'm engaged, Susannah thought, *to a man too cocky for my father's taste.*

She was glad of it. She had always wanted to marry a man as strong as her father.

44

"Good lord, what a fuss," Susannah said, looking out of the window at the huge back lawn of Willow Hill. The gazebo was banked with flowers, and rows of gilt chairs were arranged like soldiers on either side of it. From her bedroom window she could see parts of the yellow and white striped tents scattered along the sides of the freshly cut lawn, where gentlemen in morning dress and toppers strolled with ladies in pastel summer gowns and hats. "It's a wedding, not a coronation!"

"You know you love it," Katherine Morley said. "You wouldn't look that way if you didn't." Katherine smoothed the folds of her pale yellow organdy gown.

Gemma Phelps looked anxious. "You *are* happy, Susannah?"

Susannah walked back to her dressing table to put the finishing touches to her makeup. She was wearing only white silk stockings and sandals and a white satin teddy trimmed with the palest primrose-yellow lace. "Of course I'm happy," she said.

Mary Jane Carlton hovered over the cap and veil carefully spread on the bed. "We all have to get married," she said with matronly conviction. She had married the week before and delayed her honeymoon trip for Susannah.

"That's right, M.J.," Susannah said, trying to choose between two colors of lip rouge. "And as long as I have to marry someone, I'd as soon it was Charles."

"I hope you didn't tell *him* that!" Katherine looked surprised.

"What do you mean, 'have to'?" Gemma demanded.

"It's either that or stay home and be a spinster, my girl. Mrs. Charles Benedict will be able to do a lot of things Miss Susannah Slayter can't."

"Such as?" Katherine said.

"Such as work, if she likes. My father won't have anything to say about it now—only my husband will, and he's all in favor of career women."

"Are you certain?"

"Oh, it'll take time," Susannah assured Katherine. "It's a matter of decorum. A married woman doesn't have to be sheltered like a spinster."

"What'll you do if you get pregnant?" Mary Jane asked in a hushed voice.

Susannah blushed. "I don't intend to."

"You mean you won't make love with Charlie?" Gemma was incredulous.

201

"Making love doesn't have to lead to babies," Katherine said primly. "Haven't you heard of Margaret Sanger?"

Susannah glanced at the tiny diamond-studded watch on her wrist. "Would you mind discussing reproduction some other time? I'm getting married in forty minutes and I ought to be wearing a dress."

There was laughter and a murmur of anticipation as the three friends helped Susannah get into her white silk gown. It was made in four tiers of tiny pleats, each tier edged with gossamer lace. Her hair was completely hidden by the white silk coif that secured a short veil of white tulle. As usual, simplicity suited her.

"Not bad," Katherine said admiringly when they had hooked Susannah into the gown and secured the coif. "I thought you'd go all Southern belle to match the decor."

"Susannah's not the type," Gemma said. "The decor will have to match her."

Susannah smiled at her, touched by Gemma's concern and glad of her support. She never had to think before she spoke with Gemma.

There was a staccato tap at the door and Jonathan's voice spoke through it. "Mother says it's time for the girls to go downstairs for their flowers, and I want to see Susannah alone for a minute."

"Come on in, Jonnie," Susannah called, and Gemma flew to open the door for him. She took Jonathan's arm possessively and paraded him into the room toward his sister, her yellow organdy dress floating against his striped trousers and gray morning coat. "Doesn't he look dreamy?" she said, to no one in particular.

Jonathan stood with her arm through his, complimenting all the young women until Susannah shooed them out. Gemma pressed a finger to her lips, then to his cheek, as she left.

"Well, well," Susannah said to her brother. "You've scored another run." She was careful to hide her annoyance at this liaison between her brother and her best friend. It had been going on since Christmas. Gemma, of all people, should have known better.

Jonathan smiled. "You know Gemma."

"Not in the Biblical sense," Susannah replied. She suddenly knew there was more than a purely casual flirtation between her brother and Gemma Phelps. "Be careful, Jon, Gemma's trouble when it comes to men."

"Don't worry about Gemma." Jonathan dismissed it. "I came to talk about you."

Susannah turned back to the mirror, making unnecessary adjustments to the folds of her thrown-back veil while Jonathan collected his courage and went on.

"I don't think you ought to marry Charles," he said.

Susannah looked at him in the mirror, truly surprised. "Why not?"

"You don't love him! You're only doing this to get back at Father, to get away from home, but you don't love Charles."

Susannah turned away from the mirror and looked at her brother instead of at his reflection. "I do love him, Jonnie. Honestly, I do. It isn't just to get away from home. Even if that's part of it, I wouldn't marry him just for that."

Jonathan watched her. He knew her so well. He was sure she was not lying to him. Still, he had to be convinced she was not lying to herself.

She walked to him and framed his face in her hands. "I'd have married him sooner or later, you know. I can't imagine being married to anyone else."

"That's just the point. This is 'sooner.' How do you know you'll want him 'later'?"

"I just know it, that's all," Susannah said, her dark eyes beginning to glow. "Charles is a very unusual man. It's hard for me to say sentimental things, but when it's the right person you just know. You'll see."

He put his arms around her, hugging her fiercely for a second. "Okay, Sassie," he whispered, "I just had to be sure. I want you to be happy."

She was very close to tears. Until this moment she had not really considered how great a step she was taking, away from all that was familiar, whether it was pleasant or unpleasant. Above all, she had not considered the separation from the one person in her life she loved unconditionally. She hugged him back. "Jonnie, you're the best little brother in the world."

They released each other and she reached up to smooth his hair. "Even if you're a yard taller than I am." Then she turned away from him and took the van Ryn pearls from the dressing table. "Now scoot. Charles will be wondering where his best man is. Do you have the ring?" Her voice was back to normal.

Jonathan patted his waistcoat pocket as he opened the door. "I'll see you at the altar," he said.

"All right, but I'm not going to look at you. I'll giggle if I do and shock everyone." They smiled at each other and Susannah sat down to clasp the pearls around her neck under the veil. When she raised her head she saw her mother.

"Come in," Susannah said, a bit tartly. "This room is like Grand Central Station. Jonnie just left."

"I saw him in the hall," Madeleine said from the center of the room. "You look beautiful, Susannah. Do you have everything you need?"

Susannah nodded, turning to face her mother. Madeleine had made an effort to be sober and matronly—dove-gray chiffon with a matching hat, elbow-length white kid gloves, and only a single strand of pearls—but it was unavailing. She exuded an eagerness that was the essence of youth.

"I suppose you've come to ask me if I really want to get married, like everyone else," Susannah said.

Madeleine was startled. "No, why should I? You've said you love Charles. He's fine man and I'm sure you'll be happy together." She paused for a moment, then her face relaxed. "You're just having last-minute nerves, darling, every bride does."

Susannah bristled. "What if I said I didn't want to marry him? What would you do?"

"I'd go down and send them all away," Madeleine said, waiting.

"I'll bet you would at that. What a scandal that would make! Think what they'd say."

"I don't give that"—Madeleine snapped her fingers—"for what anyone says and neither should you. It's your life, Susannah. Don't let the whole world run it for you."

Susannah felt her anger swelling. It wasn't supposed to be like this. Mothers weren't supposed to sleep with other men; brothers weren't supposed to question a sister's choice of a husband; fathers weren't supposed to change from pride in a daughter's intelligence to insistence that she needed a man's protection. Even Gemma seemed to have doubts about Charles—and was blithely snatching her brother from his cradle.

"You never gave 'that' for anyone, did you?" Susannah said venomously, approaching her mother. "So why did you really come here? To give me a maternal talk on the secrets of the marriage bed? We both know you're an expert—"

Madeleine's hand struck Susannah's cheek. It was a shocking blow, the only one Susannah had ever received in her life.

"Don't dare to speak to me like that," Madeleine said, through lips that were pale, even under the makeup. "You understand nothing about it, yet you presume to judge me. I was foolish enough to think you'd begun to understand, especially since last Christmas."

Susannah's flushed face was still. "You can't rewrite history," she said, finally, as coldly as she could. "I'm very grateful for all you've done, but it doesn't change anything else. I don't want to discuss it anyway. Now leave me alone. I know what I'm doing and that's more than you can say."

"You'd have been right about that on *my* wedding day," Madeleine said with immense bitterness. "But not anymore."

"What do you mean by that?"

Madeleine observed her daughter attentively. "As you said, it's not something to discuss today."

"Why not? Do you think I'll swoon away if you tell me the truth for a change?" Susannah shook her head, in command of herself once more even though her face still tingled. "That's not my style."

"What *is* your style, Susannah? To see only what you want to see, the way your father does?"

"I know what right and wrong mean."

"So do I," Madeleine said. "It's taken me a long time to find out, but so do I. I know it's wrong for your father and me to go on living the way we do."

"What way is that?"

"As strangers, not husband and wife. Your father is not—" Madeleine paused. "He is not a loving man." She saw the confusion in her daughter's face. "He was never very enthusiastic about that side of marriage."

Susannah felt painfully embarrassed. People talked freely about Freud and sex these days, but she had never heard of a marriage where it was the husband, not the wife, who wasn't "enthusiastic." Besides, she had never let herself think of sex between her parents.

"He doesn't love me," Madeleine was saying, still unlike herself, still crisp, authoritative, and as resentful as Susannah was. "He never did, not the way I loved him. He's in love with his business, his office, all of that."

"It's his profession! What did you want him to do, stay at home and read you poetry?"

"No. I only wanted him to care about me, to really know I was there when he *was* home. There's more to life than business, Susannah, for men as well as women."

"As you found out soon enough," Susannah accused her.

"Not so soon." Madeleine's face was bleak. "I waited for years. I wonder how you'd feel if you hardly saw Charles except in bed, if he never shared a single thing with you, except his body once in a while." She shrugged. "Anyway, I gave up Ned almost as soon as I found him."

"Only because I forced you to."

"Yes, partly, but as much because I kept on hoping that he—Jesse— would change. It was as much for my sake as for yours and Jon's, but you're getting married and one day soon so will Jon. There's nothing left for me in this marriage." She straightened, her blue eyes clear and defiant. "It would be wrong to keep up the pretense. No matter what you like to believe, I hate sneaky little affairs. I love Ned and he loves me. The only honest thing for us to do is marry."

"I don't think Father will agree with that," Susannah said.

205

"I can't worry about him anymore, but I do worry about you and Jonathan. I was going to start divorce proceedings after Christmas, but you were too upset, too disappointed."

"My disappointments have nothing to do with you," Susannah interrupted vehemently.

"So I see," Madeleine said flatly. "In my ignorance I wanted to help you through a bad time. You'd been counting on Slayter's since you were a girl. Your father——"

"Don't blame him for my mistakes! He never promised me anything, not in so many words."

"Well, he promised me a lot," Madeleine said, implacably frank once more. "He promised to honor me—and he treated me like a child, the way he treats all women, even you."

Susannah sat down abruptly. What her mother said was undeniable, but it was only with regard to business that Jesse lumped her with other women.

"So you've been carrying on with that man all this time?" Susannah said.

"No, I told you I'd kept my promise."

It was too obviously true for Susannah to question it. "I don't care what you do," she said, knowing Jesse would never agree to a divorce. "It's almost time for the ceremony. I'd like to be alone."

"Of course," Madeleine said, going toward the door. "I shouldn't have disturbed you." Her gray chiffon swirled around her like a cloud of mist. "I'm sorry you had to hear this today, but I think it's better for both of us. There'll be no surprises." Her voice sounded like Madeleine's again. "I hope you'll be very happy—you can believe that, no matter what you think about anything else."

Susannah crossed to the window and heard the door close behind her mother. Through the open window she felt the June air soft against her face. The scent of freshly cut grass was sweet. Its deep green expanse was bordered with yellow daisies and spangled with people beginning to take seats in front of the gazebo.

She took a deep, unsteady breath. In a little while she would be free of both her parents. She would not have to rationalize each day the hurt she felt at her father's refusal to give her a chance now. She would not have to puzzle over the change in her mother. It would be hard for Jonathan without his sister: Jesse would never agree to a divorce and the atmosphere at home would be worse than ever. But Susannah would have a home of her own where Jon could get away from them.

Not only hers, though—it would be Charles's home too.

She thought about Charles. He had promised not to stand in her way. He had promised to love her always.

She remembered his face that night, so strong and so earnest, and she smiled and moved quickly away from the window to resettle her dress and her veil. When Gemma came to tell her it was time, she was ready.

A half hour later she had crossed the broad lawn on her father's arm, past an assemblage of names from Wall Street, Washington, and other points of power, and heard Charles promise to have and to hold her from this day forward, forsaking all others for the rest of his life.

By five that afternoon they were outward bound on the *Berengaria*, waved off by a riotous crowd of young people who had followed them all the way down from Willow Hill in a fleet of gleaming cars. The last people she saw were Gemma and Jonathan, standing together and waving wildly, like a pair of children. She couldn't be angry with either of them—they looked as happy as she felt.

45

Their suite was full of flowers when Charles and Susannah came back to it after the huge liner had swept past the Statue of Liberty and was heading for the high Atlantic.

"We're three miles out by now," Charles said, pressing a button near the salon door. "There's champagne waiting."

Susannah nodded, taking off her white straw hat. "I could do with some! I don't think I've ever talked so much in my life."

She sat down and reached for a cigarette and he came to light it for her, but before he did he leaned over the back of her chair, took the cigarette from her lips, and kissed her. It was a long, tender, searching kiss, not the brief salute he had given her after the ceremony. She felt a now-familiar warmth envelop her; it was even more exciting to know that it did not have to stop, that it was the prelude to a new and different kind of warmth.

They smiled at each other, understanding, and he gave her back the cigarette and lit it for her.

"I hope you enjoyed your wedding, Mrs. Benedict," he said after a moment. "You certainly looked as if you did."

"At first I thought it was a lot of fuss," Susannah said, "but now I'm glad we had the full treatment—bridesmaids, ushers, even throwing the bouquet."

"Who caught it?"

"Gemma Phelps, of all people." Susannah's smile faded. "She's having a thing with my baby brother. I thought she knew better than that. Nothing can come of it."

"Well, you know Gemma. She loves life but she doesn't ask too much of it."

She glanced at him. "How well do *you* know her?"

He laughed. "Not nearly as well as Jon does. But there's nothing to worry about—your baby brother is no baby, believe me."

Susannah shook her head. "I don't really understand that. He doesn't love any of those women who throw themselves at him, and he ought to be in love. He has more heart than anyone I know. He's sweet and sensitive and loving. I can't understand why he's in and out of so many beds he doesn't really care about."

"Hasn't met the right woman," Charles said. "When he does he'll stay put."

"Will he know? He might be too jaded by then."

"I wasn't," Charles said seriously. There was love in his voice, in his eyes. "I knew you were mine the moment I saw you." He watched her, waiting.

"I knew I was yours too," she told him, her voice husky with the unspoken gratitude she felt and the unaccustomed freedom to express it. "I'm very glad I married you."

A knock at the door announced the steward, carrying the champagne and an invitation; then her maid was there to unpack the trunk. Susannah looked at the invitation. Captain Sir Arthur Henry Rostron, K.B.E., R.N.R. and Commodore of the Cunard fleet, invited them to cocktails in his quarters at eight P.M. She sat down to write a brief acceptance on one of the newly engraved calling cards in her travel case. Mrs. Charles Anson Benedict III, it said. She realized that not one of her own names appeared on the card and almost said so to Charles, but the maid was leaving and she gave her the note for the captain.

They were alone again, she and Charles. He was standing near the door to the bedroom, his brown hair slightly disheveled, his eyes with that knowing expression that always excited her and that smile on his face that always made the girls melt.

But she was the only one entitled to yield to that melting sensation now. She was his wife. She wasn't Susannah Bess Slayter anymore, she was Mrs. Charles Benedict.

Charles put down his champagne and held out his arms. She went to him quickly, an answering half smile shaping her mouth to meet his.

She closed her eyes while he undressed her and himself. There was none of the awkwardness she had anticipated. He even put her on the bed smoothly—she had wondered if they would collapse on it in a heap together.

She loved the way he kissed her. She loved everything he did, all of the things she had read about. For a split second it occurred to her that Charles must have made love to a lot of women to know exactly where and how to touch his bride so expertly.

She thought of two more things, clearly and in swift succession: Madeleine's shining body that day through the window of the cottage; and how the open desire she felt now resembled the hidden excitement she had felt then.

Then she stopped thinking, because now she was no longer an observer, she was a participant, she was part of Charles. She was conscious of her body and his, but without any definition, as one is conscious of light and heat but not where one leaves off and the other begins.

She had no idea what words they were saying, but at last she knew what they meant.

46

Willis Blake marshalled the objects on his desk into soldierly order before he sat down, satisfied with this review of pencils, fountain pens, pristine tablets of ruled paper and—the most important objects of all—the telephone and Jesse's calendar book.

The door to Jesse's office had closed just one minute ago on Jesse and Erhard Eppler, I.G. Farben's chief emissary to the American oil industry. Although it was well past lunchtime and Willis's stomach rumbled urgently, he did not even consider leaving his post while Jesse's privacy required protection.

Today Willis felt quite pleased with himself. His wife had presented him with another son six months ago. They lived in a style several cuts above that of their middle-class friends. The Blakes had a Ford, two radios, an electric refrigerator, and the latest in pale green enamel bathroom fixtures with colored tiles to match. The ultimate goal, of course, was one of those posh Park Avenue apartments with gold-plated faucets, but if things went on as they were that was certainly attainable.

Willis wore a Hamilton watch—"the mark of the successful man"—and felt very much entitled to it. He had already amassed the princely sum of fifty thousand dollars—on paper—by jumping in and out of the market at another brokerage house that allowed him a margin of only ten percent because Willis was private secretary to Jesse Slayter. The several serious breaks in the market in the past few months did not worry him. Those breaks had ruined ordinary men who could not meet their brokers' calls for margin money when their stocks went down, but Willis was not an ordinary man. He was an insider.

Not only did he anticipate market moves here in America, he had a pretty good idea of world conditions too. Willis knew what Jesse's interests were, and where. For a long time now he had a duplicate key to Jesse's desk; the one thing he hadn't yet dared to poke into with his snub nose was Jesse's private safe.

Wall Street was the financial capital of the world and he was right there in the middle of it. It was true that there had been nearly two bank failures a day for the past several months, but they were only minor banks. No, only the sidewalk doomsday preachers on Wall Street croaked pessimistically, like Cassandra on the battlements. Men who knew, like Jesse Slayter and Willis Blake, forged ahead with confidence.

Willis looked up when the partners' private elevator opened with a smooth whisper. It was part of his job to know which partners were in, but he was surprised to see Mrs. Slayter and shot to his feet as she approached his office.

"Is my husband in?" she asked, with no other greeting. She seemed upset, Willis thought; on the few occasions he had seen her here before, she had always been serene and polite—and she had always telephoned before coming.

"Yes, Mrs. Slayter, but he's in a very important meeting and asked me not to disturb him."

Madeleine half turned away, then her blue eyes looked questioningly at him. "Do you think he'll be very long?"

Willis glanced at his watch. "Not very. The gentleman with him said he had another appointment. Would you care to take a chair and wait?"

Mrs. Slayter nodded and Willis carefully positioned an armchair for her, as if he might make it more worthy by changing its angle. She sat down silently and Willis went back to his desk, pretending to fuss with some papers while he studied her covertly from beneath his lowered lids. He could feel himself beginning to sweat, a phenomenon that had diminished as his confidence grew and only afflicted him now when he was nervous.

Madeleine Slayter made him nervous. She was one of the few women of her class he had ever spoken to and everything about her—the perfection of her face and figure, the beauty of her clothes, and the scent of her perfume—made his own wife seem dun and ordinary by comparison.

His car and his radios and his colored bathroom tiles, even his Hamilton watch, did not really make a man successful. Having a woman like this on his arm made a man successful. He had always admired Jesse, but right now he envied him enough to kill him.

Madeleine sat quietly in the chair, unaware of the young man's scrutiny. She had half hoped that Jesse would be out. It had taken more courage than she thought she possessed to come here today, just a week after Susannah's wedding. Willow Hill had been sad since then, with the signs of revelry gone and, in place of celebration, only silence and the echo of dreams. Still, she had finally managed to get this far and was determined to go all the way, no matter what the consequences.

The door to Jesse's office opened and he emerged with a short, fat, apple-cheeked man. She hardly heard his name when Jesse, as unperturbed as if she appeared in his office every afternoon at two, introduced them; nor did she respond when her hand was raised and not quite kissed with the requisite Prussian click of heels. She said nothing until she was inside Jesse's office and seated near his desk in a chair still warm from the rosy visitor.

"I want to talk to you, Jesse," she said when he had closed the door and sat facing her.

"I assumed as much," he said sarcastically, making her feel stupid and gauche. His black eyes were expressionless when he looked at her. He was fifty-three now and the wide strokes of white in his hair and beard only made him more impressive. He waited, watching her, exuding power and contempt.

His attitude toward her had been distant since last Christmas, not merely cool. He had treated the children with indulgence for their insubordination, but toward Madeleine there had been no comparable softening. She was aware that he bitterly regretted even his small display of sentiment that night and would never make that mistake again.

"It's very simple," Madeleine began, trying to be firm and concise. "I want a divorce."

He was impassive. "My reply is equally simple. No."

She had expected that and she was ready. "You can't pretend a divorce would affect your business. The world has changed a lot since we . . . the world has changed."

"Not my world," he said. "People who handle other people's money can't get away with scandal. Slayter's partners don't divorce if they want to remain partners—neither do Morgan's."

"I know that, but you can make an exception."

He shook his head. "Why should I? We can go on as we have. Why change anything?"

"The children are grown up now; Susannah's married, Jon's a man. They don't need me, and my presence is certainly no comfort to you."

He only shook his head again. "It's another of your whims, Madeleine, like Eugene O'Neill's plays and Picasso's paintings. It will pass."

She stood up then, abandoning her businesslike approach. "No, it's not a whim," she said quietly, but with something in her voice that made him very attentive. "I can't stand things the way they are anymore, Jesse. You must believe me, I really can't. I'm forty-three and I'm lonely, too lonely now for art and music and clever people to be of any help. I need someone to love me —not just in the way you think, there hasn't been anything like that for a long time, but to be there when I get up in the morning so I can say what a lovely day it is or even that it might rain. I want somebody sitting there when the radio's on, somebody to laugh at a joke with me and hold my hand at the movies or just smile at me for no good reason."

She took a ragged breath. He was watching her carefully. "I simply can't live without it anymore, Jesse, so if you won't give me a divorce, I'll just leave you and go to live with him. A divorce would be no scandal at all, compared with that."

"Live with whom?" he asked, withdrawing again.

"Someone who cares for me. No, don't look at me like that, nothing's happened. Anyway, what does that matter?"

He lit his pipe and drew deeply on it. "I'd ruin any man you consorted with openly in order to force me into divorce." His voice was hard, although his eyes were hidden. "He'd be drummed out of whatever profession he's in, anywhere in this country. I can do it—you know I can."

"That won't matter, either," she said, the tears still glistening unshed in her eyes. "He doesn't care and neither do I. We'd go away. I really mean it, Jesse, I'm not trying to be mean or spiteful or even to hurt you." Her hands began to shake. "It's simply that I—I can't—go on—like this."

He got up, all traces of anger or skepticism gone. "Sit down, Madeleine, sit down before you faint." He poured some water from the carafe on his desk and handed her the glass. She had to hold it with both hands and he watched her, a frown drawing his heavy brows together. He waited until she had sipped some water, until her hands stopped shaking, until she accepted a cigarette and let him light it for her.

"All right, Madeleine," he said. "It's an impossible situation for you—and me—but I think there's a better way around this for both of us."

She waited listlessly for him to go on, her cigarette held so loosely in her fingers that he thought she would drop it.

"We could try again," he said quickly, his dark eyes holding hers when she looked up, startled. "We were content together once, we could be again."

She looked too confused to speak, as if she could hear him talking, but didn't understand what he said. The listlessness had vanished.

"Do you think I liked the way things have been all these years?" he said, his resonant voice very low. "I had the same hopes for this marriage that you had—you were the only girl I ever wanted to marry, from the second I saw you." His voice dropped even lower and he looked away. "I never understood what happened. I couldn't believe it when you told me . . ." He looked up at her again. "But that doesn't matter anymore, it's in the past. We have two children we both care about, maybe grandchildren soon. If you don't want to try again for our sakes, try for theirs."

She had hidden her face in her hands, crying freely now, and he hesitated. "Madeleine?"

She was torn between the wild hope that what she had always longed for was happening now—and the fear, very real, very strong, that she might lose Ned only to resume a barren marriage of convenience. She hesitated, not moving, even her telltale hands still now as she lowered them to look at him, as if she could read him, his heart and his mind.

He took a deep, quick breath, aware of all that hung in the balance. "Madeleine," he said, and his body half turned from her, as if some part of him had to hide what he felt, even now. "I need you. I don't know how to say it any other way. I want you. Come back to me, Madeleine, so we can try again."

Doubt left her and so did hesitation. "Oh, Jesse, yes, yes. I've been waiting to hear you say that since the first time I saw you. It'll be different now, I know it will."

She stood and her eyes summoned him. He walked to her side and reached for her hands, then suddenly, on an impulse he could not master, he put his arms around her and held her close for what seemed to her both an eternity and a split second. She caught the scent of pipe tobacco, crisp linen and the odor of his skin beneath the mild cologne he wore. It was like coming home.

"I'm glad," he said finally, his voice uncharacteristically uneven. "I'm glad for both of us." He took the handkerchief from his breast pocket and handed it to her, then went to the small bar in his private bookcase to pour a brandy for each of them. "Here," he said, coming back to her, "drink this. It'll make you stop shaking."

She took a mouthful of it, shuddering a little as the fiery liquid went down, then looked up at him. "I don't know what to say, I don't know how to behave, it's been so long."

"I know," he said, going back to his own chair. "It won't be easy, it will take a while, but it's worth it."

"Oh, yes, Jesse," she whispered, holding his handkerchief. "It's worth it." She reached for her handbag. "I must look terrible."

"No, Madeleine, you're the only woman I know who never looks terrible."

She almost cried again at that, but she swallowed hard and dabbed some powder on her nose, under her eyes. Then, with nothing else to say or do, she got up to go. "I'll see you at home," she said. It was a simple, everyday phrase, but it sounded very strange to both of them.

"Why don't we have dinner out and go to the theater?" he said, just as she got to his office door.

"Yes, Jesse, I'd like that." She looked back at him, her smile tentative, but sincere.

When she had gone, he finished his brandy and went back to work. He wrote briskly for a while, then suddenly he put down the pen, his face livid, as if he had run frantically to escape danger, and sat holding his head in his hands for a long time.

47

"You can't be serious," Ned said, his eyes widening in disbelief. He put down the cup he was holding so quickly that the coffee slopped over the rim into the saucer.

"Ned, I went in there and told him I'd leave him if he didn't divorce me—and he believed me, I know he did. Then he said we ought to try again, that we could make some kind of life together."

"And you agreed, like a star-struck kid with a Hollywood talent scout!" He made a visible effort to calm himself, to speak more softly in the coffee shop in Greenwich Village where they often met, where he had been waiting nervously for her since early afternoon today. "Can't you see what he's doing? Scandal is anathema to him and all that Wall Street crowd—that bunch of hypocrites who carry on like pagans in private. He'd do anything to avoid scandal, even to taking you back, but he doesn't love you! Madeleine, how can you be so blind?" He was whispering feverishly.

She looked at him with a mixture of fear, regret, and determination. "Maybe that *is* why he's doing it—in part, anyway—but there's more than one side to him and part of him means it."

"Aren't you forgetting last Christmas and the way he manipulated your own children so cleverly, the way he manipulates everyone, even you when you were too much in love to see it? Are you still in love with him?"

"He'll be different now; he couldn't fool me anymore."

"He'll find a way," Ned said, his eyes bright with anger. He lit a cigarette. "And what about us? How much do you think I can take? I've waited years to see you, months to hold you in my arms again." He looked around, wary of the people at tables near them. "Do you think I'll be content just to sleep with you while you play at being Jesse Slayter's wife?"

Madeleine shook her head. "We can't talk about it here. Let's go for a walk in the Square."

He nodded, quickly paid the check, and followed her out, along Eighth Street to Fifth Avenue, then over to the Arch and through it into Washington Square. It was sunny and mild, one of those rare summer days when the city was bearable.

Madeleine felt his hand at her elbow and knew she still desired him, still loved him, but she could not abandon her marriage just when Jesse was willing to try to make it work.

"We can't see each other, Ned," she said. "You'll hate me, I know, but I

219

care for you too much to offer you the half life we had before. You deserve more than that."

He stopped on the path. "What will you do for love, Madeleine? You're too young and too loving to live without it."

She blushed. "I've done without it for seven years, and I know he meant love, too, when he asked me to try again."

"My God," he said, incredulous. "Don't you remember what you said sex was like with him, how he did it the same way he'd say 'steel is down ten points, RCA's up two.' Is that what you want for the rest of your life, when you know how it can be for us?"

"Ned, please, you know there's more to it than sex. There was more to us than that."

"I damned well thought so," he said angrily. "I thought you loved me."

She looked at him, wanting to comfort him, hating to hurt him, afraid to lose him. "I did love you, Ned, I do love you, but I have to do this."

"Why? Because of your bloody obsession with him? It's already ruined half your life."

"I know that, I know, but it could be different now. He's willing to change. Maybe it was Susannah's getting married, I don't know."

He shook his head. "People don't change at his time of life. Are you going to risk everything we have on a gamble like that?"

Her blue eyes were alight with her irrepressible hope.

"Jesus," he said, appalled. "I thought you'd finally realized what kind of man you were dealing with. He's not capable of the kind of love you want." His face set into absolute misery. "You're reaching for the moon, Madeleine."

She touched his face. "Ned, my darling Ned, maybe you are too. I do love you, that's why I want you to make a life for yourself and let me put my own back together." She took his hands. "Listen to me, if I didn't try again with Jesse he'd always be there between us."

He pulled his hands free. "He always was," he said. "You put him there." Then he flushed. "I wish to God I could stop you, Madeleine. We were meant to be together." He stepped back, his face drawn. "But I can't fight your own creation." He looked at her intently and with a longing that broke her heart.

"Forgive me, Ned. I didn't mean it to be like this. Forgive me."

"Never," he said. "Never." Then he turned and walked away and she knew he was taking himself out of her life with every step. She would never see him again.

She started to call him back, but Jesse's voice was stronger than hers. "I need you, I don't know how to say it any other way." It was what she had waited to hear for twenty-five years, and she knew she would not call Ned back because every word of it was true. If she left Jesse now he would retreat into his private wasteland, but Ned could manage without her. Ned was complete. And she had hurt him enough, she had hurt them both enough. Sometimes it seemed no matter what she did, she would hurt someone—and always herself.

She stood in Washington Square uneasily until he was out of sight. She felt lost, like a lonely child. Then she got into a taxi and went home to wait for Jesse.

48

"Oh, yes, Jonnie, yes, love me, love me."

She always talked when they made love. Sometimes she said the most outrageous things, things no decent girl was supposed to say, not even a girl who had once slept around as much as Gemma.

"Oh, please," she gasped, swinging her hips wildly over him. "Hurt me, Jonnie, just a little." Her eyes were closed and her curly brown hair was wet with perspiration.

She always aroused him, but there were moments, like this one, when she was more perverse than tender, that made control almost impossible. If she said another word it would be over right now.

He pulled her down to him. "Shut up," he whispered, and kissed her full mouth to soften the command. Then he rolled them over until she was under him and he had more control. His body arched and flattened against hers and his hands held hers down. He felt the velvet ridges inside her begin to contract and close tight around him and heard that familiar sound from her that was almost agony and always came just before she stopped moving and seemed to retreat into another realm of consciousness, too intense for sound or movement, as if she must be very still and not frighten away the ripples they had summoned from her depths.

When he heard that sound he knew he could let his body have its way, let loose the fierce, powerful eruption that he rode mindlessly for seconds. He often thought he would die of its intensity if it lasted any longer.

They moved tentatively against each other once or twice when it was over, as if their bodies clamored to have it back again. Then he collapsed over her, supporting himself on his forearms until she pulled him down.

"Let go," she sighed. "Relax. I love to feel all of your weight on top of me."

He let go, pillowed in the softness of her breasts and belly as he was pillowed in the depth of her body. He had been sleeping with Gemma since last Christmas and the longer he knew her the more he liked her. It was the sheer pleasure she got out of the simplest things she did—the way his mother was before some mysterious calamity clouded her days. But he worried because "liking" did not begin to describe Gemma's feeling for him.

She was stroking his hair, her arms and legs folded around him. "I love you," she crooned, rocking him as if he were her godlike child. "I'll never love anyone else."

He was silent. He did not love Gemma. He loved her laugh, her gusto, the rhythm of her rolling hips, the feel of her hands, and the incredible artistry of her mouth. But he did not love Gemma and he could not say he did. Yet his silence after each of her declarations of love made him ashamed of himself.

She knew it and held his face gently between her hands, looking up at him. "Don't be sad, Jon. I don't want to make you sad. It's all right if you don't love me yet. Just keep making love to me and someday it'll happen."

He wished mightily that he could love her. She was a wonderful girl, as generous with her feelings as she was in bed and wise in a way most other women he knew were not. But the farthest he could go beyond a primal lust to copulate with her was gratitude for what she was and all she had taught him about women—what they wanted of men, even the best ways to please them in love.

He smiled down at her and then dropped his head on her shoulder again with a feeling of well-being that overshadowed his remorse that he was somehow taking advantage of her.

After a while he lifted himself from her, rolled over on his back, and lit two cigarettes. They lay smoking peacefully for a time, the ashtray nested in the dusting of blond hair on his flat belly.

Gemma inhaled the smoke of her cigarette with keen appreciation, as she did most things. People often lit up after watching her relish a smoke, or got hungry when she ate something with obvious enjoyment. "Susannah and Charlie will be in France by now," she said. "I hope they've had as good a time this past week as we have!"

Jonathan drew deeply on his cigarette in lieu of a reply.

It didn't escape Gemma. "What's the matter? Don't you like thinking of Susannah in bed with a man—even as a duly wedded wife?"

He moved uncomfortably. "It isn't that. I just hope Charles is right for her. Susannah's special and she has very definite ideas about how people ought to behave." He shook his head. "She's not like me."

Gemma laughed happily. "Or me. Oh, we're a wicked pair the two of us, but I can't say I'd want to be saintly or chaste." She didn't let him challenge that. "It's okay, dear heart, you don't have to defend me. We both know there hasn't been anyone else since you, and I'd rather be your lover than your sister. Still, I have a feeling that old Charlie will light Susannah's furnace and then she won't be nearly so definite about how everyone ought to behave. Maybe she'll even forgive me for loving you. I know she's angry at me for it."

Jonathan cast about wildly for a change of subject. He was virtually certain that his new brother-in-law had been to bed with Gemma, but he didn't want to hear it said. It would make his intimacy with Gemma vaguely incestuous—and create a secret he'd have to keep from his sister. "I think they'll go right down to the Riviera," he said.

"Ah, yes, to show Charlie off to the legendary Uncle Daniel."

"He's not legendary," Jonathan smiled. "Just terrific."

"Not the way Susannah tells it." Gemma gestured for another cigarette. "But he doesn't sound a bit like old Jesse. That was really rotten of your father, wasn't it, to mess up Susannah's dream like that?"

Jonathan's face took on a wary expression as if the subject had to be handled delicately lest it explode. "He didn't see it that way, he explained it to us. He didn't do it on purpose. He didn't know she felt like that."

"He ought to have known she felt like that." Gemma drew on her cigarette. "He's a smashing-looking man, your father, but he doesn't think much of women."

"Why should he? He has Mother."

"From what I've seen, he doesn't think much of her, either."

Jonathan turned his head abruptly, a denial rising to his lips, but Gemma's eyes stifled any futile attempt to varnish the truth. It would be a relief to talk about it. "I know," he said to her finally, turning his eyes back to the ceiling. "I never knew why."

"I like your mother. She gets such a kick out of things."

"She used to. It was an adventure just to be with her. But then . . ." His voice faded.

Gemma crushed out her cigarette and turned to cradle him. "Listen, Jon, there's something I think you ought to know about your mother. She might need your help."

He frowned. It was dishonorable to gossip about his mother, yet if she needed his help . . . "You'd better explain that, Gem."

"All right, but don't go all pious and Victorian, will you? She's not just a wife and mother, you know. She's a person too."

He waited, his heart in his mouth.

"I think she has a lover—that Dr. Driscoll who just came back from Vienna."

He wanted to hit her, but that would mean he believed what she had said. He vaulted out of the bed and strode naked to the window of the bedroom overlooking Washington Square. "That's enough, Gemma," he said angrily. "Anyway, how would you know?"

"I saw them together a few times here in the Village, and the way they are with each other I could tell they're not just acquaintances."

He kept his back to her, looking through the curtain at the trees in full summer leaf. "That's a filthy assumption to make on the basis of a few public meetings," he said sharply. "Gemma, if you were a man——"

"Oh, stop it, Jonathan! You sound like a bad play. Why shouldn't someone love her if your father won't? She's human, like you, like me—all right, maybe not like me, but it's worse for a woman like her. She was brought up in the good old bad old days. She wouldn't have looked for someone else unless she was lonely enough to die. You must know *that.*"

He was caught between anger and compassion. "What have you got, X-ray eyes, to know so much about my mother?"

Gemma sat up in the bed, her full breasts bouncing. "You know more about her than I do, so tell me she's been happy with your father. Tell me she'd risk this kind of reaction from you and Susannah if she weren't desperate."

He clutched the curtain at the high window, remembering so many moments that could only be explained by what Gemma was saying, so many silences between his parents, that attitude of coldness on his father's part and that sad and poignant yearning on his mother's. There had been something wrong between them for many years, even if Susannah pretended he only imagined it.

"My God," he whispered. "Do you suppose that's why Father treats her as if she isn't there? Because he knows?"

"Jonathan, please look at me." She waited until he turned to her, reluctant but resigned. "Couldn't it have been the other way around? Maybe she needed someone *because* of the way he treated her!" She got out of bed and came to him. "Jonnie, it's hell to love someone who doesn't love you, ask me, I know." There were tears in her eyes, she who always joked about herself. "There must be other kinds of hell, I don't know. Maybe she has a special one. What difference does it make why it happened, who did what first? All I know is that she might need you to understand that it's not her fault, no one's to blame. Do you think people decide whom to love? It just happens, the way it happened to me."

He averted his face in a painful confusion between regret for her and shock over his mother. He could not bring himself to imagine Madeleine with a man, not even with his father. But whatever Gemma's falls from the state of female rectitude, she had an enormous capacity for love and an insight about men and women that had always amazed him. When he looked down at her again, he saw her eyes pleading with him to understand what she was saying, not for her own sake but for Madeleine's. It was infinitely touching to him that she cared so much about a woman she hardly knew.

"Why do you care so much about my mother?" he asked.

"Because I care about you and you love her and—oh, hell, Jonnie, I didn't want you to be hurt if you heard it from someone else."

He put his arms around her, as much for his own comfort as hers. He was as close to falling in love with her as he had ever been; certainly he loved her for her candor.

"You're a great lady, Gemma," he said, trying not to cry from heartbreak for her, for his mother, for himself.

"Sure," she said. "Much too great to marry."

"Don't say that!" He shook her gently. "It isn't you, it's me. I—I care for you more than I've ever cared for a woman, but it's not enough, it's not all it should be. It wouldn't work, you know that as well as I do."

She held him fiercely, her face hidden in the curve of his neck. "Of course," she lied. "I shouldn't have said that. It'd be cradle robbing anyway. You have two years to go at Yale, and here I am trying to take you away from that sordid place and give you a life of social ostracism. Come back to bed, all of this has worn me out."

"It's late," he said, thinking about Madeleine. "I ought to be getting home."

"You've hardly been home all week. A few more hours won't matter." She looked sad and sounded worried.

"All right, but I'd like a drink."

He went out to the mirrored living room to fix two highballs, wondering how on earth he would be able to face his mother when he did go home. He knew Dr. Driscoll by sight; people were curious about him because he was a psychoanalyst and that meant Freud and sex. He colored deeply. And that man was his mother's lover. God in heaven, what would Jesse do if he found out? Of course his father didn't know! He would never have stood for it.

Jonathan had been planning a trip to Europe next month to see Victor and Daniel, but if Gemma was right—and he knew she was—he wanted to be around if Madeleine needed him.

Jonathan had always gone to his sister about family things, but he could not have told her this, even if she were here to tell. No, this was something he had to face by himself. He hoped he would never have to speak about it to his mother; if he had to confront his father, anything might happen because of this new rage he had felt since Christmas. He had pretended that life was back to normal, but it was far from that.

He carried the drinks back to the bedroom, following the trail of clothing they had dropped heedlessly on their impatient way in. Gemma's anxious eyes were watching him, trying to fathom his state of mind.

He handed her a tall, cool glass. "It's okay," he said, "I'm glad you told me."

"No, you're not, but it's better to know."

He touched his glass to hers. He was thinking of so many things he knew about his family now, things that would change his life because he could never escape them, and he nodded soberly. "Most of the time you have no choice."

49

Jesse pretended to consult his notebook, but he watched Madeleine covertly as she crossed the restaurant and approached their table, accompanied by the flustered maitre d'. Most men behaved like that around her. There was only one polite word to describe his wife: gorgeous. There were an infinite number to describe what impulses she aroused in him, but he could not have used them in mixed company. And they had gone out a lot with others ever since their reconciliation.

He stood to greet her and kissed her hand, catching the light, clean fragrance she always wore.

"Am I late?" she asked, her blue eyes happy to see him.

"No, I was early. I've already ordered." They sat down. "That's a lovely dress. Worth?"

"No, Poiret," she smiled, glad of his interest. The dress was a sheath of gold tissue faille, heavily embroidered with white beads, like frosting on a golden cake. "I bought it when I went to Paris for Susannah's trousseau. It's a looser fit now."

"You ought to eat more, Madeleine, you'll get thin." No dress could hide the deep curves of her body. She looked succulent.

"I hope I will, it's the fashion."

The waiter served them filet of sole amandine and the green salad they both liked, then poured the Muscadet. Jesse tasted it and nodded. "Damn the fashion," he said. "You have to make your own, as I do." It was easier to talk tonight, he was exuberant about the market. "According to *my* magazines, there hasn't been a boom like this one in the history of civilization."

"Susannah was worried that it wouldn't last, and that was over two months ago."

"Of course it won't last," Jesse said, unconcerned, "but before it goes back to normal it will have pushed America farther into the twentieth century than any other country in the world. We'll have accomplished an industrial expansion and achieved a production technology no one will be able to match."

"Yes, but will people be able to keep up with all the changes?"

He smiled. "Your Freudian friends are needlessly concerned. Progress won't affect the national psyche. They worry too much." He glanced at his watch. "Coffee? We don't want to miss the curtain."

"No coffee, thanks—but, Jesse, won't there be another panic when things 'go back to normal'?"

"What do you know about panics?" he asked, pleased that she knew anything at all.

"There was a panic the year we were married, and quite a few since then. I never know when one's coming."

His answering smile was broad and confident. "Some say it takes a lifetime to know that; some say you have to be born with an instinct for it."

"You were born with it," she told him. He knew she meant it, that it was not idle flattery. She had been sincere with him about the things they had discussed since the day they decided to try again. The trouble was, there were too many things they avoided—one in particular.

He never paid any attention to the plays they saw. He was sure she didn't, either, that she knew why he suggested so many evenings out besides their crowded social calendar. It was to put off the moment each night when they went home together and climbed the stairs.

Throughout any play or review they went to see, he wondered whether he would approach her that night, whether he had enough control not to make a fool of himself with the kind of abandon that still flooded his fantasies of her. There had been other women over the last seven years. His sex drive might be as carefully regulated as his business, but it was strong and constant. His experiences had changed him, as hers had changed her. Would she think of another man when Jesse finally made love to her? Would *he?*

Again tonight, on the way home, the easy flow of conversation slowed, then faltered, and finally stopped by the time they reached the top of the stairs. He had intended to kiss her cheek and wish her another restful night, but suddenly the way she stood there, waiting, overpowered him. He reached for her and kissed her with a fierce appetite.

"I can't wait anymore," he whispered. "I know we should take things slowly, but I want you, Madeleine. Let me stay."

She leaned against him. "Yes, Jesse, stay, please stay."

He followed her into the bedroom, his hands undoing her clothes, then removing his own. The vision of her that had invaded his imagination for so many years was here now, under his eyes and hands, voluptuous and warm. Her fragrance mingled with the musk of her body, intoxicating him, and he knelt over her as he had in his sexual reveries, driven so much by his erotic imaginings that he forgot she was his wife and took her as a woman.

He was carried away by her, as he had never been by any woman except, in his thoughts, by this one. He was eager for what he had touched so many times, but had never feasted on except in fantasy.

Her soft mouth kissed him, her body opened to him, letting him go where he would. Things he had never before summoned from her told him she was utterly possessed by him, that he had mastered her, and the triumph of that held him long astride her until he was taken by an endless surge that turned him inside out, and her with him. He had never ventured so far into and out of himself.

She clung to him then, still trembling. "Stay close to me," she begged. "Sleep here tonight."

He settled near her, one arm around her, the other flung across her. She drifted off to sleep, imprisoned by him, and he listened to her soft breathing.

He was glad he had forgiven her, grateful that she had accepted his forgiveness so readily. Free of the burden of revenge and invigorated by passion, he felt exactly as he did in his own world, where he could control, direct and dominate. He was an arbiter of desire not, as in the past, its victim. He had the key to her now. She was another proof of his power and he loved her for that. It was love enough for him.

Madeleine, breathing in the fragrance of two dozen red roses the next morning, expected the high pitch of sexual excitement to wane. It was impossible to sustain that degree of intensity with a husband—she neither sought nor expected that—just as it was embarrassing to blush like a bride whenever she thought of him, of the two of them together. Yet, since he was often away on business for several nights at a time, the excitement lingered. She felt that it must be apparent to anyone who knew them.

Susannah and Charles would be back from their honeymoon soon. Surely Susannah would see that something had changed between her parents. Jonathan, apart from canceling his summer vacation in Europe, seemed to be unaware of anything, but Jonathan had never known about Ned and men were rarely as perceptive about such things as women. Jonathan had been doubtful of his father's motives since last Christmas, and Madeleine knew her son was too disillusioned to mask his anger—and still too young to accept that his parents were not perfect beings, but compounded of both faults and virtues, and even those not always constant.

It was the sort of thing she wanted to talk about to Jesse, but there was still much distance to be bridged between them. In the meantime, there was this wordless union, unexpected, unhoped for, amazing at their time of life. She thought it would lead to a deeper relationship.

"You were very quiet this evening," he said one night when they returned home from a party. "Aren't you well?"

"Of course I am. It's just difficult for me to speak to you in public without being obvious."

"About what?"

"You know perfectly well what."

"Don't talk to me then," he said, touching her. "In public, just look at me."

"And in private?"

"Show me—like that."

It was the beginning of what she had always wanted from him, to notice her, just to be aware that she was quiet or happy or troubled or glad. It had been more than she hoped, to arouse him to this passion she had been so long without and had never known from him. Passion was proof of love, surely, proof enough for any woman.

50

She missed her profession, Susannah thought, watching her mother. *She should have been an actress.*

Madeleine, lovely as always, seemed very comfortable at her daughter's dining table, quite at ease as a visiting mother, chatting easily with Susannah and Charles, Jonathan and Gemma. She was even rather persuasive in her role as a wife. Of course she hardly spoke to Jesse; for that matter, he hardly spoke to *her.* That was normal behavior for them, except for one thing: They glanced at each other frequently, where they had always avoided doing that in the past, and there was a different kind of tension between them that Susannah could not quite assess.

And then, as Susannah watched herself watching all of them, it occurred to her that she wasn't such a bad actress herself. She was playing a part too, in this happy family scene in the dining room of her new town house. It was a classic grouping—superficially—to welcome the newlyweds back and warm their new home.

"It'll be just a little out of perspective," she had said to Charles earlier, "like the new art. My mother and father don't much care for each other; my little brother is sleeping with my best friend and he's not even engaged to her; and I'm pretending to know nothing about any of it."

Of all of them, she thought now, only she and Charles were really happy. Or was she hopelessly naive about Madeleine? Her determination to divorce had obviously been blocked by Jesse, as Susannah had predicted. Yet Madeleine looked relaxed, even radiant. That forced air of calm was gone. If Jesse were any other sort of man, Susannah might have suspected a reconciliation. By the end of the evening she concluded that was exactly what it was.

"That was a successful dinner party," Charles said when their guests had gone and they were upstairs in the silver-gray and black-lacquered bedroom, the most modern room in the house. They talked while they prepared for bed, Charles from his dressing room and Susannah at her vanity table.

"When you consider that everyone was at odds with everyone else, yes," she said, removing her jewels.

"By everyone you mean your father and me." He sounded amused.

"Well, is it such a bad idea for you to be counsel for Slayter's?"

"The worst. I'm not about to be chained to Jesse Slayter, not even to

233

guard Slayter's for you. I'm a lawyer, my darling, not a watchdog. Besides, your father is not content to hire people, he has to own them. Jon looks like he can't wait to escape to New Haven after a summer in Siberia."

Susannah finished placing her jewels neatly in velvet-lined cases. "He's stuck on Gemma," she said.

"What of it? She's stuck on him."

"At first I thought he gave up his summer vacation to start at Slayter's—and high time too," Susannah said, creaming off her makeup. "But anyone can see he wasn't happy there." She patted her face with astringent-soaked cotton and picked up a silver-backed brush. "He didn't stay in New York because of Gemma, either," she went on. "If he were really in love he'd be happier."

"Oh, Susannah," Charles called to her. "You really disapprove of them, don't you?"

She shook her head at herself in the glass. Gemma was her closest friend and she couldn't disapprove of her just because her father did.

"No, of course not," she called back. "It just looks odd because he's still in school and she's older, don't you think?"

He laughed softly and she glanced in the mirror of her dressing table. She caught a glimpse of his naked back, dim in the distance of his dressing room, and a streak of heat raced across her lap. She knew now the frailty of appearances where passion was concerned. Even her parents' reconciliation had been unexpected, rather than shocking. She didn't understand it and she couldn't ask either of them about it, but it had come as a relief. At least she wouldn't have to tell Charles about her mother now, probably not ever.

"Oh, to hell with all of them," she called to him. "It's no concern of mine. To hell with everyone but you."

In the mirror she watched him coming toward her in burgundy silk pajama bottoms, the jacket slung around his shoulders like a tennis sweater. "Woman," he said, his voice different now, not amused, not patient, "I love it when you say things like that."

He came to stand behind her, dropping her dressing gown to let the bare skin of her back touch the warmth of his belly. They watched each other in the mirror while his hands lowered the gown, exposed her breasts and stroked them until the tips were rigid. He bent to kiss the back of her neck and she trembled with anticipation.

"Take me to bed, Charles," she whispered. "Hurry, please."

"I'll take you to bed," he said, kissing her mouth, "but I won't hurry."

She could even luxuriate in her avid desire, knowing it would be well-satisfied, only to become desire again. Sex was another of life's surprises—

one of the few things better in the reality than in the anticipation. She could let go in bed as she was unable to do anywhere else.

She moved against Charles. "All right, take your time, take all the time in the world." She turned to put her cheek against his stomach.

"Oh, yes," he said after a moment. "You wonderfully wanton woman."

He pulled her up and they walked to the bed, the dinner party quite forgotten.

Charles was gone in the morning before she was fully awake, and she lay awhile, thinking of the warm bliss of the night. She reveled in the way he made her feel, as a woman and a wife. She was amazed at how much more she loved him each day.

Love made her feel beautiful. The feeling was intoxicating. She had never thought of herself as beautiful. Her father had told her often enough that she was not, not in a conventional way, and no other opinion carried much weight next to his.

Susannah had decided that a woman with brains and style *did* have something better than mere beauty and, what was more, would have it all her life. Brains were a long-term investment, rather than a short-term speculation. Yet Charles somehow endowed her with beauty without diminishing her other qualities.

She was frightened by how much she loved him. She needed him now and that made her vulnerable. No matter how badly her trust had been repaid in the past, she had to trust a man she loved so profoundly.

How would you feel if you hardly saw Charles except in bed, if he never shared anything but his body with you?

Demolished, was the answer. Devastated and abandoned by the one person who should have understood her and protected her from the hurts and disillusions of life, with all its lonely places. The only safeguard was to keep her need of Charles a partial secret, to hold back something of herself if ever she should need to fall back upon it.

Her mother never had, she gave everything. But her father must have had a reason to behave so to his own wife!

She shook off the depressing riddle of her parents' marriage and rang for breakfast before she got out of bed and went to bathe.

She dressed quickly while she ate, in gray silk underwear and a gray Chanel knit suit—a vivid red and gray striped oversweater with a solid gray skirt and loose hip-length jacket. Her deep felt cloche was red, her silk stockings, shoes, and lizard handbag gray. She liked things to match or blend and she loved to wear red.

One of these days, she told herself, as she draped a stone marten fur around her shoulders and ran downstairs to the waiting Packard, *I'm going to wear the reddest red dress I can find.*

She was eager for another cup of coffee when the car reached the Plaza. "Good morning, Miss," the doorman said, handing her out.

Susannah smiled to herself. She was only half accustomed to being called "Mrs. Benedict" and wondered when, if ever, people would automatically assume she was a matron and no longer a "miss."

She passed the Palm Court, empty at this hour behind its white marble columns, and entered an ornate elevator. "Good morning, Miss," the attendant said, and Susannah smiled again and asked for the fourth floor. It was only eleven o'clock and she would have a half hour to herself before Gemma arrived.

The paneled door of the suite was unmarked and opened readily. A clattering of tickers invaded the silence of the carpeted corridor, and Susannah stepped inside and closed the door behind her.

There were not too many women seated in the opulently decorated room yet, and none whom she knew. Two young girls in neat gray smocks stood on ladders near a large blackboard that had been fitted to one wall of the suite's former living room; they were entering the latest changes in the most popular stocks—telephone, steel, radio, automobiles. It was an unusual atmosphere, rather like having a brokerage office in a drawing room, but by now the women had grown accustomed to it.

It was one of several luxurious "women's shops" maintained in the best hotels of the city by the biggest investment firms. Lady clients could relax as they never did when there were men around; they could watch their investments, telephone their brokers, and meet their friends.

There was a well-stocked bar and a coffee urn in the adjoining room, and the Plaza offered an excellent menu if the women were too absorbed in stocks or gossip to go out to lunch. Gossip was at a minimum here, though; there was too much money to be made when a stock rose as much as ten or twenty points in a day.

"Black coffee, please," Susannah told the uniformed maid. She studied a ticker for a moment. The volume of trading must be enormous today; the ticker was well behind already.

With a worried shake of her head she went toward a pair of chairs near a window where she would wait for Gemma. She tossed her fur over the back of the chair, sat down, and began making notes on a small pad in an enameled case—a gift from her mother-in-law. The senior Benedicts were pleasant people, fortunately addicted to sports and unlikely to interfere in Susannah's life. Now that she was married, Jesse had no right to interfere, either. Soon she would start looking for a job on the Street.

She looked up when Gemma came in, with a little wave to show where she was sitting. Gemma was very soberly dressed in a black broadcloth suit and white satin blouse—Jonathan's influence—but her face was aglow, as usual, and she seemed ready to burst with vitality.

"Sorry to be late," Gemma said in her breathless way. "I stopped by to see Mary Jane and had to hold her hand until the morning sickness went away." She sat down and waved to the maid for coffee. "What's going on here?"

"Nothing very good," Susannah said, eyeing the board again. "It looks like the start of a small panic to me."

Gemma pushed her white satin cloche back from its fashionable perch over her eyebrows. "How can there be a small panic? That's like being a little pregnant."

Susannah looked at her sharply, the board forgotten for the moment. "Oh, God, Gemma, you aren't pregnant?"

Gemma blushed deeply. "No, of course not." She looked painfully embarrassed, avoiding Susannah's eyes.

Susannah bit her lip, anxious to clear the air between them without putting her foot in it. "Listen, Gemma, if you're going to keep on with Jonathan, there's no use our pretending you're only his tennis partner."

"But you hate it," Gemma whispered, still looking at an unlit cigarette. "You haven't said anything, but I know you hate it." Finally, she lit the cigarette. "Don't you?" she insisted, when she exhaled the smoke.

"I think it's damned ridiculous, if you want to know, carrying on with a junior at Yale, but I don't hate it. Anyway if you both feel the same way, what's it got to do with me?" She knew Charles would have been proud of her for an answer like that.

"I'm not carrying on with him," Gemma said more steadily. "I'm mad about him. I have been since last Christmas. I can't think of anything or anyone else. I almost failed my finals because of it, and now I don't care what happens to me as long as I can see him whenever he gets down from New Haven." She inhaled deeply and fiddled with the catch on her handbag. "And you know this has something to do with you," she went on. "It makes it even harder for us if you're against us. You know I wouldn't ever go up there to see him, I know the kind of thing those boys would say, but I love him. He's the most wonderful man I ever met—and he *is* a man, young as he is."

Susannah was startled by the passion in Gemma's low voice. She knew

Gemma was, as Charles had seen last night, in love with Jonathan, but it was in a desperate, painful way Susannah hadn't been aware of until now.

"I'm not against it," Susannah said finally. "He doesn't seem happy about anything but you."

Gemma welcomed the coffee with relief, used cream and sugar liberally, and sipped it twice before she answered. "I don't think he likes banking much," she said.

"That's no secret to me, but he has no choice. Slayter's is meant to be Jonathan's. It's his responsibility and he's always known it. Even if he could forget that, he wouldn't let Father down."

Gemma was silent, drinking her coffee.

"What I can't understand," Susannah went on, "is why he decided to give up his summer in Europe. At first I thought it was to stay with you."

"No, I gave up my trip to stay with him," was all Gemma said.

Susannah shrugged. "Perhaps he'll cheer up now that classes are beginning. Anyway," she said, looking squarely at Gemma, "at least we don't have to play games with each other."

Gemma nodded, relief evident on her face.

There was a stir in the room and Susannah looked up at the board, glad to close this particular conversation. She caught her breath. U.S. Steel was down again. It had been sinking steadily since last month, but this was an alarming slide. If U.S. Steel went, it could take everything down with it. Bethlehem was down to ninety-five. General Motors had dropped ten points since the opening. A lot of people were losing a lot of money.

Susannah went quickly to the tickers. A glance told her they were seriously behind. She returned to Gemma and spoke anxiously. "I think something awful is happening down there. The way prices are dropping is crazy."

"But my father says it's been crazy for weeks and he still has everything invested in the market."

Susannah wondered suddenly if Jesse had sold everything while she was on her honeymoon. It was impossible to tell whether he had sided with the pessimists, like Joseph Kennedy and Baruch, or with perennial bulls like J. J. Raskob and Jesse Livermore.

"Not as crazy as this," she told Gemma. "If there's not a big recovery tomorrow, there'll be more sellers than buyers. The brokers will never recover the margin from their clients and there'll be another sell-off to save what they can. And the banks will never recover the loans they've made to the brokers." She stopped abruptly. "I'm going to call Slayter's."

She reached for the telephone and waited impatiently to give her father's private number to the hotel operator. The two friends waited, a tiny corner of tense silence in the turbulent room, where one woman had fainted over the swiftness of her losses. Finally Susannah said, "It's Miss Slayter, Willis, what's happening?" She listened, nodded, and listened impatiently again. "I'm coming down," she said, and shook her head at his reply. "Never mind what he said. When he gets back to his office just tell him I'm on my way." She replaced the receiver and looked at Gemma. "Willis says it's a real break, not just a correction this time."

"What's going to happen?" Gemma asked in a small voice.

"Everyone who's in the market might be ruined." She hoped frantically that her father had sold out.

"But everyone's in the market," Gemma protested. "The whole country can't go broke."

"Yes, it can," Susannah said. It was possible that all of the women in this suite, women as accustomed to money, ease, and privilege as Susannah and Gemma were, would find themselves penniless in the space of a few hours. Some already had, and this was only the beginning. If this was a real collapse, it could take months before the country recovered from it.

"Willis said they're meeting now—Morgan's, National City, the Chase— to see what can be done."

"Then it'll be all right," Gemma said, relieved. "Morgan's has saved many a day before this, even I know that."

"I doubt if anyone can save this day." Susannah gathered her furs, pulled on her gloves, and reached for her handbag. "I must go."

"I'll come with you."

They left together hurriedly. The lobby was curiously empty when they passed through it on their way to the Fifth Avenue exit. There was some activity around the telephones, but outside Fifth Avenue seemed normally active for a cloudy Thursday in October.

Susannah hailed a cab—there was no doorman to do it for her—and climbed into it, a silent Gemma in her wake.

They passed Thirty-fourth Street, where the old Waldorf-Astoria was being demolished to make way for John Jacob Raskob's Empire State Building. It seemed to Susannah that the elegant old hotel represented an era that was threatened with a brutal end. Building a skyscraper on the rubble might hide the wound, but would never heal it.

"You look terribly worried," Gemma said.

"I am."

"Did you really mean it—that the whole country can go broke at once?"

"If the market keeps sinking like this, it will."

"But what would we do?" Gemma said, more to the air than to Susannah. "How would we live without money? I never even carried money until I went to college—it was always taken for granted that I had it."

"I don't know what we'd do, Gem." Susannah was too apprehensive to explain to Gemma, who seemed more like a frightened child now than a woman in love. It was exactly how Susannah felt. She had no specific plan in mind; she simply wanted the comfort of her father's presence and thought he would like hers.

She kept a tight grip on Gemma's hand as the taxi rushed through city streets that seemed to be sleeping for a few last warm moments before cold reality swept in to rouse them from their dreams.

"Look at all those people," Gemma said. The taxi was slowing to a stop near Pearl Street, but they could see a large crowd two blocks away at "The Corner" near the Stock Exchange, the angle where Broad and Wall met.

"They're always there," Susannah said. "They've been coming every afternoon since the boom started." She paid the driver and the two got out. "Maybe not so many as today."

"They're awfully quiet," Gemma said. "They don't look like investors, either."

"They're not. They're tourists, sort of. They come to look, as if this place were King Solomon's mines." She started toward the office entrance. "Come on, Gem, I want to find out what's happened."

She had never felt so anxious as this. The corridor between safety and ruin was so narrow; she glanced at Gemma, hoping Simon Phelps didn't really have "everything" invested in the market.

Charles had resolutely sold whatever stocks he owned before their wedding. Susannah's holdings were in Jesse's care. The point was, anyone who owned, say fifty thousand shares of Westinghouse, had lost one million dollars since this morning. Multiplied by as many more shares in many more companies, such as her father held in his private portfolio—never mind in trust for the company's clients—that could mean disaster. Jesse was not accustomed to disaster and neither was she.

Her panic increased when the elevator door opened on the sixth floor. The habitual hush was gone. The clerks huddled in little groups, talking nervously. The sound of tickers and telephones was constant. It seemed to Susannah that the very jangle of the bells was louder than normal.

With Gemma following her, Susannah went quickly down the hall to Willis Blake's desk.

"Is my father alone?" Susannah asked him, disturbed by the moisture on Blake's balding forehead, the sickly pallor of his skin.

"Yes, Miss Slayter," Willis said weakly. "I'll tell him you're here."

"Never mind, I'll go right in." In her apprehension she forgot Gemma, who still trailed close behind her when she went into Jesse's office.

The difference was unmistakable, as if the current fueling the noise outside had been cut off at the door. Her father was standing near the ticker, passing the tape through his fingers. He looked up as the two girls came through the door.

"Susannah, what are you doing here? I told Blake——"

"He tried, but I had to come when I saw what was happening. Father?"

He walked to his desk, sat down, and gestured the two girls to chairs, only nodding a greeting to Gemma.

"You're pale, Susannah, are you ill?"

"Father, for heaven's sake! Tell me—are you—is everything all right?" In the face of his calm her voice sounded theatrical, even to her.

He glanced at Gemma again. "Yes, of course. We'll have some losses, but nothing to fuss about."

"Then you got out?" Susannah said softly.

"Last May," Jesse said, "for the most part."

Susannah's eyes closed. "Why didn't you tell me?"

"You were busy with your wedding preparations."

It almost seemed a reproach, but she had married so soon only because he wanted her to! Her eyes opened and she gave him that look of skeptical appraisal he knew from her childhood. "So you didn't want me to worry my pretty head," she said, with more than a little acid in her voice. "My poor little wits would've been addled with too much to think about."

Gemma giggled and Jesse, after a moment, smiled broadly at both of them. "Foolish of me, wasn't it?"

"Yes, it was," Susannah said. She did not return the smile. "I almost had a heart attack at the Plaza today. I came pelting down here to see if you were all right, and there you sit, as if the market weren't going crazy, laughing at me for wanting to be with you."

His face changed as he leaned across the desk. "That's not true, Susannah, I'm very glad you're here, but that crowd's been gathering since early morning and there's been mayhem on the floor of the Exchange since eleven o'clock. Wall Street is no place for unescorted girls today." He leaned back, reaching for a pipe. "I *am* a little surprised you were that worried."

She relaxed. "I shouldn't have been," she agreed. "I've told Charles often enough how brilliant you are about the market."

He looked enormously pleased at that, then there was a knock at the door and he called, "Come in." Blake brought him a sheet of figures and went out, silent and pale. The room was quiet while Jesse studied it. "There's been a slight upturn," he said to Susannah. "That'll be because of the 'buy' fund the bankers created."

"Then everything will be all right," Gemma breathed.

241

"No," Jesse said, with the total assurance Susannah had always admired. "Not for long. It will leave a mess behind when it bottoms out."

"What will you do?" Gemma said, mesmerized.

Jesse was silent. He never discussed his plans before strangers.

"We'll have to wait and see," Susannah said, filling the gap. Her father would tell her nothing more today, but she knew that fortunes were made as well as lost following a big break. She was avid to hear his views and half sorry she had brought Gemma. More than that, she was ashamed of her panic, it *had* clouded her brain. She felt remorseful too, for having stayed in bed so long this morning, mooning about Charles and love and sex. She should have been here with Jesse, watching history.

"Well," she said, standing up, "I think the situation is well in hand." She walked around the desk to her father and bent to kiss him. She was not often demonstrative with him and he looked up at her, gratified but curious.

"You're really wonderful," she said, very softly. "I'm glad you didn't need me."

He took her hand. "I'll always need you," he said. Then his voice became audible to Gemma. "We'll be all right, no matter what happens. So will Slayter's." He pressed a button on his desk panel. "Blake, have Harris bring the car around," he ordered. "I want him to take the young ladies home."

"We can take a taxi," Gemma suggested, still awestruck by the man, the setting, the panic outside and the quiet within. Nothing bad could happen if Jesse Slayter said it wouldn't. She would have given anything to make Jonathan's father really like her.

"No, not today," he said. "I don't like that crowd. They're sending in police, just in case."

"What's ailing Willis?" Susannah asked, putting on her gloves. "When I saw him I was sure something awful had happened."

"He's been dabbling in the market on margin—through another broker-age house, needless to say, since I won't allow it here—and he's lost all of his paper profits and more besides. It will teach him a lesson; he was getting entirely too cocky for my taste."

He walked to the door with them and held it open with his courtly, old-fashioned bow. They went down the corridor and into the elevator, saying nothing until they had reached the street and were in the waiting car.

"Now I know," Gemma said, "why bankers get more mash notes than movie stars these days. What a glamorous man!"

"Oh, Gemma," Susannah said, smiling, "for heaven's sake!"

"No, honestly," Gemma persisted. "Your father frightens me, but he's so —so powerful! No wonder you're clever, you'd have been terrified not to be." If *she* had been Madeleine Slayter, Gemma thought, it would have taken something pretty awful to make her want another man, and she wondered what the "something" had been.

Susannah was quiet. If the upward turn didn't continue—and how could it once the emergency "buy" fund was exhausted?—the out-of-town banks would have to call in their Wall Street deposits to cover. The New York bankers would have to block the hole it would make in the money dike.

"I think it'll be months before we get out of this," Susannah said reflectively, biting her lip. "Father said Slayter's was safe, but what about all the investors who'll have to learn the same hard lesson as Willis Blake?"

"Are you still going to work in a brokerage house? How can you dare, he'll be so angry."

"I'll dare," Susannah said, her resentment at being locked out rising again. "Wall Street isn't going to be a big gambling casino anymore, where anyone can play. The possibilities for real investment are enormous after a break when prices are low. I want to be there, where I can learn something."

A few days later, after Sunday sight-seeing buses had toured the area on which the eyes of the world were riveted, after Monday brought a surge of optimism and Tuesday the selling avalanche that finally broke Wall Street, she knew she wouldn't have to face her father's anger. So many brokerage houses had gone under along with their overextended investors that there would be no room for women in the slim job market that remained.

Much later than that, after the break was called a "Crash" and the Crash had deepened into the Depression, she started going down to Slayter's every day again as a matter of course. She knew she was welcome only as a daughterly observer, but she felt lucky to be there at all in times as critical as these.

"I can't just do nothing," she told Charles one Sunday morning when they were having breakfast in bed.

"I haven't objected to your going there," Charles said.

"Then why do I feel that you'd like to?" She picked up a pitcher as she said it and poured too much cream into her coffee.

Charles shrugged. "It's just that he's only humoring you again by letting you hang around, the way he did when you were little."

"What if he is? It's better than nothing. It's challenging, Charles, and fascinating too." She glanced at him over her cup. "Don't smile, it is, to me. For example, have you heard of the Bank for International Settlements?"

"Vaguely. It's an inside club for big banks. I don't know what they do."

"They manage German reparations payments, among other things."

"It's the other things that make me wonder. We don't need every central bank in the world just to manage capital transfers."

"Of course not—there's a lot more to it. It's things like that I want to know about and I love it!" Susannah was animated, her eyes as eager as her voice. "It's the most exciting thing in my life."

She wanted to take the words back the moment she said them, but they were poured out now, like the extra cream in her cup. Charles had been buttering a slice of toast, but he put it down with a tight expression.

"I didn't mean that the way it sounded," she said.

"I hope not. It sounded rotten." He wiped his fingers much too carefully on his napkin.

She searched for something to say that wouldn't sound stupid and mean. It *was* the most exciting thing in her business life, in the hours that she spent apart from him.

An awkward silence descended. Finally she said, "I'm really sorry, it was a foolish thing to say, but don't punish me for it as if I were a naughty little girl."

"I'm not your father." He put his tray on the floor and she thought for an anxious moment that he was going to get out of bed and leave her there with only her remorse for company. Then he took her tray away too. "And you're not a little girl anymore," he said, reaching for her. "As I'm about to remind you."

She relaxed against him, relieved that the argument was over, eager for him as always. She could say anything to him when they made love. She didn't even want to control what she said or did, and for some reason it was not a weakness to show how much she wanted him. "I love you," she whispered, holding him. "I love you so much."

In a while she begged him, "Don't stop, Charles, please don't stop."

Then he moved back over her, kissing her, claiming her. "Tell—me—now," he panted, matching his words to the rhythm of his body, "who's the most exciting man in your life?"

"You are," she breathed, her voice deep with passion, "you are, you are, you are."

244

51

Charles heard voices in the hall when he came out of the bedroom, and he went downstairs, wondering who could be calling at half past eight in the morning.

"Madeleine!" he said, glad to see her as always. "What brings you here so early?"

"Hello, Charles. Jesse dropped us off—I've brought Daisy to help me finish the nursery." The maid smiled at Charles over a pile of boxes from Harrod's in London. "We have to finish everything today if you're going to bring them home Sunday." She fanned herself with a lace-trimmed handkerchief. "I hope this heat breaks by then."

"All that stuff from Harrod's is from Philippa, I suppose. Kind of her."

"She's a kind-hearted woman under all that pepper," Madeleine said, dropping her straw hat, white gloves and handbag on the hall table and starting up the stairs with Charles. Daisy followed behind with the boxes.

"That's not what Jesse says about her."

Madeleine smiled faintly. "You never pay the least attention to what he says."

"True." Charles smiled back and followed her up a second flight to the nursery. The boxes were opened and he nodded appreciatively when he saw the yards of white lawn, edged in *broderie anglaise* beaded with blue ribbon. "How'd Philippa know we'd have a boy."

"She left the ribbons to me, of course," Madeleine said. "Now either stop distracting me or make yourself useful."

"I'm on my way to the hospital to see Susannah."

Madeleine nodded. "Jesse's over there now and I'll go when I've finished here." She walked over to the white wicker bassinet, waiting for its liner, skirt, and hangings. "That baby will grow out of this in no time," she said happily.

"Mister Jonnie only stayed in his for two months," Daisy said, her hands deftly lining the bassinet.

"It must be strange to remember someone like Jon as a newborn," Charles observed. "How can you treat him as a man?"

Madeleine shrugged. "It's difficult. You keep wanting to protect them."

"I hope you don't think you have to protect Susannah from me."

245

"No," she said, patting his cheek. "I think she's in good hands. Now be off with you, we have work to do."

He kissed her affectionately and went back downstairs.

For a while the two women worked silently in the freshly papered nursery. It was predominantly blue, with touches of garnet in the narrow stripe of the paper, the pattern of the rug and the chintz upholstery of two inviting rockers.

"Do you realize I'm a grandmother?" Madeleine said to Daisy after a while. "It seems a very august title for me, I don't feel nearly grown-up enough."

"You don't look the part," Daisy said, "that's a fact."

Madeleine sat down in one of the rockers while Daisy attached the skirt of the bassinet. "I didn't mean looks. It's how I still feel about so many things, you know, old songs and lilacs, sentimental things like that."

"And why not?" Daisy said. "It's sentiment keeps a woman going."

I suppose so, Madeleine thought, *it certainly isn't passion.*

It was still there between Jesse and her. They were getting older, of course, and it happened less often, especially since the Crash. He seemed to build to a pitch of anger—or perhaps it was a sense of failure that he had not predicted the extent of the crisis more accurately. Then he would come to her to drown his self-reproach in sex, the way a drunkard drowns his sorrows in alcohol. The rest of the time, he worked and worried.

"Can't I comfort you?" she had asked him one night, wanting just to gentle him. It was a night when desire did not impel him to her. He looked drawn.

"But you do comfort me, my dear," he told her absently at the top of the stairs. He had kissed her hand and gone to his own room, charming, gallant and distracted by other things.

Still, they had achieved what they hoped for, a restored marriage and a kind of intimacy. She had always thought that this particular intimacy engendered every other kind, that it was the best proof of love. She knew now that this was not so, although she did not know why. She was sure Jesse had been sincere that day, in his way, when he said he needed her, but it seemed more and more that his way and hers were not the same.

She wondered, as she had begun to do again lately, what Ned would have made of all this. She knew from casual gossip that he was practicing in Vienna. He had always had deep insights about people; now he was a skilled explorer of what drove human beings together—or tore them apart. Did that help him to understand what had happened to the two of them, to her and Jesse, and what there was about Jesse that kept a dark curtain between them?

246

"There, now," Daisy said, and Madeleine came out of her reverie to see the once-bare bassinet looking as soft and cozy as a white cloud in a blue summer sky.

"Oh, that's lovely, Daisy, I'll write and tell Lady Pip about it tonight. Now let's clear up. I have to go and choose the flowers for Sunday and then I want to see my grandson before his lunch."

"I'll clear up, Madame," Daisy said, "you run along and see both your babies."

"Yes, she is my baby still, new mother or not," Madeleine said. Putting on her hat in the hall downstairs, she thought about the wonder of her baby having a baby. Susannah was happy, too, happier than she had ever been in her life. No matter how much time Susannah spent with Jesse on Wall Street, it was Charles who had moved slowly but steadily to the center of her life.

Now that she had his son, Susannah would probably stay at home with the baby for a while. She would love him as devotedly as she loved her brother and her father, as passionately as she loved her husband, and with the added, ineffable love that is only a mother's for her child.

I wish I knew how she feels about me, Madeleine thought.

It was a subject both of them had avoided since Susannah's wedding three years ago, but Madeleine knew there had been a change. People who were genuinely in love were a lot more forgiving, and Susannah was deeply in love with Charles.

"I wonder if Jesse realizes how much," Madeleine said softly to herself. Then she got into a taxi and gave the florist's address.

"What will you name him?" Jesse asked Susannah.

"Charles Anson Benedict the fourth," Susannah intoned, looking down at her tiny son. "It's a lot of name for such a little person, but I'm sure he'll grow into it."

Jesse moved in the uncomfortable, too-small chair. For once he felt the heat. The ceiling fan in the large, flower-filled hospital room did little to move the soggy air. "Surely three Charles Anson Benedicts were enough," he said sourly.

"The more the merrier, as far as I'm concerned," Susannah said happily. "Isn't he marvelous? I never thought he would be so *marvelous!*" She looked at her father. "What else should we have named him?"

"He's a Slayter too, after all."

She was quiet for a moment. "It's a Benedict tradition, Father."

"Our tradition's a lot older than the Benedicts'." He shook out a fine cambric handkerchief and pressed it to his forehead.

"Well, we'll name the next one John Slayter."

Jesse watched Susannah with the baby. She looked very young, far too young to be a mother. Her dark hair had grown in from that idiotic twenties bob, and was tied back with a ribbon, the way she had worn it as a girl. He had to admit she had been a great comfort to him down at Pearl Street over the past two years. She was never intrusive, always attentive, and both ready and able to reduce a set of complicated figures to relevant essentials.

He had missed her during her pregnancy, and now she was talking blithely about the next baby!

"What time is it?" Susannah asked him.

"Almost nine. Why?"

She smiled. "I'm waiting for Charles."

It was the way she said it that startled him. Her voice was soft and her smile had a quality he had never seen before.

"When will you be well enough to come back to the office?" he asked brightly.

She hesitated. "I don't know that I will, just yet." The baby waved his hands and she looked down again. "He's so little."

"Nonsense," Jesse said. "It's not like you to be sentimental. He'll have a nursemaid and a nanny to take care of him. Babies sleep most of the time, you know. Once you're up and around, you'll be bored with nothing to do all day."

"I thought I'd like to watch him grow," she suggested, a little doubtfully. "Anyway, I really don't do much at the office, and now you have Jonathan."

Jesse smiled at that, his large body relaxing. "Jonathan still has a lot to learn—I know you do half his work for him behind the scenes." He folded his handkerchief. "That's not the point. I wanted to offer you a junior desk, dealing with the international side of our affairs. You have a keen grasp of the world banking system."

He watched her face take on a different kind of delight and stood up, gratified. "You don't have to decide this minute, but I'll need someone in a month or two. Think about it." He came toward the high hospital bed. "I suppose you want to ask permission of Charles."

"Of course not," Susannah said. "I'd just like to discuss it with him."

Jesse nodded. "He's a lucky man. With a wife like you, he'll never be bored." He leaned over to kiss her. "I'll see you Sunday evening at home. I have some gifts for you—and for him." With the tip of one well-manicured finger he stroked the baby's cheek until the infant smiled.

"He's smiling!" Susannah said, bedazzled.

"Just a reflex," Jesse told her, "but I used to wake up the household to come and see when you did that."

She looked up at him, very moved by his love for her and his inability to express it directly. It was a difficulty the two of them shared. Her eyes filled.

"You must rest now, my dear girl," he said. "I'll telephone this evening." He kissed her again and she watched him leave.

She looked at the baby, wishing she had told her father sooner about his name. He had been hurt by that, and he had enough to cope with these days without any disappointments from her.

She felt very tired and was ready to surrender her son when the nurse came to take him back to the nursery.

Charles had decided to walk. He was hatless, as many young men were these days. Correct dress did not seem important in the midst of the Depression. Even Jesse Slayter had abandoned his buttonhole and pearl stickpin!

The heat was oppressive as he headed up Fifth Avenue. He could feel it, a damp, heavy blanket around him. He would take a taxi to his office. A chauffeured Packard was one luxury Charles felt he should forgo in times like these. He didn't like seeing hungry men from inside of a limousine; it was bad enough to see them on a full stomach. He had kept only one car and chauffeur for Susannah's use.

He whistled softly as he stopped for flowers and a fresh copy of *The New York Times*. By the time he turned off Fifth Avenue, the *Times* was limp and the flowers had begun to wilt in their waxed green paper, but nothing could dampen his spirits, not even the sight of his father-in-law, just emerging from the hospital.

"Good morning, Jesse," Charles said buoyantly. "How's my little woman?"

Jesse returned the smile. "An odd way to describe Susannah, but she's fine, just a little tired."

Maybe you tired her, Charles thought. "Probably the heat," he said. "The doctor says she's recovering faster than is usual."

"Naturally," Jesse said. "She's no ordinary girl." His dark eyes were shaded by the brim of his straw hat. He seemed more jaunty than usual as he got into his car—the Depression hadn't changed anything for him. "We'll see you both—or, I should say, all three of you—on Sunday."

"Fine," Charles said, and watched the car as it went off down the street. He would never really like his father-in-law. He was a financial wizard, though, there was no getting away from that. Jesse had been surprised by the magnitude of the Crash, but he had emerged from it relatively unscathed. He would profit from the Depression in the end, men like Jesse always did.

Some people they knew, like Gemma's family, had lost every cent. Simon Phelps was a suicide and now Gemma worked at Saks Fifth Avenue, her meager salary supplemented by Jonathan so she could keep her apartment in the Village and live decently.

"I wonder why he doesn't raise hell with Jon over that," Charles had said to Susannah not long ago.

"I suppose he thinks it'll come to an end," was Susannah's reply, "the way most affairs do."

"It'll be three years this Christmas," Charles reminded her. "That's too long for a casual affair."

"But still not long enough for Jonnie to marry her," Susannah said, and added, much to his surprise, "it's very unfair of him."

Charles had gone to kiss her, his hand resting gently on her swollen belly. "That's one of the things I love most about you, your sense of fair play."

Now he went into the hospital and got into the elevator. There were so many things he loved about Susannah. She had humor, intelligence and drive. She was not the "girl" Jesse persisted in calling her, but a deeply passionate woman. Charles knew she did not give that impression, and it excited him to watch her being cool and crisp and witty in public, while he thought of the warmth and abandon she showed with him. He sometimes wished he knew exactly when their son had been conceived, whether on one of their lusty nights or one of their supremely tender ones. Then he shook his head at his own foolishness and went to peer at his son for a moment before going down the hall to Susannah's room.

She was dozing and he stood watching her. Her skin was translucent, with none of the blotches he'd heard some pregnant women had. Her mouth was soft, not as firm as it usually was. She did look very young. He was overwhelmed with love for her, and a fierce desire to adore and protect her and their child.

Susannah stirred and opened her eyes. She smiled to see him there and gestured to the flowers and the newspaper he still carried.

"Why are you standing there with all that?"

He went to put the flowers and the *Times* on a table, then came back to kiss her. "I was looking at you. I forget everything else when I look at you."

She touched his face tenderly. "That's a lovely thing to say. It'll be easier to look at me now that I'm not a group." She smoothed the sheet over her abdomen.

"My love, you're always a group. You're the ten most wonderful women in the world rolled into one."

She began to cry, covering her face with her hands and leaning against him when he put his arms around her. "I don't know what's the matter with me," she apologized after a few seconds. "I burst into tears whenever you say something sweet."

He rocked her gently until she dried her face with his handkerchief. "Have you seen the baby this morning?"

He nodded. "He's in fine fettle. I can't wait to get the two of you home. Madeleine's got the nursery all fixed up and the nurse is installed, a Mrs. Hummel. Madeleine found her through one of her volunteer agencies. Seems a cozy sort of woman."

"I hope she has more energy than I do."

"You'll perk up as soon as the heat breaks. Now just lie back and I'll read you the *Times*." He took off his jacket and sat down in the same armchair Jesse had used, unfolding the paper. "Well, well, Hoover wants to cancel German reparations payments—he's afraid Germany will collapse under the burden."

Susannah looked thoughtful. "Father says that the Communists will take over in Germany if the Weimar Republic falls."

Charles rattled the paper as he read on. "Not if this fellow Hitler has his way. He's busy fighting German Communists already." He looked up. "Not much to choose between Hitler and the Communists, is there?"

"No. That's depressing. Read something else."

"Astor won a sixteen-million-dollar tax case—that ought to cheer your capitalist heart—but on the other hand the country's got a nine-hundred-million-dollar deficit." He lowered the paper. "It doesn't get better, it gets worse. At least I stopped two foreclosures this week."

She nodded, somewhat comforted. Like many of their wealthy friends, they were stricken by the country's complete collapse. Even though they had escaped the worst of the Depression, they were not immune to the hopeless atmosphere that hung over the country like a pall. Charles offered his legal services free of charge to forestall small business bankruptcies and mortgage foreclosures and Susannah supported his efforts. They both avoided telling Jesse about them. Jesse thought people should fend for themselves no matter what conditions prevailed. Susannah and Charles thought government had a bigger responsibility in times of crisis.

"Enough bad news," Charles said, tossing the paper aside. "I had a marvelous idea while I was shaving this morning. We're going off to visit Daniel as soon as you're up to it."

Susannah's face changed. "Oh, yes, I'd like that."

"I thought you would. We'll go directly to Tourlaine and get some

251

Mediterranean breezes. We can do the Paris collections on our way back, and stop in London to find a nanny for Junior."

"Don't call him 'Junior.' He'll hate it."

"Any better ideas so you won't mix us up?"

"Something will come to me the minute we sail."

"Fine," Charles said. She seemed more upset than a name warranted, but he was glad to see her lassitude lift. "Now, what ship would you like?"

"Any one that floats! We haven't seen Daniel and Dominique since our honeymoon." She stopped for a moment. "What'll Jonnie do without me?"

A pinpoint of anger stirred in Charles, but he suppressed it. "He'll coast along; he might even make some decisions on his own."

She looked at him. "You don't like my helping him, do you?"

How could he tell her he was jealous of anyone she helped? "It's not doing either of you any good. Isn't it time he just told your father he doesn't want any part of Slayter's?"

"He can't do that! It's his!"

Charles moved restlessly in the chair. "By what criterion? Divine right? It's only his if he wants it and we all know he doesn't."

"Well, he won't leave Father now, not with the Depression getting worse by the minute. Even if Jonathan doesn't do much yet, he's moral support."

"Do you think Jesse *needs* moral support? And if he did, do you think he'd accept it from anyone, even Jonathan?"

She was quiet for a moment, then she shook her head, putting it aside. "I still wish I knew what was worrying Jonnie. It isn't just Slayter's and it isn't Gemma either. He always used to tell me everything."

"For God's sake," Charles said, getting out of the chair. "Stop treating him like an infant. He's a man, he has to deal with his own problems."

"I wonder if you'll say that when the baby's his age."

"The baby's our *son;* you are not Jonathan's mother."

They looked at each other angrily before he half turned away. "I'm sorry, Susannah, I didn't mean to argue with you over it."

"Oh, yes you did," she said softly, still very angry. "You just hoped you wouldn't have to do it now. You hoped I'd sit here like a Madonna, in raptures over motherhood, without caring about anything or anyone but the baby and you. Well, I'm not like that—I never was and you certainly knew it. I adore the baby, but he doesn't change the way I am or cancel out my feelings for my father and Jonathan."

"How long will it be before I can join that select club?"

"Damn it, Charles," she said after gazing at him in astonishment. "You know how I feel about you."

"No, I don't. Tell me!" He was ashamed of himself even as he said it.

252

"I married you, wasn't that enough?"

"Only because your father let you down."

"That's not true! I was in love with you long before that. I'd have married you sooner or later no matter what happened. I used to worry that you wouldn't wait . . ."

He turned to look at her. "You did?"

"Ask Gemma if you don't believe me."

"Never mind Gemma. I believe you." He looked at her plaintively. "I don't know what got into me."

She sat against her pillows, unbending for a minute, then she smiled. "I feel much better. I was spoiling for a good fight. You've been treating me like an earth mother for months."

"It's no easy thing waiting to be a father."

She laughed. "Try changing places."

"No," Charles said, kissing her hand. "I like things just as they are."

By the time he left for his office, things were back in balance for them, but Susannah knew he still saw himself as an outsider, excluded from the magic circle of her father, her brother, and herself. His jealousy frightened her. Just this morning she had felt a lovely rush of openness, of peace and blissful trust in the man who lived with her, slept with her, loved her—a man she loved. Yet it was wiser not to give in to that feeling; it was obviously too risky.

She closed her eyes again. This was no time to tell him about her new position at Slayter's. Time enough when they were back from France.

52

Susannah settled herself on a lounge chair next to Dominique and stretched gratefully in the sun. They could hear Charles and Daniel talking as they went off toward the stables. Then the voices faded and the somnolence of September settled over the pool at Tourlaine, Daniel's estate in the Maritime Alps behind Cannes. It was the perfect house for Daniel, as Dominique was the perfect woman, Susannah thought, not for the first time.

It was the way Daniel had described her to Susannah when he came to Montreux to collect her for her first midterm holiday.

"You're going to meet a lady who'll be with us for a while. Her name is Dominique Celestine Amadée Rochefort de l'Ile, the Condesa Montoya-Vargas."

Susannah had expected to have her uncle to herself. "That's a very impressive name," she said, trying to be gracious about still another mistress. Weren't grown-ups ever bored with sex?

"Most women couldn't live up to a name like that," Daniel had agreed, "but she surpasses it. She's the perfect woman."

Dominique was very French, Spanish only by marriage to a grandee who led his own life for many years—"And obligingly left me the villa in Monaco when he died," Dominique once said. Susannah had gathered there had been no love lost between them.

Dominique was daintily elegant, with the small bones and high breasts that made Frenchwomen wear clothes so well. She had well-turned legs, not long and racy like Susannah's; her face was triangular, with tilted green eyes. She and Daniel led a happy life together, in her villa or here at the Château de Tourlaine. They traveled to London, to Biarritz and St. Moritz, to the Greek islands and the Scottish highlands. They went to large cities whenever Daniel's expertise as an art historian required it. Most of the time they just lived.

There had been no other woman in Daniel's life for several years now and Susannah often wondered why he didn't marry her.

"Maybe he doesn't love her enough," was Jonathan's guess—incomprehensible, Susannah had thought at the time, until she realized that Jonathan was thinking about Gemma. He didn't love Gemma enough to marry her, whatever he supposed "enough" might be. Susannah made no such distinctions. You either loved or you didn't.

Dominique turned over on her lounge. "I hear your son," she said.

255

"Hungry again," Susannah murmured, placing a large straw hat over her face. "He's always hungry."

"*Bien sûr,*" Dominique said. "He's a man."

"I hope he's not too much of a nuisance."

"*Mais non!* Your uncle dotes on small creatures, as I do. You and Jonathan are still small to him. He has missed you very much these last summers."

"I wish he'd marry you," Susannah said impulsively.

"Why?"

"Why not? He loves you. I wish Jon would marry Gemma too."

"Human nature is so perverse," Dominique said lazily. "What use is proof of what one already knows?"

"Not much," Susannah said, after a pensive moment. "Charles knows I love him, but he's still jealous of my father and Jonathan."

"Love is love," Dominique said, echoing Susannah's thoughts but with a different interpretation. "He wants to be everything to you—husband, lover, brother, father."

"And probably uncle too!"

Dominique laughed. "Considering such an uncle, very likely."

By teatime the men had come back from their ride for a swim in the pool. It was another in a series of languidly fulfilling days for the four of them with only one subject on which they disagreed: Daniel's ideas about international politics.

"Why does Hoover concern himself with German recovery?" Daniel demanded over cocktails that evening. "More to the point, why do you and Jesse agree with him?"

"You can't do business with pauper nations," Susannah said, "and business makes the world go round."

"I thought it was love," Dominique said, trying to change the subject.

Susannah smiled at her. "I wish it were, but don't look so gloomy, Daniel, business is a fair substitute."

"The idea of German recovery is unappetizing to me. I don't trust a rigid mentality like theirs, and there are some new elements inside Germany that are dangerously attractive to fanatics."

"That Austrian?" Charles said. "I don't think we have to worry about a little rabble-rouser like Hitler. We have much bigger problems at home."

Susannah agreed. She had wondered before if Daniel knew how much of his personal income came from German investments. He never went to Germany himself. Now she knew he could have no knowledge whatsoever of his portfolio—he left it all to Jesse.

"Do you think you should tell him?" Charles asked when they were alone later that night.

"No, he's a very intelligent man. If he doesn't know it's because he doesn't choose to know."

"Should people be told only what they want to know?"

"Adults have that option, don't you think?"

He watched her warily as he got into bed. "Do you mean there are things you wouldn't tell me unless I asked?"

"Yes."

"But you'd tell me the truth if I did ask?"

"Yes," she said again.

He absorbed that in silence as she got into the vast canopied bed beside him. She laughed softly and moved closer to put her arms around him. "You see, Charles, there *are* some questions you won't ask me because you don't want to know the answers." He had avoided the subject of when she would return to work at Slayter's, and she had decided to wait until he asked her.

There was one very important question she would never ask *him:* Had he ever slept with Gemma and did he still want to—with Gemma or any other woman?

She kissed him. It was an ardent invitation to sex. She had expected childbirth to diminish desire, not the contrary. She didn't even wonder tonight how he had become so expert in love, or with whom. Tonight she simply did not want to know.

Book V

53

1936

Susannah stuffed a pile of folders in the center drawer of her desk, squashed some financial journals into a cabinet, and straightened the objects on the desktop. She was always neat herself, but she could never manage to keep her desk the way Jesse wanted it. At home her maid kept her closets and bureau drawers in perfect condition, but here at the office she hid her jumble of papers at the end of each day to keep a general impression of businesslike order.

She picked up a photograph of her son—they called him Cab, for his initials—and kissed it. "You're going to have a brother, my little love," she said. "We'll call him John Slayter—unless he's a girl, then we'll call him Bess." She rubbed the smear of lipstick off the protective glass, set the picture down, and took another look around the office. Except for the personal things on her desk, it was exactly as she had found it four years ago.

"The last thing I want," she had told Charles then, "is the kind of office they'll call 'feminine.' "

"What are you going to do about your own upholstery? They're bound to notice you're a woman."

"Maybe, but they won't accuse me of acting like one."

She couldn't have done anything more female than to get pregnant again. She didn't know what her father would think of it.

She glanced at her watch and pressed a button near her telephone. "Willis, is Mr. Slayter free yet?"

"Yes, Mrs. Benedict," Willis's voice said through the intercom, "I was just about to buzz you."

The hell you were, Susannah thought, releasing the button. She had never liked Willis Blake and her opinion had been confirmed many times since her days as a mere observer right after the Crash.

"Don't go wringing your hands and bowing Uriah Heep style around me," she muttered to herself as she settled a small black straw hat forward on her smooth, chignoned hair. "You're a nasty little sneak, no matter how efficient Jesse thinks you are."

She had taken to calling him Jesse to herself—sometimes to his face, if the mood was right. Most of the time, though, he was still "Father."

She put on the jacket to her dress—a Mainbocher black and white silk check—picked up her handbag, a file folder, and a copy of British *Vogue,* and went down the hall to Jesse's office.

"Hello, Father, I just wanted to give you the translated notes on Buna rubber in case you need them over the weekend."

"How does it look?"

"Farben's going ahead with a new Buna rubber plant at"—she flipped through the file—"Schkopau. Hitler's economic advisor, Wilhelm Keppler, is in charge of synthetics and he's in favor of it, so Farben's virtually certain of a government subsidy, even though it will cost ninety-two marks to make a Buna tire as opposed to eighteen to make one of natural rubber." She looked up. "The tire manufacturers, of course, are against it. So are the military: they say it doesn't wear well. And so is the government financial director, Hjalmar Schacht. That doesn't sound like a brilliant investment, does it?"

Jesse looked thoughtful. "The quality can be improved by this new research plant. That will satisfy the military, if not the finance minister." He looked up, with that move of his head that always meant a decision. "We'll wait to see who carries more weight with Hitler, I.G. or Schacht. Schacht is a financial genius, but Hitler is not."

Susannah nodded and handed the folder to him. "All right, then, I'm off."

"You're leaving early today," he said. His heavy brows were still black against the gray streaks in his hair.

"I have an appointment," she said. "I told you." She was purposely evasive; the pregnancy had come at an awkward time, just as Jonathan was taking his first European vacation in several years.

Jesse pointed at the magazine. "Nothing serious, to judge by that."

She laughed. "Philippa sent me a copy of English *Vogue.* It has their first photo of Mrs. Simpson in it. They've kept her a deep, dark secret up to now."

"So now they're publicly lionizing that divorcée in England!"

"Come on, now, Father, divorce isn't such a scandal anymore."

He shook his head. "It is to me. There'll never be a divorce in this family." He looked at her, aware of her stylish elegance. "Where *are* you going?"

"Not to an adulterous rendezvous." Susannah laughed. "If you must know, I'm going to the doctor to confirm an attack of pregnancy." She smiled very brightly, waiting for his reaction.

"I see," he said.

"Aren't you pleased?"

262

He stood up. "Naturally, are you?"

"Yes, yes, I am. Cab needs a brother—or sister. It won't upset things very much," she went on quickly. "I can still fill in for Jonnie while he's away on vacation. I won't show for at least three months more." Her gloved hands lifted, as if to convince him. "And I'll come back before you know I'm gone."

He nodded. "I suppose this was planned?"

"No," she said, quickly again. "It was rather a surprise." That wasn't exactly true; they had been hoping this would happen for about a year now.

"Well, it's a pleasant surprise," Jesse said, "as surprises go. Charles will be cockier than ever about it."

Susannah looked at her watch again. "I must go or I'll be late. Don't worry, Father, I'll be back for good by next May at the latest." She blew him a kiss and left the office, passing Willis once again, with no acknowledgment.

She stopped at Jonathan's office, looked in, and raised her right hand to make a large O with her thumb and forefinger.

"So you told him," Jonathan said. "Everything all right?"

"Fine. He didn't fire me. I'm off to get my gestating instructions from the doctor. See you before you leave."

She went off happily to the doctor's office and from there, an officially expectant mother, back home and upstairs to the second floor. She walked through the rooms with more attention than she had given them in years. They would have to make some changes upstairs, move Cab out of the nursery to a room of his own, get a nursemaid until Nanny could see to the new baby too.

She loved the house. It was just the right size: twenty rooms and eight bathrooms, easy enough to be handled by five live-in servants with help from a laundress, a seamstress, and a chauffeur.

Her eclectic taste had made something special of it. Gray-green taffeta drapes dressed the windows of the living room and the adjoining dining salon, where a crystal collection was displayed in velvet-lined cabinets equipped with interior lighting. There were stained-glass windows in both rooms, unusual and perfect with the Italian furniture, marble-topped or upholstered in pale gray and green water tints and tapestries.

The library was across the hall, done in dark burgundy leather and paneled and shelved in violet-ebony wood. Apart from the rare eighteenth-century prints, wedding gifts from Philippa and Elton, the library's only decorations were its books—leather-bound and snug in shelves that went from floor to ceiling—and the Bechstein grand piano shining in solitary splendor at one end of the room. Jonathan always played it when he came over. She glanced at her watch. He would be here soon for a brief good-bye to Cab before he sailed tonight.

July sunlight filtered through the stained-glass windows of the living room as she sat there, lounging in the armchair, her long legs resting on a marble-topped coffee table. She was very happy with the room, with her life. She and Charles were utterly mingled in marriage by now, like their books on the library shelves. They were not individuals any longer and for the most part Susannah liked the merger. She loved being married to Charles, yet there was a drive in her that marriage and motherhood did not totally absorb, and she would never understand why he should feel threatened by that, although he made every effort not to let her know it.

She heard the doorbell, then her mother's voice in the hall and Madeleine's steps climbing the stairs. "I'm in here," she called, still sprawled comfortably in the big chair, glad that her mother had come.

"What happened?" Madeleine asked, the moment she came in.

It usually annoyed Susannah that her mother always knew when something was going on—and didn't hesitate to ask—but today she didn't mind.

"You come right to the point, don't you? Is that a Chanel?"

"Yes to both questions." Madeleine sat down and fitted a cigarette into her black holder. The dress was a silk muted plaid with a soft bow at the neckline and a flared ankle-length skirt that did not hide the fact that Madeleine was still slightly more full-bodied than fashion now allowed. "But I refuse to compress myself into a corset," she had told Susannah. "I had enough of corsets as a girl."

Her small straw hat was tilted to one side of her head. She always looked much younger than fifty and, most days, as if she had just discovered the world and was delighted with everything in it. She had been this way for several years now, ever since that change took place between Jesse and herself. They couldn't be called a happy couple, in Susannah's opinion, but there was something between them that had not been there before. It was the sort of thing you sense when two people have some kind of need for each other, not necessarily physical, although that must have something to do with Madeleine's air of youth.

"Where's my grandson?" Madeleine asked.

"Still napping, I suppose." Susannah was usually amused by Madeleine's enthusiasm as a grandmother, but today she wished she could be on the same warm terms with her mother. "I'll tell Nanny you're here so she'll bring him down as soon as he wakes."

"She knows," Madeleine said. "I'm here every afternoon." She puffed on her cigarette with appetite. Usually it made Susannah want to smoke too, but this morning it had made her sick to her stomach when she lit a cigarette.

"You still haven't told me what's happened," Madeleine said.

"What makes you so sure anything has." Susannah had no idea that her mother came *every* day.

"Well, here you are, home in the middle of a Friday afternoon and looking very pleased with yourself . . ." She stopped and stood up. "You're pregnant!" she said delightedly.

Susannah nodded, as her mother came toward her, leaned over the chair impulsively, and put her cheek next to Susannah's. "I'm happy for you, honey, very, very happy."

Susannah felt the softness, breathed in the familiar scent Madeleine had always worn, and almost raised her arms to put them around her mother, but it had been too long since they had embraced each other.

Madeleine retreated to the couch. "You've been to the doctor? Everything's all right?"

"Perfect."

"When are you due?"

"March." Susannah decided to try a cigarette, after all. "I'll still be able to fill in for Jonnie."

"Will Charles object?"

"I don't see why. I'm very healthy." The cigarette tasted good, as if to confirm what she said. "Jesse doesn't mind, so why should Charles?"

Madeleine was silent—a woman who had learned not to say everything she thought. Susannah realized it happened often when Jesse's name came up.

"Father's very busy these days," Susannah said, probing.

Madeleine nodded. "Still trying to run the world—angry when it won't do as he tells it."

"You can't blame him for that," Susannah countered. "He's usually right."

"He can make mistakes, everyone does. He's only human, after all."

It was exactly what Susannah had told Jonathan often enough in their discussions about their father, but coming from Madeleine it was suspicious. The old infidelity still rankled and this sounded like an excuse for it. If Charles were ever unfaithful to her, it would be inexcusable, like death.

"There are mistakes and mistakes," Susannah said tartly, sorry she had started this.

"No, there are just people who make different kinds."

The two women looked at each other. They had been civil for years, but civility was not what Susannah wanted today. She wanted to talk about her

265

pregnancy, to figure out a tactful way to make Charles believe that wanting to work was no reflection on him or their marriage. Madeleine knew about things like that, she had a way with people.

It was too late. The habit of distance gaped between them. There seemed nothing else to talk about—or too much ever to say.

"Is Jonathan all packed?" Susannah said. He was the one person, apart from Cab, they could always talk about endlessly.

Madeleine nodded. "I'm glad he's going. He needs the rest, but it'll be hard on Gemma."

"I know." Susannah shook her head. "That just goes on and on."

"I don't think he'll ever marry her," Madeleine said.

"He's with her all the time. I won't like him very much if he doesn't. What more does he want, for heaven's sake?"

"Maybe he doesn't love her in the right way."

"He's giving a fair imitation," Susannah observed wrily.

"But he ought to be madly in love, he has the nature for it. In fact, everyone ought to be madly in love at least once in a lifetime. I'm glad you are."

Cab's arrival stopped the conversation, but Susannah was still puzzling over the last remark of Madeleine's while she dressed for dinner. Had her mother been madly in love just once? And was it with Jesse or Ned Driscoll? Once she would have been sure of the answer, but now she knew that love had too many ambiguities. It didn't add up neatly, like a balance sheet.

Lately, it seemed, she could not get a clear perspective on anything. Her feelings for Madeleine wavered crazily, like a demented barometer. Her love for Jonathan was tinged with disappointment at his lack of direction in his professional and personal life. She adored Charles, yet she was so aware of having to treat him carefully that she often blundered. Things came out sounding the opposite of what she meant. Her father was consistent, but their close business relationship pointed up some things about him that jarred her. He had curious prejudices, unfounded and violent. He was reticent with his affection and that, once a bond between them, sometimes hurt her. He might have shown some real enthusiasm about the baby, the way Madeleine had.

"He only said it was a pleasant surprise—as surprises go," she told Charles over dinner that night. "I suppose I ought to be glad he didn't pack me off to breed at home like a lady."

He poured wine for both of them. "Would that be so terrible for you?"

"Yes! I'm strong as a horse. I'm not going to lie on a couch with a lily in my hand for all those months."

"You'd have Cab and me to amuse you."

"I adore Cab," Susannah said carefully, "but he's not interested in capital growth and currency markets and I am. You're out all day . . ." It was turning into one of those discussions again, she could never seem to avoid them. She looked up from buttering a roll. "What's wrong?"

"Cab and I don't seem to be enough for you."

Susannah put down her roll. "Come off it, Charles, that's nonsense. One thing's got nothing to do with the other. If you think it's such fun to stay home, just you and the servants and the baby, then you do it. Being a husband and father isn't enough for *you*. You don't need money, either. You work because you want to. So do I."

After a moment he nodded with a rueful smile. "I can't even say it's different for a woman. I always knew it wasn't different for you."

She smiled radiantly, relieved. "That's one of the things I love about you, you never try to wriggle out of what you've said." She raised her wineglass. "Here's to our new baby, Charles. I hope it's a girl this time."

They were having coffee when she said, "Let's go down to the Village and see where Jonnie and Gemma are going tonight. I'd like to hear some jazz."

"Let's stay home and make violent love instead."

She started to smile her agreement, then she caught the expression on his face. Her smile faded and her lips parted. It was going to be one of those nights; it always was when he looked at her like that. She had never been able to resist their wildness and the promise, always fulfilled, of something different, something unexpected even by her compliant body.

They started sex together, but in the end it was Charles who was in control, of himself and her. She suddenly understood that there were times when he needed to assert his mastery over her and this was the only way he could do it. She thought it was an unnecessary gambit—she loved him as a man, not a master.

Then he got up to come toward her. Thought vanished. Anticipation crowded every corner of her flesh.

54

Jonathan tried to concentrate on his book, but his eyes kept moving to his father. Jesse sat in his favorite wing chair, holding a glass of brandy and reading the newspaper.

An evening alone with his father made Jonathan uncomfortable. He wanted to see Gemma before he sailed, but Madeleine was at a political meeting tonight and he thought he should be here to alleviate any tension when she came in. Jesse was furious with her for supporting Roosevelt, however much he belittled her effectiveness.

Things were the same between his parents. For several years they had lived together in a way that was still puzzling, but far more comfortable than the coldness that had gone before. Madeleine had no lover now, Jonathan was sure of that. She was not miserable, that was all he cared about. Jesse was pretty much the same, as far as Jonathan could see.

"I can never figure him out," he told Susannah. "That's because he never does anything for the usual reasons. He's always got some motive of his own that we can't see, as if we were all chessmen being pushed around on a board he designed."

"Well, he's only human, he doesn't relish being a fallen idol."

She was right about that. The bankers, once American heroes in their striped trousers, cutaways and toppers, had been cartooned and caricatured without mercy since the Crash, and it angered Jesse not to have the respect that was his due. Case after case of embezzlement, fraud and larceny had been uncovered and trumpeted in the press.

"It's a political ploy," Jesse kept saying. "They want to curry favor with the working man."

"Well, no one else ever has," Charles kept answering, "not as a voter, not as an object for concern. You money lords are being forced to change and that's what you resent."

Jesse always lumped him in with Franklin Roosevelt's Democratic administration. "Damned Bolsheviks, the lot of you, giving money away."

Jonathan sighed to himself, impatient to get away on his first European vacation in years. He was going to England, then to Berlin to meet Victor, whom he hadn't seen since graduation, and finally to the south of France to see Daniel and Dominique.

He had done all he could to please his father through the worst of the financial crisis. He lived at home, although he had come into more than enough money at his majority to have his own apartment and do nothing at all. He worked diligently at Slayter's, with Susannah's help, to master a business he still didn't like and never would.

The one thing he would not do, even to please Jesse, was leave Gemma. He was going to marry her, anyway, but he wanted to make the final decision while he was away from her during the summer. It would take a better man than he was to renounce Gemma while she was within reach, and yet he knew a marriage shouldn't be based on sex alone. He loved Gemma, but there had always been something missing in that love, or so it had seemed. Now he was not so sure. Either way, he refused to let his father rule his personal life too. Resentment stirred in him. He looked up when Jesse shook his paper in disgust.

"Roosevelt 'nominated by acclamation'! Hasn't he done enough harm already? Minimum wages, maximum hours, public works, collective bargaining? He's a traitor to his class." He threw the paper aside angrily. "He's interfering in free enterprise, the rock America was built on."

Jonathan answered out of his resentment, without considering his words for once. "The country seems to have foundered on its rock. Except for Roosevelt, we might have had violence here, with all the bread marches and soup lines. People aren't just hungry anymore, they're out for blood."

"If they don't take care, blood is what they'll get," Jesse said, getting up to refill his glass. "We're not Red Russia, to be ruled by a mob of Communists."

"Do you want them to shoot more striking veterans? You sound like Veidt's Nazi friends." Jonathan was somber. "I detest that man more each time he comes to the office."

"Then you're an ignorant puppy," Jesse said, sitting down in his chair again. "Veidt represents German industry. All they want from Hitler is money for research."

"They got thirty-five million dollars from Standard Oil in return for world rights to their oil conversion process. Wasn't that enough?"

"That was years ago and they're still experimenting with synthetic rubber, but I'm glad to see you're paying attention. You know how vital such materials are."

"Only for war in the quantities *they* want," Jonathan said curtly. "Is that why they always need money? Will they sell out the whole world again?"

"That depends upon what you mean by the whole world—or have you been listening to your Jewish friend?"

"I resent that," Jonathan said, rising from his chair. "Victor says nothing about I.G. Farben in his letters, even if he dislikes Veidt as much as I do."

Jesse smiled cajolingly. "Did you know that the chairman of I.G.'s managing board fell out with Hitler five years ago by defending their Jewish scientists?"

"Do you mean I.G. was trying to protect its Jewish colleagues?"

"More or less," Jesse said. "Hitler told him then that Germany could get along without Jewish scientists. He still won't enter a room if the I.G. chairman is in it." He leaned forward, making his point with the brandy glass. "But he does support I.G. research."

"And of course," Jonathan said disgustedly, "I.G. supports *him.*"

"That, my boy, is the point. No matter what our people's personal preferences, they do what's best for industry and, as I keep reminding you, Veidt represents industry."

"German industry," Jonathan specified.

"Where's the harm in that?"

"There's a potential danger," Jonathan insisted, pointing to Jesse's discarded paper. "Hitler's still saying Germany needs more territory in Europe. He's reinstated compulsory military service. Nazis in Germany, Fascists in Italy, it sounds like war to me. Whose side would we be on?"

"The winning side," Jesse said. "Politicians come and go, borders change, but money and power and spheres of influence remain steady. When the wars end we always take up where we never left off. We direct things without the blundering passion of patriotism, and the world benefits as a result."

Jonathan looked away. There was no point in arguing with his father, particularly when Jesse was somewhat the better for brandy and more expansive than usual. He turned to another subject.

"Susannah's very happy that she can stay on through the summer," he said.

"Might as well indulge her," Jesse said. "She's not too far along and it won't hurt to keep her away from her husband's influence a little longer."

Jonathan's blue eyes were intent. "What's wrong with his influence?"

"He's a New Deal Democrat, as you know perfectly well."

"So what? So am I, so is Mother."

"Yes, well, I can't do anything about your mother—anyway, she's harmless—but I can keep Susannah on a steady course." He eyed Jonathan as an obviously hopeless case.

"I see. Is that the real reason you lured her back to work right after Cab was born?" Jonathan had a curiously heady feeling of power, talking to his father like this.

Jesse sipped his brandy. "It was what she wanted. I was merely honoring my promise to her."

"What if I told her Charles's influence had more to do with it than your honor?" If he was hopeless, Jonathan thought, he might as well be honest.

Jesse glanced at him. "I know you won't do that. She'd be hurt."

"Jesus Christ," Jonathan exploded. "Are you ever anything but calculating with people?"

Jesse's face changed. "Is that what you think I am?" he asked softly, watching his son as if Jonathan had begun to assume another shape before his eyes.

Jonathan's expression was disdainful, almost contemptuous. "Isn't that what you've always been?"

"No," Jesse said emphatically. "I've only done what was best for you and your sister. I never denied either of you anything."

"I'm not so sure." Jonathan stood opposite his father, taller than Jesse, slimmer but just as muscular, with that amazingly handsome face that was so alien to anger.

"Rubbish," Jesse said. "If I were as calculating as you say, I would have been very different toward both of you."

"What would you have done to me, try to get me away from Gemma?" It was out in the open, finally, in a way Jonathan hadn't planned or expected, had deliberately avoided. It was only the tip of the iceberg, anyway; he wanted to confront his father about himself, not about Gemma.

They were watching each other guardedly, in heavy silence, when Madeleine came in.

Madeleine's eyes went from one tense face to the other. "Hello, you two," she said.

Jonathan glanced at his father's face, then at his mother's, still as animated as it had ever been, despite the faint traces age had begun to make. The room felt less confining and the atmosphere less oppressive because of her.

"You're looking very smart and efficient," he said, admiring her gray linen dress and coat.

"We have to be efficient," Madeleine said, with a wink. "It's the only way to win elections."

"A lot can happen to that power-mad Bolshevik before the election," Jesse said.

"I'm aware of that." Madeleine smiled. "I hope it's all good."

Jonathan stirred, straightened his tie and buttoned his jacket. "I think I'll go out for a while, it's still early." He kissed Madeleine, waved at both of them and went out.

"What happened?" Madeleine asked.

"I don't know what's got into him," Jesse snapped. "He's behaving like someone else."

"He's tired," Madeleine temporized. "He needs a rest."

"Tired! His last night at home and you know where he's going, don't you?"

Madeleine moved away to pour herself a glass of sherry. "He's twenty-eight years old, Jesse."

"He doesn't show such ardor for activity in office hours."

"I'm not surprised and neither are you," Madeleine answered. "It was never what he wanted."

"Then what *does* he want?" he demanded viciously. "To spend all his days, as well as his nights, in bed with his trollop?"

"That's a filthy thing to say. She has nothing to do with Jonnie's career—and she's not a trollop."

"Isn't she? She sleeps with a man she's not married to, even if he *is* my son, and he gives her money for it. It's been going on for years. She's no better than a prostitute!" Two red spots appeared on his cheeks and his eyes glittered.

Madeleine put down her sherry. "You'll lose him if you go on like this. You know that, don't you?"

The soft words were like a dash of cold water. He stopped talking and a quiet pervaded him that was familiar to her: it meant he was thinking furiously, appraising the problem from every angle and looking for a clever way to resolve it to his satisfaction.

She was under no illusion that he had changed in any basic way, but if she no longer hoped the inner man would ever emerge, at least she could manage to live with the present facsimile. She could never have intervened with him for her son the way things were before they reconciled.

"You have to let him live his private life as he likes, Jesse. He gives you his best in business."

"His best is less than I expected."

"That may be, but it's better than not having him with you at all. Once he settles down, with Gemma or not, things may improve—or," she added, "you may decide to let him go."

"Never! You're a fool even to suggest such a thing."

She stiffened. "Don't talk to me like that, Jesse, I won't stand for it!"

He quelled his temper immediately. She thought it was out of his need for her as an ally, rather than out of contrition, but it gratified her nonetheless.

"I apologize," he said formally. Then he shook his head. "But I don't understand him—he's lost all sense of obligation to his heritage, to his family, to me, damn it, to *me!* I'm his *father!* I never forgot my responsibil-

273

ity to *my* father." He shook his head again. "The world's gone crazy. The business life of this country is being threatened by a tidal wave of regulations, my family fortune leeched away by taxes, and my only son has no sense of loyalty or direction."

"He's loyal, Jesse, you know that. With time he'll find his own direction. At least Susannah has hers, that ought to be a comfort to you."

"Thank heaven for her," Jesse agreed, his manner less rigid. "She understands geopolitics."

"I meant the new baby," Madeleine said.

"Yes, *she's* having children, when it's Jonathan who should be."

"Come on, Jesse, let's go up, it's late."

"You go along. I'll be up soon."

She knew he would stay there, brooding far into the night, but she left him and went upstairs. She might never get to the best of Jesse, but she could certainly keep the worst of him at bay. Somewhere between the two extremes was the man she had to live with for the rest of her life.

Daisy was waiting to help her undress and prepare for bed. She always matched her mood to Madeleine's, but tonight she was unusually quiet. It was not until Madeleine got into bed and saw the Boston newspaper, folded to the society page, on her night table that she understood why.

Dr. Edward Randall Driscoll, the newspaper said, had returned from Vienna for a brief visit to his parents. He had been accompanied by his Austrian-born wife and their three-year-old daughter.

Madeleine looked at Daisy, unsure of precisely what she felt.

"I came by it accidentally," Daisy said apologetically. "One of the girls comes from Boston and takes it regular. I didn't want you to be surprised by the news."

"It's all right, Daisy. I'm glad you showed it to me."

"Oh, Miss Madeleine, it's never a real love match," Daisy offered plaintively.

"That doesn't make any difference," Madeleine said.

"I know," Daisy whispered, "I know." She paused for a moment. "Can I get you anything, Miss Madeleine?"

"No, thank you, Daisy, I have everything I need. Go along now and don't worry, it's all right."

Alone in her bedroom, Madeleine turned out the light. "Oh, Daisy, what a liar I am," she sighed softly in the dark.

55

Jonathan spent a week in Kent with Philippa, her amiable husband, and her large and fashionable brood. He was very comfortable with his Uncle Elton, a handsome squire with a silver mustache and a kindly air. Philippa asked a lot of questions, but Elton never pried.

He cut short his time in Paris. He was eager to see Victor after so many years, with only letters to keep the friendship alive. He had never met Victor's family and he was filled with anticipation when the train finally rolled into the Berlin station, with its roof of opaque glass panes, and came to a ponderous halt at *Bahnsteig* number one.

He spotted Victor and waved to him from the rolled-down window of the carriage. Then he ran along the corridor and down the iron steps.

"I thought you'd never get here," Victor said, with a bear hug. "You look older," he added, standing back. "Is everything all right?"

"I *am* older," Jonathan laughed. "So are you. By God, it's good to see you again. Letters don't really do it."

"No—but come on, we'll arrange to have your bags sent on to the house. I have a new Aston-Martin—bought in your honor—and we can't ruin its lines with baggage."

Minutes later they were in the blue sports car, driving through Berlin. It was bristling with new construction for the Olympic games. Again and again they passed the Nazi banner, blood red around a white circle with a cruel black symbol at its heart.

"Das Hakenkreuz," Victor said. "The hooked cross."

"Ugly thing," Jonathan said, frowning. "Doesn't all this Nazi business worry you?"

"I worry sometimes, but not my father. He has an aristocratic contempt for popular heroes, like the rest of the establishment. The financiers are afraid of Communism; the generals are monarchists to a man and afraid of the Weimar Republic; and all of them are afraid of Russia. They think Hitler is a lesser evil who can be controlled."

"And his mania about Jews?"

Victor shifted gears and the car's roar changed to a purr. "We're part of the German industrial establishment. No politician can survive without us, not even Adolf Hitler."

"My father called him 'that Austrian rabble-rouser,'" Jonathan said, "when the Jewish war vets marched to protest German anti-Semitism."

Victor glanced at him. "Surely old Jesse hasn't developed any love for Jews."

Jonathan's smile was bleak. "Hardly. He gives an even wider berth to the lower classes. He says Hitler's appeal is to the masses and 'our people' will use him for a time and then dispose of him."

Victor nodded. "By 'our people' he means the munitions and chemical industrialists—and synthetics researchers, like me." He threw back his head and laughed. "Does your father realize I'm one of 'his' people?"

"He knows the Kastenberg Chemie has been virtually absorbed by the I.G. Farben cartel, along with every other chemical plant of any value in Germany."

"Well, there you are, Jon, old man, we're safe. Now never mind all this, tell me about Susannah and Gemma and your mother."

He told Victor about Susannah's summer work, about Madeleine's political organizations, and about Gemma. "I think I'm going to marry Gemma."

Victor revved the powerful engine twice by way of approval. "That's great! When?"

"There's nothing definite. I haven't told her yet."

"Ah," Victor said. "Then you're still not absolutely certain! You ought to try someone else."

"I have," Jonathan said, "now and then, but it's the damnedest thing, I don't want anyone else. That should be enough for marriage."

"It would be for me, if I could find a Gemma," Victor answered, shifting down as the car turned into a residential area of broad, shaded boulevards. "But you *believe* all the fantasies they spin, the books and ballets and the operas about fairy princesses."

"Not really," Jonathan said. "Not any more." He smiled. "I really am older, Victor. Perhaps it's just as well."

The car stopped on the wide, quiet Bundes-Allee in front of an imposing house, set well back behind iron gates in a leafy park splattered with roses. It was built of stone similar to the brownstones in New York, but it had weathered differently. It was straight and spare and devoid of extraneous decoration, and it was apparent that wealth and culture lived here, and a long tradition.

"Home," Victor said.

"Stately. Doesn't look a thing like you."

Victor agreed, getting out of the car. "We hope I'll grow into it when I mature and take life seriously."

A footman in a striped apron appeared to take the car and the two young men started up the walk to the door.

The hall inside was very wide, paneled in wood, and sparsely furnished for its size. A great refectory table, polished to perfection, was almost lost against one wall. A huge Flemish tapestry—very fine, Jonathan thought—hung above it.

On the other side of the hall was a low, round table surrounded by four severe brown plush chairs. An enormous carpet in muted Oriental design covered the marble squares of the floor. In a recess on one side of the wide center staircase a marvelous clock surveyed the hall, more like a prime minister than a grandfather. The companion recess on the other side of the stairway held a slim, exquisitely shaped marble urn, some six feet high.

"It's beautiful," Jonathan said, looking around him.

"A bit old-fashioned after the new world," Victor said, "but I love old-fashioned things."

"So do I," Jonathan said. "I've always felt comfortable over here. It has charm. It's not so brash and busy as America."

"Come into the garden and meet Mother and Marietta."

Jonathan followed him toward the back of the mansion and through curtained French doors, open to the fine weather. The garden was large and informal, with several venerable trees scattered over it to shade a comfortable chair here, a swinging settee there. Like the house, it had been planned for comfort and weathered by time.

At the far end two women were seated near a table, one sitting upright with needlepoint and the other on a lounge with a book. They looked up when Victor called to them.

"Here he is at last. Mother, this is Jonathan Slayter."

Jonathan bowed to Frau Kastenberg and saluted her extended hand. He spoke to her in German and she smiled. She had a sweet face and the serenity of a woman who had been cherished all her life. He could not help comparing that to his own mother's very different experience. He straightened, charmed by the warmth of her welcome.

"This," Victor said with unmistakable pride, "is Marietta," and Jonathan turned.

His easy social smile deserted him. He looked down at an unconventionally lovely face with dark brown eyes heavily shadowed by long lashes. She smiled and extended her hand and he took it, feeling as young as she was.

"I've heard a lot about you," he said. Why hadn't he paid more attention to news of her in Victor's letters?

"As I have about you." Her voice was low and husky.

He remembered his manners and released her hand when he turned to Victor. "What have you told her?"

"I forget. Would you like tea or lemonade?"

277

"He calls you the playboy of the Western world," Marietta said in English. "He says no woman is safe with you. I couldn't wait to meet you." Her eyes smiled at him, but carefully, from a distance, he thought.

They spent that first evening at home and Jonathan was immediately aware of how different this family was from his. They were happy, they enjoyed each other.

He was very much aware of Marietta too, the way her heavy, shining hair moved, the faintly accented way she pronounced his name, the subtle distance she kept between them, as if she were not sure precisely what kind of man he was.

It disturbed him; no one had ever questioned the role he had always assumed: that of an attractive, carefree man who preferred diversion to the glum realities of business. He had never really questioned it himself.

He played tennis with Victor and Herr Kastenberg the next morning, the father like a large square model from the same maker as his sleek and sporty son. They had a swim and lunch at the tennis club and Jonathan met some of the young people Victor had invited to a party that night.

Jonathan was not in the big salon when Marietta began to play that evening, but somehow he knew it was she and he went into the room to listen, overwhelmed by the quality of it. He had supposed she was too young, too innocent to play with such a depth of passion.

From the ceiling-high window where he stood watching her, an awareness came to him of the personality behind Marietta's classic profile, the quiet strength of it and its purity of purpose, qualities he already admired so much in her brother. It disturbed him to see that a young man, introduced earlier as Franz something-or-other, was turning pages for her when she had no need of notes. Jonathan realized, now that he thought of it, that this Franz had been at her side all evening.

A while later, he managed to speak to her at a little distance from the others.

"I had no idea you played so well," he said, and realized how pompous he sounded. "I wish I were half as good," he added.

"I'm sure you're much better," she said politely, but her velvety brown eyes still regarded him warily. He stood there, at a loss; then suddenly he knew why she was wary of him and he had to explain.

"It isn't true, you know," he said, his expression entreating her to believe him. "That 'playboy' business, I mean."

The look in her eyes changed and she regarded him for a long moment, then nodded. "I know, it's just something that's expected of you, isn't it?"

"Yes," he said, knowing all at once that this was so. "Yes, but I'm not like that at all, it's just that I never met a girl like you." He broke off and colored, incredulous that his sophistication should have deserted him. For the first time since he was sixteen years old, he did not know what to say to a woman.

Someone—he saw with annoyance that it was Franz—called to her and she waved back and turned to Jonathan to excuse herself.

"Don't go," he said urgently, not suggestively as he usually did when a woman interested him. He said it as if he needed to see her there.

"I must go," she said softly, reluctantly, and then her hand touched his and he wondered if she were as enchanted as he. "Tomorrow," she said before she left him, "we'll talk tomorrow."

But on the next day it was hard for him to find anything to say, and the same reserve seemed to have descended on her. Instead, they played music together on the two massive, glossy black pianos in an airy corner of the salon, and it seemed to Jonathan that he was closer to her through music than he had ever been to any woman, without so much as a kiss. And still he hadn't the courage to ask her—except with his eyes—if she felt the same chord between them.

Later that day, in the garden, in the midst of animated talk, Jonathan was filled with sadness and knew that despite his surface gaiety he had always been. He had always felt as if his heart had no place to call its own. Gemma was a haven for him, but not what he hungered for, although he didn't know why.

It came to him when he was dressing for dinner. He needed Gemma and love should not come from need alone but of itself, because it just had to be. A shadow passed over his face. It was too late for him. He had long since lost the innocence for the kind of love Marietta would offer and expect in return. It would be better if he did not prolong this dream of love.

Yet it went on, the speechless, powerful communication between them when they were at the pianos together, until it was time for the Kastenbergs to leave for their summer chalet in Zurich. They were not staying in Berlin for the Olympics. "We're not particularly comfortable near crowds," Victor had told him, and there had been enough incidents involving Jews to explain why.

"Must you go?" Jonathan said to Marietta as they were closing the pianos. It was a foolish thing to ask.

She looked at him with those exquisite eyes he had committed to memory and already missed in anticipation of leaving her. "Come with us," she said, and looked away, half embarrassed by her boldness.

"Yes," he said immediately, "I will," and felt that he had been granted a reprieve.

He drove to Zurich with Victor while the Kastenbergs and Marietta took the train. It would give him an opportunity to talk to Victor about her.

56

The countryside was the loveliest in Europe, but it was scarred for Jonathan by the hooked cross erupting like an insult in every village.

"What will you do if Farben deserts you?" he asked Victor.

"Wait for it to blow over. Not all of them are insane."

"Do you think that would be safe for Marietta?"

Victor glanced at him. "You like my little sister, don't you? I noticed."

Jonathan nodded. "I wish you hadn't told her I was a playboy."

"Just playing it safe, old man. All women fall for you. I can't have my sister losing her heart."

"Why not?" Jonathan rested his head against the car seat and watched the blue sky rush by. Victor glanced at the handsome face again and realized that this was no laughing matter to Jonathan. He shook his head. "No, Jon, it wouldn't do at all."

"Why not?" Jonathan said again.

"She's too young, to start with, only nineteen. Remember how you felt when Susannah got married, and she was twenty-two and a lot more sophisticated than Marietta."

Jonathan crouched down out of the wind to light two cigarettes and pass one to Victor. "I don't think that's your real reason. I'd like to know what it is."

The wind whipped Victor's hair for a moment before he answered. "Not your wild oats, certainly. Not *you* at all, as a matter of fact. It's your father."

"My father?" Jonathan looked at him in surprise.

"Can you imagine how he'd treat a Jewish girl? I handled it, but I'm a man and I was used to it. Not Marietta; she takes things seriously."

"Religion too?"

"Enough to marry her own kind."

"Damn it, Victor, you sound just like my father! All this talk about one 'kind' or another is stupid, no matter who's talking."

"I grant you that, but that's the way things are. It's academic, anyhow, isn't it? You said you'd decided to marry Gemma."

"There's nothing definite."

The Aston-Martin took a sharp curve in the mountain road, then another before Victor spoke again. "I'm sorry to say this, Jon, but I'd like your word that you won't put any romantic nonsense into Marietta's head. It isn't as if you were sure of your own feelings." Victor waited anxiously.

Jonathan nodded. "If that's how you feel."

Victor put a hand on his arm briefly. "Please don't take it like that, old man. I feel Victorian enough as it is. You'd have done the same for Susannah if a spectacular blond socialite got off the train practically married to one woman and then got sentimental about your sister."

Jonathan smiled despite himself. "I suppose I would."

"Give it time," Victor suggested. "You don't even know each other well enough to see that it wouldn't work."

They left it at that, but Jonathan knew Victor was right. Marietta was the only woman he had ever thought of in quite this way, but because he was Jesse Slayter's son it was pointless for him to pursue the feeling. His father's prejudice was not the only hold on him; there was Gemma too. He was suddenly not proud of how he had treated Gemma, never mind that everything had always been honest and open between them.

The chalet, in the hills behind Zurich, was perfection. When he was not sailing or swimming with Victor, he was with Marietta, often playing the pianos in the chalet's music room. Every time he looked at her he yearned to take her in his arms, feel her softness close against him. He did not dare.

That brief exchange with Victor on the road from Berlin censored everything he said to her too. He knew it confused her. With her exquisite sensitivity she sensed both the yearning in him and the holding back, but she could not, he must not, tell her either feeling because, in all honor, he did not have the right.

On his last day, when she turned from him to say what she could not keep from saying, he knew he loved her.

"Must you leave so soon?" she said in her husky voice.

Come with me, he pleaded with her silently, *come with me, never leave me,* but he thought of Jesse and of Gemma and all he said was, "I've stayed too long already."

He saw her deny that with a shake of her head. "Perhaps you'll come this winter for the skiing," she said, still unable to look at him. He was devastated by her confusion with a man. The women he knew suffered no such embarrassments.

"I'll try," he said, and thought, *I want to hold you, I want to know you, I want to love you for the rest of my life.*

The thought of returning to New York, to the dreary figures of his working day and the demands made upon him in his father's house, was appalling to him. He knew he would turn to Gemma for comfort and that appalled him too, because it was so utterly selfish.

When he left the chalet and the car pulled away to take him to the train, the last thing he saw was the sun on Marietta's hair. He thought about her constantly while he was with his uncle and Dominique, but each time it was with regret, not hope or anticipation. He felt everything had been decided for him long ago. He must have known he would walk into a strange garden one day and find her, the one woman who had made all the others, even Gemma, seem not quite "enough" by comparison.

But Jonathan knew that no Jewish girl would consider marrying into a family like his. He would have to remember those three weeks of summer with her as he would an enchanting play now finished, the curtain rung down and everyone gone except himself. That was how it would be, no matter how long he stayed in the darkened, empty theater of his life, hoping for the play to begin again.

He knew now why he had not married Gemma, and before the *Ile de France* was two days out on the return voyage, he knew he never would.

57

1938

"When did *he* get here?" Jonathan asked Willis Blake. He pointed to Karl-Dieter Veidt's wide-brimmed felt hat and fur-collared coat on a chair.

Willis rose from his desk. "Just a few minutes ago, Mister Jonathan." Willis was apologetic. "Mr. Slayter wasn't expecting him." He made haste to put the hat and coat in a closet.

Jonathan turned toward the door of his father's office and Willis held his breath. He relaxed when Jonathan moved away. "As soon as he leaves, I'd like to see Mr. Slayter," he said over his shoulder.

Willis made nervous little gestures of assurance as Jonathan went back to his own office. It was even money that the young man would call his sister about this. He always did when something important came up, and Willis knew that Jonathan considered visits from abroad important. Visits from German nationals had made him particularly peppery since his trip to Europe two years ago, and the sound of angry voices, even muffled by the heavy door to Jesse's office, were audible to Willis after every one of them.

"I don't know what's got into him," Willis would say that night to his colorless wife. "He never argued with the old man before. Nobody argues with Jesse Slayter."

Mrs. Blake, dreaming of Gary Cooper's embrace, always shook her head and wondered what the world was coming to.

"Nothing good," Willis grumbled, alarming his wife, as he had intended. "I know—I'm lucky I still have my job, but the bonuses have stopped, haven't they, and the yearly salary increases."

His wife's observation that 1938 would be another bad year for everyone infuriated him. "Not for the rich!" he shouted.

"Maybe you'll move to a broker's desk next year," was his wife's idea of comfort.

"Shut up," Willis told her. "What do you know about it? I'm Jesse Slayter's chief clerk and I will be—if I'm lucky—for the rest of my life. And I care about it! I'm not like Jonathan Slayter, who doesn't even want what's being handed to him on a silver platter, or that sister of his who's not content with what she already has."

Someday he was going to get his own back from Jesse Slayter for all he had lost in the Crash. No sympathy, either, not from him, but Willis wasn't interested in sympathy, he was interested in the little deals Slayter pulled that no one knew about, not even his snotty daughter.

Karl-Dieter Veidt changed little over the years. He had always been a chill, pale presence. He was still spare and wiry and he exuded more power each time he came to see Jesse.

"My dear colleague," Veidt purred from his usual seat across the desk from Jesse. "Such a pleasure to see you."

"Unexpected," was Jesse's pointed comment. Few people dared to call on Jesse Slayter without an appointment.

The point was not taken. "Just so. I was passing through and thought to give you my observation of developments."

Veidt's observations had consistently channeled profits in Jesse's direction. Most of Veidt's business in New York was with the oil industry, and in each step of that intricate gavotte there was money to be made.

Veidt began to polish his glasses, speaking very softly as he did.

"You have heard of Butyl rubber?"

Jesse nodded. "Standard's answer to your Buna. I understand you've already been given the Butyl technology."

"Just so, but it has been decided to halt the development in the United States of this technology."

Jesse's eyebrow rose. "So the exchange of know-how remains a one-way street."

Veidt closed his eyes briefly in assent.

They chatted a few moments more before Veidt left, but the business of the day had been accomplished. The information meant he would invest massively in I.G. Farben's rubber research because there would be no competition from Germany's chief challenger in the field. I.G. was ready to share the markets, no doubt, but not the know-how, and it was in the production of a vital material that the greatest profits lay.

Jesse was smiling to himself over that prospect when Jonathan came in.

"But you're letting politics cloud your thinking again," Jesse said to Jonathan, trying to control his temper. Jonathan had been meddling in things that did not concern him since he returned from Europe. "Bankers have no politics. Our sole function is to make profits, not moral judgments."

"*Your* sole function, perhaps, not mine." Jonathan spoke in that resolute tone he had recently acquired. "I'm not a complete fool, you know. You're heavily invested in German industry. I don't trust them any more than I do that slimy little character, Veidt."

Jesse's voice rose. "You sound like a child! There are many Germans, not just the types currently in the public eye. The real power is still in the right hands, where it's always been. Veidt is part of the Establishment and the German Establishment is *using* the Nazi party."

"Not anymore. It was Nazi policy to invade Austria. It was Nazi policy to use Spain as a proving ground for new weapons. It's all Hitler—I hate the man and his filthy theories."

Jesse ignored the reference to war. "This is what comes of your association with that Jewish boy."

"He has nothing to do with it. I have a few original ideas of my own, you know." He glared at his father. "You dislike Irish Catholics as much as Jews, anyway. Why?"

"They're alien," Jesse said. "They have foreign notions, like all immigrants. The Irish Catholics are crazy and the Jews are Bolsheviks."

"What a first-class bigot you are!"

Jesse leaned forward angrily. "And you're an ignorant young puppy."

"So you've been at pains to tell me often enough."

They eyed each other. Jesse had a sense of déjà vu: Daniel and Jethro had faced each other years ago in just this way, here in this very office. The father had prevailed then and he would now.

"I find your sudden interest in my affairs curious," Jesse said in his coolest voice. "You've never come up with an original plan for the firm, not even a sound acquisition, which is supposed to be your area. Your sister does it for you—don't think I'm not aware of it—and all else aside, I want that to stop. Pay more attention to what's going on here. International investments are my affair."

Jonathan shook his head in disbelief. "Doesn't it concern you at all that your own brother is in Spain, fighting against Franco and his Nazi backers?"

"Daniel always wanted a ringside seat at an apocalypse. It was to be expected," Jesse said loftily. "I don't base my decisions on your uncle's opinions—or yours."

"Then it won't matter if I leave this company." Jonathan got up.

It was the first time he had ever made such a threat, and Jesse was alarmed because it was clearly not an idle one. A split between Jesse and his son was unthinkable. It would be the subject of gossip throughout the banking world.

"Jonathan, listen," he temporized. "You didn't even look behind the scenes when you were in Germany. Veidt is only an errand boy. Why don't you go back on a working trip now, meet our associates, talk to the banks

287

yourself? Is it reasonable for you to decide critical investment policy without taking a closer look?" He saw the idea beginning to take hold of his son and leaned back in his chair. "Be fair. It's been two years since you were abroad."

Jonathan's blue eyes narrowed doubtfully, as if he were looking for another meaning behind the words.

"Jonathan, please," Jesse said. "A son means everything to his father, someday you'll understand that. I need you, I rely on you." His eyes dropped in embarrassment. "I speak harshly sometimes and it hides my affection for you, but that's just my way."

Jonathan accepted; like Madeleine, he had never been able to resist anyone who loved him.

On the whole, Jesse decided, it had been a good day's work. He was still mulling it over, and only remembered that Madeleine was giving a party when he got home and saw the flower-decked entrance hall. The occasion was frivolous, like everything else she did: it was a party to celebrate spring. She'd probably put on that Stravinsky thing later, a barbarous piece of music, pagan in every sense of the word.

The idea of a party annoyed him; he had planned to sit at his desk and think tonight, but he went upstairs quickly to bathe and change. It would not look well if he were not downstairs to receive with his wife.

It was a word he liked to use now in reference to Madeleine, but he was not really thinking about her. He was concentrating on the infinite possibilities of a rubber monopoly during a war, and he felt a thrill of anticipation, an almost sensual shiver.

58

"Oh, Jonnie, you're exaggerating," Susannah said. "Slayter's isn't subsidizing the Nazis." She kept her voice low, even with the party noises of the house. She and Charles were in a corner of the dining room, talking to Jonathan and Gemma.

"We help finance I.G. Farben; it amounts to the same thing."

The four were silent for a moment, among the well-tailored men and beautifully gowned women who filled the ground floor of the mansion.

"Veidt was in again today," Jonathan went on. "He's a typical I.G. Farben man. They'll support any government that supports them, no matter how barbaric it is." He looked around the small circle. "I told Jesse I'd resign if he kept on."

Susannah's face showed fresh surprise. "You must have had one whale of a fight. How did it end?"

"He suggested that I go back to Europe." This time Jonathan looked at Gemma. It was rotten to break it to her like this, but he had lacked the courage to tell her when he picked her up for the party. "I agreed."

"But what can you possibly change by going to Europe?" Gemma said, trying to make it a question, not a plea.

"Father says I didn't meet enough I.G. people last time to justify making such a decision."

Charles smiled. "You'd have to meet God Almighty for him to listen to anything you said, and even then I wouldn't count on a fair hearing."

Susannah was impatient. "Don't, Charles. This is far too important for you to score points against my father." She turned to her brother. "It's probably a good idea for you to go. At least we'll know more about what we're involved in. Sometimes I don't like the whole thing."

"And if it's as Jon thinks, what could either of you do about it?" Charles persisted.

"If I.G. is just a Nazi subsidiary now, then Slayter's can't back I.G.," Jonathan said, determined.

Susannah looked doubtful. "I don't think Father would agree. The Nazis were elected legally."

"Not to start a war! I'll get out of Slayter's," Jonathan said angrily. "It's called J. Slayter and Son, damn it, and I'm not lending my name to people like that, not even from behind a desk."

289

"You'd have a lot better chance of changing things if you stayed," Charles said. "You'll have no control over him at all from outside the company."

Jonathan stopped to think about that and a faint change of expression crossed Susannah's face, but neither of them said anything. It was Gemma who spoke.

"Calm down, darling," she said. She had never seen Jonathan so furious, and her life was devoted to making him happy, at no matter what cost to herself. "Wait until you've seen for yourself."

Jonathan let it rest. At least he had Susannah's support and the hardest part of the evening—telling Gemma—was over. He wanted to enjoy his mother's party and excusing himself, he went to ask her to dance with him.

She enjoyed dancing, but she always had. He wondered how her face would look if she were dancing with someone else. He had never told her that he knew about Ned Driscoll.

He whirled her smoothly to "Linger Awhile." She was a marvelous dancer, full of rhythm, and a quick follower. Marietta must be a beautiful dancer too.

"I'm going to Europe on business," he said suddenly, although he hadn't intended to say it in the middle of the dance floor. As superficially as possible, he told her of his doubts about the German government's policies.

"Then of course you must go," she said. Madeleine was what Jesse called a Bolshevik sympathizer and what Susannah called a romantic Socialist. She called herself a liberal, to Jesse's disgust, and she didn't like Hitler "because he wants to tell people what to do."

"What does Gemma think of your trip?" she asked him.

He colored. "I don't know yet, I just told her a few minutes ago when I told Charles and Susannah."

The music ended and they walked toward the drawing room. "Not very gallant of you, was it?" she said.

"No, but we're not married, after all, and she knows we won't be."

"If you're not going to marry her, then stop seeing her."

"I've tried. She says she doesn't care about marriage, she's content to go on as we are."

"She loves you, Jonathan! Don't you know she'll accept any arrangement in order to keep you and still go on hoping for marriage when you stay."

He was silent, thinking it was a cruel habit of humankind to go on hoping. His mother watched his face, handsome and remote, drained now of the candor of youth. "Is there someone else, Jon?" It was the first time it had occurred to her.

His eyes met hers briefly, full of pain.

"Oh, Jonnie, who is it?" she whispered, looking at his stricken face.

"No one, nothing, a kind of dream," he said, shaking his head. "It's an impossible situation."

She assumed he was in love with a married woman and he was too young to settle for such a liaison. He must be suffering the same kind of desolation as Ned throughout their half life together.

"Maybe going away is good for more than one reason," she said.

He only nodded and kissed her hand before he left her. He felt terribly guilty. He had not arranged this trip to Europe, it was entirely his father's suggestion, but since that afternoon he had let himself think about Marietta again.

Yes, it was cruel to go on hoping. He understood now how it was for Gemma. He had to tell her it was over between them.

"Didn't they look gorgeous dancing together?" Charles said.

Gemma took another glass of champagne from a passing tray. "Susannah and her father, or Jon and his mother?"

"Both, actually, but I was talking about my lady and Rasputin."

Gemma giggled, despite her hurt that Jonathan was leaving. "Does old Jesse think you talk about him like that?"

"Old Jesse doesn't think of me at all. I'm merely a consort to his princess."

"Well, you do your job! Two strapping sons!"

"By no means an extraordinary number." He smiled to Susannah across the dancers and raised his glass to her.

"From the look in your eye you're planning to have more."

Charles glanced at her. From anyone else it would have been an invasion of privacy, but Gemma was genuinely interested in her friends. "I shall approach Susannah and sound her out on the subject," he said.

That provoked a hearty laugh, the first from Gemma this evening. "I always knew you'd liberate the real Susannah," Gemma said with satisfaction. "I'm glad for both of you."

Gemma was an unusual girl, Charles reflected. It did not seem to matter that they had once been to bed together—and they had been memorable occasions too—because she never alluded to it, not even with that perpetual pride of ownership most women show around yesterday's lovers. Anyway, it had been years ago, before Susannah and Jonathan Slayter came into their respective lives and made them both forget that other men and women were alive.

291

"I wish I could say I'm as glad for you," Charles told Gemma, really meaning it.

"One of these days, maybe," was all she said.

Gemma's going-nowhere affair angered Charles sometimes. He was fond of Jonathan, but there was an area of weakness in his nature that was unexpected, considering who his father and sister were—and Madeleine had a mind of her own too, when the chips were down. After all, Gemma had lost her father, her financial security, and her place in society—the last because of Jonathan. If Jon made her life a little easier, he certainly owed her that, but she deserved far more.

"Well, just remember I'm around if you ever need help. Come on, I'll take you over to Jon and retrieve my wife."

But Jonathan was talking to some of his father's Washington connections, and Gemma, who always felt uncomfortable around her dead father's erst-while colleagues, went off to find some friends, leaving Charles and Susannah together.

"You look sensational," Charles said, leading Susannah expertly into a tango.

"I feel sensational. It's this red dress. Do you think it's too flashy?" She spun away from him. She loved the tango and tonight she felt particularly festive, even after her brother's troubling news.

"It's not the color," Charles said when they came together again. "It's you." When the dance ended his eyes admired the slim satin sheath with its low-cut back and deep cowl bodice. She had never worn red before and it suited her. She wore only earrings—rubies set in seed pearls—and the wide white-gold bracelet, rimmed with diamonds, he had given her when John Slayter was born two years ago. It was engraved inside with the baby's birth date and the words *Always and all ways, Charles.* He thought he *would* like another child, a daughter, like her.

"That was a beautiful tango," Madeleine's voice applauded as she approached them. "Everyone was watching you two." She hesitated. "What do you make of Jon's news?"

"I think it's a good idea," Susannah said carefully, not sure how much Jonathan had told her about the clash with Jesse. "He might like the international side of finance."

"I don't think he likes any side of finance," Madeleine said, "but a change will do him good." She was preoccupied, even as she turned away to talk to some guests.

"It's amazing," Charles said, watching his mother-in-law. "She must be the most glorious grandmother in the world and he"—he inclined his head in Jesse's direction—"hardly leaves his office to look at her these days."

"For heaven's sake, they've been married for almost thirty-four years. By then you won't look at me either."

"Only if I'm dead," Charles said.

"There," Susannah said, relieved. "He's dancing with her now."

"Glory hallelujah!" Charles said. "Can you imagine what they were like when they were young?"

"I don't have to imagine, I can remember."

They watched the older couple dancing to the "Merry Widow Waltz." Madeleine had never worn the skinny dresses that were in fashion. Her evening dress was black chiffon made with a full skirt and a wide bertha of filigree lace. Her magnificent shoulders rose like cream from the cloud of black. There were diamonds at her ears, throat, and wrists. Jesse's tail coat emphasized his height and his dark eyes. His linen was as snowy as his hair. They were a striking couple and they danced well together.

"I was wondering when you'd get around to me," Madeleine said.

Jesse smiled. "I had to do my duty dances first. Charles's mother has no sense of rhythm, and the less said about my partners' wives, the better."

"The less said about your partners, the better. Now that I've finally got you to myself, tell me about Jonathan. Why is he going away?"

"I need some information," he replied easily. "He wants to go and get it for me. What's he been telling you?"

"Pretty much the same thing," she said, and it seemed to him she was not quite convinced. "I just wondered," she went on. "He's so unhappy lately."

"Unhappy?" Jesse shrugged. "Only a fool expects to be anything else these days. You fuss over him too much."

"I wish he'd marry," Madeleine said. "He needs a wife to fuss over him."

"He can always marry *her.*" Jesse never referred to Gemma in any other way, and Madeleine had never asked him why he had suddenly stopped plaguing Jonathan about Gemma.

"You're still the best dancer in the world," she said. "I love waltzing with you."

"You could have done that without inviting half New York to watch."

"You wouldn't be here except for this party. It was the only thing I could think of to get you home before ten o'clock—and even then you'd forgotten about it."

Jesse said nothing, but a slight move of his head indicated that she was right.

293

"Anyway," Madeleine went on, "it's a better party than the stuffy ones we usually go to, where you and all the great goddamns talk about nothing but finance. Why are businessmen such cultural illiterates?" Her smile took the sting out of the words.

"That doesn't follow simply because they don't like those filthy books everyone's reading and that wild music they call 'modern.' Why don't they bring back pagan rituals and have done with it?"

"I wouldn't mind being pagan in the least," she said. "As a matter of fact, it's been quite a while since we were."

He glanced quickly at the dancers near them. "This isn't the place to talk about that," he said, more pleased than not.

"We didn't talk about it the first time we danced together, but it was on both our minds."

"You don't care what you say, do you?"

She shook her head and winked at him wickedly. "Not at my time of life."

"Do you suppose we might finish this in silence?" he said. When she was like this he didn't know quite what to do with her.

She inclined her head with a polite smile and they went on dancing. What she said had made him more aware of her physically. He could feel the warmth of her body under his hand, and he was very conscious now of her beauty, which seemed never to change and always to tempt him. It kept a man young to be aroused by a woman. "A woman," someone had said, "is a dish for the gods, if the devil dress her not." Madeleine had been "dressed" by the devil, but she was a dish he planned to savor when this party was over.

Madeleine danced, thinking once more that it was nicer to seduce Jesse than to anger him. There had been so much anger between them in the past; there would probably be more when she discovered what he was up to with Jonathan. There was no point in pretending that Jesse wasn't always up to something.

I don't care, she thought. *They're playing all the songs I love in waltz time and I don't want to think about anything.*

She was having a hard time blinking back the tears in her eyes. She was dancing as she had long ago, when she was young and in love for the first time with the same man who held her now. She could remember when Jesse was her Wonderful One, when she knew he would love her always.

I suppose he does, she thought, *in his way. I don't think he knows how to love in my way.*

Suddenly she was thinking of Ned. Ned had known what she meant by love. Where was he now? Once in a while, over the years, his name was mentioned by someone who knew him. He was in Europe; he was back and teaching somewhere in New England where he had his practice now; he was in Europe again for a symposium. He was one of the best-known men in his field.

It was hard to believe that she had once been ready to leave Jesse, divorced or not, to go away with another man. It was hard to believe that another man had ever held her in his arms with a different kind of rapture from what Jesse felt.

She was suddenly heavy with a sorrow she did not want to understand, that it would be dangerous to investigate.

Then the set ended and she left Jesse and went to smile and talk to her guests, thinking that she would go to see her grandchildren every day while Jonathan was away, that she would spend more time with Gemma.

She hoped Jon would settle something with Gemma before he left for Europe. Either way, Gemma was going to need a friend.

59

It was almost two o'clock when Jonathan and Gemma walked into her apartment in the Village and sat down formally in the living room, as if they had never shared their bodies before.

"I'll be going back and forth to Europe all the time now, Gem," Jonathan said. "I'll see you less and less."

"I could go with you," she said, barely audible.

"That would be too much for my father." He felt sick at his own duplicity.

Only one lamp burned in the living room. Gemma clutched her evening cape around her as if she were cold and reached for a cigarette from an alabaster box on the end table. The heavy box slipped out of her hand and fell to the floor with a thump, scattering Camels on the carpet. He came to help her pick them up, but she had hidden her face in the sofa cushions and her shoulders shook.

He sat next to her, determined to end it now for both their sakes. "Gemma, we've got to put an end to this. It isn't fair to you, it never has been."

"No," she said tightly, trying not to cry. "But I never asked that it be fair. Just don't leave me, Jonnie, please don't end it unless there's someone else." She waited a breathless moment before she asked, "Is there?"

He hardly knew what to tell her. Could he say he was drawn to Marietta in a way he had never known before? Could he say he needed time to see where it led him, that marriage was what he wanted with Marietta and a marriage between them was impossible?

Could he say any of it, knowing that Marietta had not brought him one tenth the loyalty and pleasure he had known with Gemma and might never do so? His hopes were worse than foolish. They were doomed, and he needed Gemma as much as she needed him.

"No," he said, "there's no one else." It was a half truth or a half lie. He could be proud of neither.

She turned to him the moment he said "no." "Then have me," she begged him, "stay with me."

"Gemma," he tried again. "I don't want to hurt you anymore. I've hurt you so much already."

"Oh, no," she whispered, coming close to him. "That isn't true. You never could, only if you left me. I love you so."

297

He had so little love for himself that he was grateful for hers. The touch of her mouth when she kissed him felt good, warm and familiar and good. She led him to the bedroom and undressed him, as if he were the one who had cried. She was more tender than ardent tonight and he more protective than erotic. He had the feeling, sad and romantic though he knew it to be, that they were two lost souls who turned to each other for a ray of shared light in a twilit world.

He made love to her very gently at the start, but he was unable to resist her sensuality. It seemed the only way she could give full expression to her stormy nature and he was carried along with her. His sorrow for both of them put a finer edge on every sensation and finally he was possessed by passion, lost in her and startled by the force of his release.

He held her long after she was asleep, thinking of Marietta and wondering if a man could love two women.

Book VI

60

1938

Later, Jonathan remembered the next months as the longest succession of days he had ever lived, when time, like a worn elastic, had lost its pull and day struggled after endless day. By the time he was ready to sail it was August. Even the crossing was interminable. Every mile of distance from Gemma brought him closer to Marietta, and he could not gallop the hours quickly enough to satisfy his impatience.

He called Victor the moment he arrived in Paris. "I'll stay here for a few days," he said, "then come on to Berlin. How is everyone?"

"They all left for Zurich yesterday."

Jonathan said nothing, utterly disappointed. He couldn't tell Victor he had hoped Marietta would wait for him, and he could hardly invite himself to Zurich. But he *must* see her!

"Never mind," Victor said, "I'll arrange my work so we can both go for a few days' holiday when you've finished your business here."

In the end Victor was delayed and Jonathan, too agitated to wait idly, decided to go ahead to Basel en route to Zurich.

"That's where I.G.'s big chief Walter Schmitz is," he told Victor while he packed. "That seems to be where they all are. I'll bet it's a meeting of the Bank for International Settlements."

Victor sat down on the bed. "Who's with Schmitz in Basel?"

"As far as I know, von Schröder, Emil Puhl—he's the real power behind the Reichsbank now—and Walter Schellenberg."

"He's Gestapo," Victor said. "What's he doing at the B.I.S.?"

"That's what I'd like to know. He's also a director and shareholder at I.T.T."

Victor whistled softly. "You can't tell the bankers and industrialists from the Nazis without a program, can you?"

"No, unless you know where to look. The B.I.S. is owned by First National Bank of New York—a Morgan affiliate, by the way—and the banks of England, Italy and France, among other central banks. Including the Reichsbank. I should say *especially* the Reichsbank."

The two young men looked at each other. "The Nazis are into everything, like vermin," Victor said. "Maybe that's where the Austrian gold went after the *Anschluss,* into the B.I.S."

Jonathan's face was rigid with the implications of all of it. "My father only intended me to see Farben people here in Berlin. It's pure coincidence I heard about Basel. The Nazis' power is even greater than I thought."

Victor agreed. "We've both had our heads in the sand. We should have known this would happen."

Jonathan snapped the locks of his large suitcase shut. "Knowing is one thing, acting on what you know is another." He turned to Victor. "I wish you'd all get the hell out of here. Bosch tried to protect I.G.'s Jews, but he's not the real head of I.G. anymore, Schmitz is, and he'll do as the Nazis do."

"If it were your country, would you just hand it over to the Nazis to run?"

Jonathan asked himself that question all the way to Basel. His meeting there was banal and inconclusive, as had been the few meetings he had in Berlin. These men were urbane, smiling, gracious; they had a talent for saying little and telling nothing—the way Jesse did, Jonathan thought, wondering what he would do when he saw his father again. Jesse certainly knew far more about the whole thing than he would ever tell his son. Jonathan even asked himself how much Susannah knew. Still, she would never have tried to dodge a direct question and keep the facts from him, as Jesse had.

He put it aside when he left Basel for Zurich, like a stubborn knot he was too preoccupied to unravel right now. All he could think about, as night closed in around the polished Swiss train, was Marietta. What would she say? Had she been thinking of him at all? Why had she left Berlin when he was expected?

"I should have written to her," he whispered in the taxi that took him from Zurich's Bahnhofplatz to the chalet in the hills. He had sent polite messages to her in his letters to Victor, but he had resolutely put his dreams of her in the closet with his travel cases the moment he got home. He had taken up his old life and his old habits, and the old, anonymous misery he had no right to claim because he had everything a man could possibly want.

It was past nine o'clock when he got to the chalet. The Kastenbergs had dined out tonight, the maid said, but Miss Marietta was at home—and she rushed off to deal with his baggage, leaving Jonathan in the hall.

A pair of Marietta's monogrammed gloves lay on a table near the stairs and he touched them softly, as if they were a part of her. It was then he knew he would marry her, no matter what anyone said—if she would have him, if only she would have him.

His heart thudded and he could not stand still. He moved down the hall to the music room at the back of the house. If he played she would know he was there and come to him.

He had reached the doorway of the darkened room when he saw her, sitting at one of the grand pianos. She turned her head to look at him and light from the corridor behind him illumined her: the wide, tender mouth and dark eyes, the heavy, shining hair.

"What—why are you sitting here in the dark?"

"Waiting for you," she said. "Oh, Jonathan, I thought I'd never see you again."

If a hundred women said his name, he would have known which voice was hers. He moved to her side and drew her up to him across years of dreaming it.

"I love you," he said. "I love you, I love you."

He had never known a kiss could mean so much, had never known such longing for a union that went far beyond the erotic.

"Say it again," she whispered.

"I love you."

"When did you know that?"

"From the first moment—before that, even, always. I've been looking for you all my life, Marietta."

"Then why . . . ?"

"I don't know, darling, I don't know."

"Was it Gemma?"

He was glad she knew. "She means a lot to me, she made my life bearable, but it's not the same. How could I have known what love was until I knew you?" He kissed her again. "Marry me, my love, no matter what anyone says."

"Yes, Jonathan." She seemed not to have heard the warning he could not keep himself from uttering, and yet he could not make the glow in her eyes begin to fade, not yet, not so soon. Somehow it would all work out, it had to. He had wasted two precious years of her, in the grip of some fear he could not really understand. It was gone now and he would not waste another minute.

They went into the living room and sat together, talking sometimes, although he could never remember what they said, only that they had resolved to keep their secret for a few hours, to have it to themselves, untarnished, before the world and its judgments ruined it.

Marietta's returning parents were the only reason they parted for the night. If she had been in that house alone, Jonathan knew, he would not have had the will to say good night and leave her side, not even for a few hours. The next morning he blessed the delay that would keep Victor from arriving until late afternoon and from sailing on the lake with them today. Victor would have known what had happened in a second.

The sun had never been so delicious, the lake and sky so blue, even the mighty Alps so friendly, as on this summer day.

"There's the cove," Marietta called to him when they had been out for about an hour. "Bring her about and we'll picnic there."

That was another thing he could never remember: what they ate on the blanket under the trees in a little glade about one hundred yards from the lake shore, or if they ate anything at all. He only remembered Marietta near him, the sound of wavelets lapping the shore, and a bird calling amid the rustle of leaves.

Marietta stirred against him on the blanket as he held her in his arms. "Jonathan, I'm afraid."

"Of what, darling?"

"I know they'll try to keep us apart. My father"—she glanced up at him —"or yours."

"Nothing can keep us apart, I swear it."

She came closer into the circle of his arms, as if it were the only place where nothing could threaten her. "I love you so," she said. "There is such sadness in you. I want to take it all away and make you smile as much with your eyes as you do with your mouth, your beautiful mouth." She touched his lips with hers, gently at first, then passionately. "I don't care how many women have loved you, not one of them has loved you the way I do, Jonathan. I will love you forever, only you, my darling, no one else."

Her passion stirred him, and the lily scent of her in the sunlight. He knew that she was totally innocent of the rapture she invited and he would have been willing to wait until they married, but she would not let him wait.

"Love me, Jonathan," she begged him. "Make love to me."

Her eyes held his while she undid the buttons of her dress, and he forgot the vows of honor and friendship that a man makes to himself. The message in her eyes, of passion still untapped and love the first time offered, called to him.

He kissed her—deep, gentle kisses that explored the fullness of her mouth, the satin of her breasts, and the silk of her hair. He would not let his body claim him before she could follow with him; his hands played over her lovingly.

The warmth of her secret flesh overpowered him when he was within it, and only then did the dream and the reality become one for both of them.

"I love you," Jonathan said. "I have always loved you."

They were like newborn infants, with no past but the moments they had just lived in each other's arms. They believed in every touch and every word.

"I love you," Marietta whispered. "I will love you forever."

61

Victor Kastenberg, his face reflecting uneasiness, berated himself while he bathed and dressed for dinner. It had been disturbing, when he arrived that afternoon, to learn that Jonathan and Marietta had been out on the lake since early morning.

"But that doesn't mean Marietta's in love," he told himself, without much conviction.

Jonathan was, that much was obvious. Jonathan had always been an open book to him, but it didn't need Holmesian powers of deduction to put a few facts together and reach a conclusion. Jonathan had not married Gemma; more important, he had avoided speaking of Marietta all the time he was in Berlin.

Then Victor forced himself to smile. Marietta was a lot more level-headed than she looked and she knew, as well as Victor did, that such a marriage would have distressed their parents even before Hitler.

"They picked a rotten time to get more serious about religion," he said to himself.

If Victor had not been so clever at research, his family would have been barred from professional posts with the rest of the Jews, or frightened into leaving. Privilege had made it harder for him to desert his country.

"And it *is* my country, every bit as much as Hitler's," he muttered, jerking the knot in his tie viciously. "More. I've been a German longer than he has."

He settled his collar, put on his jacket, and went down the stairs and into the living room to mix himself a whiskey and soda. It was so early he thought he was the only one down, until he saw his sister on the terrace that bordered the chalet. He started toward her, but something in her attitude made him stop.

He looked at her intently, with that keen observation that made him such a fine scientist. She was very dear to him, an unexpected flower that had bloomed into his life when he was a big boy of nine, ready to cherish a baby sister. Suddenly he thought of Susannah and Jesse, and then of Jonathan. His eyes narrowed, watching Marietta, because he saw her for the first time, not as a sister, but as a woman.

"She's in love with him," he whispered, as if he had discovered something fearful.

He wanted to go to her, to warn her that she, who had never known

305

anything but love and kindness, was risking the wrath, if not of God, then certainly of Jesse Slayter. One way or another that man would be the ruin of her, of his own son too, if that were necessary for Jesse to have his way.

At the very least Victor wanted to tell her not to wait like that, so vulnerable and so intense, with a longing even he could see.

It was too late. Jonathan had come onto the terrace from the far end and Marietta felt his presence before she even heard him. Victor could tell that, by a gathering of her body and a turning toward the tall blond man who approached her. He was moving with that masculine grace that made Jonathan irresistible to women, and Victor saw the look on his sister's face, saw her hold out her arms, melt into Jonathan's and kiss him with such a craving that there could be no doubt of what had happened between them.

"God help us, they've become lovers," Victor said, and turned away from the window, for this was intimacy too deep for any but the two of them to share.

After a long moment he heard Jonathan say, "We must tell them, darling," and he went out onto the terrace, his dark eyes saying that he knew what had happened between them out on the lake before he said a word. Instinctively they drew closer together.

"You know this is impossible," Victor said in a low voice, mindful of his parents' open windows above them. "At least Jonathan knows it."

"Papa will give in as soon as he knows Jonathan better," Marietta said, with more hope than certainty.

"It's not so much our father as his," Victor told her, forgetting to be gentle in his urgency. His eyes went from Jonathan to Marietta as he spoke, rapidly and vehemently. "You don't know what you'd be getting into, Marietta, his father is not like ours." Seeing them unconvinced, he could only appeal to Jonathan. "Leave her alone, Jon, give her a chance to be happy."

"How can she be happy in a country that thinks Jews are an inferior race?"

"They think the same thing in your country, they just haven't made a law about it yet. There are a lot of places in America where you couldn't take a Jewish wife—notably your own home."

Jonathan shook his head. "That won't be true once we're married and he meets her."

"No!" Victor whispered sharply. "Promise me you won't marry her until he's met her. You owe her the chance to make that decision after the fact, not before it."

"Oh, Victor, darling, please don't look that way." Marietta left Jonathan's side to go to her brother. "If that's how you feel, of course I'll meet him first; it won't make any difference." Her brown eyes looked at Jonathan for confirmation and he nodded.

"All right, then," Victor said, only a little mollified. He took a deep breath. "You'd better tell Papa and Mama tonight."

It was a long evening for Victor. He watched his parents' disapproval begin to melt in the face of Jonathan's love for Marietta, but even more, Victor thought, because of the safety such a marriage would provide for their daughter. They did not worry in quite the same way for Victor. He was a man and valuable to the Nazis' war plans, but no Jewish woman was safe in Hitler's Germany.

"You see?" Marietta said to him softly after dinner, when they were by themselves for a moment. "They're beginning to love him too."

Victor smiled. "Little sister," he said, stroking her hair, "it wasn't their reaction that worried me, it's Jesse Slayter's."

"He can't be a complete monster, with a son like Jonathan."

"You don't understand, Marietta! That man has blighted his entire family. He never cared what he did to his own wife and daughter, never mind someone else's. He won't permit this marriage, you don't know what he's like!"

Marietta's smile was a masterpiece of determination, quiet and implacable. "We're both of age, we don't need his permission," she said, "and he doesn't know what *I* am like, either." Then she kissed him and went back to her parents, leaving Victor to wonder if Jonathan would really challenge his father for the first time in his life and, with bitter regret for his own disloyalty, to hope he would not.

"What about Gemma?" he asked Jonathan as soon as they were alone that night.

Jonathan's face changed. "I'll tell her as soon as I get back." He lit a cigarette and leaned back against the sofa pillows, his buoyancy dissipated. "I can't tell her in a letter, it's not the honorable thing to do."

The word fell between them like an ax and Jonathan flushed. "You'll never forgive me for what happened today, will you, Victor?"

"Don't be a fool, Jonnie," Victor said roughly, looking away. "I know you didn't set out to seduce her. It's going to make things more difficult for both of you, though." He got up to fix himself another drink. "Want one?"

Jonathan nodded. "How do you mean?"

"It won't be easy for you, wanting to be alone together. That can't happen in my father's house, or yours."

"I know that, Victor, not until we're married." Jonathan quelled his temper and took the drink. The ice in it made the only sound in the room.

He made no direct reply to Victor. The same thing had occurred to him.

307

It seemed utterly unnatural for Marietta to be separated from him ever again, to sleep anywhere but in his arms, not after today. She belonged to him now.

"I've been thinking," Jonathan said after a moment. "I'm going back to New York next week, as planned. I want to tell my family, give Mother a chance to do whatever it is women do to celebrate engagements, before you bring Marietta over." He drank gratefully. "Then we'll come back to Berlin to be married as soon as possible." He spoke very quietly, but there was the same determination in his manner as in Marietta's. "When you come, I'd like both of you to stay at Susannah's."

"You see," Victor said grimly. "It begins already."

They were silent again, aware that things were not the same between them and might never be again.

"I think it's time to turn in," Victor said finally, putting his nearly full glass down on the table.

Jonathan looked at him squarely. "I love her, Victor. I've never loved anyone like this."

It was Jonathan's absolute decency, more than what he said, that was impossible to resist. Victor nodded and put an arm across Jonathan's shoulders as they went toward the stairs. They parted for the night without the formality that had soured the evening for both of them.

When Jonathan left for New York, Victor knew that his major preoccupation was not his father and the ominous signing of the Munich pact, nor even the temporary parting from Marietta. What worried Jonathan was Gemma, and Victor did not envy him the prospect of telling her he wanted to marry another woman.

62

The sky was heavy when Jonathan's ship came up the Hudson River, with thunderheads shrouding the city in humid, threatening gray. He cleared customs and took a taxi, first to Fifth Avenue, to leave his baggage and a message for Madeleine, then downtown to the Village. He looked at his watch. He would get to the apartment about the same time Gemma got home from work.

The storm broke when he passed Fourteenth Street and the arch in Washington Square was barely visible through the rain when the cab turned into Gemma's street.

His hand went to his pocket automatically as he climbed the stairs. Her key was still on his key ring, and he realized with a pang that he must take it off and leave it when he left her tonight.

The apartment was in its usual jumble when he opened the door. Gemma's books and magazines spilled out of shelves all over the room, as undisciplined as she was: *Vogue* and *Photoplay,* the *Times* and the *New York American,* every fashion magazine she could find, domestic and foreign.

The bed was always spreadless, ready to lie on. Her weekly maid never put away the peignoirs and mules scattered around the bedroom, or the hats and gloves that accumulated on the hall table.

He got ice from the refrigerator and poured himself a stiff drink, then sat, without drinking it, on the edge of a chair near the door, as if he wanted to bolt. Finally he heard the street door slam—Gemma never closed a door quietly—and the sound of her running up the stairs, and he got to his feet and squared his shoulders, knowing he must tell it to her quickly, or he would never be able to tell it at all, knowing, too, that he would hate himself for the rest of his life for what he was doing to her.

"Where is she?" Gemma said.

"She'll be here in about two weeks. Victor's bringing her."

"Are you really going to marry her?"

"As soon as possible."

She began to cry quietly, without sobs.

"Gemma, don't," Jonathan pleaded. "Please. I never said it was going to be forever, I never said it could be more than just what it was."

"Then 'it' meant something very different to you. I love you with all my

309

heart. There's nothing I want but you." She was still wearing her hat, still sitting where she had collapsed when he told her what had happened in Europe, the joy on her face crumpling into sorrow.

"Please, please," he begged her. "Don't make it worse than it is." He was close to tears himself.

"How could it be any worse for me?"

He turned away, raking his hair with his fingers. "I didn't fall in love with her to hurt you. I'd have done without you and all you've given me all these years if I'd thought there could ever be anyone else, if I'd known I was going to hurt you like this. You were the one good thing in my life, but I couldn't help falling in love."

"No," she whispered. "You can't help it. All you can do is hope things end at the same time for everyone, all neat and tidy with no ragged ends."

The wind blew outside and rain splattered the windows. It was autumn, suddenly. It was very still in the apartment. The fireplace looked forlorn. How many nights had they lit a fire here while they read or talked or made love? He had been coming here for ten years; it was the closest thing to a feeling of home he had ever known before he found Marietta. He would love Marietta to the end of his days, but he could never forget this place, either, or the woman who stood a few feet from him and yet had never been so far away.

"We had some good years, Gem. I'll never forget them—or you." He wished mightily that it were a lie, but it was the simple truth.

She shook her head. "That only makes it worse. I wish I'd never known what it means to love someone like this."

He turned to her, speaking softly. "No, you don't mean that. It's something no one as wonderful as you are ought to miss."

There was a look she had never seen before on the face she loved so much and thought she knew so well—a luminous quality. His disposition had usually been sunny, but determinedly so. For a second he had been happy inside, for himself, not to please or placate or protect anyone else.

Her heart turned over with sorrow that she was losing him, but she could not deny him such a feeling, even if she were not the one responsible for it. She had always said she would give him anything; she had only one thing left to give.

She went to him as she had done so many times and reached up to put her arms around him. He returned the embrace hesitantly.

"No," she said, "I wouldn't want you to miss it. You ought to have everything. It's all right, Jonnie, don't worry, I'll survive."

His arms tightened around her, his face pressed close to her tear-stained cheek. She knew he felt affection, respect, gratitude, and the kind of love for

310

her that some people feel only for themselves. It was a terrible thing to know because there was no passion left in it.

He kissed her hair. He held her close and she heard him say "thank you." Then he released her. "I must go. I'll call you, I promise." Then he left her with a last good-bye. She heard him going down the stairs and knew he wouldn't call her, ever again.

63

"That'll do, Daisy," Madeleine said. "The dress will look fine when you've hemmed it."

"It's elegant, Madame," Daisy said, helping Madeleine out of the gold and blue brocaded tunic and long black crepe skirt she had been pinning up. "I wonder what Miss Marietta will wear tonight. Such a pretty girl."

"More than pretty," Madeleine said, slipping into a housegown. "She's like one of those Roman statues Jonnie used to stare at in the museum. He always believed they came to life at night, when everyone was gone—and now one has, just for him."

She went downstairs to check the table. Except for the flowers, everything was ready. The engagement dinner was for twenty-four people—Slayters, van Ryns and Benedicts—with a large party afterward. The one person who would be conspicuous by her absence was Gemma.

She was glad to hear Susannah's voice in the hall minutes later, telling Harris to bring the flowers into the dining room before she came in herself.

"I picked up the flowers for the table," Susannah said, explaining. "I wanted to be sure they'd done exactly what I'd ordered."

"I'm glad you came," Madeleine said. "I was too nervous to stay upstairs by myself." One of these days she and her daughter would have to talk to each other about themselves, not other people, but not now, not when she was so worried for Jon and Marietta.

Susannah waited while Harris brought in a dozen floral arrangements and put them on the sideboard. "Nervous about what?" she asked, as soon as the man had gone.

"Jesse," Madeleine said, not bothering to be careful.

"I thought he was behaving very well," Susannah said, none too certainly.

"Too well. All of us—except, I hope, for Marietta—know he doesn't want this marriage."

Susannah did not dispute that. "But they're engaged now, he can't interfere with a *fait accompli*."

"What happened in Germany?" Madeleine asked. "Did Jonnie decide anything?"

"I don't know. He's avoiding the subject. Too much in love to bother about it, I suppose."

313

"No," Madeleine said. "He just doesn't want any open disagreement at this point, I'm sure of it."

Susannah looked at her watch. "I'll stay and place the flowers, if you'd like me to."

"Of course—it's not every day Jonathan gets engaged, is it?" She sighed. "I just can't stop thinking about Gemma."

Susannah moved quickly, putting the sprays of yellow roses and calla lilies along the center of the long table. It was draped with white lace over ivory velvet and set with van Ryn gold-bordered china and heavy Slayter silver. "It's a nasty situation. I don't know what'll become of her."

"She wouldn't harm herself?" Madeleine was alarmed.

"No, Gemma's not the type. I just don't think there'll ever be anyone else for her."

Madeleine nodded and moved a plate, then moved it back. "Where's Marietta today?"

"At the beauty parlor. Father said he'd pick her up and take her to tea before he brought her home." Susannah's face, as they looked at each other down the column of flowers, reflected her mother's.

She's as worried as I am, Madeleine thought.

"There's really nothing to worry about," Susannah said, as if Madeleine had spoken, and went on with the flowers for a second, before she added, "nothing at all."

No, this was obviously not the day for them to tell each other what they really thought.

"You like Marietta, don't you?" Madeleine said.

"Very much—and she's perfect for Jonnie. I've been waiting for years to see him happy like this. I'd like her for that, if nothing else."

"She reminds me of myself at that age," Madeleine said. "We were so sheltered then, you know, the way American girls will never be again."

"And a good thing too," Susannah said, squinting along the line of flowers to be sure they were perfectly aligned.

"I suppose so, but whatever became of romance?"

Susannah smiled, a secret, personal smile that changed her face. "It's still alive and well," she said. "It just doesn't show so much."

Madeleine smiled too. Charles and Susannah were lovely to see together. "Yes, but you'd still rather do the tango than the jitterbug, wouldn't you?"

"Sure," Susannah said, "but the important thing is to dance, no matter what tune they're playing." She straightened up, satisfied. "Well, that's done. I'd better scoot, it'll take me at least three hours to get ready for tonight and all those peering relatives."

"Me, too," Madeleine said, following her into the hall.

"No, you could come to a party in a burlap bag and still be the most beautiful woman there." Susannah picked up her bag and gloves from the marble-topped table in the hall, and let the butler help her into her blue fox coat. "See you at eight o'clock sharp."

"Come earlier, if you can," Madeleine said from the stairs. "I'd like the moral support."

"Fine," Susannah said, "so would I." Their eyes met for a second.

"I'm so glad you came by," Madeleine said softly.

"Yes," Susannah said, "so am I." Then her heels clicked across the marble floor of the entry hall. She turned at the door while the butler opened it. " 'Bye," she said. "And don't worry."

Madeleine went slowly up the stairs, feeling more certain than ever that things were changing for the better between them. Now that Jonathan was getting married, it would be wonderful to have her daughter back.

Daisy, going to her own little sitting room after settling Madeleine down for a rest, hummed as she put the kettle on for tea.

Bob Harris, in his chauffeur's livery, paused on his way out the door. "What's the meanin' of all the merriment, and the whole house in a scramble to get ready for tonight?"

Daisy smiled at him. "A regular visit they had, in there over the flowers. She's as happy as a lark about it."

Bob shook his head. "It's unnatural, the way they've been goin' on all these years."

"Never you mind," Daisy said. "It'll all come right now."

"But will the other? I'm off to get him now. He's takin' Mister Jonnie's young lady to tea."

Daisy's smile evaporated. "He wouldn't have the heart to spoil it!"

Bob Harris sighed. "That's just what he hasn't got, my girl, is heart." He rubbed the visor of his cap and put it under his arm. "I'm off then," he said, and went out, leaving Daisy with a frown on her face.

"You're looking very pretty," Jesse said.

He made Marietta uncomfortable. He appraised her dove-gray suit, silver fox fur and tiny veiled hat as if he were going to bid on them. *I ought to make him like me,* she thought.

"The beauty salon deserves all the credit," she said. "Milk or lemon?"

"Nonsense, they just gild the lily. Milk, please."

She prepared it for him, in the genteel hum of Sherry's, glad to have something to do with her hands. American women didn't pour tea for a man in public, but she did it before she remembered that. It was hard to watch every move she made.

"Are you enjoying your visit?" was his next question, and this time he produced a smile.

So handsome—that white hair and those heavy brows—he doesn't care two pins. "Why don't we talk about Jonathan, Mr. Slayter," she said, suddenly abandoning her maidenly air.

A faint gleam in his eye rewarded her. He did not like small talk, either. He tasted his tea. "What have you to say?"

"I'm going to marry him," Marietta said, acutely aware of her slightly accented English. "That says everything."

"Not quite." Jesse set down his cup and took out his pipe and tobacco pouch. "Please understand that I don't question your affection for my son in the least. In fact, I'm counting on it to make you do the only thing possible for both your sakes."

Inexplicably, she nodded, as if she agreed with him.

"It has to do, of course, with the unfortunate matter of your religion. I am totally indifferent to religion myself, but the world is not. I'm afraid," he said, pausing between phrases to draw on his pipe, "that you—would—find life—very uncomfortable here because of that."

Her own father had said virtually the same thing to her many times before she followed Jonathan to America, but not like this. "No more so than in Germany," she said.

"At least it's out in the open over there," Jesse said. "Here it would be subtle, but you would be hurt and Jonathan's whole future compromised by it—his social position, his place in banking, in short, everything that matters to him."

None of that matters to him!

"I don't see how you could be happy, knowing he had lost everything because of you. It's a burden no woman should have to bear and no man could tolerate." He paused, waiting for her to agree with him.

Victor was right, he'll never let Jonathan marry me.

"Then, too," Jesse went on reluctantly, as if pushed to it by her stubborn silence, "there is the ugly fact of Jonathan's liaison with the woman everyone expected him to marry. It pains me to tell you this, but he will never give her up, not even when he does marry, eventually. The affair has gone on too long." He watched her a moment, puffing on his pipe, then added, "She was the first person he went to see, straight from the ship, when he came back from Europe."

Don't cry, you mustn't cry. She twisted her gray suede gloves in her lap, biting her lip. *He stops at nothing, even this.*

"I've been against it for the past ten years," Jesse said, "but he's always been stubborn about all of his women. You're a fine young lady, I wouldn't want to see your life ruined by him. Some men are simply like that."

He was still watching her, waiting for an answer, this handsome, powerful man who hated her. She was better off with the Nazis—at least she knew what to expect from them. She choked back the outrage she could never express to anyone, above all not to Jonathan, and then anger stiffened her back.

"I only want what's best for Jonathan," she said.

He touched her arm, a generous winner, and she made herself sit still for it. "Whatever you do for his sake will be amply rewarded. I have a little influence in your country."

Victor? Was he why Victor had been so suddenly deluged by work that he could not come with her? No, he was not that important, no one was.

"It is getting late," Marietta said, rising with all the dignity she could summon. "I must prepare for this evening." An engagement party for an engagement that would be broken, very quietly, as soon as she went back to Germany.

He was obliged to stand when she did, to empty his pipe and put it away, to follow her through the labyrinth of linen-covered tables, to sit by her side in the Rolls-Royce and talk about the people she would meet tonight as if he were not the most despicable man she had ever known.

While she was dressing at Susannah's, her mind raced frantically, looking for a way out. She loved Jonathan with all her heart, but she was not blind to his relationship with his father. Jesse had a hold on him that was as old as Jonathan and would be difficult to shake off.

She was hardly aware of the people she met at dinner and knew she seemed aloof, very tall and proud in a white crepe gown with her hair piled on her head. It was not how she felt.

"Are you all right?" Jonathan asked her when the endless dinner was over. She smiled at him then. It was the first time she had really smiled that evening.

"I have something to tell you," she said, "it's all I can think about."

"Tell me," he said later, when they were dancing.

She put her hand on the blond hair at the back of his head and felt him tremble at her touch. "I love you," she whispered, "I want you." It was difficult to say it, she had not been brought up to this kind of frankness with a man, not even after their one precious day together on the lake shore at Zurich.

"I know, my darling, so do I," he said, his cheek against hers.

"Find some place, Jonathan, any place, so we can be together."

He held her closer, whispering. "I won't take you to some sleazy hotel, like a thief in the night."

"You could if we were married."

"Yes," he said, "soon, darling."

"That place you showed me, near Wall Street, where people get married quietly?"

"City Hall."

"Take me there and marry me." She would not let him look at her, she held him close. He couldn't see her worried face, he could only hear her voice, warm and inviting.

"But you wanted a real wedding, with your family and all your friends, in Berlin," he said.

Her lips touched his cheek and she whispered urgently, "Yes, darling, we'll have that later, as soon as you get there, but marry me now, Jonathan, please, just for us, the two of us, so we can be together even just a few times before I sail, with no one to watch us or listen to us, so I can feel your arms around me and love you with nothing between us, not even your conscience. I love you so much, Jonathan, say you will, please say you will."

"Yes," Jonathan said, "yes, my darling, yes."

64

It was only seven in the morning when, two weeks later, Jonathan came to take Marietta to the pier, but Susannah and Charles were halfway through breakfast in the small dining room.

"Have a cup of coffee," Charles said. "Marietta's not down yet. We'll drop you at the pier."

"I have Harris waiting with my bags."

Susannah looked up sharply. "Your bags?"

"I'm going with her. I booked a cabin a few days ago. I can't let go of her, not now, not ever again." He stopped talking, as if he had said too much.

Susannah nodded. "Have you told Father?"

"From the look of him," Charles said, "he's leaving that little chore to you."

"You can tell him if you like, but I'll wire him from the ship in any case." Jonathan put sugar into his coffee. "I'd have been leaving in another month for the wedding, anyway."

Charles shook his head. "He'd have been right along with you then; he'd have had you in tow."

Jonathan's answer was not quite as cordial this time. "I'm not tied to him, Charles. That seems to have escaped your notice, as well as his."

"Then why haven't you talked to him about Germany?" Susannah said.

Jonathan lit a cigarette. "Because it's going to end in a break and I wanted to avoid that before the wedding, for Marietta's sake. It'll be awkward enough as it is."

"You're really leaving Slayter's?" Charles asked him.

Jonathan leaned forward, speaking intensely as he explained his reasoning. There was no doubt whatever in his mind, nor in Susannah's now, that I.G. and the Nazis were hand in glove, that this nasty partnership was leading straight to war, and that Slayter's was an accessory, no matter how indirectly. "I won't help manufacture the gun that might kill Daniel in Spain," Jonathan finished. "I won't help Germany start another world war."

Susannah shivered slightly, torn between pride in Daniel and resentment at her father's part in the trouble brewing in Europe.

"What do you want Susannah to do?"

"She's agreed to vote my proxy if it comes to a fight and I'm not here to do it." He took a document from his breast pocket. "I have it here."

"What good will that do?" Charles wanted to know. "Jesse controls Slayter's."

"The family controls it. He's been voting our shares up to now. Along with Daniel's shares, and Philippa's and Mother's, we'd control the voting shares in Slayter's."

Charles looked from Jonathan to Susannah. "You'd need Susannah's too. Would you do that, vote your shares against your father?"

She nodded, uncomfortable, but determined. "If there's a war and he doesn't break with Germany. I'll vote the boys' shares too, if you agree."

Charles whistled softly. "Of course I'll agree—and good for you. Hitler won't like having a steady supply of money cut off right now."

"It isn't that much money," Jonathan said. "Two hundred million, more or less. Other firms have floated larger loans. It's the patents that worry me." Briefly he told Charles that some of the giant American companies, partially financed by Slayter's, shared important patents with I.G. Farben, regulating the production in America of strategic materials like magnesium and aluminum. "They're vital for modern armaments and, of course, Farben kept them, and the technology to produce them, under German control, with limited production permitted elsewhere. When production is restricted, prices rise." He shrugged. "That's what monopolies are for."

"So we can't manufacture much in the way of modern armaments for anyone—not even ourselves—if we honor the patent agreements. But American companies wouldn't honor them!"

"Wouldn't they?" Jonathan asked. "Wouldn't they?"

Charles looked at Susannah. "Did you know all this?"

"Yes, but their research is light-years ahead of ours. It was good sense to finance them with loans and invest in the companies here that shared the patents." She looked from her brother to Charles. "No one was thinking of war."

"No one?"

"Certainly not Father. Neither were all the people who participated in the loans we underwrote."

"How would they know where their investments went, anyway? The final destination of that money is hidden behind holding companies and interlocking directorates." Jonathan looked grim. "Ambrose-Sentinel is a case in point. The public invests in a prestigious, bona fide American company, but that money travels everywhere—it can ultimately be controlled by a Dutchman or a Swede—or a German."

The conversation stopped abruptly when they heard Marietta coming downstairs.

In the flurry of the lovers' departure, Susannah's preoccupation with the

320

problem was not noticed, but once in the Citroën that drove them each morning, first to Charles's office, then to Pearl Street, Charles took her hand.

"Would you really do it, Susannah, try to take over from your father?"

She was startled. "I don't want to take over; I couldn't, not even with the proxies. I don't want to control the company, anyway, just this one policy."

"It comes to the same thing. Whoever controls its policy controls Slayter's."

She shook her head. "This is a single issue; all Jonnie and I want to do is change this one thing." She shook her head again. "Anyway, I hope it won't come to that. I hope the war never happens and Jonathan and Marietta settle down right here in New York after their honeymoon."

When she got to her office, Susannah put her things away and sat down at her desk. She had a few matters to straighten out before she went to her father for their informal morning conference and, resolutely, she put her brother's departure out of her mind until then.

"Face it, Mr. Tillotson," Susannah said into the telephone an hour later. "You have to deal with us or go under."

When Ambrose-Sentinel, the vast and diversified holding company owned by Slayter's, decided to take over a company, there was no other choice.

"I know that, Mrs. Benedict," the man said wearily. "I just don't want to abandon my plant and my men. Take me over if you must, but let me stay on to run the place with my own people."

Susannah had come across men like this before. Bad times forced them to sell out, but they wouldn't take the money and run. She admired them for it —and knew she would have trouble with Jesse over it.

"All right, you have a deal. I'll have the papers drawn up."

"You won't regret it," he said before they hung up.

She was beginning to regret it already; she did not relish these run-ins with her father about Ambrose-Sentinel's burgeoning acquisitions, and she had more than that to tell him today. She knew she was right about Tillotson, though, and she kept saying that to herself until she could say it to Jesse.

"Being right isn't always profitable," Jesse said with a too-familiar frown. His heavy brows hadn't whitened completely along with his hair, and they lent a Machiavellian look to his face, still as strong and impassive as ever.

"You'll get a better product out of Tillotson Tool and Die if he stays on to run it," Susannah said. "That *has* to mean something."

"We may get a lot of interference, as well, if we decide to change the product. Did you consider that?"

She hadn't, but she had seen the pattern of Slayter's recent takeovers. Most of the companies could easily be converted into the production of war matériel or the machine tools to make it.

"Why would Tillotson care what he made?" she asked.

Jesse observed her with a mixture of pride at her ability and annoyance at her naiveté. "He's an isolationist, that's why."

She was amazed. "You really investigate everything about a company before you take it over, don't you?"

"So should you. You don't leave a man like that in charge of a product that might irritate his tender principles."

She shook her head slowly, a half smile on her face. "You're a remarkable man, Father. I admire you, but sometimes I wonder about your beliefs."

He raised a quizzical eyebrow.

"If you have such contempt for idealists, what must you think of Daniel?"

"What I would think of any lame man in his prime who goes off to fight a civil war in Spain. He should have had enough of other people's battles by now."

Susannah kept her temper. She had been worrying constantly about her uncle since he crossed into Spain to join the Loyalists. Now the international brigades had disbanded, but Daniel still had not returned to France.

"That sounds like contempt to me," she said. "Wouldn't you concede that an aversion to Fascism might be a good thing?"

"*You* claim an aversion to it, I believe. So does your brother and your husband. You still haven't gone off to risk your lives. Obviously you realize it's only a new name for an old form of government."

"That's not why," Susannah said, feeling helpless in the face of her father's cynical logic.

"As a woman you can't go, of course," Jesse answered, "but what is their excuse?"

She had no answer.

He nodded. "There is a difference between carrying a popular flag and charging into battle with it."

"Damn it," Susannah said, finally showing her temper. "Charles and Jonathan are anti-Fascist out of conviction, not because it's a popular cause. That's true whether or not they pick up guns to prove it."

Jesse shrugged. "Have it your way, Susannah." He was sardonically forebearing. "But what, pray, is your husband doing in Washington so often these days?"

"That has nothing to do with Spain! He's interested in labor law."

"On whose side?"

"The federal government's. With all the new laws someone has to sort things out between management and labor."

"I see." Jesse smiled. "I'm sure the administration will look more kindly on him if he agrees with their foreign policy. Roosevelt liberals favor the Spanish Loyalist side, everyone knows that."

She felt herself flushing again. "I know how Charles thinks and he doesn't form his convictions to further his career."

"Come, come, Susannah, people make compromises every day. Charles didn't really want you to work, but he said he did to persuade you to marry him. When I gave in he was hoist with his own petard."

"Why *did* you give in?"

He smiled again, busy with some papers. "Times had changed—Jonathan hadn't. You're still doing most of his work."

"I must go," Susannah said. She stood, slim and chic in a wide-shouldered suit. "I gave Tillotson my word," she reminded Jesse firmly.

"Yes, yes," he said. "Don't forget I'll pick Cab up at one o'clock sharp on Sunday."

"Oh, yes, to take him to the zoo! Good, he's been talking about it. He really adores you, Dad," she said.

"Why shouldn't he, I'm his grandfather. By the way, did Miss Kastenberg get off on time?"

"In plenty of time," Susannah said, wondering if he would ever call her Marietta. "Jonathan went with her."

Jesse looked up, no longer occupied with the papers on his desk. "You're joking," he said.

"No. It was a last-minute decision. He said he'd wire you from the ship. He just didn't want to be so far away from her and that's understandable."

"Not to me! It's inexcusable."

Susannah got up from the chair. "I only wanted to tell you about it, not listen to Jonathan's lecture for him."

After a second Jesse shrugged. "No, of course not. Well, there's nothing I can do about it now, we'll see him soon enough at the wedding."

He sat there when she had gone, forcing himself to put anger aside and deal with the problem of a marriage that must be prevented. He was not to be defied by a schoolgirl. She had certainly used her charms to entrap the boy—he was besotted by her, anyway. Jesse realized suddenly that she could probably persuade him to leave Slayter's once they were married.

He lit his pipe, his fingers polished the bowl. Then he opened the panel in his desk and unlocked his private safe. He looked up a number in a small directory, replaced it, and picked up his personal telephone.

"I want to call Berlin," he told the operator, and gave her the number. "It's urgent. I'll wait."

65

If Jonathan could have chosen just one week of his life to relive, it would have been their ocean crossing from New York to Bremerhaven in this November of 1938, when they were alone together at last on a great ocean liner. It was a world apart for the days of its passage.

Elsewhere on the planet, the panzers made ready to roll and the jackboots to march, but they heard only each other. In Berlin, truncheons rose and fell, blood ran, windows shattered, but they knew nothing of it.

It was only when they were in the taxi, driving home from the *Bahnhof* in Berlin, that reality forced its way between them, like a rude jailer.

The streets were strangely quiet, although small knots of people clustered here and there. They saw shop after shop with broken windows. Shattered glass and broken objects lay on the pavements.

"All those shops are Jewish," Marietta whispered suddenly. "Look!" If the signs above them had not said so, the yellow-painted slogans on the door fronts marked them clearly.

"What's all that about?" Jonathan asked the driver.

"Some trouble with the Jews," the man said.

Marietta's warning look kept him from asking more and their anxiety mounted when the car stopped in the Bundes-Allee and Victor, not the footman, came to unlock the iron gates.

"What happened!" Jonathan demanded once they were inside the house and Marietta had run up the stairs to her parents.

"A riot—what the Nazis are calling a 'spontaneous demonstration.'" He looked haggard; there were deep circles under his eyes and his hands moved nervously. "We don't know everything, but there isn't a synagogue left standing in Germany or a Jewish store with its windows intact."

"Jesus," Jonathan swore softly. "You have to get out of here, all of you."

Victor shook his head. "They won't let us go. It's because of me, it's what I know, the work I do. All that research is in my head and they want to keep it here." He leaned against the balustrade of the great staircase. "Jon, do you realize what could happen to my family because of me?"

"Nothing's going to happen." Jonathan put a hand on Victor's shoulder. "We're married, Victor. We were married in New York. No one else knows it yet, but it will help to change their minds about keeping you here. Marietta can claim American protection by marriage."

Victor's grim expression had softened slightly as he listened. "I should have known," he said, "when you made the crossing with her." He took the cigarette Jonathan offered him, and the light. "I'm glad for you, Jonathan, but I don't think it'll help."

"Yes, it will. I know Hugh Wilson, the ambassador. I'll have him call my father from the embassy."

"Your father? Why would he help?"

"Of course he'll help, Victor! He's a bigot, I know, but he's not a monster. He'll find a way to get you all out. He knows a lot of people in Washington." He laughed ruefully. "And then he'll do anything he can to make me divorce my wife, even though the idea of divorce is anathema to him."

"Not as much as the idea of Jewish grandchildren," Victor said morosely.

Jonathan looked at his watch. "It's only two o'clock. I'll go right over there now." He willed Victor to believe him. "It'll be all right, I promise."

"I'm not so sure," Victor said. "The Gestapo have been around, asking questions. My father and mother are frightened to death, and so am I." He looked ashamed of himself. "It's terrible, what fear does to a man."

"I must go," Jonathan said. He had never seen his friend like this. "Tell Marietta where I've gone, will you? I'll be back as soon as I can."

Victor nodded, saying nothing, and Jonathan searched his face. "Victor, I love her, I'll never love anyone else as long as I live. Don't be angry at us."

"Angry?" Victor almost smiled. "Who in the world has ever been angry at either one of you?"

"My father's going to be," Jonathan said. For a second he looked at the stairs, wanting to comfort Marietta, to see her face once more before he left, but there was no time. "Don't worry, Victor," he said, and left the house. He was out on the street when Victor went upstairs. He was running for a taxi and well out of earshot when Marietta tried to call him back.

An hour later Jonathan sat in a room at the American embassy, his voice as strained as his face.

"Do it, Father," he said. "You know you can. Just call someone in Washington and do it. Now."

Jesse's answer crackled furiously over the trans-Atlantic wire. "Don't issue orders to me. You left here without so much as a by-your-leave."

"I don't have to ask your permission to leave home," Jonathan said angrily. "That's not the point, anyway. I want my wife and her family out of this madhouse!"

"Your *wife?*" Jesse's voice was cold and quiet now.

Jonathan's head dropped into his free hand. "We were married in New York, Father, at City Hall, about two weeks before we sailed."

The silence between them was almost humming with what they must not say to each other, until Jonathan spoke again, his attitude more moderate. "I haven't got time to explain. The situation's too serious here."

"What can I do about it?" Jesse insisted. "I have no influence with the Nazis."

"Oh, yes you do!" Jonathan shouted into the telephone. "You're one of Hitler's major stockholders. How would that look in the papers, next to the headlines about beatings and fires and broken glass?"

"Are you threatening me?" Jesse was incredulous. "Those people have turned you against me!"

"My God," Jonathan said, desperate now. "You're my father, no one could turn me against you. Why are we talking like this? I'm asking for your help, I need you."

After a moment Jesse's voice came through in its familiar calm. "Jonathan, it would be better if you made the request personally, in Washington."

"I know that, but I won't leave her, not ever again." There was fear in his voice, and renewed desperation. "You can't imagine the atmosphere here, no one's safe." His voice broke. "Victor's afraid of arrest as it is. If they arrest her, I'm going with her. I won't let her go to one of those concentration camps without me."

"Get hold of yourself, Jonathan," Jesse said quickly. "They're only trying to frighten them. What would the authorities want with her?"

"Not just Marietta, all four of them, because of Victor."

There was another silence from New York while, his anger partly spent, Jesse's sharp mind made the connection between Victor Kastenberg's knowledge and Farben's closely guarded technology. "I see," he said, and Jonathan had a vision of a roulette wheel spinning inside his father's head and a small white marble skipping from option to option until it finally settled into a choice. "I see," he said again. "All right, Jonathan, I'll do what I can. Stay at the embassy so I can call you back easily. The service to Germany's been irregular since those riots."

"I will, but hurry, please. And Father?"

"Yes?"

"What I said before—I didn't mean that, I'm sorry."

"You're upset, you don't know what you're saying. Just wait there, I'll take care of everything." The connection was broken.

Jonathan waited, smoking continuously. He could hear the noise of people asking, then pleading for the papers that would get them safely out of Germany. The brutality of the riots had been recorded on front pages around the world, he had learned, and the American ambassador had been recalled in what was fast becoming an international incident.

327

It was not a time, Jonathan reflected, to be an ordinary citizen. Privilege had gone largely unnoticed in his life, but in this private office, given to him because of his father's influence, he felt its cloak and was glad of it.

Time labored by. Once in a while he managed to make the clock advance by thinking of Marietta and the days they had just lived together at sea.

He could hardly wait to see her face again, to talk to her. It was so much more than desire, but it was desire too, to feel her close to him and hear her in her passion for him. In all of his many moments with women, no voice had ever reached his soul as hers did.

He wanted to take her riding in Central Park, swimming at Southampton. He wanted to dance with her to Glenn Miller's music at the Glen Island Casino, take her to Cafe Society Downtown to hear Billie Holiday. He wanted to tell her how he felt about so many things, because he knew she could understand him, not only in the flesh as Gemma did, but with her well-ordered mind and in the light of her own opinions.

After another hour, when he was sure his watch had stopped, he left the small office to ask if the telephones were in order. The frenetic bustle in the embassy struck him again, and he went back to the telephone and broke open a fresh pack of cigarettes, too nervous to do anything but wait for it to ring, unwilling to tie up the line by calling Marietta, and anxious lest their telephone be tapped. Finally the telephone rang and the embassy operator announced a call from New York.

"Jonathan? I've arranged it. There will be diplomatic visas issued for the four of them."

"Thank God," Jonathan whispered. "When?"

"They've cabled instructions already, they should arrive by tomorrow." He waited. "Jonathan?"

Jonathan wiped his forehead with a handkerchief. "Yes, I'm here, I'm relieved, that's all. You can't imagine what it's been like, waiting here."

"When will you be back?"

"As soon as a ship can bring us." He hesitated. "Father, I know you don't approve, but for my sake don't be cruel to her."

"When have I ever been cruel to anyone?" Jesse asked.

Jonathan left the embassy, after a brief exchange with the ambassador's harried secretary, and found a taxi. Driving back to the Bundes-Allee, he reflected that his father never *had* been cruel to anyone. It had often felt that way, but how could you condemn a man for your secret perceptions of him? It would be like claiming to read his mind.

The taxi stopped in front of the Kastenberg house and Jonathan paid the man, got out, and knew the instant he entered the unlocked gate that something was wrong. The silence in the house was too intense; it hung in the air like ether. He started to walk across the hall, but suddenly he was running up the stairs, calling to Marietta, to Victor, looking into every room, even though he knew there was no one there.

They had either fled—or they had been taken away. He went back to the bedrooms. Closet doors were open, drawers half pulled, as if they had packed in a hurry. It was not an unusual circumstance in Germany today. Victor might have been warned to leave, but where had they gone?

He went downstairs again, shaken and unsure. Finally he left the house and found another taxi. He gave the driver Karl-Dieter Veidt's address in the city's financial district.

Veidt's smile faded as soon as he saw Jonathan's face. He listened carefully, his agitation growing.

"I regret, Herr Slayter, but I know nothing about them," he said, apparently bewildered.

"But you can find out!" Jonathan insisted.

The pale gray eyes dropped. "It might be a Gestapo matter."

"What have the State Secret Police to do with it? The Kastenbergs are I.G. Farben people, not criminals!"

"The Gestapo has to do with everyone now," Veidt said, his eyes shifting again, and a part of Jonathan's mind remembered that a member of the Gestapo had been at the Bank for International Settlements in Basel. Veidt was not lying, Jonathan realized; he was afraid. Jonathan stood, lit a cigarette, walked around the office with its carved desk and heavy furnishings, redolent of wealth and security, like his father's office. If this man was not safe, God alone knew what had happened to *them*, to Marietta.

He turned back to Veidt. "If you can't help me, who can?" He had accepted the utter uselessness of asking more.

He made the calls Veidt suggested. He spent the day trying everyone he knew in Berlin, making shameless use of his father's name. Jesse had never used the power of his name except at the top; now Jonathan used it in every government office and every police station, making it clear, in his fluent German, that he was very rich—Germans respected wealth as much as anyone else—that he was an American—they had been warned about "annoying" foreigners, particularly Americans, after the riots they were now calling *Kristallnacht*—and that he was an ardent supporter of the Third Reich looking for his wife. More than once it was obvious that they approved of him, but thought him well rid of her.

At night, exhausted and shaking inside, he went back to the house, dark and sad in its emptiness, the warmth of its heart gone. It was impossible for him to stay there; he packed his things and moved to a hotel, ready to continue his search the next day.

His father knew nothing. "Have you seen Veidt?" Jesse asked on the telephone.

"He's too frightened to ask anyone; he thinks it may have been the Gestapo—you've heard about *them*. I feel like I'm living in a nightmare."

"Jonathan, listen to me," his father said, gently, reasonably. "You're too tired to think. Come home and rest; then we'll see what can be done."

"I'm not coming home until she comes with me," Jonathan said. "Have you called anyone?"

"Of course I have! They won't risk an incident over one family. The world's on a tightrope as it is. Be reasonable, Jonathan, come home."

"Would you have left Mother in a place like this?" Jonathan asked before he hung up.

Finally he returned to a vice-president of Slayter's correspondent bank who had seemed more sympathetic than the rest.

"There is absolutely no record of their arrest—I was able to inquire. They must have gone before they could be—detained."

"So quickly?" Jonathan asked. "Within hours?"

The man looked at Jonathan sadly. "These days, Herr Slayter, people like the Kastenbergs are lucky to have a few minutes' warning."

A faint hope awakened in Jonathan. Was it really possible they had been warned? He remembered the signs of hasty packing, and all he had heard of Jews taking flight from Germany with little more than what they could carry. Ten days after he had arrived, Jonathan left Berlin for Switzerland, the most logical place for them to have gone, although the telephone at the chalet had rung unanswered for a week.

He found no trace of them in Zurich or anywhere else in Switzerland. Frantic, he went to Holland, where the Kastenbergs had cousins, but they could tell him nothing. The search was difficult and very slow: they might even have changed their names and papers.

When finally he journeyed to the south of France, Daniel was home from a cruel civil war that had scarred his face and the heart of Spain forever. It fell to Jonathan to burden his uncle still more by asking him for his proxy and explaining the reason for it.

Daniel listened, sitting close to Dominique, while Jonathan told him about the close connection between Slayter's and I.G. Farben and the cartel's one saving grace, the protection of its Jews, now obliterated in the violence of *Kristallnacht*.

Daniel, thin and white, breathed deeply at the end of the recital. "I would have known it long ago if I'd taken the trouble to find out. It's some kind of poetic justice that I was in Spain when the Nazis tried out their new arsenal."

He got up and walked to the window, leaning more heavily on his cane than he used to. "Bilbao and Durango and Guernica—the carnage was terrible, but what can you expect of Germans? They were taking blood oaths when the rest of Europe had moved on to the Renaissance—and the SS are still taking blood oaths today."

Dominique and Jonathan watched without a word until Daniel turned back to them. The scar that slanted from his left cheekbone to his chin was livid in the sunlight. "My proxy is little enough to atone for my part in all this. I'll have it notarized and give it to you this afternoon."

"Make it to Susannah," Jonathan said. "She's sure to be there to use it."

"Where are you going?"

"To look for Marietta," Jonathan said.

His two companions turned to each other in alarm, then back to him where he leaned against the mantelpiece.

"Jonathan," Daniel said. "You've got to face it. The Nazis have them and there's nothing you can do about that for the moment."

"I can't just—give her up." Jonathan held on to the mantel, his arms stretched out, looking into the empty grate as he spoke. "I'm going back to Germany. If I don't find her there, I'll just keep on looking. My God, she may be sick, or cold, maybe those bastards hurt her, maybe—" He stopped for a moment. "She wanted to have a real wedding. It's why we came back, you know, so she could be married, like Susannah was, with all her people there, not just in some grubby public chapel in City Hall. I shouldn't have brought her back, I should have known better." His shoulders shook. "I can't see her face," he said, as if he couldn't quite believe it. "I can't visualize it. I know every feature of it, every expression, but I just can't seem to see her face."

The two people watching him listened sadly, without protest.

"I have to find her," Jonathan said. "I have to."

331

66

1939

Jonathan sat in a coffeehouse near the Unter den Linden in Berlin, as he had done many times before, but even the August sunshine depressed him. There were still some tourists about, apparently unconcerned, although German troops were in the Sudetenland, in Czechoslovakia, in Memel; Hilter and Mussolini had signed their "Pact of Steel"; and a German-Soviet pact had been made four days ago in Moscow.

For Jonathan the smoke of impending battle obscured the sun. He was here because he wanted one more meeting with Karl-Dieter Veidt before he left for England, one more chance to make the little bastard tell him all he really knew about Marietta's disappearance.

The terrible suspicion that had taken root in Jonathan's mind nine months ago had gone full term, to be born like a devil and rend him with its horror and his own abysmal stupidity. He had no one to tell it to but Madeleine and ugly as it was, he would have to do that before too long. Susannah would never believe him, but his mother would; his mother knew what kind of man Jesse really was.

He heard someone give an order at the next table in fluent German, but with a slight American accent, and he looked up, eager for even the smallest hint of home. The man looked up too, and with a mixture of feelings he could not have named, Jonathan recognized Dr. Edward Driscoll, still bearded and conservatively dressed.

The doctor smiled, rose, and approached Jonathan's table.

"It's Jonathan Slayter, isn't it?" he said, extending a hand.

Jonathan took it briefly and flushed. The other man stood there, obviously waiting for an invitation to sit down at Jonathan's table.

"I don't think," Jonathan said with difficulty, "that we have anything to say to each other."

Ah, Ned Driscoll thought, *so Madeleine was wrong, he did know about us.*

"On the contrary," he said, still standing there. "I think we have a lot to say. May I sit down?"

Jonathan made a gesture that showed his indifference to where the doctor sat.

"What are you doing in Berlin?" Ned asked.

"Looking for my wife," Jonathan said, on the brink of tears. It was the first time he had said those words to someone other than a totally uninterested official. As tersely as he could, he told Dr. Driscoll the circumstances of Marietta's disappearance.

Ned shook his head in sympathy. "If it's as bad here for the Jews as it's been in Austria since the *Anschluss,*" he said, "she'll be difficult to find."

Anguish overwhelmed Jonathan. "I don't need you to tell me that," he said rudely.

Ned was silent for a moment. "Look here, Jonathan, I appear to anger you for some reason."

"Your—your affair with my mother is what angers me," Jonathan said explosively.

"Why should it? We were happy together for a little while. Madeleine didn't have much happiness in her life. I'd think you'd be glad of any she managed to find." The voice was calm and the manner gentle; even the words were logical and persuasive. "After all," the doctor continued, "it's not your responsibility to defend your father's property, and that's all she was to him."

"Defend him?" Jonathan had heard nothing beyond that. "I hate him! I'd like to kill him!" His hands were shaking.

Ned Driscoll said nothing, waiting.

For a moment Jonathan struggled with himself, the tendons in his neck straining to keep back what no one outside his own family should ever know, but what he felt for Jesse was too much for him; it had always been too much.

"I think he was responsible for Marietta's arrest," he blurted, gripping the edge of the table with such force that his knuckles went white. "I think he called someone, I don't know who, while he kept me waiting in the embassy that day. He knew when he called me back that they'd been arrested and taken away. That's why he keeps telling me to come home; he knows it's hopeless." His blue eyes blazed in his haggard face. "If I go home, I'll kill him."

After a moment Ned put a hand on Jonathan's arm, and this time the younger man did not avoid his touch. Then Jonathan's face twisted into a cynical, tearful grimace. "What do you make of that, Doctor? Don't all sons want to kill their fathers?"

"Perhaps," Ned said. "Listen, Jonathan, you look terribly strung out. Come and walk with me a while, talk if you like. I want to hear the rest of it, if you want to tell me."

Two hours later, when they parted, Jonathan to see Veidt and go to England, Driscoll to his home in Vienna—"Until it gets too hot over here," he said—Jonathan felt as if an enormous weight had been lifted from him.

Nothing had changed, but the telling of it, all of it, to this clever, sympathetic man had made it possible, somehow, for Jonathan to keep going.

He thought suddenly of all the people he was supposed to love and didn't, and of all the people he was supposed to hate and couldn't.

"I can't thank you enough," he said earnestly to Ned, not knowing precisely what it was he thanked him for. "I'm sorry I was so—so stupid back there."

"How is she?" Ned asked. The doctor vanished and a man in love stood in his place.

My God, Jonathan thought, *no wonder she fell in love with him!* Driscoll was the most genuine man Jonathan had ever met and in a world of pretenders that was extraordinary. A woman like Madeleine would have seen that in him and loved him for it; she was like that herself.

"She's well," Jonathan said. "Content, in a way she never was before, but I don't think she's really happy. She's still very beautiful."

The doctor nodded, his eyes made sad by memory.

"I'll write and say I saw you," Jonathan said, touched by the feeling the man still had for his mother.

"Yes, I'd like that," Ned said. "And if I see her when I get back to the States, I'll tell her we met. She always loved you very much."

Enough to stay with my father, Jonathan thought.

They looked at each other with nothing to say that would not take a lifetime. "Don't stay in Europe too long," Jonathan said.

"No. I wish you luck, Jonathan. Be careful."

With a last clasp of hands they parted, walking in opposite directions, two men who had lost the one thing in life that makes it bearable.

Book VII

67

The way she measured time told the story of Susannah's life. As a child, her birthdays and Jonathan's were her markers, and later, her Saturdays at Slayter's. Those were superseded by wedding anniversaries and her sons' birthdays. It was when, early in 1939, she received the proxies from Jonathan that she began to measure time by the events that were leading the world to war and her brother to a destiny she had never foreseen.

His letters were heavy with cynical foreboding and something that troubled Susannah even more. "He's making it a personal vendetta," she said to Charles, "against the German war machine and the men behind it—Jesse in particular."

Charles was glad she had abandoned the filial "Father" when the proxies came from Europe, as if she knew she must distance herself from the man if she were forced into fighting him.

"Jonathan wants you to use those proxies all by yourself," he told her then. "That's not fair."

"I can't use them! There is no state of war in Europe and what we have here is a neutralist, isolationist country—with anti-Fascist sympathies in some corners. I need more than that to make a successful stand against him."

"You can't change anything," Charles warned her. "He'll never surrender control of that company, no matter what happens."

He knew she would never use those proxies without fair cause, and that was just as well. Her involvement at Slayter's was enough for Charles to handle now; he didn't like the prospect of being married to a chairman of its board.

On the September day in 1939 that Jonathan left Berlin and Germany invaded Poland, Susannah and Charles were at Southampton with the boys for a long weekend. The declaration of war against the Third Reich by England and France early Sunday morning brought them back to the city. Susannah was tense in bed that night; he didn't have to touch her to feel it.

"Susannah, you don't have to confront Jesse tomorrow. You don't have to do this all alone. Wait for Jonathan. Now that war's been declared he'll come back."

"No, he won't, not without Marietta. He has a stubborn streak a mile wide."

"But he'll never find her now! We'll be in this before too long and his passport won't take him all over, like a magic carpet. He'll have to come home."

She moved restlessly next to him. "And when he does, how will I face him if I don't keep my promise? I made it for my sake, as much as his. No, Charles, I have to do it and I have to do it tomorrow. Just hold me, Charles. I need you; you're the only one I can trust."

She dropped him at his office the next morning and Charles watched her pull away in the open convertible, admiring the way she handled the car—with efficiency and authority, the way she handled everything except her father. He spent a useless few hours, waiting to hear from her, but at eleven o'clock his secretary said she was outside, waiting to see him.

"It was easy," Susannah said as soon as the door to Charles's office closed behind her. She tossed her bag onto one of the clients' chairs facing his desk and sat in the other. "I went storming in there with a big speech about I.G., ready to threaten him with those proxies if I had to."

She stood again and wandered around the office aimlessly, picking up a book, an ashtray, straightening a stack of law journals as she went. "But he had anticipated me, as usual. He showed me the cables to I.G. advising that Slayter's would undertake no further business for them."

Charles hid his relief. "It was the clever thing to do and Jesse is a clever man."

"But he did it even before Roosevelt went on the air about getting the arms embargo lifted! He did it before Germany invaded Poland!"

Charles watched her circling around his office. She was trying to figure things out. Figuring things out was a passion of hers. Maybe someday she would figure Jesse out and see him as he was, but Charles wanted that to be her own discovery. She was getting closer to it.

"The factories are tooling up for armaments already," he said reasonably. "He holds commercial paper and shares in all those corporations. Why would he support a cartel that restricts the very supplies they'll need?"

Susannah sat down finally. "It was just too easy," she repeated, worrying it like a bulldog with a bone.

Charles waited.

Susannah shook her head. "He wouldn't mislead me about a thing like

340

this," she decided. Her dark eyes challenged him to dispute that. "He's still furious with Jonnie," she went on, "but he wouldn't do that to him either." She seemed convinced, and more relaxed than she had been in a long time.

Charles got up from his desk. "Come on, I'll take you to lunch. I think you just had the wind taken out of your sails. You went in there rigged for battle and he had already surrendered." He put his arms around her.

"I guess he yielded to the inevitable," she said. "If I knew where Jonathan was, I'd write to tell him."

Charles was glad she couldn't see his face. Jesse Slayter *yield?* "Would a letter reach him with a war on?"

"It's not much of a war yet," Susannah said.

It was the time in 'thirty-nine journalists would call "the phony war," a few months' lapse between the declaration itself and the start of serious hostilities.

But then, one by one, the countries fell to Hitler. Poland surrendered in three weeks and then the year turned again. May of 1940 brought not rebirth but the fall of Holland and Belgium. By the end of May the British Expeditionary Force was pinned down on Dunkirk Beach in France, and still there was no sign of Jonathan's return. It was at Willow Hill that Susannah began to despair of ever seeing him again.

"Are you all right?" she asked Madeleine, when she came upon her one afternoon, alone in the music room. Her vitality was gone and her blue eyes looked dull with fatigue.

Madeleine was silent for a moment, her hands moving idly across the polished veneer of the closed piano. "Susannah how much did Jesse have to do with Hitler?"

Susannah, startled, considered before she answered. The papers had been full of the federal suit against Alcoa for restricting the aluminum supply in America; everyone knew that. Alcoa was involved with I.G. Farben. Still, she was not sure how much Madeleine knew about Slayter's dealings with the vast German monopoly.

"At one time, quite a lot," she said, "indirectly, of course, through I.G. Farben, but last year Father cut his ties with them."

"How did you make him do that without my proxy?"

"I didn't have to make him do anything," Susannah said, surprised at how much Jonathan had told his mother. "Jesse did it first."

"Are you sure?"

"Of course I'm sure!" Susannah said, nettled that her judgment was in question. "Jesse draws the line somewhat later than we do, but he does draw it." When Madeleine made no reply, she asked, "Don't you believe it?"

Madeleine bit her lip as if she preferred not to say any more, but finally

341

could not stop herself. "Susannah, I've had the most terrible letter from Jonathan."

Susannah waited, trying to govern her panic, until Madeleine went on with tears in her eyes.

"He thinks Jesse had something to do with Marietta's disappearance. That's one of the reasons he won't come home, he says he wouldn't be able to keep from—from killing Jesse."

"Oh, no," Susannah said, and her eyes closed briefly against the ugliness of it. "He must have gone a little crazy."

Madeleine nodded, her misery palpable. "I know Jesse is a lot of things, but he's not bad enough to send that girl and her family to one of those concentration camps—just to keep her away from Jonathan!"

"My God, of course not!" Susannah said. "May I see the letter?"

Madeleine handed it to her and she read it swiftly, with the heartbreaking feeling that her brother was lost to her. He had been brooding about Marietta for so long that he was locked into a nightmare where none of them could reach him. "It would've been better if he'd told you about this sooner, instead of nursing it all by himself," Susannah said.

"I know," Madeleine said. "My poor Jonnie, I can't bear for him to be tormented like this."

Susannah's heart turned over for her mother, and she went to the piano bench. "Look, we all know Father hates the idea of this marriage, but from that to—it's absurd and we have to convince Jonathan of that." She sat down next to Madeleine. "Please don't cry, it'll be all right," she whispered, and knew it would not.

"Try to find some way to make Jonathan come home, Sassie, you're the only one who can," Madeleine said, drying her tears because Susannah asked her to.

"I'll convince him that it isn't true," Susannah said, and knew she could never ask her father to deny such an accusation.

"Maybe Daniel can persuade him to come home," Madeleine said. "If the war goes badly for France, maybe they'll come home together." She looked at the door, as if they might suddenly appear in the music room.

France fell at the end of June and there was no sign of them, as the world held its breath and waited for Hitler to invade England. There were letters from Philippa, who had taken refuge in Kent in anticipation of a lightning war—a blitzkrieg—centered on London, and was now a reluctant hostess to a score of children evacuated from the huge city. Jonathan came and went, she said, withdrawn and bitter, unwilling to listen to reason.

Then the Battle of Britain began in July and there was another marker: Jonathan joined the R.A.F.

For Susannah there was only one good thing about the summer of 1940: that day at Willow Hill with Madeleine. She knew she had forgiven her mother years ago, but until she could tell her so, she would not forgive herself.

68

"I knew he'd join the British forces," Gemma said when Charles and Susannah took her to dinner one night during the Thanksgiving holidays. She looked exceptionally well, Susannah thought. Her velvet-brown eyes were steady and her hair curled mercilessly in the wet weather. It suited her, no matter how much she hated it.

"But Jon was never a warrior."

Gemma's full mouth closed around a cigarette and Charles held a match for her. "You two think he's just a lover, don't you?" she said, looking at them with the kind of patience a mother extends to a dear but slightly limited child. "He's always been a lot more than that."

She inhaled deeply and took a sip or two of the wine before she went on. "He's always known the truth about himself, even if he didn't do anything about it. He's fighting in this war because he believes he must. If you don't know that, you don't know him."

Driving home after they had dropped Gemma off, Susannah wondered at her. "At first I thought she'd go to pieces, and now I know why she didn't. She talks as if he weren't married, as if he's just been away on a trip, not looking for his wife. It's not good." Susannah shook her head. "She has to accept things as they are."

"People can't turn love off, like a faucet," Charles said. "Especially not Gemma."

"Why 'especially'?"

"You know Gemma," Charles said. "She's always had a man around. She's the kind of woman who needs one."

Susannah suppressed the question she had never asked him and put another. "Do you think she's sleeping with someone?"

"I doubt it—she's still too gone on Jon. I think she's right about him too; he's fighting because he feels he must."

"Damn it," Susannah said, "he should have left Slayter's years ago. I feel responsible for that. He'd have been happier."

"Well, he's left it now," Charles said, pulling into their garage. "He'll never go back." He turned off the ignition and the car gave a gentle shudder before it stopped. "What'll that do to your father?"

"I don't know—and as long as Jonathan gets home safely I don't really care." She got out of the car and they went into the house.

345

He waited until they were in bed to pick up the conversation. "I didn't know you didn't care about your father anymore."

"That's not what I said. Everything's relative—I don't care by comparison with Jonathan's life."

"You wouldn't have said it ten years ago."

"I wouldn't have said a lot of things ten years ago."

"Such as?"

"I wish I knew Madeleine better. I've steered pretty clear of her for a long time. How do I get chummy with Mummy now?"

"Just tell her you want to," Charles said. "Tell her you think she's a helluva woman." When she didn't reply he said, "Oh, Susannah," the way he always did when he thought she was wrong.

"Put yourself in my place, Charles! She was unfaithful to my father." It was still hard for her to say it, even to him.

Charles dropped his equable manner. "Unfaithful to what? His idea of love is to live all your lives for you. He takes everything you have to give him, and gives you nothing in return, not even freedom. Love can't exist in a half vacuum, Susannah; it has to be shared to be real."

Susannah propped herself on one elbow and turned toward him, although she couldn't really see his face in the darkened room. "Maybe controlling people is his way of loving them. Don't you think he may feel more than he shows? I'm a lot like him, you know. I've always loved you so much more than you ever believed. I just don't show things in exactly the same way you do."

He reached for her and she lay down again with her cheek on his shoulder. It was easier to say things like that in the dark.

"What are you thinking about?" she asked Charles.

"Washington. When the war starts they want me at an intelligence desk."

"Oh, shit," Susannah said, in one of her new lapses into vulgarity. "I might have known they'd want you. All your school buddies are in F.D.R.'s brain trust." She was restless suddenly. "When?"

"When the war starts."

"Would you have to live in Washington?"

"Of course—will you come with me?"

She hesitated to say it, but she knew she wouldn't move to Washington. It would be impossible to go on working at Slayter's if she did. She felt too close to him tonight to ruin things by saying so.

"I'll think about that tomorrow," she said. "Wasn't it wonderful when all we had to worry about was whether Rhett would come back to Scarlett or the king would marry Mrs. Simpson?"

He didn't answer. The closeness was evaporating. Once she had supposed

346

that a man and a woman understood everything about each other after they were lovers. She had learned that deep communication only happened when lovers were actually making love; otherwise the barriers between them remained as impenetrable as ever.

She pushed back the bedclothes covering them; they were both naked and she moved over him, her hair brushing his stomach. She knew what excited him and she loved him—it excited her too. In moments she could feel him responding.

"Oh, yes," he said, "do that. Be Sassie for me."

69

"My dear sir," Karl-Dieter Veidt said, holding out his hand to Jesse. "Such a delight to see you again. It has been entirely too long."

Jesse took the hand briefly, then sat back in the Rolls-Royce. He didn't think much of such cloak-and-dagger arrangements, but in this winter of 1940 discretion was the better part of business. Veidt could certainly not appear at Slayter's; his staff, especially his own daughter, would have made a fuss over it. To all intents and purposes he had had no business with Veidt since last year.

With barely a whisper the great car moved off, headed uptown toward Central Park. The heady aroma of two gardenias, one in each of the vases affixed to the sides of the car, began to give Jesse a headache.

"I trust your family is well," Veidt purred pleasantly. "The last time I saw your son he was, shall we say, distressed. He requested a service of me which I was unable to perform. I hope you have assured him I was utterly helpless under the circumstances."

"I haven't seen him for over two years," Jesse said frigidly. "He was searching for his wife until he joined the R.A.F."

Veidt was visibly surprised. "I made it clear to him in Berlin that it had become a Gestapo affair. He knew Victor Kastenberg was a talented chemist; the Fatherland no doubt persuaded him to keep his knowledge at home."

Jesse rolled the window down a few inches. "I thought you had only been persuaded to keep my good will, not to go farther."

Veidt's spectacles glinted as he looked at Jesse. "We have no control over the Gestapo."

"You have lost control of Herr Hitler, as well. He is not popular with the public here, no matter how much pro-Nazi propaganda you pay for in the American press. It could interfere with business."

"Not, I devoutly hope, between us. Our organization has always dealt in good faith with yours."

What Veidt said was true, but they were no longer on an equal footing. In Germany the government controlled business; in America it was still the other way around.

Veidt rested a slender hand on his crossed leg. His bony knee pushed at the pale gray worsted of his suit. In all the years Jesse had known the man, he had never worn any other color. Today, however, his underlying calm seemed to have deserted him. He must really want a lot of money from America—but for what?

Finally he began to explain the reason for this meeting, the first in some time. "Rubber has become more vital than ever under present circumstances," he said.

"When does Hitler plan to invade Russia?" Jesse returned. He took out his pipe and tobacco pouch.

Veidt smiled his admiration of this man's perspicacity. The German-Soviet pact had come as a surprise to the public—Hitler, after all, was a rabid anti-Communist, the concentration camps were full of them—but men like Jesse had understood the reason for Hitler's pact with the arch-enemy in 1939. His gains in western Europe had to be consolidated before the German armies could turn east; the refusal of the *gottverdammte Engländer* to surrender posed the possibility of a two-front war. Eventually Hitler would wipe the Bolsheviks off the face of the earth. Even those who disapproved of Hitler's theatrics preferred him to the Communists. The Soviets were a threat to all vested interests.

"I cannot presume to anticipate the Führer's plans," Veidt said primly, with a confirmatory smirk.

"And if Japan should come into the war against Britain, rubber supplies from the Far East will be cut off," Jesse said. He had filled and tamped the bowl of the pipe and now he lit it.

Veidt sighed. "Alas, yes."

Jesse sniffed the pipe smoke gratefully. The gardenias were beginning to curl in the heat of the car.

The German was talking again. "I.G. is planning construction of a huge new plant for the production of Buna rubber—one of the synthetics Victor Kastenberg was working on, by the way. It will be financed and owned privately, we have decided, independent of government assistance. We are prepared to invest the equivalent of two hundred and fifty million dollars."

Jesse puffed a few times. If I.G. Farben was willing to invest its own money, the projected profits must be enormous and the success of the venture certain. "There is a fortune to be made in synthetic rubber," Jesse said, "both during the war and after it."

"Just so, a fortune," Veidt agreed. "We are almost agreed on the site—it has good rail access, plenty of water and Silesian coal for the high-pressure techniques required in both the Bergius and Buna processes. We hope, with this plant in addition to those at Huels and Schkopau, to bring our annual Buna tonnage to one hundred and fifty thousand, enough for any offensive."

Jesse was impressed. "With a war on where will you get the labor for such an effort?"

Veidt stirred slightly in his seat and uncrossed his legs. "We shall use prisoners from a concentration camp the SS plans to develop in that area—undesirables, political dissidents, mainly Communists." He tittered faintly. "There is a certain poetic justice in having them work out their sentences by laboring to squash the Soviets." He crossed his legs again in the opposite direction. "I should add that the site—it is at a place called Auschwitz—is in eastern Poland, making a good supply depot for our armies when they begin a move in that direction."

He removed his glasses and wiped them carefully with a scented handkerchief from his breast pocket. "More to the point, imagine what an enormous market will open to us once Russia is persuaded to abandon the evils of Communism."

Jesse glanced at Veidt. "Would you mind if we got rid of those gardenias? The scent is overpowering."

"My dear sir," Veidt said apologetically. "Of course! I had no idea."

Each of them leaned forward to remove a gardenia and toss it out of a window. By the time they had settled back, Jesse was ready to proceed.

"You want us to handle part of the financing. That is no longer as simple as it once was. There is a great deal of anti-Nazi feeling in this country, and that Jewish farmer Morgenthau is breathing down American I.G.'s back already. When there is war between us"—he brushed aside Veidt's mild protest with a wave of his hand—"no American firm could risk an open connection with a German monopoly. I refer you to the case of Alcoa. We would be dealing with patriotic fanatics, not men of affairs."

It was Veidt's turn to wait now, while Jesse considered the problem. He had no ready-made front like the company I.G. Farben had set up to distribute Bayer aspirin and Phillips Milk of Magnesia in America. The next best thing was to form a new company and make sure it was well hidden.

Jesse Slayter was a master at constructing pyramid holding companies. The corporations at the top were fronts; the real owner was buried somewhere at the base of the pyramid. "How much do you want from me?" Jesse said finally.

Veidt named a figure. Jesse refused. The sum was lowered. Jesse proposed a rate of discounted interest and a share of the future profits that Veidt termed exorbitant.

"I am not asking for shares or options now," Jesse said. "Given the circumstances, that is impossible. The discount is my guarantee against profits far in the future, since we are agreed that rubber will be vital no matter who comes into this war and no matter who wins it."

They reached an agreement, finally. It was the kind of thing Jesse did every day—float a bond issue to raise investment capital for ostensible use in America.

That posed no great problem, either. The bonds would be issued for Ambrose-Sentinel, that gigantic umbrella controlled by J. Slayter and Son. The capital Jesse raised, less his healthy discount, would trickle down through the maze of wholly owned subsidiaries to end in an account at the Bank for International Settlements in Basel. The account would be called Sertes and no one, not even Jesse's partners, would have any idea what Sertes represented.

"I wonder," Jesse said to Veidt when it was all decided, "is Kastenberg interned at this place—at Auschwitz—with his family?"

Veidt removed his glasses again and repolished them. "You understand we have nothing to do with police matters," he cautioned. "I could make inquiries, although I doubt if the authorities would let him go—if, of course, he is there." He replaced his glasses. "Your daughter-in-law, perhaps . . ."

Jesse watched the bustling city outside the windows of the car. "I doubt she would leave her family now," he said. "She is apparently very loyal to them—an admirable trait."

Veidt inclined his head briefly and they left it there.

When Jesse got out of the Rolls he took a taxi back to Pearl Street. He had some business to discuss with Susannah—not Sertes, of course. She had some womanish sensibilities, largely because of her brother, and Jesse did not intend to rouse her ire. He was grateful for her presence. It helped fill the gap Jonathan had left, not in his empire but in his life.

He had never been able to reach his son, although he had certainly tried. As a result he had been overindulgent and this was his reward. The R.A.F.! That pack of heroic fools!

Jesse's hands clenched as he rode up in his private elevator. This was his son in danger, his only son! Somehow he must be brought back to safety. He had hoped that when Jonathan could not find the girl he would have come to his senses and forgotten her, as he had the Phelps woman. A good thing, too, she was no fit wife for a Slayter, either.

Jesse stopped at Susannah's office on the way to his own. "I'd like an hour of your time," he said, admiring the neatness of her desk, the crispness of her style. She was a handsome woman—and a clever one, a real credit to him. It was amazing that he had produced two such different children, but given the character of their mother he had been fortunate.

"One more telephone call and I'll be there," Susannah said, smiling at him.

He withdrew, gratified. He knew how to handle his daughter. She loved the private conferences in his office; they were an easy sign of his confidence in her. And more than ever, he knew she loved him. He had that to comfort him whenever he had enough time to want comfort.

70

"Look at this room!" Gemma said to Madeleine. "It's straight out of *House and Garden.*"

Madeleine agreed, looking around the living room of the senior Benedicts' vast new apartment on Park Avenue. The expanse was broken by Coromandel screens into comfortable four-chair "conversation groupings." The Chinese wallpaper and the Savonnerie carpets were works of art. There was not an ashtray or an ornament that had not been carefully selected to accessorize the room.

"I feel like scattering some dog-eared old magazines around," Madeleine said.

"What do you think we can take out of here to put into a Bundle-for-Britain?"

"Money," Madeleine said. "It looks like the Colony Club has moved in with the Racquet for this do." She flagged down a waiter and the two woman helped themselves to champagne.

"I was always glad Jonathan didn't bother much with his men's clubs," Gemma said, savoring her champagne.

Madeleine didn't answer. She agreed with Susannah that even after all this time Gemma had not come to terms with Jonathan's marriage. It wasn't healthy, but no one had the heart to belabor the point with this woman who had meant so much to Jonathan for so long. She appeared to be going on with her life—she worked hard at her job, went skiing in the winter, played tennis in the summer—but she was always alone. In a world full of couples that was difficult. For a woman like Gemma, it was preposterous, but she was not the only woman to do preposterous things.

Madeleine spent a lot of time at Gemma's apartment, even when Gemma was at work. It was cozy, not a great, empty shell like the mansion on Fifth Avenue that Jesse stubbornly refused to close down for the duration of the war in Europe, while Jonathan was gone.

Madeleine needed a place where she could relax completely. On the rare evenings Jesse spent at home alone with her, it was hard to keep from asking him, point blank, if there were any grounds for Jonathan's terrible suspicions about Marietta. She needed to relax from the strain of it.

Usually she thought they were only sick imaginings, brought on by Jonathan's loneliness and worry, and totally absurd. Even Jesse could not hide his constant anxiety for his son. It was ridiculous to suppose he had contributed to Jonnie's agony in such a loathsome way.

Jonnie was safer now, thank heaven. His Uncle Elton had arranged for him to be attached to intelligence headquarters in London. But in the private war Jonathan was fighting, there was no safety.

Madeleine's eyes roved over the room while she talked to Gemma and she saw him the moment he came in. He was alone: there was no expectant glance around for someone he was meeting. It was a very large room and Ned was not a big man, but she knew him immediately from the way he stood, the set of his shoulders, the tilt of his head. She was startled to see that his hair was completely gray. Then she thought to herself, *there are a lot of silver threads among my gold too.*

"I see Susannah and Charlie over there," Gemma said. "Shall we?"

"You go ahead, there are a few people on the committee I want to talk to."

Gemma left her and Madeleine walked over to the door. He smiled when he saw her coming, a smile as tentative as hers, and he took her hand.

"How long has it been?" he asked. "A dozen years? One hundred?"

"A long time." She looked at him, not really noticing anything but his eyes. "I've thought a lot about you."

"What did you think?"

"I wondered if you were well, if you were happy, if you were still married."

He nodded. "That's exactly what I wondered about you." He leaned forward. "Let's not stay here. I only came to give them a Bundles-for-Britain check. I can mail it."

Madeleine smiled. "All right, but I ought to tell the woman I came with."

"You'll never find her in that mob. She'll assume you couldn't stand this social watering hole. You never liked this kind of thing."

They found a taxi on Park Avenue and Ned gave the address of his brownstone.

"You've moved back to New York," she said, feeling on the brink of something.

"I'm in the process. I had already decided not to stay in Boston, and when my tenant didn't renew this lease it seemed to be a sign, so here I am."

He hadn't once said "we"—married people always said "we." She knew she was being foolish, but she was glad of that.

The taxi stopped and she realized she had never been to this house before, but he made no attempt to show it to her when they were inside. They went into a comfortable living room, with the lamps still lit and a low fire almost gone in a grate behind the screen. He took her coat, dropped his own, and

356

went to stir the fire, adding two logs while he talked to her, asking about her children, hearing about her grandchildren. Then he came to sit next to her on the deep couch in front of the fire.

"I saw Jonathan in Berlin last year," he said.

"Yes, he wrote he had run into an old friend of mine—with a beard." She smiled briefly. "I'm glad it's gone." Her face clouded. "How was he, Ned?"

Ned shook his head. "Not very well, I'm afraid. He's a man pursued by very special demons."

She clasped her hands. "He told you?"

"Yes, he did."

Madeleine sighed. "I don't know what there is about Jesse that arouses such horrible suspicions." Her blue eyes beseeched him to make little of them.

"Jonathan makes a good case against him," Ned said, "but I'm sure an equally good one could be made in his defense if Jonathan wanted to hear it. It's not a healthy thing to speculate on, is it?" He lit a cigarette for Madeleine and then subsided. They had suddenly run out of conversation.

"I have a hard time just chatting when I'm with you," he said.

She nodded. "What do you want to know?"

"What happened. If your 'try' succeeded."

Madeleine looked at her hands, turning the sapphire ring she always wore. "In a way, yes. Jesse and I always had this chemistry for each other, even if nothing much came of it the first time. Then for some reason we discovered a kind of—I don't know what to call it—I guess it was a mutual excitement. It was very strange, coming twenty-five years into a marriage, instead of at the beginning."

"Is that love?"

"I'd have thought so when I was a girl, when I was blinded by desire," Madeleine said, "so I thought it was love for a few years while it was happening." She studied him. "I couldn't say that to anyone but you."

"What changed it?"

She shrugged. "I realized it didn't mean to him what it meant to me. I think it was just a better way to control me. It was some kind of bond between us, anyway; you can't rule out sexual delirium, no matter what you want to call it." She twisted the ring. "And then—well, I thought I could help a little with Jonathan. Susannah has Charles, you see." She nodded proudly. "She has grit, my Susannah. She's one of those people whose promise you can bank on." She shook her head. "That was a poor choice of words."

"This excitement—is it over?"

"Excitement's tiring. It burns out."

He just stood there, watching her. She knew what he wanted to ask her, ridiculous as it was at their age and after so many years. He wanted to ask her if there was anything left of the love she had once felt for him, which had been so real. But it was too soon—and it was too late, anyway.

"Where are your wife and daughter, Ned?"

"In Boston. We're emotionally separated." His hands rose, then fell back into his lap in a hopeless gesture. "It was my fault. I never loved her." He looked up. "I loved you."

"Oh, Ned, how you must hate me."

To his everlasting credit, he did not deny it. He just kept looking at her, with the same longing she had seen on his face that day in Washington Square—and a profound sadness.

"I don't know how I could have ruined so many lives," Madeleine said, "without trying to. Susannah's, Jonnie's—he tried to protect me from Jesse at one point, you know, it must have been so hard for him to stay at home—and yours." She seemed resigned, but astonished. "How can that happen, Ned? I loved all of you so much. How could I have hurt you so?"

He leaned toward her, as if to defend her. "You had help, Madeleine. You didn't do it all alone. You had him. You can't fight something so alien to you, something you don't even understand."

"Will you ever forgive me?"

"No, but what does that matter? I still love you." He took her hands. "I wasn't there by coincidence tonight, you know. I knew you were on the committee. I've tried to keep from coming to New York to find you since I got back from Europe." He shrugged. "Now I've moved here. It's ironic. I know all about obsessions, I can even cure them sometimes, but not this one, not my own."

"Oh, don't cure this one, Ned, please don't."

He put his arms around her in a tender passion to protect her from anyone or anything that might hurt her, and she ached with love for him and all the years she had let go by without it.

"I won't leave you again, Ned."

"No." He held her close. "We have to find whatever happiness we can in the ruins. I used to demand everything, but I know now I can't have it all the time. I love you, Madeleine, you're the sweetest dream I ever had."

"I've been a dream too long, Ned, make me real again."

She had known many sublime moments in Ned's arms, she had survived for many years on the mere memory of them, but when he touched her it surpassed her memories. They were locked in love, not some kind of combat, and the joy of it was electrifying.

358

She only thought of Jesse for an instant, but he was the death of her and she wanted to live.

She lay in Ned's arms, quiet at last, and watched the fire with him.

"You haven't changed, Madeleine, you're still the most wonderful woman I ever knew."

"Yes, I've changed," she said. "I know what kind of man I'm holding in my arms and I'll never let him go."

A few weeks later she signed a lease on a small apartment off Gramercy Park, furnished it, and moved a few of her treasures into it. Ned kept up his semblance of a marriage. "For my child's sake," he told Madeleine, and she respected that decision. She had done the same thing herself.

She spent many contented hours alone at the apartment, reading or writing long letters to Jonathan, to Philippa and her nieces and nephews in England.

Ned came whenever his practice permitted, and she only slept there when Jesse was away in Washington. She made no special attempt to keep the apartment a secret, but only Ned and Daisy knew about it.

"At least she's happy for a few hours, now and then," Daisy told Bob Harris, never mentioning Dr. Driscoll to him.

"She won't be when Himself finds out," was Bob's doleful prediction.

"Himself!" Daisy sniffed. "He doesn't know she's alive. There's nothing wrong in having a little place of her own."

"And Miss Susannah?"

"Miss Susannah loves that woman a lot more than she thinks," Daisy said, "and one day she'll come to know it."

71

1942

"I wish we wouldn't argue about it anymore, Charles." Susannah left the bedroom of the hotel suite and called "Come in" to a knock at the living room door. The waiter wheeled in a table with a large pot of coffee and some covered dishes on it, along with a copy of the *Washington Daily News* for March 27, 1942.

"You never argue, you just do as you like," Charles said, following her into the room. He stopped talking only until the waiter left. "There's no reason for you to live in New York and commute to see me whenever you can get away. Away from what? You're not holding the country's hand through hard times—the war has cured the Depression. You can't even pretend it's the boys—they're both in school now."

Susannah sat down at the table and poured herself a cup of coffee. She looked at Charles. He was sleek and handsome in his uniform; he carried a cap and jacket with an Army major's insignia on it.

"Be reasonable, for heaven's sake," she said. "My work is in New York, yours is in Washington. You chose to make the move, I didn't. Why should I leave my career for your war job? There'll be no C.O.I. when the war's over, but Slayter's will still be there."

Charles dropped the jacket and cap on an armchair and sat down across from her. "It's a damned peculiar kind of marriage, being together for a night or two whenever you can make it."

She uncovered a plate of scrambled eggs. "I don't know about that. I think it's kind of exciting. So did you, last night."

"It's the rest of the time that bothers me; I wonder why it doesn't bother you. Probably because your heart still belongs to Daddy."

She put the cover down. "I stay to keep an eye on him, you know that. You wanted it as much as Jon when he asked me to do it."

He helped himself to some eggs. "Aside from that, you love it."

"Yes, I do! I love the excitement of Wall Street, the electricity that sparks along like chain lightning when something big is in the air." Her chin came up. "And I'm proud of what I did—little things, but they add up—to help steer this country through the Depression. I'm not just another rich girl who sat on her tuffet." She looked at him imploringly, even in her pride.

361

"Surely you, of all people, can understand that!" She waited, looking at him, pale and anxious, but indomitable too.

"Yes, of course," he said, giving in and furious with himself for doing it, with her for asking it on perfectly logical grounds. His love for her had nothing to do with logic.

She came to sit on his lap and nestle in his arms for a moment. "I love you, Charles," she said. "You're the only man I know who's honest enough to be fair, even when he hates it." She kissed him and went back to her breakfast.

Charles lit a cigarette, composing himself, then changed the subject. "I had some particularly bleak news from Elton yesterday," he said. The paths of Britain's Special Operations Executive and America's Coordinator of Information crossed often these days.

"Marietta?" She was very intent.

"No, and from what they're saying, I doubt very much that we'll ever hear of her again. They tell us conditions in those camps are unbelievable— worse than anyone suspects—and Marietta led a sheltered life."

She moved again to stir her coffee, disappointed but not surprised. Then she looked up at him, impelled by the irony in his voice. "A sheltered life— like mine?"

"Not quite. She didn't have a Jesse to show her what the world's really like. He casts a long shadow—only the strong can survive it." His tone, even more than the cynical words, betrayed his still-smoldering anger because Susannah was going back to New York.

She looked at him in disbelief. "You resent strength. It's amazing! You'd like it if I weren't so—whatever it is I am—wouldn't you, if I were just an extension of you, a life tenant, like one of those birds that ride around on hippos' backs? But that's not why you wanted me; there were plenty of girls like that to choose from."

He sighed. "I'm sorry. I wanted to tear down those fine defenses that hide the inviolate you from me."

"I have no defenses against you!"

"Yes, you do." He smiled, trying to make light of it. "There's still the essential you behind a last veil."

"Maybe the essential me and the veil are one and the same; if you destroy one, you destroy both. Remember Salome and her seventh veil, the last one."

"She dropped it once, for love of Jochanan."

"And had to have his head on a plate in return! What kind of bargain is that?" Her eyes closed in exasperation. "And what kind of conversation is this? Listen, Charles, I love you so much it sticks out all over me, like tinsel on a Christmas tree."

He smiled at her again, then glanced at the train case and the coat that proclaimed her departure. "Sometimes it does, when you're with me."

"Then I promise to be with you more often. I'll be back next weekend and I'll stay till you beg me to go back." She went to kiss him good-bye. "Mind if I take the paper?"

He shook his head and she slipped it into her train case and snapped it shut. Then she kissed him again and left, swinging her sable coat around her shoulders. A trace of Arpège stayed in the room with him.

He started to pour another cup of coffee, then set the pot down so sharply that the coffee slopped out of the spout, making an ugly brown stain on the white tablecloth. He didn't want to drink his coffee alone in the morning, he didn't want to come back here alone at the end of the day. He wanted to be with a woman, any woman; they were all the same except for Susannah.

There were so many open invitations in Washington since the war had started. They were in the women's laughter, in their eyes, in the way they pressed against him at the endless cocktail parties. There was one, in particular, who would make him more than welcome.

He hesitated a moment, looking at the door Susannah had just walked through, and wished mightily that she hadn't left him alone today. Then he set his jaw and went to the telephone. He asked the hotel switchboard for a number and waited until there was a comforting click at the other end of the line and a sleepy female voice said "Hello."

"Hello," Charles said, with what Susannah called his Mona Lisa smile— "Because a woman can't tell whether you're inviting her to dinner or to bed"—"this is Charles, Charles Benedict. Is that invitation still open?" He waited for a moment, then nodded and smiled. "Fine, I'll pick you up at six." Then, the smile fading, he hung up, put on his jacket and his cap and left the hotel suite.

On the train Susannah went into the club car. It was crowded and full of smoke. It smelled of perspiration, whiskey and men. She sat in a swivel chair and tried to sort out her emotions. She knew Charles objected to their separations, but not how much. Her promise to stay in Washington until he asked her to leave was an exaggeration, but she wasn't sure he realized that. Then she shrugged slightly. He would, when he'd seen her sitting around doing absolutely nothing for a few days.

She took the *Washington Daily News* out of her case and looked at the front page. Her eyes stopped on the Senate hearings about the rubber crisis and the connection between the shortage, Standard Oil, and I.G. Farben patents on the synthetic process. She gasped in shock at one line from a Standard memo, written as they received two thousand patents—obviously for "safekeeping"—from I.G. in 1939, just after the war in Europe started.

> We did our best to work out complete plans for a *modus vivendi* which would operate through the term of the war whether or not the U.S. came in.

It was unbelievable! Standard Oil had received those patents to *protect* them from seizure by the Alien Property Custodian when the United States got into the war—and even then they had evolved a "method of living," actually a means of mutual cooperation that ignored war and necessity and treasonable dealing with the enemy!

America had a serious rubber shortage, not because she was incapable of making synthetic rubber, but because I.G. Farben, Hitler's monopoly, held the patents on it and Standard Oil, an American company, protected them.

Susannah hardly heard the noisy crowd in the train. She was unaware of the men's glances and she brushed aside offers to buy her a drink. She sat stone still in the churning car, and wondered if there were other men in America who had reached a *modus vivendi* with the Nazis for the duration of the war, no matter who came into it and no matter who won.

My God, she thought, *if Jesse's one of them, I don't want to know*—and realized she wouldn't rest again until she knew for sure.

72

1943

Sometimes Lord Lucas was convinced that everyone had gone mad. If this struggle was Britain's finest hour, as Winston had so nobly said, it was also her gayest and most thrilling. He could tell already that people would look back on the war years with nostalgia, as much as anything else, and that meant they *had* gone completely insane.

"Nostalgia!"

The Earl snorted as he unlocked the inner drawer of a safe in his office at S.O.E. headquarters, withdrew a file, and sat down at his desk with it. He glanced at his watch and shook his head in gloomy anticipation of what the January morning would bring. No matter how he tried to keep back alarming information, Jonathan always got it out of him, down to the last detail—and they were grisly details these days.

There had been enough escapes from the concentration camps for the Allies to concede officially that Hitler was, indeed, killing the Jews of Europe and that some protest had to be made or the Allies would have to answer for their silence after the war.

It would have been pointless for him to keep anything from Jonathan. London was awash in goverments-in-exile: Poles, Finns, Czechs, Greeks, the Free French. He supposed it was why the Allied Declaration on the mass murders was prepared right here, where all the evidence was collected.

He moved restlessly, his silver hair and mustache gleaming in the bare light overhead. It was hard to believe such random slaughter, no matter how many reports and documents and smuggled escapees surfaced to confirm it. No one wanted to believe it; they didn't even want to hear it. Good God, they'd come within an ace of losing the bloody war until the British victory at El Alamein, only two months ago. Now they could just begin to hope they'd win it. There was the whole continent of Europe to retake, a huge effort to mount in the Far East. No one had the time to worry about prison camps with foreign names in Eastern Europe, no matter what horrors were going on there.

"Insane," he said, "they're all insane."

He ruffled the papers in the file without looking at them; he knew what they said. This line of work was called "intelligence," but it seemed to Elton that he was gathering data on a nation of psychopaths. The survival of one young woman in that vast asylum was almost impossible, but the hope of it was all that kept his nephew going.

"He's obsessed," Elton had told Philippa back in 1940 when Jonathan joined the Royal Air Force. "Other men have lost their women in this war and a lot more will. He's got to accept that and go on with life, such as it is in wartime."

"You'd be obsessed too," Philippa returned, "if you thought your own father had something to do with your wife's disappearance."

Elton had consistently rejected that possibility. "The man's a father, like me. He's a cold fish, I'll give you that, but he wouldn't do such a thing."

"Wouldn't he?" Philippa said. "Wouldn't he?"

Elton refused to believe it, it was arrant nonsense to him, but Jonathan went on monitoring every scrap of underground information about the prison camps he could get his hands on, as if he were preparing a legal brief with which to try his father. He was like his uncle, a hero who had found his cause. At fifty Daniel was running a Resistance cell in the south of France, and now that the Axis had occupied the "Unoccupied Zone" he would be in considerable danger. An American was still an American to the Gestapo, even with a name like Slayter.

The door opened and Jonathan came in. Exchanging nods with him, his uncle reflected that the son had all of the heart his father lacked and none of the power, only determination, now fueled and buttressed by hate.

"Anything new, Sir?" Jonathan asked. He was still in R.A.F. uniform, as a sop to military convention, although now he worked exclusively for Special Operations Executive, where his French and German were particularly useful. Elton thought he looked like a poster for armed forces recruitment.

He moved the file on his desk. "Not much. The Allied Joint Declaration had some effect."

Jonathan's mouth twisted into cynical disgust. "What good can a declaration do? That news about the camps has been in the papers all along and no one's done anything."

His uncle shook his head. "As rumor, not as fact. This has established the truth."

"And no one will do anything," Jonathan said.

"What *can* we do but win the war and put a stop to it?"

"It'll be too late by then for—for a lot of people. They have to do something *now*."

Elton looked uncomfortable. "It is not politically expedient to do anything now."

"Is that your phrase or theirs?" Jonathan's blue eyes were merciless.

"It is the consensus. We can't turn this into a Jewish war."

"Why not? Hitler has." Jonathan sat down, lit a cigarette, and gestured with it at the file in his uncle's hands. "What's that?"

"Information about the biggest camp of all, at Auschwitz. There's a rubber plant there, it's called the Bunawerke." He pronounced the German word with distaste.

"Buna?" Jonathan was nervously alert. "It must be owned by I.G. Farben, they hold all the patents."

His uncle nodded. "It's called I.G. Farben-Auschwitz. They have their private concentration camp for Farben slave labor; that's called Monowitz."

Jonathan swallowed. "Anything—anything else?" He put out a hand for the folder.

"No names, no mention of any Jewish research chemists in the plant." The Earl fell silent while Jonathan read the notes. When he was finished, Elton said, "You have got to give it up, my boy. You know better than anyone else, they could not have survived, any of them."

The younger man put down the file and, still holding his cigarette, lowered his head into his hands. The smoke curled up idly from between his fingers. Finally he raised his head and nodded, almost imperceptibly, and Elton thought for a second he had accepted the truth at last.

"I want to go to France," Jonathan said.

"What?"

"I want to go to France, to the south where Daniel is. They're bringing out a lot of refugees that way."

"A lot! A pitiful handful," Elton said. "The place is swarming with Italians and Gestapo now."

"There's still a Resistance. We're in and out of there like tramcars, dropping couriers. Let me go."

"And if I do? What can you possibly accomplish there?"

Jonathan crushed out his cigarette. "Uncle, please! They need people. I can help Daniel, I can do something. After all those years when I just stood by, I *must.*"

Elton hesitated, but there was no use trying to stop him, no use at all, his guilt was too monumental.

He nodded. "I'll arrange it."

"Thank you, Uncle," Jonathan said. His shoulders relaxed and he lowered them.

"For what, sending you to risk your life?"

"No, for never asking too many questions, not even when I was little."

"Nonsense, it's British phlegm." He paused, touched and terribly worried. "I'm about to ask one now."

367

Somber and polite, Jonathan waited.

"Does Susannah know about this?" Elton tapped the file about the Buna plant at Auschwitz.

"No."

"Are you going to do anything about that?"

"Yes, I'm going to tell her," Jonathan said. He went out, closing the door behind him, and Elton pressed his lips together and thought that nothing good would come of this for any of them.

Susannah gripped the receiver until her fingers ached. "Are you sure?" she asked. "Jonathan, are you sure?"

"Absolutely. It's taken me two weeks to find the courage to tell you."

"It makes me sick," Susannah said, "but it still doesn't implicate *him.*"

"Maybe not, but I want to find out for sure. He was always keen on synthetic rubber." He made a small, contemptuous sound. "More than on any of us." Then he went on in a crisper tone. "They didn't start building the place until March, 1941. If they raised foreign capital for it, they'd have done it the year before."

Susannah hesitated, her own hidden suspicions joining with his. For a long time she had been sure he was a victim of emotional shock, but he was not talking about Marietta now, he was talking about a business venture by I.G. Farben that differed significantly from the others: The plant was in a concentration camp where people were being killed by the thousands. Not many knew anything about it. Few who knew could believe it. Yet there was incontrovertible proof, she knew that from Charles.

"Susannah?"

"Yes, I'm here." Her voice faltered. "Jonathan, are you all right?"

"Well enough. Will you find out about it?"

"Yes, Jonnie, yes, I will."

"You haven't told him about the proxies?"

"No, there was no need."

"It's just as well, he won't have been on his guard."

"Oh, Jonnie, forget about *him* for just a minute. Talk about you. There's something you're not telling me, I know it." She was afraid she would cry. "I miss you. It's been four years."

The line was quiet for a moment. "I know, Sassie, but it's better not to think about it. Listen, I won't be calling for a while. I have to go—on a mission."

It was like a death knell in her heart. "No," she said. "You mustn't."

368

He ignored that. "I'll keep in touch somehow. Tell Mother for me, I can't tie up this line to make another personal call. And Susannah . . ."

"Yes?"

"Promise me you'll follow through on it, all the way if you have to. Do that for me. You're the only one I can trust."

"Yes, Jonnie, I will, I promise."

"Good-bye, Sassie."

"Good-bye, Jonnie, be careful." She sat looking at the silent receiver with an ache in her throat. She was going to find out about Jesse and right away, now, tonight, as if by doing Jonnie's bidding she would keep Jonnie safe, wherever his "mission" took him.

She remembered a night when she was about seven years old and feverish, when she had been convinced by a dream that her parents would be killed in a car accident unless she could unsnarl all the threads in Nanny's sewing basket. In her fevered little mind their fate and survival had depended upon her vanquishing a challenge, any challenge. She felt the same way tonight.

She had thought about it long enough to know she would have to get into Jesse's private safe, and she even knew how to do that. He was in Washington this week, as he was very often lately, more than she was, but Charles had stopped arguing about it after that day last March. Just nine months ago, that was, long enough for a woman to have a baby and for the world to get itself so enmeshed in war it seemed the planet would cave in from the force of arms. Time enough too, to know she must find out the truth about her father or go to pieces.

It was January dark outside the office windows, that winter night that falls so precipitately between one moment and the next. She pulled herself together and went out into the corridor and down the hall to where Willis Blake sat at his post, bald and pudgy, an animated fixture.

"Come in here," she said as she went past him into Jesse's office. "I have something to say to you."

He was afraid of her, she knew that, and she played on it, leaning against Jesse's desk, her arms crossed, to confront him with a nonchalance she did not feel.

"Close the door, Willis," she said. She had always called him "Willis" because he didn't like it. "I want something you have."

His face was startled in the reflected light of the desk lamp. He stood waiting to know what she wanted.

"I want the key to my father's safe."

He drew his breath in sharply, but she cut him off. "Don't deny it, Willis; I know you have a copy of it. Just give it to me."

"Has—has anything happened to Mr. Slayter?" he faltered.

"No," Susannah said, "but someday it will and then my friendship will be very valuable to you."

They stood in silence for what seemed a long time while Willis considered that. "What is it, Willis, do you want money for it?" She said it sneeringly, but she was quite prepared to pay him whatever he asked. Her dark eyes bored into his.

At last he shook his head. "I couldn't set any price on your friendship, Mrs. Benedict," he said. He put a hand in his vest pocket.

"You're a clever man, Mr. Blake."

He handed her a small key and she took it, avoiding the touch of his fingers. "You can go home now, it's late. I'll close up here."

He stood for a minute, looking at her with expressionless eyes; then he inclined his head, said good night and left her. Still holding the key, she went to the closed bookcase where her father kept the brandy, poured herself a little and drank it down. Then she went to the desk and sat there, while she waited for the noises outside to quieten, for Willis Blake to leave so she could be about her nasty business, feeling as rotten and deceitful as he was.

Feeling like someone else, not her father's daughter, not anyone she wanted to know, she unlocked the safe and started to read.

For a while the contents of the safe were what she had expected: notes in her father's neat script about conversations, in person or by telephone, with some of the most influential men in the world. There was a small telephone directory filled with private numbers that were unobtainable by the public. Finally there was the Ambrose-Sentinel register she had often seen in Jesse's hands, with a page or two for each entry and a clipped sheaf of balance sheets.

She started with the notes. Jesse kept most of his files in his head, doing his more sensitive business orally, but these notes formed a brief, comprehensive record of everyone's affiliations with everyone else in Slayter's world of business and banking, and the complex Ambrose-Sentinel network in particular.

She wondered what the press would make of some of the corporate titans who "donated" their services so generously to the wartime government at a salary of a dollar a year and, behind the scenes, kept a healthy international trade flowing with the enemy through the obscure companies they directed. How would the public feel if they knew American companies had indirectly fueled some of the planes that shot down their sons and dropped the bombs over London and Liverpool?

"They can't be arrested," she murmured to herself. "There wouldn't be a corporate board left intact to keep the war effort going, never mind what it would do to morale."

It was frightening, even to her, to see how deeply the connection between I.G. Farben and American business went—British business too—and how vital the giant chemical industry was in a war.

"They can't run a war without Standard Oil," her father had said. They couldn't run it without I.G. Farben, either, but he had never told her that.

After a few hours Susannah's head ached and her shoulder muscles complained about poring over documents in the silent office. From time to time the grandfather clock in the corner wheezed out the quarter hours. It was almost eight o'clock and she had found nothing she had not known or guessed, except the magnitude of all of it. Only her promise to Jonathan made her look at the balance sheets inside the register.

A few were for a company called Sertes. Her father had never mentioned it to her, but there were many companies he was involved in, or even only investigating, that he kept to himself.

The balance sheets looked perfectly straightforward until her practiced eye noticed a constant between the dates they were drawn and a list of Slayter's outstanding loans in the register. Taken alone, the register had told her nothing. With this particular set of balance sheets she saw that a loan to Sertes was canceled every year in December and renewed again in January so that it would not appear on the company's balance sheet.

Susannah forgot her headache abruptly when she saw that Sertes had been formed in December 1940 and that its official address was care of the Bank for International Settlements in Basel.

She knew that the B.I.S. was controlled by the Nazis now. "But what has Sertes to do with I.G. Farben?" she asked herself, sure that she had stumbled onto something.

There was no term to the loan and the interest was staggering, far too high for any normal business transaction. The risk must be enormous, yet Jesse did not take enormous risks. The payback date then, must be unknown and that could only mean "s.c.h.—subject to the cessation of hostilities." Terms like that could only apply to a foreign corporation on the other side of the conflict. The annually canceled loan was meant to hide it all from the auditors.

Finally, there was a penciled note, almost a doodle, on the first sheet that stung her like a swarm of yellow jackets: "Buna."

She knew she needed more to prove it, but she knew, too, with a dull, smothering certainty that needed no proof, that Slayter's had done business with the Nazi war machine long after her father said he had stopped.

"My God," Susannah said, covering her face with her hands. "My God,

Father, how could you do that, with Jonathan in the war? How could you lie to me? Is profit more important to you than I am? What am I to you anyway, just part of the collection of people you use when it's convenient for business?" She shook her head, wondering why she hadn't known it before.

"I'm not a bank or a corporation, Father," she said, the tears burning her eyes, anger stopping them unshed. "I'm a person and I believed you, I never doubted you once, no matter what anyone said, Jonathan and Charles and Mother. And they were right! They knew! But I loved you, damn it, I loved you so much I believed everything you said and everything you taught me, even about love, so I could do to Charles what you did to Mother and Jonnie —and me."

She shook her head, trembling. She wanted Charles desperately. She wanted to tell him she knew now and that she was sorry to have been so blind for so long. It was what Charles had always wanted of her—to see the truth about her father. He wasn't jealous of the time she spent with Jesse, but of her blind faith in him.

Even now, sitting here with the proof of her folly in her hands, she knew that the hardest thing to do was let her illusions die.

"Jesus," she said, staring at the papers from the safe as if they had come alive to poison her. "What am I going to do?"

She knew she had to try, at least, to use those proxies. She had promised Jonathan. It would be a doomed effort. Taking Slayter's from her father was virtually impossible unless he let her do it, out of some guilt of his own.

"But what would you know about guilt? And what did you really have to do with Marietta?"

She wanted someone she could talk to. Charles was out tonight; he had telephoned to tell her so before Jonathan's call came through. Jonathan was gone, on some nameless mission that filled her with dread. Jesse—and she marveled at the power of habit, that made her turn to him always, like a flower to the sun. But she was not a flower, she was a person, a thinking reed, Pascal had said, and it was *not* enough to have a good mind, the main thing *was* to use it.

Jesse would be out of town until the end of the week. It would give her time and she needed it. She was bright, but she wasn't prepared to run a multinational, multi-billion-dollar corporation all by herself. She would need his partners if she went through with it.

Wearily, she put the papers back into the safe, arranging them exactly as she had found them. She was exhausted by disillusion and remorse and the weight of tears she had never learned to shed. Having Jesse Slayter for a father was no preparation for being his daughter, or Charles's wife. All she wanted right now was to go home, soak in a hot bath and go to sleep.

It wasn't until the next morning, when Charles did not answer, either at his hotel or his office, that she called Madeleine.

73

Madeleine walked along a path in Central Park, just behind the Metropolitan Museum. She hated exercise, but Ned insisted it was good for her and walking was the least onerous form she could find. Even that had been a bore until Ned gave her a dog. Now she could talk to the setter puppy who bounded along at her side on his still-oversize paws.

She patted his head and he rumbled with love. "Blarney, you're the nicest present I ever received, even if I have to tell everyone I bought you myself. You're all warm and furry, like Ned, and you have a sweet face too, like his."

Ned was her best friend, not only her lover. She had never had anyone else to whom she could tell everything, not even Daisy. It was easier to be a man's friend when life had channeled passion, just as it was easier to go sailing on a calm day. There were still the wind, the sun, the blue skies—everything but the waves of drunken desire that had dragged her from the shore. She would never be its victim again and she was glad of that, glad that she had been cured of that particular torment. There was nothing left between Jesse and herself now. She wouldn't leave him—Ned was not free and he had a young daughter to consider—but there was nothing left of all that.

"I only want my Ned," she told Blarney, "and presents like you."

Funny, how few personal things she had taken to the little apartment on Gramercy Park. Jonathan had once carved a lopsided bird for her out of a piece of wood. Susannah had offered up her one effort at sewing, a grubby needle holder with uneven stitches, before abandoning the domestic arts forever. And Jesse had given her a magnificent sapphire and diamond necklace she never wore, on the night she forfeited a reconciliation between them. It had been worth it; the one that came later had been on more equal terms. She frowned; she was thinking like a businessman herself lately.

How quickly they came and went, the Christmas gatherings that marked the end of a year and the private celebrations she could share with Ned now, at the start of each new one. She felt safe and sure with Ned, but uneasy everywhere else. The war was always with them.

"My poor Jonathan," she said aloud, and Blarney perked up his ears and glanced at her before he went back to snuffling along the path. Philippa had called to tell her Jonathan was leaving England, but not where he had gone. They thought it must be to Daniel, but the Axis had occupied all of southern

375

France to guard against invasion across the Mediterranean from North Africa, and the danger was tremendous.

Time was rushing past again. It was a lot like recent years; they all ran together. It seemed she had always been placating Jesse, waiting for Susannah and worrying about Jonathan. The nicest thing about Christmas last year had been Cab and John Slayter and the puppy—and then the boys had gone back to school until Easter.

"But I have you, Blarney, that's a good boy. Keep an eye out for Susannah, although why she wants to walk in the park in winter is beyond me. Maybe we can go somewhere afterward for a hot chocolate." She looked at the dog doubtfully. "If they'll let you in. They'd let me in with a lot of other inanimate presents not worth half of you, the idiots." Then she thought of taking Susannah to her apartment, but it might not be the day for such a surprise.

A group of children went past and a little girl stopped to pat Blarney's dark copper coat. A wave of nostalgia overwhelmed Madeleine at the sight of the smiling little girl in a snowsuit, mittens and a cap. Her shiny dark hair spilled out over her shoulders.

"Susannah used to laugh like that," she told Blarney when the child had gone. "She was a rambunctious baby too, until she decided to imitate Jesse —you know how he is, all restrained and dignified. Lately, though, she's not just restrained, she's damned unhappy."

Once again Madeleine ticked off to herself the possible reasons for that. It wasn't Jonathan. Worry was one thing and misery another and Susannah had been miserable for months.

Charles? He was working for the Office of Special Services in Washington and absorbed in his job. Aside from his resentment over long-distance living arrangements, everything seemed the same between them. Their only problem was Charles's desire to have Susannah all to himself, but they were good for each other.

"I've always liked Charles," Madeleine said to the dog. "He has pizzazz and that's what makes a man exciting. You have to be born with it, Blarney, like that skinny singer who had the girls screaming over him at the Paramount."

She stopped talking to wave to Susannah, coming toward her on the path in a silver fox jacket and slacks. Susannah had pizzazz too, enough to wear unlikely outfits like that and make them look chic. She was hatless, as she often was these days, and her hair was loose and full around her face. It made her look softer, not so businesslike, but her eyes, when she reached Madeleine, were even more troubled than usual.

"Thanks for coming out to meet me on such a gray day," Susannah said. "I couldn't sit still."

"No more can I, with this dog around. He's taken a fancy to Jesse's chair and sits in it like a sphinx. I have to keep heaving him out."

Susannah played with the jumping puppy for a moment, then straightened and began walking at Madeleine's side. "I'll come right to the point," she said. "I'm going to need that proxy of yours after all."

Madeleine took a breath, grateful for the cold air. "What happened?"

"Jonnie had some other suspicions, about Jesse and I.G. Farben, but these are true. I got the information by going behind his back," Susannah said with disgust. "I had to use that slimy little maggot Willis Blake." She told Madeleine about the company called Sertes that Jesse had set up in 1940 and the connection she was certain it formed between Slayter's and I.G. Farben-Auschwitz.

"But that was before *we* got into the war," Madeleine said. "You can't get his partners to object to that."

"Blast the partners," Susannah said. "He did it *after* he told me we were finished with Farben. I don't understand him anymore! How could he lie to me like that when he knew how I hated it? And Jonnie! Do you know what Auschwitz is? It's a concentration camp; worse, Charles says. For all we know, the Kastenbergs are there. What if Marietta dies there?" She ran her hands through her hair. "I can't stand it, I just can't stand it."

"Can you really take control away from your father?"

"I have to try," Susannah said in a rush. "I wouldn't trust *him* as far as I could throw Jon's piano, not anymore, not ever again." She stopped and looked at Madeleine as if she needed approval from her. "I trusted him. The least I expected in return was the truth. I deserved that much from him after all the years—" She stopped abruptly. "That's what I wanted to tell you. That's why I'll want your proxy as soon as I'm ready to use it."

Madeleine nodded. "Does Charles know?"

"Not yet." Susannah looked even more stricken. "But he'll be against me. He'll think I'm doing this out of spite." She stopped again and fixed Madeleine with her dark eyes. "Do you think that's true?"

"No, I don't," Madeleine said without any hesitation. "You're a lot of difficult things, Susannah, but you're not spiteful."

"I think I'm going to cry," Susannah said.

Madeleine took a handkerchief from her coat pocket and held it out. They resumed walking while Susannah cried quietly into the handkerchief.

"You always use the same perfume," she said when the tears abated. "You don't change much." She blew her nose. "Not in any way that matters."

"Neither do you," Madeleine assured her.

"That's not true. I was rotten to you for years."

Madeleine conceded that. "But you didn't like being rotten. It was a question of loyalties. It was a terrible thing for you to have seen us together, you were so young. You had to be loyal to your father."

"Mother," Susannah said, and the word was new and lovely in her mouth. "Do you still love him? I mean, after all he's done?"

"It's what he's always done, Sassie. We just didn't want to see that."

"I feel so—so used," Susannah said. "It's a rotten feeling."

"I know," Madeleine nodded. "I once felt that way myself."

They had come out of the park onto Fifth Avenue and a gust of wind lifted Madeleine's hair. Susannah saw how wide the streaks of gray had become. Madeleine was getting older and Susannah had just begun to really know her. Tears filled Susannah's eyes again. She put an arm around her mother and leaned against her, ignoring the impatient dog and the passersby on Fifth Avenue.

"Lord, I'm sorry," she said. "I'm so sorry. I should have helped you somehow. I've wanted to tell you that for a long time. I don't know why it was so hard to say."

"Don't cry, Sassie," Madeleine said, "not about that, anyway. Come on home and I'll fix us both a drink."

Susannah shivered. "I can't go into that house, not today."

"I meant my apartment." Madeleine's blue eyes were steady, as if she expected a blow and was prepared to weather it.

"I don't understand, what apartment?"

"Just a small one on Gramercy Park I rented for myself. I couldn't stand rattling around in that mausoleum anymore, not without Jonnie." Her eyes glistened.

"Does he know?" Susannah said quickly.

Madeleine shook her head. "He doesn't notice what I do."

"God," Susannah said, "you must have been the loneliest woman in the world, married to him." She stopped again and turned to Madeleine. "I'm sorry I was so stupid about Ned when you needed him so much."

"He's back in New York," Madeleine said. She watched while a look of understanding broke over her daughter's face like a wave, smoothing all the other reactions—surprise, some embarrassment, and an echo of disapproval —away.

"Well, I'm glad he's back," Susannah said after a moment, "and that's the only comfort I've had today. Yes, let's go to your apartment." Susannah linked arms with her mother and hurried along by the bounding puppy, they went to hail a cab together.

74

Mist spilled over the mountains soaring high behind Monaco. Daniel watched gratefully from the terrace of Dominique's villa as it rolled like foam down the craggy slopes of the Maritime Alps and frothed along the road separating Monaco from France. It would make things a little safer for his men. They had business tonight that could not wait.

Last summer had been hot and humid, as if the elements knew what was coming. The Germans had always been doubtful of the Vichy government's ability to insure French neutrality; they had assigned this *département* and seven others to the Italians when they moved into Unoccupied France, but the Gestapo kept a watchful eye on their allies.

Daniel left the terrace and crunched along the gravel path that led from the villa to what used to be a rolling lawn and was now a vegetable garden. He walked toward two men working at the far end of the field—a grizzled old man with apple cheeks, a beret and a corncob pipe, and a younger man, blond and hatless, who stayed within earshot but was silent while the other two spoke. The conversation sounded harmless enough to other men working in the field, but every word of it carried a simple message.

"Christophe, *bonsoir,*" Daniel said. Phrased this way, the greeting meant "Any changes?"

"*Monsieur, bonsoir.*" Had the old man reversed those words it would have signaled some alteration of their plans for tonight.

Daniel's head tilted up toward the evening mist. "What kind of weather does that mean for the winter?" *Any enemy patrols on your route?*

Christophe's eyes narrowed. "Maybe more snow than we expected." *There are more patrols than usual.*

Daniel considered that. They had to get a man out of France on the chance that he had picked up information to help the Allied effort. Whether such scraps of intelligence had ever been worth the risks they took to get them was open to question.

He glanced at the younger farmer, and Jonathan's blue eyes looked back at him, dismissing old Christophe's caution as only a hopeless man can dismiss danger.

"*Je m'en fous royalement de la neige,*" Jonathan said. *I don't give a royal screw about the patrols.* He spoke French as well as he spoke German, but in any language his meaning was clear to his uncle: Don't try to stop me.

For a split second Daniel wanted to cancel the mission. It was madness that these men, the old and the young, should go skulking through the night, hiding from other men who would kill them if they could, in order to rescue still another man whose life was already forfeit because he did not share all of the religious convictions held by the Western world.

"*Tant pis,* Christophe," Daniel said. "We can't be put off by a little snow. Better get out more shovels to be on the safe side." *Go ahead, but take more men in case some of you don't get through.*

The old peasant nodded and paused to rekindle his battered pipe before returning to his work. Daniel looked at his nephew again, then turned and went back toward the house with the uneven gait that was the gift of other Germans twenty-five years before. He glanced at his watch. They would be leaving soon, under cover of twilight, to meet the Nice-Marseilles *rapide.* The train would be held up by sabotage on the rails outside Nice—nothing serious, but enough to allow the man they were meeting to slip off the train and disappear into the darkness.

There would be four teams—the "shovels"—of two men each placed along the line to intercept "Samson" before the patrols did. Aside from what Samson might tell London about troop movements in the East— intelligence he had gathered from the underground that helped him after his escape from Auschwitz—Daniel knew Jonathan wanted other information. Samson might know something about the Kastenbergs. It had been a well-known name in Germany once. If they were at Auschwitz they might still be alive, or so Jonathan told himself.

In the back of Jonathan's mind, Daniel was certain, was the idea that if men came out, men could get back in. He wanted desperately to speak to Samson.

"It's terrible," Daniel said often to Dominique. "Why must he, in a world full of war, be unable to acknowledge death?"

"Because Marietta was there one moment and gone the next," Dominique said, "as if she had dropped off the edge of the world. She'll always be waiting for him, around the next corner or through the next door. He can never stop looking for her until he knows for a fact that she's dead."

Or he is, Daniel thought. He sighed when he reached the terrace and stopped automatically to scrape the mud from his boots on a stone step. Dominique was waiting for him on the other side of the terrace, the mist clinging like gauze around her feet.

"He's not a hero," Daniel said, putting his arms around her. "He's not a soldier, either. He was just a lovable man with a gift for making people happy. Now he keeps a dead German's cap and tunic in his knapsack as some kind of grisly souvenir! He'll be shot if he's even found with it. How can I let him risk dying, no matter how much he wants to?"

"Hush, darling," Dominique said. "There's no way to stop him, no way at all."

Jonathan crouched in the culvert and listened to the faint sounds of Christophe and his men moving away. He peered at his watch in the dim light of a half-moon—there was no mist on this side of Nice.

"It's a good half hour yet," the man beside him said in a low voice. A strong aroma of garlic drifted over to Jonathan.

"Pierrot," he whispered. "You have eyes like a cat and you smell like a sausage."

Pierrot shrugged. "I'll stay downwind of the *milice* if they ever come around."

Jonathan nodded. He, too, wondered why they had encountered no one on the heavily patrolled coast road. Once out of the hills they had been easy targets. There was so little cover down here. The road ran along the Mediterranean, a silent sea that barely moved except when the winds whipped it. There was no wind tonight, just the sound of the water gurgling against the stony beach across the road. The railroad track was behind them, about fifty yards from the culvert.

Jonathan settled back and gripped his stolen Schmeisser machine pistol. He and Pierrot were the first of the four teams to drop off along the line. No one knew exactly where their man would get off the train. He had been instructed to follow the tracks back toward Nice, but in any action it was impossible to know if every link in a long chain had functioned perfectly. For all they knew, he might not be on the train at all.

It was a risky plan, but the man code-named Samson was used to taking risks. He had escaped from a death camp and that meant he was not only a survivor, but a fighter. His destination was Spain and then London, and they had needed an ingenious plan to get him across southern France to the Spanish border, now that the area was occupied.

Hiding him by letting him go in plain sight had been the best they could manage under the new circumstances. They were even more heavily policed by the French than by the Italians.

"*Merde,*" Pierrot muttered.

"What's wrong?"

"Nothing—I was just wondering what Pauline's up to."

"This is no place to think about one of your women!"

"*Et alors?* You want me to think about this Jew we're going to rescue?"

Jonathan's expression changed. "If you feel that way about Jews, what are you here for?"

Pierrot wiped his mouth with the back of his hand, a habit he had when he spoke more than a few words. "What do I know about Jews? I hate Germans, is why I'm here, and I'd rather think about *la petite chatte de Pauline* than the whole lot of them."

"Well, think about it if you want to, but shut up while you're doing it and listen for that train."

The other man subsided with a faint expletive and Jonathan shook his head in the dark. Pierrot was as uncomplicated as a loaf of bread. He sat in a drainage ditch by the seaside waiting to rescue some unknown man from out of the night—and to pass the time he thought about Pauline's pussy! No great guilts for Pierrot, no need to expiate a crime he didn't commit, but hadn't prevented, either. What did he care about Jews, no matter how many were being murdered in the camp Samson had escaped? He just hated Germans and what he called the "real deportations"—of Frenchmen now being sent to work in German factories. The Resistance had been swelled by an influx of men when rumors of that decree got around. Better living in the *maquis*—the bush—than in a labor camp in Germany.

The sound of motorcycles split the quiet.

"How many?" Jonathan whispered.

"Two."

They flattened their bodies against the culvert, waiting for the cycles to pass. The stupidity of it struck Jonathan: that he and Pierrot should lie in a gutter while two strangers drove along the road, ready to kill anyone they found. A man had a right to know his killer.

Pierrot was wiser than he; all of them, the Germans included, ought to be home, in bed with their girls or drinking wine at the café, or walking along Fifth Avenue looking at Christmas windows.

But the windows were too far away. Much closer were the boxcars that were rolling out of Drancy in the north, packed with Jews for "resettlement in the East." Jonathan was determined to find those tracks after he had spoken to Samson and to follow them east, and he didn't care where they led him.

His hand ached from gripping the Schmeisser. Poetic justice if he could shoot a German with a German gun! And a finer irony if one of them killed him with a weapon made with Slayter money.

The sound of the motors built, reached an apogee, then passed and faded. The two men relaxed.

"Sometimes I wonder why in hell everyone's so scared of Germans," Jonathan whispered when the night was completely quiet again. "They're only men, after all."

Pierrot shook his head. *"Drôle d' espèce.* How many of our species like to bash out babies' brains?"

"Men have been bashing out babies' brains since the world began," Jonathan said. "History is a record of slaughter."

Pierrot grunted. "I wasn't around then." They all knew what was happening all over France when the Germans dragged Jews away to fill their boxcars for the terrible trip from Drancy to—where? East, they said. Death, they said.

"The Italians won't do it for them," Pierrot went on. "Italians aren't worth shit in a battle, they have no balls, but they don't do much German dirty work, either." He wiped his mouth again with the back of his hand.

They lapsed into heavy silence. Jesse had done some German dirty work, even from far away, even indirectly, but Jonathan couldn't think about his father. Red rage would suffocate him, take his mind off what he was doing, make him less alert. He had a job to do, he had to think about Samson.

What would Samson say if he knew Jesse Slayter and his son had helped a pack of murderous jackals come to power and threaten the so-called civilized world?

Jonathan was desperately ashamed of it. It was something he would always keep hidden, like a curse.

He pushed it away and tried again to see Marietta's face. For a long time now he had lost all clear visions of it. It was like a puzzle—he had the pieces, but he could not put them together. He simply could not conjure up her face, only her eyes and the way they had looked at him, a look more intimate than words, more voluptuous than sex itself, as if sound and touch were not enough to say all they meant to each other. How did she look? He knew exactly how she felt, her skin, her hair, her body so soft and sweet and open to loving, but he simply could not see her face.

"Le voici," Pierrot said. "Here it is."

75

The train waddled steadily in the direction of Marseilles. The passengers were quiet, a habit with them since France surrendered. They never knew who might be listening and the French *milice* were as rotten as the Gestapo. But after all, a man had to accept the inevitable. With a little luck he might even profit from it.

Things were getting worse each day, though. Food was short, medicine and soap nonexistent. There was no dancing, even on fête days—that old cockerel Pétain believed moral laxity had caused the fall of France in the first place and had decreed three days each week without any alcohol as a kind of penitence! No, there was not much to talk about that wouldn't get a citizen shot for undermining morale, or, at the very least, sent off to become a slave laborer in Germany.

Except for some German uniforms and a few men in raincoats and dark hats, the passengers were a threadbare lot. The small man standing and apparently dozing against a window in the carriage corridor blended in with the rest of the crowd. Only Moses Feldman's left forearm would have identified him had anyone seen it—a number was tattooed on it. He kept his cap on his head; the night air was chilly and although his code name was Samson, Moses was bald as an egg—*a Samson after the fall,* he thought to himself.

He had none of the features the Germans called "Jewish": His nose was not prominent, nor his lips thick. Even the lost hair had not been kinky. He was circumcised, but so, probably, were some of the Catholics standing near him, and certainly any Moslems who had escaped the Nazi net.

Moses had no intention of displaying either of his telltale parts. He would use the Mauser strapped to his shin if any German came near him.

He had stolen it from his underground contact two nights ago. It was not a decent thing to do to a man who had risked his life to get Moses to the south of France, but fear had drowned his decency. He was not going to be taken again by Germans.

The train was redolent of tobacco and sour-smelling humanity, but by comparison with the stench of the crematorium in the place from which he had come, it was a delight.

His hands moved. He would have liked to wash his hands, but he had learned to control the impulse. All his life from now on he would want to wash his hands.

385

It couldn't be helped. A *Sonderkommando's* job was an unclean business. After the bodies came out of the gas chambers, dripping with the excreta of a ten-minute death by choking on gas fumes, their gold teeth and fillings had to be wrenched out of their mouths, their orifices searched for concealed gold and diamonds, before they were burned. The SS was a business and these were its profits.

But it had been his only hope, his last chance, when he was caught, after two years in hiding, and sent to Auschwitz—to the camp called Monowitz. Monowitz had been built to spare its workers long marches from the main concentration camp at Auschwitz I, not out of kindness but because it was better business to use whatever energy they had for working, not marching.

I.G. Farben was a harsh slave lord with a high death rate—even the SS sometimes complained. Day by day his strength had left him. He could see it going when his hair fell out in clumps and his skin began to shrivel. The hours were long, the food poor and meager. Sooner or later he would be weak enough to be sent to Auschwitz II, the extermination camp known as Birkenau.

Before that day came he volunteered for the *Sonderkommando* at Birkenau, thinking it was better to tend them after they were dead than work for the people who killed them, thinking it was nasty work but a *Sonderkommando* lived a little longer for doing it, thinking that the barbed wire might not be strung so closely behind the new crematorium and a man might escape if he were willing to take the risk and wait his chance.

After one day he knew he would lose his mind if he waited. After one day he was talking to the bodies as he worked over them, and then he was crooning a lullaby his mother used to sing about *roshinkes* and *mandlen*—raisins and almonds—sweetmeats in that incredible stink—singing softly to each of them as she had to him, sleep, my little one, sleep, my darling one, sleep, oh my precious one, sleep. Oh God, I must have lost my mind already because who would want to kill such helpless tender ones. The women and children and the *babies*—who would want to kill them?

Moses shook himself and propped his head against the cold window and shivered, trying not to think of it. There were men risking their lives to get him away from the Germans so he could warn everyone.

But of this part of his story he would tell nothing. He was ashamed of it.

What would normal men say if they knew what he had done, even for one day?

His eyes peered through half-closed lids at the countryside. It was almost time, he could sense it. He was fairly certain that the man between him and the door of the car was Gestapo—he was pale, but too well fed and dressed to be French. Gestapo was bad, but it was better than a uniform. He had to control his terror at the sight of a German uniform. His dreams were not only of naked innocents done to death; he dreamed as well of shooting clean-cut young men in German uniforms and watching them die. In his dreams he never saw their faces, only their uniforms. He never heard anything but the crack of a bullet and its thud into flesh.

There was a small explosion at the forward end of the train and it jolted to a halt.

"*Scheisse!*" one of the German soldiers said. "Those French pigs are blowing up the rails again."

The soldier led two of his companions out of the car, shouldering the passengers roughly aside with his rifle butt. Four others left by the door at the other end of the carriage, followed by the Gestapo and a few curious passengers. Among them was Moses Feldman.

"Wait a minute!" Pierrot warned. "I hear something."

"I hear it too," Jonathan said. They were lying in the bushes just above the culvert, listening intently, the stalled *rapide* was not more than a mile away. Shouts echoed through the still night air while the track was being repaired, but there were voices coming toward them from the other direction.

"It's *Boches!*" Pierrot said. "It's a *German* patrol!"

They looked at each other, anxiety taut between them.

"If he bumps into them . . ." Jonathan said.

"Maybe he was picked up by Christophe and Morin down the line," Pierrot offered.

"And maybe he wasn't." Jonathan struggled out of his knapsack. "Give me a hand," he said hastily, dropping his jacket and tugging the knapsack open. He took out the crumpled tunic and cap that had been taken from a dead German and put it on.

"Pierrot, go toward the train, keep low. If you find him, just stay with him until I fool this bunch into taking off. Then I'll join you."

Pierrot nodded, dropped the canvas bag into the bushes, and took off toward the train, crouching low over the rails, keeping on the seaward side of the tracks so he could roll down to the road if he had to. He could hear Jonathan shouting something in German and the patrol answering. He stopped a second to look back and felt the barrel of a revolver behind his ear.

"That's right, don't move," a voice said in heavily accented French. "Who are you?"

The accent could have been German, but a German would have hit him by now. Pierrot took a chance. "*Dalila,*" he said.

387

The pistol was lowered. "You're a noisy bugger," Samson said. "I heard you all the way down there."

"Quiet!" Pierrot whispered. "You must be quiet. There's a German patrol down the road. My partner's trying to get rid of them."

Moses Feldman's pistol came up again. "How? He can't shoot the whole lot at once."

"Be quiet! Get down and shut up, *nom de Dieu!*"

Moses dropped to the ground behind the Frenchman, wondering how one *maquisard* was going to get rid of a German patrol. After the train the air smelled sweet and fresh and the gurgling sound of the sea was delicious to his ears. He had to keep from running to wash himself clean in the saltwater. But as he lay there, waiting, the familiar terror crept back over him at the thought of German uniforms in a group—brutal, menacing and all-powerful. He was glad of the Frenchman's bulk and he stayed behind him, peering over his shoulder.

They lay there, straining to hear and see. There was a sound of running feet from the other side of the tracks and a German uniform came over the rise. In the moonlight Moses could see him clearly. He looked like posters of the ideal German Moses had seen in Vienna so long ago. His blond hair glistened under his cap. His triumphant grin showed white, even teeth, just like the guards outside the gas chambers who smiled over the terrible sounds of dying that came from inside to hang upon the fetid air of Auschwitz.

This time Moses did not have to crouch behind another helpless victim. This time he and the Frenchman would not be beaten and burned by a sadistic German bastard with the face of an angel.

He raised the Mauser and fired only once before the gun was knocked from his hand.

Jonathan lay where he had fallen, his bloody head pillowed in Pierrot's lap, unable to tell him he had sent the patrol off in another direction, thanks to the dark and the uniform and his impeccable German. He could feel Pierrot's hands on him, smell the garlic on his breath, hear him cursing and hear the sound of a man sobbing, was it his father?

The last thing he heard Pierrot say was *"Pauvre Juif maudit!"* and for a second he wondered why Pierrot would call him a poor accursed Jew.

Then he closed his eyes and smiled the way he had when he was young because he could finally see Marietta's face and hear her say to him, "I love you, I will love you forever."

76

The office was quiet, cold despite its opulent furnishings, with none of the comfort Jesse had always found here. He could feel his father's eyes on him, eyes as slick as the varnish over the canvas, eyes that had followed him all his life, but he did not turn to look at the portrait because there was no comfort there, either.

A telegram lay on his desk and he stared at it. It had arrived moments ago from one of Jesse's business connections in Washington. The man must have heard about Jonathan from Charles to have fired off a message so soon. Charles himself was en route from Washington to be with Susannah.

"Condolences," the telegram said. The word seemed as empty as the world to Jesse. Something absolutely essential had been taken from him, the only real extension of himself.

Yet he was angry in his sorrow; Jonathan had gone to a pointless, unnecessary death, driven by romantic fervor and a childish notion of guilt. There was no guilt in business. There was profit or loss, that was all.

The door opened and Madeleine came into the room, breaking the chilling silence, assaulting his self-control just by the way she stood there, clinging to the doorknob. Her blue eyes—Jonathan's eyes—tormented him.

"Jesse, are they sure?"

He only bent his head.

"But people make mistakes, even Daniel," Madeleine insisted, her voice denying what she said. She was twisting one glove in her fingers. "Oh, Jesse, I can't bear for him to be dead."

She walked to the desk and looked at him appealingly. He represented such power to her. He was omnipotent. Surely he could put things right and bring Jonathan back.

He raised his head, his eyes deep-shadowed by those heavy brows. She had not looked at him, really looked at him, in so long that she was surprised to see how old he was.

"Jesse," she whispered, "what are we going to do?"

"Do?" He sighed heavily. "I don't know."

It was the first time he had ever failed to have a solution, give an opinion, take a stand. He seemed as vulnerable to her as he must have been once, when he was a boy, and his place in his father's life had been threatened by a new wife, by new children.

She touched his hand wanting to help him. "Jesse, we have to remember

389

that together, when we were young and miracles were possible, we made a wonderful boy. Now he's dead, but he was ours and you're the only other person on earth who knows exactly how I feel."

Sorrow filled his empty face and he nodded slowly. "Sit down, Madeleine, I'll get you a brandy."

She watched him, tall and white-haired, still vigorously handsome, the kind of man people had always turned around to watch and ask "Who is he?" *Oh, my poor darling,* Madeleine thought, crying, and didn't know whether she cried for the son or his father, both lost to her.

"He fought me to the end," Jesse said.

She was attentive. "That's not true. He had his differences with you, that's all."

He looked almost wary. "What did you know about our differences?"

Madeleine drank some brandy, her eyes filling again. "I don't want to talk about German industry today."

"Oh, that," Jesse said, sitting back in his chair. "I see." He sat there quietly for a moment, then he read the telegram again, leaned forward, and pounded the desk with his fist. "He didn't have to die, damn it! There was no reason for him to go."

"He had to find his wife," Madeleine said, the tears beginning to roll down her cheeks.

"His wife! He only married her to defy me."

Madeleine looked at him, her expression changing. "He loved her. You had nothing to do with it."

"Then why did he sneak away to marry her? Why didn't he tell me about it?"

Madeleine's voice was muffled by her handkerchief. "You thought there was a religious problem."

Jesse nodded emphatically. "An insurmountable one. Most of my friends would never have accepted her. I tried to warn her but she wouldn't listen." He shook his head angrily. It was only when Madeleine's silence seemed unnatural that he looked up.

Her blue eyes were electric with anger now. "I wouldn't call anyone a friend who didn't accept her—including you." Jonathan's suspicions goaded her. "What did you tell him when he called you from Berlin?"

He flushed. "What difference does it make what I told him? It was irrelevant after she disappeared. Why did he wander all over Europe, risk his life, wind up dead in France doing the devil knows what?" He stood so suddenly that the chair behind him rocked nervously with a little sound of leather and springs. "He would never have found her!"

Madeleine looked up at him from across the desk, white and breathless, while the chair rocked, getting slower and slower until its sound and movement stopped.

"How did you know that, Jesse, how could you be so sure?"

He put his hands in his trouser pockets, a rare gesture for him. "It's an obvious assumption to make, the way things are in Germany."

Her voice was barely audible. "I don't believe you," she said, standing up. "I think you *knew* all along. I think you could have told Jonnie where she was, whether she was alive."

His face settled into its habitual impassivity and made her sure she was right. "You're talking nonsense, Madeleine," he said impatiently. "Even if I had known, I wouldn't have told him where she was. He threatened me"— Jesse's hand grabbed the receiver from one of the telephones on his desk— "he told me on this very telephone that he would go to a concentration camp with her." He smashed the receiver back into its cradle. "Would you have wanted that? Well, I didn't—so no, I wouldn't have told him anything." His dark eyes flashed at her. "Get hold of yourself, Madeleine, you're hysterical."

Madeleine bent to take her gloves and handbag from the chair. "I'm not in the least hysterical," she said. "If you had ever done or said anything spontaneously, because you loved or hated someone . . . But you've always planned and plotted about everything, including me and the children. So I don't believe you didn't know. I know my Jonathan and he didn't believe you didn't know, either."

His head went back with that imperious look of denial she knew so well, denial of anything he did not want to know.

"Why do you think he wouldn't come home?" she asked him with all the contempt she could summon. "He knew what you'd done. He said he was afraid he'd kill you if he ever saw you again."

"Sit down and be quiet," he said. "You have no proof of what you're saying."

"I know that. I couldn't prove you stood by and let my father be ruined, either, but I know you did. He died too soon because of you—and so did Jonathan."

"Be quiet," he snapped again. "Jonathan's dead. There's nothing we can do about it."

"I can leave you," she said, with infinite relief.

"You're too old to leave me."

"I'm too old to look at you every day, knowing what you did to my son. Jonnie might still be alive if I hadn't believed you years ago, if I'd left you then."

"I forbid you to say that," he whispered venomously. "I've always done what was best for my son, and I had nothing to do with his death."

She started toward the door. "I can't be sure of that." She turned to look at him. "Can you?"

He crumpled the telegram and threw it into a wastebasket. "Go on, Madeleine, leave me. I'll be happier without you."

"Happy?" She shook her head rapidly, her face contorted with grief. "People are happy sometimes, but not you—you're a machine. I used to think there was something real and warm inside you, but there's only more you. You're capable of anything—anything—but not of happiness. Live with yourself, Jesse, it's the best punishment I can think of for you."

His hand went up in a gesture that stopped her momentarily. "Are you going to Susannah with this—this nonsense?"

"No," Madeleine said, torn between pity and contempt. Whatever Susannah's quarrels with her father, they had to be her own. "She's had enough grief because of you already."

"Because of me? You don't know what you're talking about."

She couldn't risk another word. She slammed the door behind her, ignoring Willis Blake's stare that followed her all the way down the corridor and into the elevator. She thought she would stop breathing if she didn't get out of this place and away from the man in that corner office, on whom she had wasted so many acts of trust and love—and her only son. And for what? For some empty pride of purpose, such a hunger to be right that she could not accept what was true.

She got into the waiting car and Bob Harris closed the door behind her, then waited in the driver's seat for instructions. Madeleine bit her lips and struggled with herself in the back of the car, too full of death and the death of love to be able to speak. It was the pain of lost illusion and the waste, the awful waste of most of her life that broke her, and she cried.

Bob Harris let her cry in peace. Then, his face wet with tears for her and Mister Jonnie, he put the car in gear and drove her to Dr. Driscoll's house on East Seventy-ninth Street.

77

Susannah stood in the center of the music room at Fifth Avenue, aware that she had been running away from death. She had left her own house, right after Charles telephoned from Washington to say he was catching the next train, and then she had walked as fast as she could because it was beyond her to be still, to sit quietly with sorrow and wait for it to drown her.

When some need brought her to this house, a tearful Daisy told her Madeleine was out, at Pearl Street, she thought. At first that was a shock, but then Susannah realized that Jesse was Jonathan's father and such authorship would outweigh love and hate.

She walked over to the piano. There was a book of music on the rack, and with a pang of recognition she saw that it was Jonathan's. She had seen it so often here or at Willow Hill. On the cover, in faded ink, Jonathan Slayter was printed in a child's hand. There were a few smudged finger marks too, made by a blond boy years and years ago, a boy whose smile made the angels sing, Nanny always said.

She could see him bending over the keyboard when he was little, his legs still too short to reach the floor. She could see him in the grace of young manhood, smiling up at her when he played one of her favorite pieces, or holding her hands to calm her when she was angry, or laughing with her at some joke only the two of them shared.

He was real enough to touch, as if the old book of music held some magic that brought the essence of him back to this piano, where he could be happy doing what he wanted to do.

"But it isn't genius," she could hear him saying ruefully, "just talent."

"Oh, Jonnie," she told him, "talent was enough, you were enough, I should have said that to you when I could." She hugged the music to her.

She had no idea how long she sat there, only that the light was beginning to fade when the door opened and she looked up to see her father.

"What are you doing here?" she said dully.

"You weren't at home. I thought I might find you here." He took a few steps toward her, but she waved him back.

"Don't come near me," she said.

He stopped, looking at her carefully. "It's terrible for me too, Susannah."

"It must be worse for you. I don't have Sertes on my conscience."

Even though the light was dim, she saw that he was alerted by that name. Then he shrugged. "That has nothing to do with Jonathan," he said.

She realized it was irrelevant to him how she had found out about Sertes. That was like Jesse, to ignore extraneous details. "Do you treat all your crimes so casually?"

He walked to the window seat and sat down heavily. Light from the street made silver of his white hair. "One company more or less is not a crime."

"Like one lie more or less." She put the music down. "Jonathan and I were solidly against helping the Nazis, even through Farben's good offices, and you knew it. I'll never forgive you for lying to me about that, for using *my* effort for something I despised."

"That still has nothing to do with Jonathan."

The anger in her began to swell. "Of course it does! For all we know, Slayter money made the gun that killed him."

"That isn't true!" His voice rose sharply.

"It's very probably true. He was in the Resistance with Daniel. He was killed on a mission."

"How can you possibly know that?"

"Through Charles. Elton's British Intelligence, Charles is O.S.S. Your son's a hero," she said with quiet disgust. "He might even get a posthumous medal engraved *Dolce et decorum est pro patria mori.* But he didn't go to France to die for his country, he went because of Marietta, and that was your doing. What did you tell her that day you took her to tea? What kind of man *are* you?"

"You've been talking to Madeleine," Jesse said, in quiet fury.

"Not today—but she wasn't the first to suspect you, Jonnie was. That's why he wouldn't come home."

His head dropped into his hands. "But it was an unacceptable marriage," he said, as if that explained everything.

"You mean it wasn't what *you* wanted." She leaned on the piano, both her hands on its polished surface. "You never let any of us have what we wanted. You're a heartless, lying bastard."

His head came up. "Be careful, Susannah. I won't accept that from you."

"Yes, you will. There's nothing you can do about it. I don't like what you are, any more than Mother does."

"I refuse to discuss her with you."

"Poor, pretty Madeleine," she said, ignoring him. "Chained to you all her life."

He said nothing, watching her from the window.

She was glad of the dusk; it hid her shaking hands. "If the Justice Department finds out about Sertes you know what a merry hell they'll put you through. Standard is still trying to dig its reputation out of the muck, and they're a lot bigger than you are." She told him about the proxies and what Jonathan wanted her to do with them.

"Never," he said, very softly. "You know you can't take my company away from me. I'll contest Jonathan's proxy for the next ten years. Justice won't do a thing about it, either; you can take my word for that."

"And the press?" It was macabre to sit there in the twilight and talk about betrayal.

"They'll use it, I suppose, as a nine days' wonder. Business will resume openly after the war, it always does, and there'll be other wars and other enemies—flying flags and marching bands. People like those better than principles. All this will be yesterday's news."

"My brother will still be just as dead."

His control abandoned him and he stood. "You'll do anything to hurt me, won't you?"

"I was taught," she said, hot tears spilling over her face, "by an expert. I loved you, Father—my God, how I loved you." She shook her head, overwhelmed by that, missing it already.

"And I love you, Susannah. You were always the brightest star in my life."

She shook her head, wanting to go to him, wanting to love him and knowing she could not love him and still love her brother, herself, or anyone else. "I didn't want to be a star. I just wanted to be your daughter, but I was never a person to you. I was only some kind of project to satisfy your pride."

"I *was* proud of you!"

"That isn't love—and the price for it was too high. I made you proud—and you made me mistrust every impulsive feeling I ever had. I never really trusted anyone but you, not even myself. There's a piece of me missing, Father, because of how you were and what you made of me—and of Jonathan."

"Susannah, please." He put out a supplicating hand and the ring he always wore flashed briefly in the gloom. "We can talk this out, the way we always have. When it all started, how could I have known it would lead to this? He was my son." His voice shook. "Susannah, don't leave me, I have nothing left, not even *her.*"

It was that one, all-encompassing, degrading syllable that gave Susannah the strength to resist him. It was almost dark, but she could see him more clearly than ever. She saw him old, she knew him mortal and she pitied him, but she had to let him go.

She picked up the music and walked to the door. "Did you really think

Jonnie's life was negotiable? Oh, Jesse, I guess there are worse than you, but they're hard to find."

She went out, then, to do what she had to do about the press and find her mother before she went home to Charles.

78

The town house was quiet when Charles got home late that evening after a noisy, crowded trip on the train. After a moment he remembered that Susannah had been on her way out to find Madeleine when he telephoned from Washington that afternoon. He mixed himself a drink and sat down to wait for her.

This was not the time to think of his own feelings, but he was still vehemently opposed to her trying to fight her father for control of Slayter's, as he was positive she would do now. She would never win and the struggle would sap her spirit, especially with Jonathan gone. Jon had been away so long, it was hard to believe he was really dead.

Charles nursed his guilt uncomfortably over a cold supper. Washington was a wild city in wartime and there had seemed to be some justification for playing around when he started it. Now it only seemed a childish, petty, despicable thing to have done, and he could only pray she'd never know about it.

In the silent house Charles wandered from the living room to the library, freshening his drink more often than usual and chain-smoking Lucky Strikes. He even disliked the white packet. Lucky Strike Green had gone to war and so had he. He felt helpless and miserable and angry. The pale, smooth whiskey accentuated each of those feelings.

He kept checking the time. The minutes crawled, but the hours raced. It was past ten and she was still out, certainly still talking to Madeleine about her brother. He was glad Susannah had made it up with Madeleine before Jon was killed. Still, it hurt to have her out like this so late. He wanted to hold her and help her, no matter what she did about her father and his bloody business.

Jesse Slayter! That icy sonofabitch had always been the reason, direct or indirect, for what Susannah did. Ever since Charles had known her she had not acted as much as *re*acted to her father. They all had, Jon and Madeleine too. It was maddening. It would be a fine comeuppance for Jesse if she did boot him out. Jesse, after all, had taught her how because Jonathan, poor bastard, had never wanted to know.

"Damn it," Charles whispered. "I loved that guy too. She ought to be here with me."

He was pouring another drink when the phone rang and he leaped for it.

Before he could speak, Gemma's voice said "Susannah?" and he sighed, disappointed. "No, Gemma, she's over with Madeleine."

"Oh," Gemma said, with a world of sorrow in that one syllable. "I just wanted to talk to someone." Her voice trailed off and she started to sob.

"Gem," he said sadly. "For God's sake, Gemma, I wish there were something I could say."

For a second she couldn't answer. Then she said, "I know, Charlie, there's nothing anyone can say or do. I just wish I could die too. I can't stand it that he's dead and I'm still here."

She sounded as forlorn as he felt. "Listen, I'll come on down there and talk to you a while. I'm not doing myself any good alone up here."

"Okay, Charlie," she said through her sobs. "Thanks."

He put down the receiver and the glass and went downstairs. He thought about leaving a note for Susannah, but he would probably be back before she was, and at the moment she probably didn't much care where he was. He grabbed the topcoat he had been wearing earlier, went out, and got into the car.

He lit another cigarette at the first red light. The Greeks used to kill messengers who brought bad news. Susannah had only left him alone, but it felt like the same thing.

He could hear the sweet sound of Harry James's trumpet playing "I Don't Want to Walk Without You" as he climbed the flight of stairs to Gemma's apartment. It was just like Gemma to play songs that reminded her of Jonnie and made her feel worse.

The door to her apartment was open when he got to it and he went in. The place had always been comfortably untidy, but now it was a mess. Gemma was on the sofa with a drink in her hand, looking as if she hadn't slept in days.

"Hi, Charlie," she said pathetically. "I'm so glad you came."

He took off his coat and turned off the record player. "Maybe you've had enough of that too." He pointed to the glass in her hand.

"What the hell difference does it make if I drink too much now?"

He moved his head in agreement. "I guess you're right." He went to get a drink himself. Then he sat down next to her. "Okay, I'm here, Gem. Let's talk about him."

They drank and she talked for over an hour about all the things that had happened to both of them, the unforeseeable turns their lives had taken, the charismatic brother and sister they both loved.

"You were lucky," she said, groggy with drink. "She married you."

"You were luckier—you didn't have to share him with a goddamn career while you had him."

"Poor Charlie, I'm sorry about that. You're such a sweet guy. I'm not, I'm a rat. I hoped he'd never find his wife. I didn't want anything to happen to her, I just hoped he wouldn't find her." It was hard to understand her. She had begun to cry again.

"Come on, Gem, you're asleep sitting up. Go to bed and sleep for real, you could use it." He got to his feet unsteadily and helped her into the bedroom and under the rumpled bedclothes.

"Don't go until I'm asleep, Charlie. I can't fall asleep if I'm alone."

He crawled across her to the other side of the bed and lay on top of the covers. "I'm here. Now go to sleep." His head was spinning and he lay there gratefully, hoping to drift off for a few minutes' nap, but the whiskey had strung him too tightly. Gemma was awake too, and crying softly.

He put an arm around her and pillowed her head on his shoulder. She clung to him with a need for physical comfort that was as great as his, and with a desire to give that, and only that, he kissed her.

He had kissed her many times before, years and years ago, when they were both very young and in love with love. They had made love then for the pleasure of it; they were making love now for the comfort it gave them. He felt bereft and he wanted the pillowy comfort of a woman's breasts and body, a cradle for his seeking flesh and a balm to his spirit. She welcomed the touch of a man's hands, the weight of a man's body, the joining and the filling up. They were old lovers, but more than that, tonight they were old friends mourning the same man and too exhausted by drink and sorrow to think much beyond the solace it gave them to be close.

He didn't hear what name she called him; she didn't care that he pretended she was someone else. They made love to comfort each other and then they fell gratefully asleep.

When the telephone rang at midnight, Charles reached for it automatically, his puffy eyes closed, his head throbbing.

"Hello," he said thickly.

"Charles?" It was Susannah, incredulous, wondering why he was there and asleep at this hour.

"Jesus," he said, opening his eyes. He glanced at Gemma, still out cold, and suddenly he could say nothing else.

She was still on the line, the silence explosive between them.

"Susannah?" He was asking her to wait, to listen to him.

The silence between them was dense and chaotic now. The paths they were on crossed and recrossed, like railway tracks, and the mere throwing of a switch could take them forward together or down two separate roads.

"No," she said. "No, Charles. I don't want to hear you. I don't want to see you. Go back to Washington, go anywhere you damned please, but don't come anywhere near me, not ever again."

The telephone went dead.

79

Grief turned Madeleine outward, to Ned first, and then to anyone who had known Jonathan—except Gemma, for Susannah's sake. It exiled Susannah to a lonely, private wasteland. In the weeks following Jonathan's death Madeleine, like a friendly spirit trying to save a haunted house, hovered close to Susannah and waited.

"She has no one," Madeleine said to Ned. "She can't stand the mention of Jesse—thank God the newspapers have finished with him now. She won't talk to Charles yet, not even about a divorce. I don't think she'll ever speak to Gemma again—and she needs a friend for comfort."

"She has you," Ned said from his wing chair at Gramercy Park.

"It's not the same. Except about Jonnie we're like new friends with each other, not old ones. When things fall apart a woman needs old friends to help her remember the first times."

"The first times?" Ned watched her in the firelight. Her mauve velvet housegown was reminiscent of another age, a gentler age than this one, when women wore such exquisitely feminine garments with picture hats and parasols, to go out in their carriages.

"Yes, the first time you began to think like a real woman or languished over a special song."

"Or went to a ball and fell in love?"

"Yes," Madeleine said, remembering it. "Or walked in a garden with a stranger and couldn't let him go." Her eyes cherished him and she wished she hadn't let him go, the first time or the second. "So you see, she does need Gemma."

"They need each other. Now that Susannah has nothing more to lose, she might be ready to take some emotional risks. As for Gemma"—he sighed— "she lost Jonathan long before he died and Susannah right after. She never loved carefully, like Susannah, always too well."

"I've thought of calling her, but it would seem like disloyalty to Susannah and I won't risk that. Do you think that someday the two of them . . . ?"

"I don't know, darling. People have different clocks for getting over things. Some never do."

Sometimes Madeleine was afraid that she would never be able to speak openly and honestly to her daughter, that what had started that day in Central Park had been brutally ended by all that had happened since. Yet they saw each other every day. They walked when the streets were cleared

401

of snow. They went to museums and thought of their own dead and living, not some other era's.

Madeleine waited for the right time to speak, but was there a right time to approach a woman who had lost a brother to war and a father to principle, only to find herself betrayed by her husband and her best friend too?

"I don't know how she's managed to get through it," Madeleine told Daisy.

"Miss Susannah has discipline, like a soldier."

"Discipline? That only makes things easier on everyone else, but it's bad for her. All of that misery bottled up will influence her decisions. She'll divorce him and she doesn't really want to."

Daisy sniffed.

"There, you see, that's what I mean," Madeleine said. "It's her pride that's been damaged, not her love for him, or his for her. In a few years that'll seem a poor excuse to have lost each other."

Yet Susannah seemed determined to do just that.

"For God's sake, Madeleine," Charles pleaded on the telephone early one morning during the Easter holidays. "Talk to her. She doesn't hear a thing I say. Make her believe me before I see her tonight, or it'll be all over. It's so damned stupid."

"You always knew she was like this, Charles. Susannah doesn't go in and out of marriage as if it were the revolving door at Saks." Madeleine blushed; it was an unfortunate allusion because Gemma had worked there for so many years. Charles didn't appear to notice.

"I didn't plan it this way, Madeleine!"

"No one ever does," Madeleine said. "I'll try, Charles, but she's been unapproachable about this."

"She'll listen to you," Charles said. "She's missed you a lot all these years."

"Oh, Charles," Madeleine said, "thank you for telling me that."

"I love her," Charles said desperately. "Those other women were just something to do."

Why was it, Madeleine wondered, waiting for Susannah to call, that most women took up knitting for something to do and most men took up women?

"I'm taking the boys to the Natural History," Susannah said when she called. "Meet me in front of the Royal Family at ten, okay?"

"Fine, I'll be there." Why she wanted to go to that gloomy old museum was nobody's business, Madeleine thought, but the boys liked it and you had to do something with children during a school recess.

She went to dress, determined to say something about the divorce business before it was too late. Susannah talked about starting her own brokerage house, but she could never do that until she had made up her mind about Charles.

I'm going to tell her, Madeleine vowed to herself, *I'm going to tell her everything and I don't care how angry she gets.*

Madeleine saw her grandsons first, gazing raptly at the mastodons. Cab was a duplicate of his father, with Charles's personality too. He was only twelve, but it was clear that the world would never get the better of its fourth Charles Anson Benedict.

"Where's your mother?" Madeleine asked.

"Over with the cavemen," John Slayter said, looking mystified. "She *likes* them." He was seven and very sensitive. He reminded her of Jonnie.

"Don't you like them?"

"No, we like the dinosaurs," Cab answered for him. "Mother said we could go see them and you'd meet us there in half an hour."

They went off and Madeleine crossed the polished floor of the museum, almost empty at this hour. Susannah was standing in front of the glass that separated the Neanderthals from their twentieth-century descendants.

"Their skins look a little ratty," Madeleine said. "I don't know why you call them the Royal Family."

"It was Jonnie's name for them."

"You're right, it was. He was a generous soul."

"I'm not," Susannah said. "I wanted to talk to you. Charles is coming tonight."

"And you want a divorce," Madeleine said, as evenly as she could.

"Yes. It'll be the first thing you and I have ever done at the same time."

Madeleine dropped a glove. "I was hoping you'd change your mind," she said, looking down at it.

"After *his* performance? It wasn't only Gemma, you know. There were quite a few women in Washington, as kind friends came running to tell me." She picked up the glove and handed it to Madeleine as if it were a gauntlet and she were responding to a challenge. It was the first time she had said Gemma's name and Madeleine held her breath. "You probably think," Susannah went on, "that it doesn't matter in the grand scheme of things." Her eyes pleaded to be convinced of it.

"Oh, it matters," Madeleine said, determined to go on no matter where it led them. "It matters a lot, but maybe not enough to be worth a divorce."

"You sound just like Charles! He calls me 'True Blue Sue.' Is being faithful so foolish? I wonder what *she* would have done"—Susannah pointed at the cavewoman—"if he'd had it off with the lady next door?"

403

"Sometimes you sound just like Jesse," Madeleine said spiritedly, turning her gloves nervously. "He wants perfection too—a perfect bank, a perfect world, a wife and children who conform to his idea of how they should believe and behave. Well, life isn't like that. You have to take people as they are."

Susannah's eyes shone with suppressed anger when she spoke again past the glassed-in family. "Why should I take him as he is?"

"He's pretty good, all things considered—you always knew that. And he loves you."

"Oh, sure, until the real thing comes along—again." Susannah took out a handkerchief and blew her nose. "I wonder what Jonnie would have made of all this."

"Not much," Madeleine said softly. "He'd have seen it for what it was and it wasn't much: a war and a separation can upset a lot of apple carts."

Susannah shook her head admiringly. "How long does it take to be broadminded about a sock in the teeth?"

"It took me fifty-seven years."

"I always wanted to be like you," Susannah said desolately, "but I never will be in a million years. I wish I were! I wish I could say the things I want to, but I can't. Emotions embarrass me. I just can't wear my feelings on my sleeve." She looked up at Madeleine, puzzled and miserable, like a little girl who has gone happily to a birthday party and come home hurt and humiliated. "There isn't a sleeve in the whole world long enough for all I have inside me, but I just can't seem to show it to people I care about."

"But, Sassie, we know, all of us who love you *know* that about you. Charles, too. Charles especially. He just wanted it all for himself."

Susannah absorbed that in grateful silence for a few minutes, then she turned, hesitated, and looked briefly at Madeleine. "I'd like to know, if you feel you can tell me, why you didn't leave him sooner. Your second try was a long time coming."

Madeleine looked through the glass pane at the Pleistocene landscape and something in her face made Susannah move closer to her.

"I just wanted someone to *be* with me in the world, like everyone else, and I thought it was Jesse," Madeleine said. "I chose the wrong man, but I couldn't stop caring just because of that. I gave him all I had, but it didn't make him understand me or need me or even love me the way I did him." She glanced at Susannah. "After a while I knew all about him, what he was, but I was so sorry for him because of all the things he wasn't, all the loveliness he missed because of what he wasn't, that I wanted to love him anyway, the way you love a battered doll—you still see it as it was meant to be, beautiful and wonderful and *yours,* your someone to be with." Her hands tightened on the guard rail. "If he hadn't driven my Jonnie away, I'd still be with him."

Susannah touched her mother's hand. "Well, he *was* something, you can't be blamed for that."

"Oh, he was something, all right," Madeleine said fervently. "He had a smile that lit up the room like Jonnie's. Jonnie looked like me, but he had Jesse's smile, with warmth behind the dazzle. And he was terribly strong, he always knew what he wanted."

After a moment Susannah leaned against the guard rail as if she were too weary to stand alone. "How can I live with a man if I don't trust him? How can I ever trust Charles again?"

"To be what? Himself, or some idea you have of him?" Madeleine confronted that skeptical gaze she had known since Susannah's childhood. "Listen to me, Sassie, your father was never what I thought. I made him up. Then I went back to him because it was the right thing to do. Society said so, and pride too—the very things that demand you divorce Charles now. I ruined my life to do what was 'right.' *Don't you do it,* Susannah! Do what you really want."

She turned back to the glass wall of the display and the stunted figures behind it. "If you divorce him, don't do it because of a fall from grace. You *know* there are worse crimes in a marriage. Do it because you don't like the kind of man he really is—and I think you do."

Susannah, leaning on the rail with her head bent, nodded slowly. "I guess he *is* my someone," she said, "warts and all." She turned a pale, but calmer face to Madeleine. "How do you forgive a man without being holier-than-thou?"

"You don't," Madeleine said, remembering Ned. "Some things are unforgivable. You get over them." She sighed, thinking of Jesse. "And some things you can't forgive or get over; you just have to live with them."

They were silent for a while, then they turned together to walk toward the dinosaurs. The museum was filling up, the gloom of its halls pierced by the voices of children, the dust of aeons stirred up by their wonder.

"If it's any comfort," Madeleine said, "I wouldn't change a thing about you. I think you're a terrific woman."

Susannah took her arm. "Even 'True Blue Sue' who still can't understand why he slept with Gemma?"

"You understand perfectly well; you just have to say to hell with it, and tell Charles to come on home."

Susannah nodded, then stopped walking and turned to her mother. "If you could change anything—apart from Jonnie—what would it be?"

"The color of my hair," Madeleine said positively.

405

Susannah smiled. "No, really, I'm serious."

"So am I. Blondes are supposed to be empty-headed creatures, designed to be vacuous, obedient and dumb. I wasn't—my father saw to it that I wasn't—but Jesse didn't know that. He would never have married me if I'd been a brunette."

"I think he'd have married you," Susannah said.

"Then he'd have taken me more seriously."

"And that's all you'd change?"

"I can think of a lot of things now, but they didn't occur to me then. Regret is too painful, anyway."

Susannah nodded, once more aware of many lost moments she might have spent in Madeleine's company, but there was just so much a woman could handle in one day. "Look, I haven't told the boys anything—except that Charles was away on war business. Would you take them to a movie this afternoon? *Fantasia*'s playing somewhere."

"I'd love to," Madeleine said, her smile hiding her vast relief. "But I'll take them to *Casablanca*. I'm dying to see it again and it's time they started learning about life."

"From a romantic movie?"

"Oh, it's more than that. It has love and betrayal, passion and honor, acceptance and pardon, courage—and just enough villainy to make it human."

"You *are* a romantic," Susannah said, glad that it was so. "Like Jonnie."

"There's a lot to be said for romance," Madeleine said, walking on. "It can ease you over the bumps." She laughed. "Just look at your sons, starry-eyed over a heap of old bones! Leave them here with me, I'll spoil them all afternoon."

"Thanks." Susannah touched her mother's cheek. "I love you, Madeleine. I wouldn't change a thing about you, either."

She went quickly away to talk to Cab and John Slayter, then Madeleine watched her leave the vast gallery and go home to wait for Charles.